Prince Habib's Iceberg

Habib, youthful and sybaritic potentate of an independent oil kingdom on the west coast of Africa, comes to London to find an engineer who can transform his sun-scorched and waterless lands with Arctic ice. Mendes, musician, mathematician, and tycoon extraordinary, responds to the challenge, but at the expense of his marriage and his peace of mind. Then, as a million cubic yards of iceberg are being navigated across the Atlantic, revolution breaks out in Habib's kingdom.

Edward Hyams's new novel shows him at top form. This is a grippingly told story with marvelously evoked backgrounds, from the icebound regions of the north to the desert splendor of Habib's African domain, and a cast of splendidly realized characters.

Edward Hyams

Prince Habib's Iceberg

W · W · Norton & Company · Inc ·
New York

For Mary with love

Library of Congress Cataloging in Publication Data
Hyams, Edward S.
Prince Habib's iceberg.
I. Title.
PZ3.H9884Pr3 [PR6015.Y33] 823'.9'14 74-14539
ISBN 0-393-08704-2

Printed in the United States of America

1 2 3 4 5 6 7 8 9 0

Part One

One

Miss Bartrum came into John Gurling's office and said, 'There's a General Abdul Aziz Hakim to see you. He says that he telephoned you at home last night.'

Gurling was standing at the window overlooking the garden: the camellias were in flower and he was thinking that they looked unnatural in a London garden. He would have preferred the greys and greens of masonry and foliage: something Italianate. The Gurling–Curran headquarters were housed in the villa which Repton had built for a Russian ambassador and which the guide books attribute to Nash. It lies in the area between Kensington Gardens and the street usually called Millionaires' Row and is hidden from the rest of London by its own trees.

Gurling said, 'Yes. I should have told you.' He crossed the beautiful double-cube room to the huge relief map of Eurasia and North Africa which had been presented to Curran by his fellow directors when he left the Bank of England's service and now covered the whole of one wall, and stared for a moment at General Hakim's small country. Gurling–Curran had never worked there: the oil installations were in American hands; the Russians had built the port, the Italians the new roads. Gurling said, 'What's he like?'

'A dish,' Miss Bartrum said.

'I thought you didn't care for Arabs.'

'There's always Omar Sharif; and this one's even dollier. I don't think he's an Arab.'

'Bring him in.'

Gurling sat down behind his desk. He recalled that Hakim was one of the Ruler's political soldiers, a member of the six-man executive which Habib Shah used to run his country; a strong-arm man of the kind Gurling disliked, though knowing what they wanted they were often easy to do business with. But when Miss Bartrum returned with their visitor Gurling, after a single glance at the man's face, got to his feet with an alacrity which he would not have conceded to the likes of General Hakim, and did not utter a word of greeting until Miss Bartrum had left the room. In fact it was the visitor who broke the silence, watching Miss Bartrum go and saying, 'What a very pretty girl.' He spoke English with a slight French-sounding accent. Only then did Gurling say, 'This is a very unexpected honour, Prince.'

'Ah, Mr Gurling, so you know me.'

'Of course.'

'Mr Gurling, oblige me by calling me Hakim. The general is good enough to lend me his name from time to time. I'm not in London officially. Your government know I'm here but are kind enough to respect my incognito. If I'm known to be away from Farzar, it disturbs my associates on the council of the oil-producing states; and if I'm known to be in London I shall spend my time dodging Palestinian bullets or Israeli journalists or one of those hazards which make my life rather more exciting than is good for me. Shall we sit in those comfortable-looking chairs by that very handsome window. What are those flowers?'

'Camellias, General.'

'Camellias, of course. Why do the English grumble about their climate? Everything grows here. They should try living in my country where two sheep compete for every blade of grass.'

Habib bin 'Ali ibn Far was known to the officials of those Foreign Offices which had business with his country as 'the

Ruler'. To his Arab subjects he was Sheikh Habib bin 'Ali ibn Far; and to his Farsi subjects – it was to their ethnic group that he belonged – as Habib Shah. The newspapers usually referred to him as Prince Habib. Fourteenth of his line, he was the direct descendant of the Persian prince who, during the reign of Shah Abbas in Iran, had conquered a part of Anatolia, taken to the sea, and carved himself a kingdom in Africa. Habib was celebrated for two things: his remarkable personal beauty, of the classic Iranian cast which had emerged in him from the past despite the fact that he certainly had Arab, Indian and Tartar blood in his veins; and for his business acumen which had enabled him, by setting the Italians against the Americans and the Anglo–Dutch, and the Russians against both of them, to keep for his country something like eighty per cent of the value of the oil which was its only asset. When it came to negotiation the world's big oil men had even more respect for Habib than for that formidable business man the Shah of Iran himself.

'Mr Gurling,' he said, after refusing a cigar and giving Gurling permission to smoke one of the *caporal* cigarettes which he always rolled for himself, 'how much do you know about my country?'

Gurling was silent for a moment; then he said, 'I know where it is, its extent and population. I know that the people of Farzar are chiefly of Iranian stock though much mixed with Berber and Arab, that the desert people are Arab and *bedu*. I know that as well as the Moslem majority you have small Jewish, Zoroastrian, Nestorian and Bahai minorities. I know that nine-tenths of your land is as barren and waterless as the Rio de Oro to your north. And naturally, I know what everyone knows, that your oil-fields look like being the richest in the world by a very big margin.'

'Good. I'm surprised that you know so much. To be frank, there is not much more to know. Have you ever visited my capital?'

'Farzar? No, sir.'

'It's not a bad place. It was for long an entrepôt in the Omani slave-trade. My ancestors got their share of the takings, and some of it went into building and as our architects were Persians, the old town is pretty. For the rest, I'm particular about the architects we employ to build our own quarters.'

While the Prince talked he was studying Gurling quite openly; the man he looked at was square-shouldered, burly without being fat, between fifty and sixty – one could get no nearer than that, with a red face, abundant hair, worn rather long, between tow and grey, an important nose, and small, very brilliant, hazel-green eyes. He was also, clearly, a man who said nothing until he had something to say.

Habib went on, 'Mr Gurling, be patient with me if I approach the object of this visit in my own way. To begin with, two propositions which I should be obliged if you would comment on.' He paused and Gurling nodded.

'One. Oil is a wasting asset.'

'Not an urgent or even immediate problem in your case, surely?'

'You think not? At the rate the Americans, you Europeans, and the Japanese, all of whom are seriously short already, are squandering oil, my country's field will not last twenty-five years. You note that I use the word *squandering*; in other words, I disapprove; but there's nothing I can do about it but exploit the folly of consumerism to my people's advantage.'

'By using your revenues to capitalize industries? Yes, I know. I have read that not even the Persians have channelled so much of their oil revenues into investment . . .'

'And I, Mr Gurling, unlike my distant cousin Aryamehr, do not tolerate bureaucratic obstructionism. I use my Jews, my Nestorians in key posts; and they are business managers, not *fonctionnaires*. Now will you tell me something else: of what use are industries if there is a fuel famine?'

'Ah . . . you're thinking of the atomic energy plant we built for the Mexicans,' Gurling said.

'I have thought of it, Mr Gurling; and dismissed the thought. I'm not impressed either with the record of efficiency or with the economics of nuclear power stations. No, for a country with thirty-seven hundred hours of blazing sunshine per annum and a vast amount of useless land, a really big solar energy plant is the answer. I have a team of Americans, steered by the M.I.T., working on that. Now, here is my second proposition; there is one fundamental industry which never lets you down – agriculture; if one can't sell the product one can at least eat it. Bear that in mind and consider this: man's most important raw material is water.'

Gurling hesitated; it was a fact that without adequate water you could have neither industry nor agriculture. He thought of the mean annual per capita consumption in Britain, something like thirty thousand gallons; a few other statistics came to mind. He said,

'One doesn't think of it that way, but . . . yes, of course.'

'I wonder you even hesitated, Mr Gurling. I tell you, within twenty-five years five per cent of the world's shrinking energy resources will be spent freshening sea water. Do you think that the admirable Miss Bartrum could bring in the rather awkward package which I left in your anteroom?'

Gurling gave the order on the intercom. Habib said, 'Water I must have. Now, Mr Gurling, where are the world's largest reserves of water?'

'The oceans, you mean. You have in mind the big desalination plant we are building for . . .'

'No, no, I did not make myself clear. *Fresh* water . . .'

Miss Bartrum came in carrying a seven-foot cardboard cylinder about a foot in diameter. Habib jumped up, took it from her, thanked her, uncapped it and pulled out a roll of stout paper which he started to unroll on the floor. Gurling came to help him. Miss Bartrum, at a glance from her boss, reluctantly left them. The map now lay unrolled on the floor, its corners secured by heavy glass ashtrays. Habib said, 'The scale is one thousand to one,' and, kneeling, with Gurling standing behind him smoking another of his thin, black cigarettes, said,

'We are not much bigger than Britain, you see. Here . . .' his finger made a circular motion to delineate a large tract of country, 'here are something like a million hectares of so-called desert. Like the real desert surrounding it, it supports at present only the *bedu* – perhaps at a density of one person per square kilometre.' The Prince looked up at Gurling and went on, 'I am thirty-four years old. Three times in my life we have, owing to some freakish conditions which I have no doubt the meteorologists understand but I do not, had rain, sustained rain. Each time, this desert has blossomed like the rose. The soil scientists whom I have brought from Israel tell me the whole area is potentially very fertile. Instead of supporting one person per kilometre it could support many hundreds per hectare . . .'

Habib rose in a single graceful movement to his feet and said,

'All I need to feed my people as they should be fed and to reap harvests which could feed – let us say half England as well, is rain, or its equivalent.'

'Desalination . . .' Gurling began; the prince waved away desalination, saying, 'Forget it. Think of the energy required. Enormous. Why should I spend my precious oil on desalination, when nature has done the job for me? You have still not answered my question . . . I will repeat it. Where are the world's greatest reserves of fresh water?'

Gurling, giving himself time to think what it was this lively visitor had in his mind, what bee in his bonnet, crossed to the big wall map and staring at it, said, 'By the way, the sun's over the yard-arm, would you like a drink, General?'

'That is kind of you. Yes, I should like a small whisky and soda. No ice. A *chota peg* rather than a highball.'

Gurling touched a bellpush on his desk; suddenly, ice was the clue. He went back to stare at the map; this man could not mean *that*: it was fantastic, a pipeline dream three thousand miles long. Miss Bartrum came in and said, 'Sir?'

'Whisky and soda for the General and, for me, water,' he said and, as the girl went to the drinks cabinet which included a small refrigerator, he committed himself as far as it was in his careful nature to do by saying as if about nothing in particular, 'It's an awful long way from Farzar, General.'

This relative boldness was vindicated. The prince said,

'Good, very good, you begin to see. It is not for nothing that one comes to Gurling–Curran,' and took his drink from Miss Bartrum, smiling his thanks with a charm which made her blush. Or it may have been the way he had of looking at her that made her blush, the deliberate taking-in of the perfection of her skin, the lustre of her red-blonde hair cut in a bob to just below the lobes of her ears. He said, 'Miss Bartrum, forgive me for asking a question so personal, and never mind your boss who will forgive both of us; do you like working here?'

'Yes, I do.'

'Of course. But you come of an adventurous race, you are in a job which entails dealing with strange lands, the gorgeous . . . it is not really gorgeous . . . east, the golden . . . it has ceased to be golden . . . west. Are you never tempted to wish that your lot was . . . should one say *were* ? . . . cast in, shall we say gaudier lands?'

'Often, sir.'

'I shall remember that and perhaps do something which Mr Gurling will not easily forgive, though he *is* a kind man. Now will you do something for me?'

'Of course, General.'

'Ah, she calls me General, shall we let her, like your Prime Minister, into the secret, Mr Gurling?'

Gurling, irritated by this flirtatious clowning, but too curious to know what was in the other man's mind to be rude at this stage, said, 'General Hakim is . . . his real name is Prince Habib bin 'Ali ibn Far, the Ruler of . . .' he nodded towards the map on the floor which took up so much room that there was hardly space to walk around it.

'Now Mr Gurling is cross with me and so has been indiscreet, but I am sure you are as trustworthy as you're beautiful. Now, Miss Bartrum . . . by the way, what is your given name?'

The girl glanced at Gurling who gave a tiny shrug. She said, 'Caroline.'

'Delightful. I wonder what it means? And what is your sign?'

'Aquarius, highness.'

Habib rose, bowed, said, 'I was born under Libra, *mes hommages, mademoiselle*. Now will you do something for me?'

'Of course, prince.'

'I want a tumbler of water in which you have dissolved two heaped tablespoonfuls of salt. Do not look so sorry for me; my digestion is robust.'

Caroline Bartrum, her face glowing, unquestioning, left them. Habib sipped his whisky and said, 'Mr Gurling, have you ever heard of two geographical features . . .' he returned to the map on the floor, indicated an area with the toe of his elegant Italian shoe, and went on, 'the Great Curzon Depression and, here, the Wilhelm Crater?'

Gurling shook his head and said, 'Sorry, no.'

'Do not apologize. We are a small country for which the English, even in their imperial days, never having taken it over, there being nothing worth taking as far as they knew, cared nothing. The crater is that of a volcano which became extinct ten thousand years ago. It was completely sealed by the final eruption and it has a capacity of three thousand million cubic metres.'

Gurling nodded. Habib went on, 'Below it, seven kilometres to the west, begins the Great Curzon Depression, so named by Elmer Hattersley – you've certainly heard of his *The Dry Lands of Q'jar* – who had no sense of humour and a great admiration for Curzon. It has an average depth of thirty-four metres, is about forty kilometres long, twenty wide, and when we do get rain it holds water . . . so does the Wilhelm Crater . . . until the sun evaporates it. In short, both are natural reservoirs . . . if we had anything to put in them. There's a fall from the Wilhelm Crater . . . by the way, it was named by Von Hölm . . . you probably know his works . . . to the Depression of 180 metres, and very nearly sheer.'

Gurling was tempted into the open by this relative wealth of information: he said,

'From the way your ideas are running . . .'

'Wait, I have not finished.' Once again Habib went to the map which covered the floor and said, 'Look at these contours . . .' Gurling followed the line of the pointing toe and after a moment said, 'This puts the rim of the crater at five metres below sea level, and the Depression . . .'

'One hundred and eighty. You'll find the whole area marked on the maps as a land depression.'

'Which gives us a gravity feed from any source at sea level. You're clearly thinking of a pipiline from the Arctic. Not impossible; but, my God, what a price.'

'I think, Mr Gurling, that there may be a cheaper way of bringing fresh water from the Arctic than in one of your pipes.'

Miss Bartrum returned carrying a glass of water on a plate, saying,

'I think it's all dissolved.'

'Caroline, you are the incarnation of efficiency. Now, please, one other prop for my little conjuring trick: a piece of ice from Mr Gurling's refrigerator.'

She brought the ice from the drinks cabinet on a saucer: he picked up a single cube and dropped it into the water: it bobbed under then floated to the top and settled, most of it below water, but a part exposed. Habib placed the glass on Gurling's desk and said,

'You must forgive my little dramatization. Let us look again at the figures. The Wilhelm Crater will hold about three thousand million cubic metres of water, the Curzon Depression a great deal more than that. I'm told that to do a good job of irrigation on my fertile rectangle – and by the way there's a great deal more than a thousand square kilometres, if I succeed with them – I need the equivalent of fifty centimetres of rain per annum – five hundred million cubic metres of water. I fill the Wilhelm Crater with water, I run it down to the lake through a turbine, generating electrical energy; from the lake, the old Depression, I pump it, with that energy, into pipes feeding the irrigation lines. Hey presto . . . two metric tons of wheat, or four of rice and God knows what else, per acre.'

'And your cheap way of bringing water from the Arctic, that is, some three thousand kilometres?'

Habib stared at the glass on the desk, the glass in which a cube of ice floated in half a glass of brine. Gurling said,

'Good God, fishing for icebergs . . .'

'Something of the kind but a little more sophisticated.' He turned to Miss Bartrum, who had taken advantage of the fact that neither man had dismissed her, and said, 'Caroline, I am alone in this great and wonderful city. I should like, this evening, to eat a nice little dinner somewhere quiet, and then to see the new *Othello* for which I have tickets. Will you take pity on me and be my guest for the evening?'

Miss Bartrum flushed, hesitated, glanced at Gurling – she was an orphan and he had for some time stood to her *in loco parentis*. Unlike her friends who had, as it were, all too much father, she had never had any. Gurling was no help; he shrugged very slightly. With a lifting of the heart she said, 'I should love to, prince.'

'Good. Let us meet in the bar of my inn – Claridges is the name, you will know where it is – at . . . would six-thirty suit you?'

'Six-thirty would be fine.'

His smile of thanks was again dismissive. When she had left them Gurling said, 'Having finished seducing the best secretary

I've ever had, maybe you'd better tell me what bee you do have in your bonnet.'

'It is a very big bee, Mr Gurling; and it has a very loud buzz which we should try to silence for a few months . . . Now hear this, as they say in the United States Navy, in their quaint way . . .'

Mr Gurling listened.

Two

By an accident of history the people of the country which lies south of and inland from Farzar, between the southern frontier of the Islamic Republic of Mauritania and the northern frontier of Senegal, are of almost pure Arabian stock; although there must have been a certain amount of mingling of blood, it does not appear. These *bedouin* are descendants of a ninth-century expeditionary force led across all North Africa by the so-called Pseudo-Calif 'Omar the Younger, whose mystical *Contemplations* laid down a way of life which gave his people a powerful sense of a special identity. The seven Sheikhs of the seven clans which compose this people all claim descent from 'Omar. They address one another as 'Cousin', and together comprise a senate of elders to preside over a régime which is remarkably democratic. Six of the Cousins recognize the presidency or leadership of the seventh, the Sheikh of the Mocktar clan which is the guardian of the shrine of 'Omar the Younger.

In 1923 Sidi Mahommed bin Mocktar became Sheikh-among-Sheikhs while still a very young man – his father was killed in a brush with a band of Mauritanian raiders – and presided over the council until his death in 1968. And this despite the fact that contrary to the will and custom of the people he showed a regrettable tendency to modernism; for example, he accepted subsidies from his sovereign in Farzar; and he lost face and influence with the Cousins and the people at large by investing the money in an irrigation scheme which was to be the basis of an agricultural settlement of part of the Mocktar clan.

The reluctant farmers ran away to the desert and joined one of the other clans; then 'Omar the Younger, who had written 'And God makes the grass grow, each blade in its place, and the sheep to eat the grass. And where there is no grass for sheep, yet shall the goats be fed. Will ye not be instructed?' declared himself on the runaways' side by drying up the irrigation wells, a contingency forecast by the Sheikh's English engineers, which was why Sidi Mahommed had dismissed them in favour of a more optimistic Italian firm. Chastened, Sidi Mahommed refused to pay the last instalment of the Italians' bill and resumed the ways of 'Omar and his fathers. But there was one sin he might repent but could not undo; his beloved and only son Allal Mahommed had been sent to the Ecole Française in Farzar; and the Sheikh was unable, or unwilling, to deny Allal the fruits of his talent and toil by forbidding him to accept a valuable Lyautey bursary to the Sorbonne.

The Cousins resolved that neither they nor their sons would ever accept Allal as their leader; but when the young man returned in 1965, preaching, albeit in new words, what amounted to death to the infidel, friendship with the new Arab republics of North Africa, and war on the Zionists, combined with respect for the ways of 'Omar, the Sheikhs and their sons realized that their resolution against him had been premature and that God had given him the heart and bowels of a true believer. In short, here was a young man after their own heart, and when the old Sheikh died in 1968 on his son's thirtieth birthday, they readily accepted him as Sheikh-among-Sheikhs.

What the Sheikhs had too little knowledge of the world to know was that Allal Mahommed had plans for them and for the whole country, above all for himself. He was a friend and disciple of Mehdi Ben Barka; had heard with his young and impressionable ears the siren voices of Ché Guevara, Fidel Castro; and, echoing resonantly across the world, of the venerable Ho Chi

Minh, and even more venerable Mao Tse-tung. He, too, would add a chapter to the handbook of revolution.

In short, Allal Mahommed, *Licensié ès Lettres, Docteur ès Droit* of whom the Ecole des Sciences Politiques had, predictably, made a politician, saw, in a subtly managed alliance of extreme Right and extreme Left, as others have done before him, a means of getting his hands on the oil-field and so to supreme power in Farzar and over all that country; saw the means to overthrow Habib's 'manageocracy' of Jews, Christians and renegade Moslems, those running dogs of the oil corporations; saw the oil road to a power widely transcending the narrow frontiers of his country. The Cousins and their people were due, ultimately, for a nasty shock; but meanwhile, they would serve his purpose which was the true purpose of the people and of tomorrow.

As for Habib, he suspected rather than knew Allal for an enemy; and there could be no sense in fighting where talking would serve. At a certain moment – only later did he realize that it had been too soon or too late – he invited Allal to spend a day or two at the palace to 'discuss the welfare of our people'. Allal appreciated that *our* might be royal, or might express or at least suggest conjuncture in rule. He accepted; as he told the Cousins, leaving it to them to tell the people, only a fool refuses the chance to visit the enemy's camp in safety. Of course, he made no concessions to the Ruler's westernism: throughout his short visit he wore the clothes of a desert Arab; prayed, a shade ostentatiously, at the times prescribed, ate only the food prepared by the cook he brought with him – it was known or suspected that Habib by no means barred eggs and bacon for breakfast – and drank neither wine nor beer nor spirits.

He was in some ways a difficult guest, for he would not drink the Coca-cola which was offered as an alternative to the proscribed liquors, being unwilling to put profit into neocolonialist pockets. And was not water good enough for any believer?

'Adam's ale,' his host agreed; Habib was always dredging up such trifles from his English education – 'Adam's ale; but at least let it be iced, there is no sin in that, Presence.' It amused him to speak thus humbly to this most powerful of his subjects. As he said to Caroline, in bed that night, 'My golden flower, standing on my dignity is just not my thing.'

As for Habib's plan to make the desert blossom like the rose – which meant that Allal's Arabs would have to learn to toil with tractor and hoe like so many kibbutz Jews – it was gracefully presented:

'Your father, Sidi Mahommed, was the pioneer; it is in his footsteps that I tread,' Habib told Allal, as they sat at coffee and watched the sun set on the terrace above the palace gardens overlooking the sea. 'It was from him that I learnt my lesson.' He went on to paint a picture of a new golden age: the people would eat their fill, would be clad and housed in such fashion as would not disgrace them in the eyes of the West. Why should the Prophet's people be less comfortable than Christians? Were they dogs to fight and snarl over meatless bones? Let their women, also, be freed from drudgery, their children be kept alive and schooled, their bodies be cooled in the great heats. Allal, who was not for nothing a licentiate of letters, appreciated the prince's sham classical style as much as did Habib himself; as he was to tell his friend, Doctor al Badr, a few days later, the Ruler abused the people's lamentable taste for rhetoric as ably as the late great Winston Churchill indulged the English taste for the Augustan style.

Habib was never a fool; only he relied too much on the charm of apparent candour, which usually worked. He said,

'I respect your ideas, Presence. But you know as well as I know what I propose to do will have to be done, later if not sooner, whether I rule or you – for the people.'

'For *some* of the people, Highness. What of those from whom you will take away the desert?'

There were moments when the strain of play-acting told:

Habib said, 'Oh, come now, *mon ami*, don't tell me it's a crime to take a *rial* from a man and give him a hundred in exchange.' But Allal refused to relax:

'The *rial* of today is tomorrow's hundred *rials*, Highness. I will be more specific: the moment the oil corporations conceded, in dollars, the demands of your Persian friends and yourself, and of the Gulf sheikhs, the dollar was devalued twice. Will you allow me to say that a man who trusts such people may be laying up merit in Heaven but is running himself into bankruptcy on earth? There are other values. You propose to take away from my people the freedom to breathe clean, dry air while they watch their beasts with one eye and with the other rejoice in the beauty of the world. Are the peoples you would have us emulate so happy? Are we, also, to have no values but those of the full stomach and the bank account in credit?'

'It was so hard for me to keep my temper,' Habib was to say to Caroline that night, just before she nearly lost hers and suggested more action and less chatter; 'the man's a bloody hypocrite.'

It was not quite a fair judgement but Habib was not to know that throughout their argument Allal was rehearsing the things he would say to the Cousins and the people. His case would not be hard to make: Habib, by setting out to transform the desert into the sown, became the natural enemy.

Habib was saying, 'A full stomach is not a bad thing.'

'I have heard that you, like myself, Highness, once had a taste for English novels. Now who was that man who wrote . . .' he changed abruptly from Arabic, which the prince, bent on being courteous, had set the example of using rather than Farsi, into English '. . . that he liked a dog provided it was not spelt backwards?'

Habib's face lit; he enjoyed a play on words. He said, 'I never heard that one before. Thank you, Sheikh. But your meaning . . .?'

'That a full stomach is a good thing so long as it does not become an idol. When I look West I see that idol, the Full Stomach, a foully bursting bag, the image of the only god they have left. What is your authority, Highness, to give me a dispensation to bow down in the house of the Full Stomach?'

Habib looked at Allal curiously and with a feeling which was genuine said,

'I wish that we had known each other many years.'

'I, too, Habib Shah.'

'But you will not help me?'

'I did not say so. I do not know yet. And there is something missing from the picture you have drawn for me.'

'I will supply it if I can.'

'Water.'

Habib nodded: candour was his policy with the Sheikh but it would be foolish to overdo it; he was chancing his arm, the man might be his worst enemy. He said, 'You may take it that I do not try to make bricks without straw. Water will be forthcoming.'

'My father's wells ran dry.'

'Mine are inexhaustible, Allal *aziz*.'

He was staring out to sea as he spoke: in the blue middle distance a Japanese tanker, a half-million tonner, was positioning itself to enter the oil port. Inshore, where the land's shadows darkened the sea, there were half a dozen fishing dhows. His meaning seemed obvious: desalination. Allal said, 'I will talk to my Cousins.'

'Talk well, Allal,' the Prince said over his shoulder, 'God forbid it should come to strife between you and me.' And, 'I think you said that you have to leave my house for Cairo this evening?'

There was no need to enlarge on his meaning; it was well known that Habib had no friends and a great many enemies in the Arab republics. Allal felt a moment of alarm: how much did this fellow know? Was he capable of . . . arresting him? He said, 'For some months I have had a persistent pain, sufficient to distract my mind, here . . .' he put his hand on his chest under the left armpit. 'I should go to Paris, or London. But, well, Your Highness knows my Cousins . . . and that those of us who are born to authority may not offend the people whose servants we are. They ask me "Are there no physicians in Islam?" And what could I say but that there is one at least equal to any European – Your Highness will have heard of Doctor Abdel al Badr?'

'Of course. A great and charitable doctor, you could not do better. But, God willing, it is nothing serious . . .'

Habib broke off as two girls and a young man came from the house onto the terrace and who were about to retreat when – seeing in them a relief from the boredom which was beginning to afflict him – he called out,

'Azizeh, Miss Bartrum, there is no need to run away. Come and meet our guest.' To Allal he explained, 'They have been away or I should have presented these friends before. With your permission, then, my sister, Princess Azizeh, who has been reading economics at Oxford; Miss Bartrum, my new English secretary; and Doctor Dirk Leuwenhoek who is doing some geophysical surveying for us. His Excellency, Sheikh Allal Mahommed bin Mocktar.'

Azizeh, bowing her head, said, 'Not economics, Presence, political economy.'

Habib laughed and said, 'There is a difference?'

'Of course, brother; and one the Sheikh will know.'

Allal looked at her sharply: there had been more than the apparent meaning in what she had said. Like her brother she was beautiful, with the large, wide-set eyes one sees in Persian miniatures, and the delicate apricot complexion. Reluctantly, Allal withdrew his attention from her to say something polite to the English girl; he had heard of her, she was said to be Habib's latest mistress and just possibly a future wife.

'You like our country, Miss Bartrum?'

'It is exciting to be here, Excellency.'

Allal turned to Dirk Leuwenhoek, a big, fair awkward man with very pale blue eyes, and asked him, in a tone which made it clear that the question was asked only as a formal politeness, where he was at work.

'The Wilhelm Crater and the Curzon Depression,' Leuwenhoek said, with equal indifference. But that seemed to interest the Sheikh who said, 'I have visited them several times. I have long believed that the Crater is very much older than the existing accounts of it make out.'

'It is,' the Dutchman replied, putting now a little warmth into his voice. 'What remains is only a stump. I'd give it between half and quarter of a million years. Moreover, the old surveys are wrong, the rim is two metres more below sea level than the contour on your maps indicates. Useful, those two metres that aren't there.' He laughed, perhaps to indicate that he had made a joke. Allal said,

'Useful, how so?'

Habib interrupted them: 'A wild idea of my own, Sheikh . . .' and gave Doctor Leuwenhoek a glance of warning. A servant came in to call the prince to the telephone – Teheran on the line. Caroline and Leuwenhoek went to the balustrade of the terrace to watch the fishing dhows make their way in line ahead through darkening shades of turquoise, into the small fishing harbour below. Princess Azizeh said to Allal, 'I have seen you before. Perhaps you will not remember . . . comrade.'

His face did not express the consternation he felt but he did look surprised and before he could speak she went on, 'Algiers, 1971. We stood in a group, eight of us, students from England and France, listening while you argued with Fidel and Danny. You're forgiven for forgetting me, we were not introduced.'

Allal had recovered; he smiled and said, 'You take me for a Marxist, Princess, and your brother for the leader of the reaction. Now who is right, I wonder?'

'Both, I expect. My brother and I are not of one mind,' the girl said; 'you have nothing to fear from me.'

No question but she was speaking the truth. And no chance to say more. Habib returned; the line had been impossibly bad. He said,

'My remote cousin should do something about his telephone service. Allal, my friend, how do you propose getting to Cairo? Let me put one of our planes at your disposal.'

Suspicion awoke again as Allal remembered the use that rebel officers had made of aeroplanes against Hassan of Morocco. He said,

'You are very kind; but I have my place on the afternoon flight . . . in fact, it is time I made a move.'

Habib walked him as far as the archway into the house, took him in his arms, kissed him on both cheeks.

'Talk to the Cousins,' he said, 'and then come and see me again.'

'If Your Highness has a fancy to shoot a leopard,' Allal said, formally, 'my house is yours.'

'My dear fellow, I'm the patron of our conservationists! If you didn't read my speech at Stockholm about our sweet little leopards, you missed a treat. But I'll come and drink coffee with you with all the pleasure in the world.'

Three

The Gamal Abdul Nasser Hospital was a model of what a hospital should be. Doctor al Badr and two associates, all Edinburgh trained and all heirs to wealth accumulated by shrewd grandfathers and fathers in the times of Kings Fuad and Farouk, had built it, managed it and worked in it. It was a free hospital for the poor; as Abdel al Badr said, 'It is right and just that wealth wrung from the fellah should be put at the service of the fellah.' He did not refuse rich patients, but to them his fees were extortionate. Nationalists, Socialists and above all idealists, supporters first of Mahommed Neguib and later of Gamal Nasser, the three doctors had presented their hospital to the State; on condition of retaining control of it.

Al Badr's admiration for Nasser did not outlast that statesman's life: the doctor became disgusted with the compromises into which Nasser was forced, with the very slow pace of progress towards Socialism; with the waste of spirit and treasure entailed by the long and futile war with Israel; but above all with the failure to do anything effective to relieve the millennia-long misery of the fellahin. He was an impatient man excepting when it came to his chosen work – diseases of the skin; and his impatience drove him steadily to the Left.

Just how much the authorities were aware of this is not clear. They would have hesitated, in any case, to treat him roughly unless his political conduct became outrageous; no man in Egypt was better respected and better loved.

He dismissed his last patient of the day, frowning as he completed a note of the problem her case presented. His secretary-nurse was hovering; without raising his eyes he said, 'Yes, yes, I will see Sheikh Allal now; show him in; and then you may go.'

When Allal bin Mocktar came in the doctor was still frowning over his notes. He pushed them from him, rose and kissed his visitor on both cheeks.

'I am sorry to have kept you waiting. It is good to see you, Allal.'

'And for me. But perhaps you will be less happy when you know my errand.'

'You need more help?'

'Yes. Abdel, I think that the time I have waited for is nearly upon us.'

'Indeed?' The doctor was non-committal. He said, 'Do you mind if we do our talking here? I'm waiting for a telephone call, an urgent matter, from the Institut Pasteur in Paris.'

'Here, of course. Your patients come first, I know. It is right that they should.'

Doctor al Badr rang for coffee; Allal asked after his wife and children; they exchanged personal news until the servant bringing the coffee had left them. Then Allal talked while al Badr listened. At one point he interrupted,

'The project is a great and good one. You are not proposing to sabotage his works? That is not the way.'

'You misunderstand. It is a question of seizing control of them for the workers, for the people. If I am strong . . .'

'Dear friend, you can be strong only in the strength of the people. I know your people, and above all I know your Cousins. Whatever *your* object, theirs will be to destroy the pipelines, burn the desalination plant, to keep the desert desert and their own.' He smiled and went on, 'I have always had reservations about that wisdom of the people which Lenin bids us trust.'

Allal said, 'Yet he was right when he wrote that man only is a socialist who relies upon the experience and instincts of the toiling masses, infinitely more valuable than the most extensive and brilliant theoretical forecasts, and my business will be to teach them to find and recognize their own wisdom, to guide them in the use of their native good sense; and of their strength.'

'Your bedouin are not what I should describe as toiling masses, Allal.' The doctor paused, looking at Allal thoughtfully. At last he said, 'Ah, well. Do you have the shopping list for me to pass on to our friends in Prague?'

Allal put a typewritten sheet of paper on the table: it was a list of weapons and explosive materials. Al Badr looked it over and raised his eyebrows, saying, 'You ask a great deal.'

'You know that I can and will pay.'

'When you control the oil, yes. Our suppliers may call themselves Communists but they are worse than the Jews when it comes to business. They are not enthusiastic about long-term investments.'

'I can pay much sooner.'

'How?'

'I had not finished what I had to say to you. Listen; Habib will pay to make sure that his works go forward without interference from my people. His associates, the oil corporations, will pay to be sure that we do not cut their pipelines and burn their booster stations.'

'Blackmail. Yes . . . you are sure that you can keep your men in hand?'

'Quite sure.'

'It will not be easy, Allal: to rouse the people so that their anger is a serious threat, yet deny them the logical expression of their anger in violence, and keep them in leash . . .'

He shook his head. Allal said,

'That is the whole skill of the leader; it is his business. I know my business, Abdel.'

'Supposing that I can procure you this hardware . . .' he used the English word, 'what is the route of delivery?'

'As before, through Senegal.'

'It will be permitted?'

'I have the General's assurances; the customary price, of course . . .' He rubbed his right thumb over his forefinger, and added, 'In Swiss francs and into his Geneva account.'

'Very well, I will do my best.'

The telephone rang; the doctor picked it up and said, 'Al Badr,' and listened and then, '*Ah, monsieur le docteur . . . oui, c'est moi . . . Bien, merci, et vous? Bon, bon. Eh bien, vous avez trouvé ce qu'il me faut? . . . Ah, je m'en doutais . . . Bon, allez-y . . .*'

He fell silent and began to write, punctuating his busy silence with an occasional word of attention.

Habib began to hear news, first from the spies he had purchased among the clansmen, then as bazaar rumours retailed in their reports by his observers in the city, of a new voice raised in the desert.

It was the voice of the mullah 'Omar bin Mocktar, half-brother of the Sheikh-among-Sheiks. It was not a loud or ranting voice: it was the voice of a scholar, and some said a saint, who did not order men, 'do this', 'think that'; did not rebuke and did not urge, but expounded. He sat in his tent, the Book before him, like the teachers of old, talked, reasoned and prayed. He bade no man come to him but said, 'Those who would be of our company of seekers, let them be welcome.' And to those who came, and they were many and growing daily more numerous, he said, 'Those who have ears to hear, let them hear.'

Soon the great tent was daily crowded so that many who wished to hear had to remain outside.

The reports which Habib received were supplemented; he sent a trained man, an intelligence officer, to hear the words of 'Omar. After ten days the man returned to Farzar and said,

'The man is dangerous.' His long report, which included three tapes recorded on a small machine which he carried concealed in his clothes, was handed to Professor Feridun Bagheri of the Faculty of Religious Law in the University of Farzar. In due course the professor, author of *The Influence of the Sonna on the Development of Capitalism and Socialism in Islam*, reached his conclusions and reported to Habib who sent for him, receiving him on the terrace where he liked to hold such conferences.

'There is nothing very new in our saint's sermons, Highness. It is all what has been said before, but he reinforces his arguments with quotations from the *Contemplations* of his eponymous ancestor, a thinker no more original than himself. He bases his case on the Koranic deprecation of *riba*, and draws, to the same end, on the *Sonna*. Similarly, he teaches the orthodox prohibition of *maysir*, and the equally orthodox condemnation of *gharar*. He derives his authority in each case from the *Companions*, of course . . . but it has, in the last thirteen centuries, been rather thoroughly . . . how shall I put it? . . . scholasticized. From the point of view of his particular congregation, his case is greatly strengthened by his frequent references to the *Contemplations*.' The professor expounded *riba*, *maysir* and *gharar*. When he fell silent the prince said,

'More Catholic than the Pope, as the Christians say?'

'Exactly, Highness. The gentle insinuation of his argument always is that his listener knows the law as well as he does; they have come together to discuss its excellence, that they may be edified; and that when the time comes they will not fail to act righteously. When the law is at stake, a believer does not shrink from violence. Where there is good precedent for righteous war, for a *jehad*, then killing's no murder.'

'Quite so,' Habib said, sombrely, 'I can almost hear him . . .' He rocked his body gently back and forth in his chair and, changing from Farsi to Arabic, intoned quietly, '*In the name of Allah, the Compassionate, the Merciful, hear now the voice of your manly hearts . . .* You know, Feridun Bagheri, it is perhaps a strange thing to say to a master of the law, but if there's one thing I'm frightened of in this life, it's a man who knows he's right. This fellow makes capitalist industrial development contrary to the law, impious, an abomination. Am I right? How much, I wonder, has the Sheikh, his brother, to do with this?'

'That is outside my competence, Highness.'

'You are too modest. Let us suppose that this work – my work for this country – were being done under the aegis of Marxism. What do the mullah of Mocktar and the six clans say to that?'

'Your Highness needs no guidance from me: *then* the work becomes a great giving of alms.'

'As I thought. Is this man a mere bigot, my friend, or is he a mere agitator?'

'Highness, the saints have generally been agitators. It is why they are such a terrible nuisance.'

The Prince laughed. More coffee was offered, and refused; the Prince saw the professor to his car, and returned to his own workroom and sent for whisky and soda and his sister Azizeh to whom he said, 'Sister, I have work for you.' He poured her a whisky and explained.

Four

Israel Mendes telephoned his wife from the Curran–Robarts drawing-office to say that he had lent himself to Gurling–Curran as consultant, had to attend a special meeting at their office that evening, would be home at four but would have to go out again at five. Gertrud said, 'There was no need to drag me to the phone to tell me that.'

'I thought it might make a difference to your dinner arrangements. I may be late.'

'Oh very crafty: never fail in considerateness and you can skip the rest. I shall dine at eight as usual.' She rang off. Miss O'Neill, Israel's secretary, looked at his face and turned her eyes hastily away: would he never learn?

He reached home at four; told his driver that he would be wanted at five; and let himself into the house. He found Gertrud in her own sitting-room, staring into a log fire and drinking gin and tonic; she had the bottle beside her. That she had had a fire lit was the measure of his guilt. On the other hand, there was the gin: Israel tried not to look pointedly at it. Her silvery-blonde hair looked dank, but the blue eyes were clear when she turned them to his and said,

'I've had a terrible fright.'

'I'm sorry. What happened?'

'Ike . . . your son, remember? . . . he turned blue, he couldn't breathe, I thought he was going to die. Marvellous how you manage never to be here when something awful happens.

You've a wonderful way of avoiding unpleasantness. Oh, don't tell me, I know it's not your fault, you couldn't know the child was going to choke nearly to death . . . just your damned Jewish luck.'

'Is Isaac all right?'

'Now, yes. No, don't go up to the nursery. He's sleeping. Nanny says he's not to be disturbed.'

He sat as far from the fire as he could; the month was May and the weather warm. He said, 'Please tell me what happened.'

'You remember when those appalling Greek friends of yours came to dinner . . . why the hell we can't take such people to a restaurant when they have to be fed, I never shall understand . . . One of them, the fat man, broke those ridiculous worry-beads he was always fiddling with, probably to prevent himself picking his nose or scratching his balls in public. The string broke . . .'

'Constantin Vafiadis . . . who happens to be one of the half-dozen mathematicians who understand the philosophy of the theory of chance in my books; but you wouldn't know about that . . . I remember the incident. What has it to do with poor little Ike?'

'*Ike* . . . Christ, what a name for *my* son. Ikey-Mo von Hoffmanstahl . . . sounds lovely, doesn't it?'

'As his surname isn't von Hoffmanstahl but Mendes, perhaps it doesn't matter. You were telling me what happened . . .'

'I should be able to tell you sooner if you didn't interrupt . . .' She poured herself another drink but he knew that though she finished the bottle she would not be drunk: drunkenness was not given to her. She said, 'One of the beads wasn't found; amber things, probably sham amber. Ike was crawling about the drawing-room floor after that bloody kitten you insisted on giving him, found the bead and stuffed it up his nose.' The picture made him smile. She said, 'You find that funny? Somehow it got through into his throat and stuck there.'

'And you got it out?'

'Nanny, not me. I was useless in a crisis, as usual. I'm saying it myself so that you won't have to.'

'That's not fair. I have never . . .'

'Oh, don't quibble. You may not say it but by Christ you think it.'

'If you'd let me try to help . . .'

'*You* help . . . oh, go to hell . . .'

'I'm going to my room to work. I'll be leaving at five and expect to be back for dinner.'

'Whatever time it is, I'll be in bed by then.'

Israel went to his room and sat at his desk and stared at his hands. Her antisemitism did not really hurt him: it was part of a general campaign of abuse; if he had happened to be the son of an earl with Norman blood she would have found a way to make an insult of that. She was not literate enough to feel herself evoking the huge crime of the past; she did her damage like a drunk striking out at random.

For three years they had been happy . . . Then, it began to be like this and for the first time he remembered her father's extraordinary letter: the old Graf had written:

> No man enters into a contract with me without knowing what he is receiving. You will do as you please, sir, but remember, on a day that will come, that her revulsion from what the Nazis did to her as a maiden, from what they taught her, will not last. Believe me, sir, that you are a Jew is nothing to me; that you are a rich one is, for the moment, everything to my daughter. Please face what you are doing. I will not be involved in a fraudulent transaction. She will hate herself first; and then you.

He could no longer bring friends to the house. The last time he'd brought a friend home it had been Jock Drummond and there'd been that shocking scene: she had picked on both of them all the evening; dinner was late because she'd wanted to go on drinking. Drummond was trying to be amusing on the subject of his children's passion for fish fingers and Gertrud had started to hector him about the enormity of letting young children eat filth from the deep-freeze. She was still at it as they went in to dinner. Fortunately it had been Elspeth, the elderly maid he'd inherited from his mother, who had been waiting on them. Drummond had become very white, which meant that he was in a rage. Israel himself was shaking by then. There came a moment when Jock had put down his knife and fork and risen and said, 'Izzy, I think I'd better be going,' and she'd abruptly screamed at him, 'Go, get out, and take your little Yiddisher friend with you.'

Drummond had stood over her, his face bloodless, suddenly thin, vicious, and said in a voice much lower than his usual tone, 'You know what's wrong with you, Gertrud? For years, because you used to be beautiful, till you started on the booze, you were the important one, and Izzy just an appendage, useful because of his money. You were the one they looked at, eh? But when you started to hear him talked of as the boy genius, when his books were talked about and his name was in all the papers as the designer of the R01, when it was him people looked at first when the pair of you came into a room and you were just another of his achievements, a pretty wife . . . it went sour on you, didn't it? The lovely, witty, *hochgeboren* Gertrud von Hoffmanstahl . . . *so amusing, my dear, and, of course, quite ravishing* . . . playing second fiddle to . . .' he glanced at Israel, and said, 'a Yid,' and then said, 'You make me sick, Gertrud. It's an effect you have on people nowadays. Try looking in the mirror tonight and see if you throw up . . .'

He, Israel, filled with horror and pity, had said, 'Jock, that will do . . .' and Gertrud had said, 'Why don't you go back to fucking your sisters in the Glasgow slums, Drummond?' and with the full swing of his arm he'd given her a slap on the side of her face that had knocked her off her chair.

Israel sighed: he rang the bell on his desk and when Elspeth came in asked her to tell him about the accident. She told him, concluding . . . 'A great fuss about very little, master Israel. I don't care for Nanny as you know, but she knows her work, I'll say that for her.'

'Thanks, Elspeth.'

He went quietly up the stairs and into the night nursery. Nanny was reading a massive volume which turned out, when he caught a glimpse of the jacket, to be *Angélique*, and this immediately made her less formidable. She rose from beside the child's bed and put a finger to her lips. Israel looked at his son; the hair was like pale natural silk, the cheeks like petals. He turned to Nanny and raised inquiring eyebrows, and she made a reassuring face. He looked at his watch: it was time to go.

There were to be four at the meeting besides Gurling. Miss Rutter, promoted to Caroline Bartrum's place, had managed to suspend the big map left behind by 'General Hakim' from the picture-rail, covering three oil paintings of the Gurling–Curran nuclear power plant in Mexico. First to arrive was Jock Drummond of Pipeline Division, a short, tubby man with a cheerful face and a temper which he sometimes failed to master.

'Anyone else here?' he asked Miss Rutter.

'Mr Mendes is in the spare office, playing his guitar.' She had been with them long enough to take that eccentricity for granted.

Drummond strolled along the corridor and stood outside Izzy's door and listened, smiling to the notes of a *chora* by Villa-Lobos. Successful himself – he had made his way from a slum to executive office as an engineer by his thirty-second year – he had an affectionate admiration for Mendes which was free from envy and wholly sweet-natured. A man in need of heroes, for him Israel Mendes was a man apart, with a mind of a special order; in short, a genius. How else could one explain his worldwide renown among mathematicians before he was twenty-four, as an original mathematical philosopher; or his accomplishment of the R01 jet engine which was soon to be powering a new generation of supersonic jumbo airliners, in his twenty-eighth year? Add to that his skill as a musician, and didn't you have something out of the common way?

While Drummond was standing in the corridor listening to Israel's playing, David Gough of the Maritime Division came up the stairs and walked past him on his way to the conference room, raising a hand in greeting. Gough was short, slight and very fair, almost girlish in appearance. He came of seafaring stock; his father and both grandfathers had been master mariners. He had preferred to become a naval architect and had been gathered into the Gurling–Curran fold after his team at a rival establishment had designed the new ice-breaker hull which both the Americans and Russians were now buying. For the time being he was doing experimental work on a new submarine hull. His reserve among colleagues was apt to be mistaken for unfriendliness.

When Israel stopped playing, Drummond followed Gough into the conference room. Miss Rutter came in with a tray of glasses, bottles, ice and sandwiches. Israel arrived looking as if he had never played a guitar in his life, and asked the girl if everyone had turned up; she said that Mr Brax was with Mr Gurling. A shade under six feet tall, he had long legs and a short body, sharply waisted, like a Cretan's. The skin was fair and the eyes grey but the hair very dark brown; he wore it long. He stood in front of the map and said,

'Does anyone know anything about this place . . . I mean, anything interesting?'

Gough said, 'I made a forced landing there once, at Farzar, flying a Comanchee up to Casablanca . . .' Then Gurling and Simon Brax came in, continuing an argument. Gurling was carrying a long roll of paper, and tapping his knuckles with it every time one of Brax's arguments annoyed him.

They took their places round the table; then Gurling rose again and went to the map with the paper roll in his hand. Miss Rutter came in with two tape-recorders, put them on the table, and switched one on. Gurling used the paper roll to point out the Curzon Depression and the Wilhelm Crater, saying, 'This is where Dirk is now . . .' He said a little about those two features of the landscape, then returned to the table and said,

'It's a question of making a feasibility study: problem, fill that crater with fresh water and keep it filled and running through a turbine into the Depression from which we pump it through pipelines to an irrigation system covering a thousand square kilometres, and possibly more, up to two thousand five hundred.'

'If it's another D-plant . . .' Brax began.

'It isn't a D-plant,' Gurling said; he appeared slightly embarrassed. He said, 'The client has an idea.'

'God help us,' Gough said, quietly; Drummond laughed. Gurling said, 'I'm inclined to think we shall need His help, but I haven't turned the idea down. I see it this way: there are minds, a few, very few, outside our world, professionally I mean, which can sometimes throw off an idea we shouldn't be too quick to reject as crazy. I think we should never forget that the history of our trade is a history of experts saying you couldn't do things which someone then proceeded to do. Think how the Brunels, father and son, were treated . . . and in our own time, Barnes Wallis; there are fifty examples. Izzy, who designed the first efficient marine turbine?'

'The Earl of Rosse, wasn't it? I see the point . . . an amateur.'

'Right. Our client isn't an earl; he's a reigning prince and a damned clever one. He gave us this idea. It's probably crazy. Let's try to find out.'

'What, in a word, is all this *about*, John?' Jock Drummond said, 'for you're being unco' shifty.'

'In a word then – icebergs. Does the name Erik von Neuberg mean anything to anyone here?'

'Yes,' Gough said, 'glaciology.'

'Good. I have here a recording of a paper he read to the Royal

Society last year, on the growth of the East Greenland glaciers and the calving of icebergs in Melville Bay. I want you to hear it; it runs to just over half an hour but it's packed with facts. You all understand German, I think.'

He touched a switch on the second recorder, switched off the first, and they settled to listen, Drummond quietly pouring drinks and handing round the sandwiches. The German glaciologist reeled off observations, statistics and conclusions with the deliberation of a machine.

When the paper was over, and Gurling had switched the tape recorder off and switched on the first one again – it was keeping a minute of the meeting – he said, 'Anyone been doing any arithmetic?' Israel said, 'You mean, of course, that a big berg can be holding upwards of a thousand million cubic metres of water.' And Brax said, 'Good God, you're not thinking of towing . . .'

'No, not towing. Izzy?'

'You're thinking of the SR zero?'

'Yes.'

'I'm not ready to say much about it yet. The prototype works at depths down to two hundred metres. Whether it would push an iceberg from the Arctic to Farzar – it's a tallish order.'

'Completely impossible,' Brax said. He was known in the whole group as the 'handyman'. Trained as a marine engineer, he had built bridges, drilled tunnels; he had seven important patents, all of them the outcome of improvizations in a crisis, to his name. He began every project with the assurance that you couldn't do it; and then did it.

Gough said, 'I must say, it sounds mad, John.'

'Forget that. We'll approach it as if it were sane. Anything else to say, Izzy?'

'Not till I have some data. Why engines? Why not sails? I suppose, David, that we can consider an iceberg as a hull?'

'Yes and no. They don't seem to be any particular shape. I

wonder, could one sculpt the ice, shape up the lump a bit, say with flame . . . very big flame guns of some kind . . . to make it more manageable . . ?'

'A cubic kilometre of ice would weigh a thousand million metric tons or thereabouts,' Drummond said. 'It's not my field, thank God, but can you shove a lump that size about?'

'Dead weight doesn't mean anything,' Israel said, 'when you're calculating the inertia of a body floating in water. For our purpose, nine-tenths of an iceberg is weightless, like a balloon exactly balanced in air. Inertia and resistance are calculable, of course, that's elementary stuff.' Brax said, 'I'm humouring you by discussing this nonsense at all. Melting loss would be enormous.'

Gurling, rolling one of his stinking *caporal* cigarettes, said,

'But not disastrously so. I've been looking into the records. Quite big bergs have been sighted at least as far south as 31 degrees of north latitude, which isn't far north of Farzar. They've been seen off Bermuda. They're not of the same order of magnitude as the kind of thing we're discussing, but remember this: they've been drifting in warm seas for many months, in some cases for a couple of years, perhaps longer. For us it would be, in part, a question of avoiding long passages in warm currents, for instance of crossing the Gulf Stream on the shortest possible course.'

He started to unroll the paper he had used as a pointer; while he did so Brax said, 'Suppose we get it, or them, to Farzar . . . which we certainly never shall, then what do we do with it?'

'That's your job, Simon . . . a dry dock.'

'A dry *dock*?'

'That's what I thought. The investment would be large but this isn't a one-off operation, it would be repeated once or twice a year indefinitely if it works at all. Float her in, pump out the sea water, the tide would help, there's a two hundred metre ebb at certain points along that coast. Then let the sun's heat melt the berg, and pump the water up into Jock's pipeline which, I might point out, will have a small incline down to the crater. Come and look at this chart.'

They gathered round him. He said, 'Here's Melville Bay where von Neuberg says most of the big bergs are calved. Now see what happens: we choose our berg here – the East Greenland Current drifts it south-west. By then we're aboard it, fitting our gear. Round about here . . .' Gurling was now using a pencil to point out the course, 'the current delivers us into the *West* Greenland Current: it's a sort of branch off the Gulf Stream and consequently warm, so there'll be some melting losses there, but it carries us round Cape Farewell and north into the Davis Strait.'

'What're these red pencil arrows for?' Israel asked.

'I'll come to them in a minute. Let me do this my own way. Now normally our berg would continue northward till the West Greenland Current makes a U-turn here, just north of the Arctic Circle. But at this point we start to shove. And we shall have the kind of help which, in practice, releases the bergs from these northern currents and enables them to get into the open Atlantic: wind.'

'The red arrows,' Israel said.

'Right. I'm assuming we do this job in June/July. We start shoving here, then, across to the Labrador Current – a cold one – which drifts us southward parallel with the coast of Labrador and Newfoundland, to a point somewhere a couple of hundred miles off Cape Race. All right? And off Cape Race the wind at that season should be steadily eastward, with a considerable northward component. I mean it's blowing from the south-west. It goes without saying that we've got to be able to steer the berg, more or less. Now the wind . . .'

Gough said, 'Wait. Any above the waterline face of a really big berg can be upwards of one hundred thousand square metres, a fine big sail I grant you. But our hull's no shape at all. I don't know, mind you, but I'd guess, that the wind simply imparts a slow rotary motion to the berg. There can't be much forward progress.'

'But some and that's where steering comes in,' Gurling said, 'and for all I know we could steer with a sail if it was big enough. How we do it is your problem and Israel's. My point is this: here . . .' he put his pencil point again on the mark he had made off Cape Race, 'we have to change direction and move the berg across the Gulf Stream roughly at the point where it merges with the North Atlantic Drift. Both warm, so we'll have more melting losses, and the currents are both going the wrong way. On the other hand, look at the red arrows again. The wind helps us into Mid-Atlantic, then starts pushing us south-west, and here . . .' he marked a point off the southern extremity of the Bay of Biscay, 'helps to move us south down the coast of Spain and North Africa and by long before then we have the Canary Current, and moreover that one's cold, drifting us the same way, down to Farzar.'

'About two thousand five hundred miles,' Israel said, looking at the chart. 'Any idea of the rate of flow of the currents?'

'Yes, about five miles an hour, and the wind usually between four and five on the Beaufort Scale. As far as I can see, we'd have the wind helping us all the way, and the currents for about seventeen hundred miles. For the other eight hundred we'd be fighting a north-westerly lateral drift but still have the wind on our side. Let's suppose we average only two miles an hour, the job will take a couple of months. I don't believe melting losses would be prohibitive in that time and even if we lost half the berg on the way we'd still have about half a year's supply for the whole scheme. Once we've done one, we can do as many as necessary, establish a regular delivery. Izzy?'

'I can't say anything useful at this stage, unless it's useful to say that I don't agree with Simon that it's impossible.'

'Do we have any figures for the size of bergs which have been at sea, in the warm currents, for months?' Gough asked.

'Not our sort of big ones. It's estimated that the berg which sank the *Titanic* four hundred miles south of Cape Race on 14 April 1912 . . . I've been doing some homework on this . . . was at least six months old, probably a year. It was about 220,000 cubic metres. And there's always the chance of a stroke of luck: for instance, according to oceanographic people in Washington, in 1973 the Atlantic Current was about sixty miles further north than usual, cutting-off the Labrador Current and causing a big cold eddy here, between the Grand Banks and the Atlantic Currect.'

Gurling looked at his watch: he said, 'I think that'll do for now. The purpose of the meeting was to start you thinking, and doing any preliminary research you can do. Just one thing. The calving season for bergs will be starting soon. I think I'll lay on a visit to Melville Bay. We might as well take a look. I want you to think of the implications if we succeed. Why shouldn't Arctic ice water the Sahara? Why shouldn't Antarctic ice fill the depression they call Lake Eyre in South Australia?'

Brax said, 'Why shouldn't pigs fly? Because they haven't got any bloody wings, mate.'

Five

Brax and Drummond left the meeting together and walked north to a public house called 'The Seven Beeches' in Notting Hill. Nobody else in the firm used it but they liked it because in its public bar they could enter a world remote from their own but round the corner from Drummond's house. It was a favourite pub with the blacks but was also used by people from the Church Street region and from that area north of Bayswater Road inhabited by impoverished and not so poor members of what used to be called the intelligentsia. More recently it had acquired a clientele of Irish building labourers.

Brax was to dine with the Drummonds who had a pretty little early Victorian house with a small garden in the tree-lined cul-de-sac which is called, nobody knows why, Wyatt's End.

Simon Brax dined with the Drummonds about once a month. They were fond of him but, like the people at Gurling–Curran, knew almost nothing about him. They did, of course, know about his life and work as an engineer; but he seemed to be one of those people who have no private life. When he wanted to repay hospitality he took his friends to a small and excellent Italian restaurant in Mayfair. With women he was easy and pleasant; he obviously enjoyed their company and they usually liked him; but not one of his friends had ever seen the least kindling of sexual fire between him and a woman. The obvious assumption, that he was homosexual, had been discounted on no particular grounds; perhaps because he never showed any distinguishing warmth towards a young man; and, as Emma Drummond said, 'He just doesn't seem queer.' As she also said, 'Why do we never allow for the people who just don't have any sex?' To which her husband replied, 'There ain't no sich animal.'

'The Seven Beeches' was crowded: Brax used his height and weight to reach the bar, and emerged with their drinks. The evening was warm and they took them outside to the little paved courtyard round a bed of tulips and wallflowers, where the landlord had set iron tables and chairs. The south façade of the house, which was an old one, was overgrown with a magnificent wistaria and Simon and Jock were discussing the legend that it had been planted by John Claudius Loudon and was more than a century old, when Simon suddenly flushed all over his big, square face, and put his hand over his mouth in a curiously helpless gesture of embarrassment. Jock Drummond was taken aback; he had never seen his friend so put out; following the direction of Simon's eyes, he saw a man who might have been any age from thirty to fifty – it depended on how much significance you attached to the tissue-papery texture of pale facial skin – who was staring at Simon and making his way, with a full pint tankard in his right hand, towards them.

When he reached them he said,

'Hallo, Simon. Won't you introduce me to your friend?' and Simon said, 'What the devil are you doing here?' in a tone which made Jock look at him with astonishment. The other man, using a tone which Jock could, absurd though it seemed, only call insolent, said,

'My dear, I'm sorry to break our treaty, but Art Leary has shifted his labour-market from 'The Swans' to this place, and as you very well know, where the carcass is, there shall the eagles be gathered together.'

Simon, who from very red had become pale, said, 'Jock, this is Jocelyn Quist, an old friend of mine; Jock Drummond.'

Quist smiled at Jock and said, 'Simon has, as they say, told me so much about you, I feel you're no stranger. Clearly you can't return the compliment.' Jock said, 'Well, I . . .' and Quist, 'Oh God, I'm being embarrassing,' and, abruptly changing his manner, 'I'm afraid that what I've just been saying is Choctaw to you. If you look and listen about you, you will perceive a lot of large, rough men with the brogue. That very powerful-looking gentleman in corduroy trousers and a tweed jacket reproducing what, if I'm not mistaken, is the Stewart hunting tartan, is Arthur *Ignashus* . . . his own rendering . . . Leary; and, in my dreary trade, a person of consequence. Whithersoever he goeth, there also shall thou find . . . me.'

All this was spoken in a slightly breathless, lilting way, with much facial expression, ending in a very wide opening of the eyes, a deliberate pastiche of naïve, boyish amazement at the importance of the man Leary.

In a dull voice which Jock had never heard before, Simon Brax said, 'Jocelyn, do we have to have that camping turn?' Quist ignored him and went on speaking to Jock:

'You see, I know I don't look the part, but I'm a building contractor in a small way of business. Trained as an architect, you know, but simply couldn't do the maths. Now I know you won't believe this, because nobody outside the trade ever does, but . . .'

Simon said, still in the same dull tone but louder, 'Jocelyn, some other time, I'm afraid we have to be going . . .' and Quist without turning to him, said, 'Don't be tiresome, darling,' and '. . . but all the building labour in this town's in the hands of Irish foremen. One makes what bargain one can with them, it's exactly like dealing with a slave-master, so many men to be on such and such a site, at such a time, day and place as the buyer requires, at such and such a rate per hour and a bloody big cut for the foreman. Our enterprise, Mr Drummond, isn't just private; its bloody well *secret*, and nothing, but nothing, to do with trade unions, government agencies, laws, rules . . . and then, you see, halfway through the job, with the first concrete not even *set*, they're off to another job, and unless one pays and pays . . .' he shrugged, turned at last to Brax and said, 'Simon, I implore you to stop looking as if you'd lost your upper *denture*.'

At which point Brax said to Drummond, 'Jocelyn and I share a flat.' And Quist said, 'In other words, Mr Drummond, Simon and I live together and I must add that I've become bored with being treated as a social *leper*.'

Jock Drummond's mind was flooded with new light on Brax. Now guided by the instinct he relied on without thought in his dealings with people, he said,

'Mr Quist, Simon's dining with my wife and me. Will you . . . I apologize for the short notice . . . join us?'

Quist's assurance, if that is what it was, suddenly deserted him and with an expression of timidity, he looked at Simon for guidance. He did not get it; Brax was shamming dead. Jock said,

'Do come, if you're free. I've always been interested in how you chaps manage the labour problem. You weren't exaggerating?'

'I'd love to dine with you and your wife. No, I wasn't exaggerating.'

They talked on, leaving Brax to himself, giving him time to recover. Quist went to buy a round of drinks, stopping on the way to talk to the great Mr Leary and to two or three building workers. There was a lot of laughter where he passed; he seemed to know how to talk to the men he depended on. Simon said, 'I suppose you think . . .'

'I don't think anything. I like Quist and he seems to like me. Why you chose to keep him to yourself is your business. I think you might have trusted Emma and me, but . . . let's forget that.'

With a visible effort, as if he were lifting an enormous load, Brax said,

'I've never quite been able not to be ashamed.'

'Of what, in God's name?'

'Ah, in God's name; maybe that's been my trouble. My

father's God didn't like . . . queers. Remember what He did to the cities of the plain?'

'That old heavenly Savage,' Jock said, and, exaggerating his accent, 'Aye, there's few things do more harm to a decent nature than a religious education. Here come our drinks.'

The three walked to Drummond's house, Jock in the middle; for the awkwardness of the evening's beginning was still lingering. Jock, determined to have done with the nonsense, said, 'How long have you been shacked up together?' It was Jocelyn Quist who answered him, 'Nearly two years. You must come and see us. Simon has no taste, we should be all leathery if he had his say, but he doesn't and I've made it rather nice. Of course, I have useful connections, wallpaper people, that sort of thing.'

Emma Drummond was not a woman to be put out by an extra guest and she took an immediate liking to Quist. They had drinks in a pleasant room which opened onto a pretty little Italian garden of grass, clipped evergreens and a small fountain. Emma talked Simon back onto terms with himself while Quist admired her looks: she was a little taller than Jock – he was only five feet seven – with reddish brown hair, a very fair, fine skin and exceptionally large, short-sighted grey-green eyes. Quist said, 'I love your garden. I'm going to give you a present for it, an Adam garden seat cut in stone; I stole it from the garden on a demolition job; it would go beautifully against that far hedge.'

'For her garden's sake,' Jock said, 'Emma will cheerfully become a receiver of stolen goods.'

The *au pair* girl brought in Emma's two little girls, one dark, one fair, both pretty, to say goodnight. They were lively, well-mannered and self-possessed; Quist remarked on it and Jock said that they'd been brought up 'old-fashioned'.

'You monster, I believe you beat them . . .'

'Only as often as necessary.'

The guests stayed, talking, till midnight. Quist was widely read, had travelled, worked at twenty trades, and talked with the kind of animated frivolity which stimulates a party. He had no prejudices, no convictions, no faith in anything but work and luck, and no illusions. For him all politicians were charlatans on the make and the only rules worth keeping kindness and generosity. As Jock said that night to Emma before they went to sleep, 'Now there's a man who's native where he walks and wise in his generation.'

When the guests left they decided to walk until they found a taxi. They did so in silence for some minutes until Simon said,

'Jocelyn, forgive me, I'm . . .'

'Sorry? Don't be; don't explain, don't talk about it. I've always understood. That pub scene was . . . a tantrum. I've had an extremely tiresome day and – I fell short. If I believed in apology, then it should be me . . .' He took Simon's hand and went on, 'I've never complained, it would have been grossly hypocritical to complain because it would've meant pretending that I didn't understand.'

Another silence until Quist said, 'Your friends . . . that's a house of love.'

'Yes.'

Israel Mendes got permission from David Gough to make use of the huge tank in the hydrodynamics department of the Group's Harpenden workshops; he needed to make some underwater experiments. Gertrud said, 'If you're going to stay out there, I shall go to Paris.'

'As you please, of course. I hadn't thought that my presence or absence were much noticed by you.'

'I need a change. I'm bored. Have you *never* been bored?'

'Never. I can imagine it's very painful. But do you forget that you have a son?'

'Nanny's better with him than I am.'

'Gertrud, tell me, do you hate it . . . being a mother?'

'I might not have done. Don't start that again. I have the wrong father for my child. It's nobody's fault.'

They left the house together the following morning. Israel said,

'I take it you'll stay at the usual place.'
'Yes. If there's any need – there won't be but if – telephone.'
'Of course. Amuse yourself.'
'I intend to. I shall buy clothes.'
'I'm sure you will.'
'Have you any objection?'
'No. And I didn't mean . . .' he shrugged, raised a hand in farewell, and walked to the bus-stop, leaving her the car and driver.

His request for permission to use the tank had been made through John Gurling, as coordinator of the project study. John had telephoned:

'You can have the tank, of course. I've squared it with David who's off abroad for a week anyway. I gather you've made progress with the SR zero.'

'Yes, John. I still don't know if it'll work.'

'As Simon would say, it's obviously impossible.'

'It may well be; I've had trouble with the waterproof jacket. I'll tell you in about a week.'

The first trial, after six twenty-hour days in the shops, blasted water and steam out of the tank in spectacular style and flooded an adjacent welding shop. Gough's assistant raised his voice in a lamentation of biblical eloquence, weakly concluded with 'I don't know what David will say.' Israel, getting out of his waterproof overalls, said, 'I can tell you. Nothing; he never does when someone makes a mess. What I need is a canal, an old stretch of canal . . .' Inwardly he was excited; he knew that he was onto something. The other man said, 'What you need's the whole bloody Atlantic.'

Israel could not get a canal, but he got a one-hundred acre lake in what had been a gentleman's park and was now farmland. The engine was mounted on the underside of a hollow steel raft which was counter-loaded by steel cables to two powerful hydraulic-pneumatic winches. The shops' senior engineer told him, in writing, that he'd surely kill himself and washed his hands of the project. Israel himself rode the raft, at the controls.

He was using a modified engine and a fuel of his own containing a liquid oxygen component. Halfway across the lake the engineer at the winch controls made a mistake, both winches jammed, and before the winch anchorage was torn away from the concrete brakes and Israel could throttle back, four acres of pasture had been flooded; Israel, hurled clear of the raft as it leaped into the air, was swimming for the bank. But he was happy, and after seven telephone calls and a minor row with Sir Edwin Curran, he was given permission to take his contrivance to sea, and Royal Navy help was procured. The first of his family of hydroturbines was born.

As often as he was not working until late into the night, dining off corned beef sandwiches, pickles and stout, and sleeping, if at all, on a campbed in the drawing office – as the senior engineer said, 'Yon fella's possessed of a devil' – he drove himself home to Regent's Park to see Ike. Ike never showed whether he was pleased or displeased to see his father: he was an extremely serious child whose expression suggested that he was occupied with matters far above such sentimentalities as filial affection. Israel said as much to Nanny, who was much relaxed in Gertrud's absence; she said, reproachfully, 'He's only three, Mr Mendes,' but allowed Israel to play with the boy. He sat on the nursery floor, detesting the self-consciousness with which he did so, and fed plastic building bricks to the younger builder. He was moved by Ike's prettiness, fascinated by the visibly growing intelligence, but could find in himself no specifically paternal feelings. Then why come home at all? Was it any more than an acted reproach to Gertrud for her indifference to their son? The gentle pleasure of these nursery sessions ended in a sense of guilt: what lack or what evil in him had transformed Gertrud, or at least released in her all the poison of her Nazi schoolgirlhood?

Gertrud was not a Nazi moral cripple; Jock Drummond had been right about her. Israel's fame was an intolerable affront to her pride; he had soared away from her power, she had come to hate him and any stick would do to beat him with.

At Heathrow, on the day she left for Paris, she saw a man she thought she knew standing at the Duty Free counter for spirits and tobacco in the departure lounge. He was slight, fair and physically unremarkable but it seemed to her that there was a hardness, a tautness about him, which set him apart, as if he were so charged with energy of some kind that his body was stiffened by it, because it imposed on him a permanent bracing of the flesh. A light from behind the counter was so placed in relation to his head and her own position, that she saw him with a halo, which made her smile; for she was certain that whatever he was, he wasn't a saint.

During the rest of the time she had to wait for her flight to be called she was trying to place him, but it was not until she was boarding the aircraft, the man being some way ahead of her, that she remember Izzy showing her the man's photograph on the front cover of *Time* magazine, in order to complain that here was another of his friends and colleagues whom he could not ask to his house because she – it was an old story to which they had been reverting in the course of a row – was as likely as not to insult them simply because they were his friends. Gertrud now recalled that the man had been featured by *Time* because, as an expert witness called by a powerful group of Senators bent on exposing corruption in the U.S. Navy's Procurement Department, to testify in an investigation into an American submarine disaster in which seventy men had lost their lives, his authoritative and devastating analysis of the faults in the vessel's hull design, and the brilliance with which he had discredited the cross-examination by the Administration's experts, had resulted in a national scandal.

At last, as the stewardess at the entry port gave her the ritual smiling 'Good morning, madam,' Gertrud remembered the man's name: David Gough.

As she made her way down the aisle of the Trident she saw

that Gough had taken an inside seat and that the seats next to him were not taken. Without specific purpose or intention she took the one beside him; later she was to tell him that she was feeling too lonely to sit alone, even on a half empty aeroplane; it is possible that this was true.

Jock Drummond, who detested Gertrud, once said that only a blind man, a eunuch, or a homosexual could come within two yards of Gertrud without being excited and attracted; he had added, 'Mind you, I suspect she's a sexual fraud. The bait's not worth being trapped for.'

It took Gough three minutes to involve her in talk; he was soon telling her that he always drank a bottle of champagne during this flight and hoped she would share it with him as there was never quite enough time to finish it; he added, 'By the way, my name's David Gough.'

'Not, by any chance, *the* David Gough?' Gertrud said, widening her eyes at him.

'I don't think so. Who's he?'

'The marine architect.'

He studied her coolly; she found his air of being in complete command of himself very attractive. He said, 'I'm a marine architect; it's unusual to find a layman or laywoman who's ever heard of the trade, let alone of me. May I know your name?'

For some reason the name of her tutor at Oxford came into her head and she said, 'Hilda Lulworth.'

'Mrs Lulworth, I see?' He was looking at her wedding ring but made the observation sound like a question.

'You're very inquisitive, Mr Gough.'

'Yes, I am. For instance, I'd love to know how you came to know about me.'

'I don't mind telling you that. During my brief attempt to become a journalist there was a sensational investigation of an accident to an American submarine. I subbed some of the reports. You gave evidence and became headline news.'

'Correct. Thank you. So you're a journalist?'

'No, I didn't go on with it. I'm an idler, the divorced wife of a rich man. Any other questions?'

'I'm sure to think of some, Mrs Lulworth.'

They were still drinking their wine when an impatient stewardess came for the bottle and glasses as they were about to land. They had talked easily and pleasantly throughout the short flight and David's colleagues would have been surprised to see and hear him so talkative. It is true that he had maintained his usual reserve to the extent of telling her nothing about himself except that he had come to Paris to act as consultant to a French member of the Gurling–Curran Group involved in trying to revive big flying boats as passenger and freight carriers, for Air France; 'A matter of hull design, you see.'

At Orly she shared his taxi and as they drove past the Rungis food-markets which have replaced Les Halles, and into the city, he asked her where she was staying; there was already a tacit understanding, almost a commitment, between them. Gertrud said, 'I haven't made up my mind,' and told him where she usually stayed. He said, 'Far too dear. Why pay four times the fair price for a comfortable bed? I use a small place on the other bank, in the rue Jacob. It's pleasant enough and they might have a room for you.'

'All right,' she said, 'I'll try that.'

The hotel clerk said that as a result of a guest being delayed twenty-four hours, they could offer her a room but only for one night. She took it; and filled up her *fiche* as Hilda Lulworth, inventing a passport number. As soon as she was upstairs, in a small but agreeable room which was quiet because it gave onto the courtyard and not the street, with a tiny bathroom, she telephoned Israel's London office, knowing that he would not be there, and spoke to his secretary:

'Tell Mr Mendes I've decided that Paris will bore me and I've gone to stay with friends at St Germain.' She gave the girl her friend's address and telephone number and then rang that number herself. Her friend answered the telephone; they exchanged gossip and then Gertrud said,

'Ecoute, chérie, si mon mari m'appelle au telephone chez toi, dis que je suis sortie, veux-tu, et donne-moi un coup de fil à ce numero . . .' She gave the hotel number. *'Tu demanderas Madame Lulworth. Provisoirement, c'est moi.'*

Then she asked her friend to lunch with her the following day, promising an explanation.

When she had finished telephoning, she felt suddenly free, safely isolated, and able to dispose of herself as she liked. Gough called her from his room, asked if she was satisfied with her own, told her that he himself had a double, and asked her to dine with him and go to a theatre. He said he had never seen a performance of *Phèdre* and although Racine was rather a bore, wanted to see it; they were doing it at the Comédie. Would she mind seeing that?

'No. I'd like to. I haven't seen or read a line of Racine since I was at school. He can't possibly be as tedious as I found him then. It will be interesting to find out.'

Gough did not consult her about a restaurant but took her to a small quiet place still decorated in the fashion of the Second Empire, on the Quai de la Mégisserie. The air, the beauty and the hard business of Paris always excited her. When they met in the hotel lobby, Gough said, *'Que vous avez l'air star, chère amie,'* and she was delighted with the compliment. As they took their places at a corner table he explained that the cooking was *classique* and, 'I prefer that because I find eating a toil and in *cuisine classique* you get small portions perfectly prepared. I can manage that.'

'You don't enjoy food?'

'Oh, it's not a case of anorexia nervosa, but, on the whole, no. But one's companion makes the meal and I shall certainly enjoy this one.'

But he liked good wine and she had not eaten and drunk so exquisitely for years. The business of inventing, in answer to his questions, a life for Hilda Lulworth amused her; she allowed herself a London house which she had just sold, and a son of three; it was easier to include some truth. At one point she said,

'Rich, you see; and selfish enough to enjoy it, David. I suppose you're going to be censorious.'

'You suppose nothing of the kind, my dear. You're very well aware that no normal man can be in your company for an hour and be censorious. Moreover, you do me an injustice. I'm neither a socialist nor an American, but a realist. We live our lives in an age which is *en pleine décadence*. It would be absurd to live otherwise than selfishly bent on enjoying work and play while we can.'

Then enjoyed *Phèdre* although in the second *entr'acte* he complained that the regular tramp of Alexandrines tended to become as absurd as the story itself. Gertrud, on the other hand, found it stirring and the story moving. 'I can't think why I hated him at school.' They became more and more pleased with each other and if Gough's colleagues would scarcely have known him in this easy, witty talker, Gertrud's friends would have marvelled at her transformation.

After the theatre he proposed that they go and drink a bottle of Montrachet and eat a dozen oysters . . . 'The French, as you know, despise our superstition about an "R" in the month.' The place he took her to was in the boulevard St Germain, at the St Michel end. They talked about the play and David said, 'Do you believe it?'

'Believe what?'

'The grand passion, the overwhelming love. One believes it until the verse grows tedious while good actors are putting over Racine's lines, but afterwards?'

'Surely such feelings are a matter of fact,' Gertrud said.

'Are they? Or have certain perfectly ordinary affairs been transformed by poets who flatter our foolish aspiration to be and feel grander than we are?'

'I am to gather,' she said, 'that you don't believe.'

'No. I don't.'

'All right, then what's your idea of a relationship between a man and a woman?'

'The giving and taking of pleasure,' David said, and grinned.

They walked back to the hotel, turning in at the rue Bonaparte beside St Germain-des-Près. That narrow street was full of cars parked on the pavement. David took her arm and insisted on their walking in the middle of the street, ignoring the line of cars forced to crawl, hooting angrily, behind them.

'We shall be run over,' Gertrud said, but she was obviously enjoying herself. David said that he had a mind to call a policeman and point out that the motorists behind them were, by using their hooters, breaking the law.

At the door of his room David said, 'You'll come in for a whisky,' and stood aside to let her enter. She went in without question or hesitation, and remained.

The next morning, when the hotel clerk told her that they would, as they had warned her, require her room that afternoon, she took extraordinary pleasure in the candour with which she explained that she would be moving in with Mr Gough. The clerk said,

'Very well, madame. It is true that he has two beds. Should we make two bills or one, when the time comes?'

'Two, please.'

Simon Brax liked Farzar, both the old town and the new; he was familiar with a score of North African and Middle Eastern towns and could make comparisons. The care which had been given to the best of Farzar's old buildings and to the architecture of the new ones impressed him. He had twenty-four hours in which to see the town before the Ruler, who wanted to see him personally, was free to receive him; in that time Simon conceived a considerable respect for Prince Habib who, when Simon was at last shown into his office which was very obviously a place of business and not of ceremony, said, 'Mr Brax, I'm delighted to see you and I apologize for keeping you waiting. I must say, you people don't waste any time. I like that. How can I help you?'

'I should like, sir, to survey the coast from the sea, fifty miles north and south of Farzar.'

'I foresaw that, Mr Brax. You'll also need expert advice on the geography and geology of the coast. I've arranged for Captain Petrus Van Kleef, who's the commander of our little corps of pilots – the men who take the tankers in and out – to place himself and his launch at your disposal for as long as you need them.'

'That will be perfect, your highness.'

'Good. You have made a preliminary study, on the charts and so forth?'

'I have, sir.'

'Then I will make a guess at the name of the place on which you've fixed your attention: Abbas Bay.'

'Exactly, sir. You obviously . . .'

'It's the obvious place for our purpose. I know the coast well,' the prince interrupted, 'and if I had the time I should enjoy being your guide. I'm fond of sailing, when I have a moment to spare; and we have rather exciting tunny and shark fishing. Tell me, from your preliminary study, do you foresee any very serious difficulties?'

'Yes, sir, I do. I think I should tell you at once that I believe the project to be impossible.'

Prince Habib showed no concern; Gurling had briefed him about Brax's way of setting about a job of work. He said,

'Why do you think that?'

'It's a question of depth of water, sir. As you know, nine-tenths of an iceberg are below the water. If we chose a berg big enough for our purpose, it's going to draw far more water than you have right up to the land at any point along this coast.'

'What depth do you need?'

'That we don't know yet, but I would guess that it might easily be two or three hundred fathoms.'

'I don't believe it's impossible, Mr Brax, or I shouldn't be paying the very large fees your Group demands for its advice. I don't believe that thorough soundings have ever been made in Abbas Bay or at some other points of the coast. At all events, make your survey and then report back to me.'

Habib touched the bell on his desk and Caroline came in from the adjoining office. Brax rose and said, 'Caroline, how nice to see you.'

'Good morning, Mr Brax. It's nice to see you, too. If there's any way in which I can be useful, let me know.'

'You could let me give you dinner one night and show me the sights.'

'I'm afraid,' Habib said, 'that Miss Bartrum's duties are so exacting that . . .' he shook his head, smiling at Simon and, turning to Caroline, 'Telephone Captain Van Kleef and tell him that Mr Brax is on the way now. And have Mr Brax driven to the pilot office.' She nodded and left them. The prince said, 'Mr Brax, will you give me the pleasure of having dinner with my sister and myself, tonight?'

'I shall be honoured, sir.'

'Seven thirty for eight. I will send a car to the Farzar Hilton. Don't dress. And best of luck in your survey.'

The first thing one noticed about Petrus Van Kleef was that he was not just fat, but magnificently fat, an egg-shaped man. He seemed to rejoice in this if his smiling eyes and cheerful red face were anything to go by. Sometimes he made jokes which were a kind of bragging about his weight; for instance, on setting foot on the deck of a tanker, he would say, 'Better take another look at the Plimsoll line, Captain.' He had no hair; the little which baldness had left him, on the great fleshy folds of the neck, was shaved. His English was good but punctuated with archaic slang.

He received Simon Brax in his office with a disconcerting roar of 'Welcome to cloud-cuckoo land.'

'Meaning the place isn't real, Captain?'

'Call me Piet. Real? Listen to me, my friend, His Nibs has told me what this is about. Somebody is potty. And it isn't me.'

'Or me, Piet. By the way, my name's Simon. I've told the prince that the thing's impossible.'

'Your name may be Simon but I see you aren't simple, eh?' The captain roared with enormous laughter, displaying a mouth full of gold teeth. 'No bats in your belfry. Never mind, it will be a holiday for us. You like fishing? We catch real whoppers here . . .' he extended his fat arms to their fullest stretch. 'Our little trip will buck me up no end.'

'You know the coast like the back of your hand, of course?'

'From Conakry to Casa.'

'You know what I'm supposed to look for. What do you say?'

'That it isn't there, Simon, that the whole thing is napoo.'

He rose and stood before one of the big charts which covered all the walls of his room, Simon lean and towering beside him. The captain explained, talking fast and clearly, '. . . shelving from zero to ten fathoms . . . average incline 1 in 440 . . . no water of the depth you need less than one hundred miles from the coast . . .'

'Abbas Bay, Piet?'

'Ah. Certainly much deeper; an old scour has scooped out the shelf to within a mile or two of the shoreline. It's really the only place worth looking at. But it's not deep enough close enough.'

He admitted that he had no record of soundings; the bay was not used by any vessel bigger than a fishing dhow or a tunny-fishing launch.

'We'll start from here tomorrow at seven,' Van Kleef said. Just before they parted Simon asked, on impulse and with no particular plan in mind, 'In the very unlikely event of my wanting it, is there any deep diving gear available?'

'*Yah.* There's a salvage firm, Dutch, working on a wreck just off the edge of the shelf, here . . .' the captain put a sausage finger on the chart. 'We could borrow their boat and gear, they're in no position to refuse.'

'I don't for a moment expect it will be necessary.'

Gurling–Curran had the right connections and John Gurling's reception at the U.S. Air Base at Thule was cordial. He had never been so far north before and the flight up the coast in a world of ice, blue water and brilliant sunshine delighted him. He was given the facilities he needed for his big helicopter, and comfortable quarters for himself, his pilot, an Icelander named Magnus Sigurdson, and Peter Grimmond, his photographer. The colonel who received Gurling said, 'Ice . . . the only use I have for ice, Mr Gurling, is in a highball. My orders are to ask no questions, so I won't. But I'm mighty curious.'

He paused. Gurling said, 'A client of my firm, a very important one, has a crazy notion of his own about how to use ice for something other than chilling liquor, colonel. He wants it kept secret. I've come myself because I always wanted to see something of the icefields.. Our client's rich enough to pay for his whims.'

'Well, sir, if it's ice he wants he's sent you to the right place. O.K., Mr Gurling. Captain Levin, here, will take care of you; and we'll meet in the mess.'

Day after day, whenever the weather was clear, Sigurdson flew Gurling and Grimmond up and down the 250-mile stretch of icebound shoreline; much of the coast of Greenland is clear of ice; but here the great inland icefield had forced its way inch by inch for thousands of years, down to and into the sea. Every fall of snow, coming under the enormous pressure of succeeding falls, was transformed into the granulated stuff glaciologists call firn and, by the growing pressure of still later snowfalls, into glacier ice. There were places where the ice was a mile thick.

Often there was fog and Gurling, landbound, made up his

notes, studied and classified photographs, looked at the moving pictures Grimmond was making, talked to London and New York on the telephone, and even, one morning, to Brax at the Hilton in Farzar. Brax said,

'John, I'm pretty sure I'm wasting time.'

'Go on wasting it for a while, Simon. H.H. is paying.'

On the whole the weather favoured them. They flew inland over a grim and lovely landscape, icescape. In places the mountains were still visible where there were towering peaks and plunging valleys of ice; in others the ice, more than three thousand feet thick, had levelled the world as far as the eye could see into one great, white tableland. If this ice were ever to melt, London and New York would lie under water, only the tall towers emerging; and half the world's great cities and fertile lands would be drowned.

It was the unimaginable weight of the ice which had forced the icefield flow down to the coastal mountains. The ice was squeezed into valleys and carried through the mountain barrier by the outlet glaciers, and so down to the sea.

Captain Levin flew him, in one of the air force machines, across Greenland to the sea terminal of the great Rink glacier and there they were lucky, flying round in a circle to watch, awe-struck, as a huge territory of ice – Levin estimated it at seven hundred million cubic metres – collapsed with a thunderous roar into the sea in the space of a few minutes. Absorbed, enchanted by the grandeur of the spectacle, Gurling said, 'How often does this happen?'

'Twenty, thirty times a year,' the pilot said. Millions of tons of solid water to feed the seas, be taken up as vapour, condensed and precipitated as rain and snow and hail, recommence the grand cycle – it must have been at about this time that Gurling made up his mind that Habib should have his icebergs to water his deserts.

The luck held: three days movie shooting from the helicopter in the region of Melville Bay gave Gurling and his team a motion picture of the most colossal spectacle Gurling had ever witnessed. An outlet glacier had reached the point in the sea where the water was deep enough to float almost a mile of its leading edge; buoyant, this great cape of ice was heaved upwards by a flowing tide, cracked in a mighty noise of creaking and groaning along a series of crevasses, torn loose from the body of the glacier, and floated free. On the third day, Sigurdson landed them on the new berg: it was fourteen hundred metres long, more than a third as wide. They took off again and flew round the berg at sea level while Gurling took the angle of its top and measured the cliff of ice which towered more than three hundred feet above the water line. The berg's draught, then, must be something like three hundred fathoms.

During the next series of days when the weather enabled them to work, they watched smaller bergs calved in a different way. Sigurdson flew them over a length of coast where the sea water, by melting the lower base of the ice-shelf, left its upper part unsupported. They watched blocks of ice as big as a village break away under their own weight to plunge with a roaring crash and form great fountains of water, beneath the sea, then to rise again, rolling over like some leviathan among leviathans, then rocking and bobbing like a floating cork, to settle at last into balance and begin the slow drift southwards towards Cape Farewell.

This was a world of white and silver and ineffable blues, of vision falsified by 'blink' and glitter, of austere and moving beauty. John Gurling began to understand the infatuation which had bound so many Arctic and Antarctic explorers, and which binds those men who work in the polar regions, to this majestic world of ice, of slow violence and sudden catastrophe, of fogs which magnified icebergs into mountain ranges of glass.

He returned to London with the outline of a plan.

Six

Dinner at the palace was not grand. Simon Brax, wearing a white silk suit which he had had made for himself in Italy, was shown by a servant onto the terrace. There was nobody to receive him but the servant said something in Farsi, bowed, left him and returned with a trolley of bottles and glasses. A moment later a young woman who was unmistakably Habib's sister, wearing an ivory silk trouser suit embroidered with gold thread, came out onto the terrace. Simon shook her offered hand as she said, 'Mr Brax, I am Habib Shah's sister. I am to apologize that he is not here to receive you. He is talking to a man in Texas on the telephone. Do please sit down. What will you drink?'

He asked for whisky. The Princess gave an order to the servant. She herself chose a Bloody Mary. She said,

'What do you think of my brother's wild ideas?'

'I have reservations, your highness.'

She sat beside him and said, 'I think I have never quite understood what you are trying to do.'

'The prince wants to use icebergs to water your deserts, your highness.'

'And you think it impossible?'

'I don't know yet.'

Caroline Bartrum, in green chiffon to the ankles, appeared in the archway from the house and Simon stood and said, 'Good evening, Caroline.' She bowed her head to the princess and then said, 'This is nice, Simon.' He thought her nervous. The princess said, with a faint air of surprise, and a slight elevation of the eyebrows,

'You are joining us, Miss Bartrum?'

'Yes, your highness . . .'

Habib arrived at that moment, saying, 'Ah, you are all here, good. Caroline, send that fellow away and give me, let me see, a vodka and lime juice. Azizeh, you look beautiful. I've hardly seen you since your return, you must tell us all about it.' He crossed to the balustrade, turned towards Simon and said, 'My sister has been staying with the Mocktar Sheikh. You know about our Arabs? They live in the territory we are going to turn into a paradise, with your help. The difficulty is that perhaps they don't want to live in paradise. They'd prefer to put it off until they die. Yet if I don't give it to them, you may be sure I shall be blamed. You know, Mr Brax, those of us who are set in authority are often blamed for doing too little for people who'd much rather we did nothing at all.'

The food eaten in Farzar and the country at large, except in the Arab quarter, is Persian: rice, cooked dry and fluffy; kebabs, chelows; and a great deal of yoghourt. It is good of its kind, but Habib had a French chef and dinner that night could hardly have been bettered in Paris. When the wine was served Habib entertained them with a lively account of his negotiations with a French syndicate who wanted to plant vineyards in the cool, mountainous north of the country and had been disconcerted by the Prince's idea of fair shares for himself. Caroline said very little; it seemed to Brax that she was being careful to give Azizeh no chance to snub her again. Habib asked his sister to tell them about her sojourn in the Arab country. She said,

'Your fears are groundless, brother.'

'Let that be for your private report. Tell us about life among the Sheikhs.'

The girl shrugged, saying, 'It is what I suppose it has always been, uncomfortable, boring, dirty and idle. But 'Omar bin

Mocktar is interesting. An anachronism, of course, a throwback.'

'By his photograph,' Habib said, 'he's a fellow of sinister appearance.'

'Not really, Habib. It's only the eye patch. He lost an eye when he was stoned by a Communist mob in Sidi Barani. He's a gentle soul, convinced that all change is for the worse.'

'A desert Melbourne,' Habib said. Nobody understood the reference and he did not explain, going on, 'And Allal, is he under the influence of this man?'

'A little, perhaps,' Azizeh said.

She had found 'Omar very far from being a simple soul: like many others who have been called saints, he was a man of penetrating intelligence. So much so, indeed, that she had warned Allal, thinking the Sheikh overweening in his confidence that he could use the mullah and then discard him. And how, she had asked, had Allal kept the mullah silent until it had suited him to let him talk?

After a bad start they had very soon come to terms with each other. He had read the letter in which Habib appointed her his envoy and, concealing none of his suspicion, wondered aloud what the prince hoped to gain by sending her.

'Information about your degree of responsibility for the mullah's preaching. He sends me as his spy. But what I come as – that he doesn't know. He's blind because he's arrogant.'

Allal was taken aback. He said, primly, 'Prince Habib has surely always been a liberal in his attitude to women.'

'Of course. His liberalism is the measure of his contempt. He thinks so lightly of women that he isn't afraid to give them rope.'

On the following days he heard about her involvement in a Black September aircraft hijacking – she was the notorious 'Jasmin' who had shot and wounded an El Al armed guard in a gun dual on Tel Aviv airport and then vanished. She told him about the P.D.F.* organization which had smuggled her to safety.

It was not these confidences alone which made Allal sure that Azizeh was not her brother's spy. It was, rather, the will to power, the burning ambition to lead which she revealed with every word she said. Habib's senior by one year, she was certain that she, not he, should be the Ruler. The very authority which she was aware of in herself seemed to her a title to power.

Answering her question about how 'Omar bin Mocktar had been silenced, Allal said,

' 'Omar would have been the Sheikhs' choice as Sheikh of the Mocktar, if they had found me as unacceptable as they'd thought I should be. When they accepted me, it was thought wise to send him away. They thought I might have him poisoned: there are good precedents. He became a sort of minor prophet in central Libya but he was glad enough to come home when I found a use for him.'

Azizeh had told him, 'He is not a fool, Allal. You think you're using him. Are you as sure that he isn't using you?'

'It'll do no harm, Azizeh, to let him think so. Political violence nowadays has its own logic. Whatever its plotted course, it turns Left in the end.'

But what she talked about during dinner at the palace was the life which the shepherds led as they ranged wide with their lean flocks of goats and sheep over the sparse, dry 'pastures' where the animals sought grass blade by blade among the stones, and which would not have been recognized as pastures by any European farmer. 'One day I rode with Allal to the place, a sort of compound of stone hovels where they milk the ewes and goats to make the *dourch* . . .'

'Yoghourt,' Habbib interrupted, speaking to Caroline and to Simon.

'. . . which they send down to Farzar for sale. A little boy,

* Palestine Democratic Front: an Arab Marxist–Leninist Movement.

son of the headman, had pulled a great pan of boiling water off the fire and badly scalded the flesh of his left leg. He was about six, I think. He stood there, like a statue of a suffering child made of bone and parchment, not complaining, not crying. They'd plastered his leg with some concoction of their own, some herb or other pounded in a mortar, mixed with earth and the urine of sheep . . .'

'They shouldn't have done that,' Caroline said, 'just clean cold water and air . . .'

Azizeh looked at her and said, 'Oh? You have a medical degree, perhaps?'

Habib said, 'You didn't interfere?'

'Of course not.'

Nor had she: a little medical science might be welcome in a desperate case but it aroused suspicion that custom was being tampered with. It was no part of Allal's policy to stir such fears until he was sure of his strength; and his policy had become hers also.

In her second week as Allal's guest, her first as his formal political ally and as his mistress, she had ridden with him and two of the Cousins and an escort of a hundred horsemen who were armed with Italian carbines, for five days through semi-desert country, through widely scattered flocks guarded by tall men who stood leaning on staffs and made no movement or sound until they were spoken to courteously. Here also each beast had to seek for every leaf of grass or herb which nourished it, and to the eye the country was all stone. As they moved south there was a little more vegetation, scrub in which antelope and wild or feral sheep got a living. For diversion and having time in hand, they hunted antelope; and one day followed a leopard into the bush until they lost it. At the end of that time they reached their rendezvous in a barren gorge where the sun heated the stones to the temperature of a bread oven, and where they met the convoy of trucks whose cargoes had been procured by Doctor al Badr; and the 170 camels onto which the guns were to be off-loaded. The loading took two days and then the straggling caravan of camels and their owners, hired for ten *rials* a day, began the long, slow journey back into Allal's country, from well to brackish well.

Azizeh had not enjoyed that journey: enveloped in the burnous of a desert Arab, the heat did not trouble her; but the camels did. She would have preferred motor transport, although given their resources and the nature of the country, and the impression which Allal wanted to make, camels were the right answer. The trouble was that camels seemed like a symbol of 'Omar's aims, and not of her own and Allal's. Camels, like 'Omar, were an assertion of the past's obstinate strength. You did not, surely, make a revolution with camels. It required all her respect for Maoism to help her put such nonsense out of her mind.

She had talked with 'Omar and was afraid of the damage he might do, as she had told Allal. Mystical maunderings, as she called them, the conservatism of mere fanatical piety, the sort of nonsense the mullah used when he talked to the people, would never have frightened her. But 'Omar's argument, when he talked with his equals in education, was rational:

'The happiness and good of the people do no lie in industrial riches, yet those who have made material riches for the people their aim are not to blame. It was reasonable to suppose that men would be better for being comfortable and free of drudgery. But only look at what has happened: wherever wealth has greatly accumulated the moral quality of men and of life has declined. Must we not learn the lesson? Why, with their example before us, should we go the same way? Let us keep our poverty as a blessing of God.'

It was, more or less, the argument Allal had borrowed for his dealings with the Ruler. It was also, of course, the old argument touching man's freedom of choice between God and

Mammon. And 'Omar said, 'Where the things which are Mammon's are not to be had he will not be worshipped.'

Gurling's telephone call from Thule had come after Simon Brax and Captain Van Kleef had spent four days in the pilot's powerful launch, poking into small bays, taking echo-soundings, conscientiously doing the less promising part of their work before allowing themselves to try Abbas Bay. Those four days confirmed the conclusions drawn from the charts: there was no deep water excepting the narrow dredged channel into the oil port.

On the fifth day they made directly for Abbas Bay, putting out a shark line baited with half a leg of pork. Piet Van Kleef had a ferocious hatred of sharks and killing them was a kind of hobby with him. There were merchants in the bazaar who would buy the skins, the flesh and the oil.

Abbas Bay, so-called, was in fact a small gulf. Its mouth was relatively narrow, a strait two kilometres across between sheer, low cliffs. Inside this strait the bay was seven kilometres across at its widest point. Once inside, Piet and Simon took in the shark line and began soundings, finding very deep water at the mouth. Piet said, 'As I told you, the shelf seems to have been scoured away here. On a line from the centre of the strait directly to the land at the nearest point, you get a reading as great as twelve hundred. I'm reading eleven hundred now. But wait . . .'

Simon took over the echo-sounder while the captain took the helm, setting a course directly for the beach and using, as a bearing to steer on, a group of what looked like branched and short-leaved palm trees immediately above a gut or small bay about twelve hundred metres wide which broke the shoreline of Abbas Bay. The readings showed remarkably little shelving towards the mouth of the gut. But at about one kilometre from the beach Piet turned the launch to port and within half a kilometre the sounder made a sudden jump to around the one hundred metre mark, then eighty, seventy, and steadied around fifty at a point about fifteen hundred metres south of the deep channel. Simon called, 'Piet, go about and steer due north, will you?' The captain did so and the readings began to rise; they crossed the deep channel again, with the sounder reading steady at about eleven hundred while they covered a kilometre, at which point came the abrupt shelving again, although not quite so sheer, the reading dropping to 250 and then shelving away until it steadied at seventy as they continued on their northerly course.

'Get back to the original easterly course,' Simon called, 'steering on those trees again.' There was something in his voice which made the Dutchman shout, 'Don't tell me we've found something. I don't believe it.'

Simon did not reply; the launch came about again and Piet put her on her original course, from the centre of the mouth of the bay to the centre of the mouth of the gut. At the centre of the mouth of the gut, with land rising close on both beams, they still had eleven hundred metres of water under them. Not until they were within five hundred metres of the small white beach did shelving begin, but then it was steep and Piet set the control to dead slow ahead and stood alert to go astern. At a hundred metres from the beach they had only two metres of water under the boat. They went back and did the run again, on a parallel course but further south: same result. They did a long zigzag run from land to the mouth of the bay and back, crossing and recrossing the channel, and found no shallow water. Simon said,

'Lunchtime. Let's anchor here, just off the shelf,' and watched the triangular dorsal fin of a big shark cruise inquisitively round them. Piet, at the anchor winch, shouted above the clatter of the anchor chain running out over the ratchet, 'That rascal smells our sandwiches.' Before sitting down to eat or even swallow his first gin of the day, he again put out the shark-line.

Simon, meanwhile, was examining the head of the gut through the captain's Zeiss glasses: a tumbled mass of rock rose from the beach to the top of the low cliff, with trees and shrubs growing in the crevasses. The land rose quite steeply to about three hundred metres before levelling off into the coastal plain. His attention was caught by the trees which they had used as a bearing. He had never seen anything quite like them: grey, squat boles carried a very complex and regular system of ramifications like elephants' trunks, tipped with tufts of big, stout, grey-green pointed leaves.

'Those trees,' he said, 'they're vaguely sinister, like something from the age of the dinosaurs.'

'So they are,' Piet said, 'the first time I saw them I thought I was having the horrors.' He uttered his usual roar of fat laughter and continued, 'They tell me they're not even real trees and not even palms, but we call them dragon-trees.'

'A good name, Piet, I think we're going to need a name for that gut. How about Dragon-tree Gut?'

'Good, very good,' the captain said, with his mouth full. Simon ate his lunch while staring at the shore. He said, 'Do you know that piece of country up there?'

'*Yah*. The dragon-trees stand at the end of a broad *arroyo* in the plain, but it grows shallow very soon inland into nothing but a slight depression which you could easily not notice at all unless you are there when the sun is very low.'

Simon nodded; he said, 'As I expected. That scour of yours, Piet, it doesn't exist. Do you know what we have here? The outfall of a river which flowed down here in an earlier epoch, I don't know which, but I'd guess the shoreline was much further west. We're anchored on top of a gorge, or what was a gorge some millions of years ago.'

It was at that moment, before Piet could answer, that the shark-line gave a violent jerk and began to run out. Piet rose – he was a quick mover for so fat a man – started the engine and began to get the anchor in. Simon jumped to the humming reel on the short, stout steel rod, but Piet bawled at him to leave it alone. 'Let the bugger have all the line, that reel's spring-loaded.'

He had the anchor clear and called to Simon to take the helm and to let the launch follow the shark which seemed to be making for the open sea. Just before they reached the mouth of the bay Piet began to reel in line and shouted to Simon to go hard astern. The line snapped taut, Piet began to reel out again as the shark dived, but not before it had driven the hook deeper into its flesh. Diving, it had gone about and was headed for land again. Simon was quick enough putting the launch about to prevent the line from fouling the propeller. Piet gave the shark more line as it continued swimming, deep now, straight for the shore. Piet shouted, 'Let her idle; he can tow us.' They did that, drawing nearer and nearer to the shore until Simon suddenly shouted,

'Piet, how much line have you got out?'

'Most of it. It's O.K., I . . .'

'Man, look at the angle and the distance from the beach.'

'What are you getting at?'

'The line's going slack. Reel in, for Christ's sake. Look, man, look! Where do you think he is, *under* the beach?'

'*Groot Gott* . . . go slow astern,' Piet said, and began to reel in fast. And presently there was no doubt about it, they were dragging the shark, as if from a hole, a lair under the land.

While the shark made another run for the open sea and they fought him with reel and engine as he tired and Piet marvelled aloud at the beast's colossal reserves of energy, an underwater picture was forming in Brax's mind. When they had the shark, four metres long, killed with Piet's harpoon gun, on the surface, lashed alongside the launch, Simon said, 'I'm going to need that diving gear.'

For four days they worked the launch and the echo-sounder on a tedious grid of courses until they had the bottom of the whole bay charted. Simon had made four protracted dives. On the evening of the fourth day he rang Caroline and said, 'Can you get me an immediate audience or whatever you call it, with your boyfriend?'

'Don't be spiteful, darling. It depends: success or failure?'

'Qualified success.'

'That should do. I'll call you back. Oh, and Simon, telephone lines here are apt to be tapped.'

'Hardly a wise thing to tell me on the phone.'

'Oh, there's no secret about it. Surely you remember the famous TV interview with the Ruler when he was asked whether his country wasn't a police state and answered that of course it is – a benevolent police.'

She rang back before room service could deliver the drink he'd ordered as soon as she had hung up.

'Simon, I'm sending a car for you. It'll be there in fifteen minutes.'

While he waited, he put his papers in order: the new charts of the shoreline and the bottom of the bay, which he had drawn with the fat Dutchman's help; the drawings of the underwater formation to which that shark had given him the clue; a report roughly typed by himself. His half-written letter to Jocelyn was the only paper left on his table; he would finish it that night, conscientiously, although Jocelyn, incapable of being interested in anything beyond a range of about four hundred yards, would read only the opening and ending lines.

At the palace he was taken not to Habib's office but out onto the terrace; it was rarely excessively hot at Farzar; the sea and the breeze off the sea usually kept the thermometer below ninety degrees Fahrenheit. But that day there had been no breeze off the sea, the air was sullen, dirty with the foul fumes from the fourteen brickworks, burning low-grade oil, which kept Farzar's busy builders supplied, and the temperature still, late in the day, at ninety-six degrees.

The prince, who was wearing loose Arab robes, the first time Brax had seen him in any but European clothes, said,

'Mr Brax, good of you to be so prompt. Would you rather go inside where it's cool? For my part I enjoy a good sweat from time to time, though the taint of sulphur dioxide is tiresome.'

'The heat doesn't bother me, sir.'

'You have been in hotter places, eh?'

'Much hotter, sir.'

'You have some news for me?'

'Yes. I've changed my mind. I can build you an iceberg dock at the mouth of a gut off Abbas Bay. At a price.'

'Never mind the price. Where is this gut?'

Simon unrolled the chart of the shoreline and, pointing with his little finger, said, 'Here. A small bay or gut 1,207 metres from north to south, 1,327 from east to west. Unless you object I'm calling it Dragon-tree Bay.'

'How surprisingly romantic, Mr Brax.'

Simon explained about the trees and Habib said, '*Dracaena draco*. There's a legend that the oldest plant in the group is two thousand years old. Like most legends, it's nonsense. Please continue.'

'The gut is the landward end of an ancient gorge. We have eleven hundred metres of water to far beyond the mouth of Abbas Bay . . .'

Simon was using the chart to illustrate what he was saying. He recounted the incident of the subterranean shark. Habib was amused. Simon said, 'So I went down to have a look, sir.'

'And?'

'I wasn't surprised to find I'm right about the gorge; that was obvious from the echo-sounder. I've explained that there's steep shelving here to shallow water at the shoreline. Well it's hollow below, that shark went *under* the shelf which is quite literally a shelf. It's the end of a stratum of granite between two strata of some softer stone. What this means is that if it were not for that granite projection there'd be deep water at the shoreline down to about one thousand metres with a bottom of clean silicaceous sand.'

Habib clapped his hands for a servant and ordered coffee and whisky. He said, 'Remarkable. Please continue.'

'The shelf's topped with two metres of mud but the stone's

actually only about fifty metres thick at the shoreline. I believe we could cut it off and drop it on the bottom.'

'How?'

'Explosives along the line of the cliff face.'

'And then what? Please help yourself to whisky.'

'Thank you . . .' Simon did so and said, 'In that case we've a natural basin of about the right size. John Gurling was right about the tide but not exactly so, there's a fall at the head of the gut of about one hundred metres. If the shelving didn't extend so far, the hollow under it would be uncovered and we should have known it was there. That hundred-metre fall is important. Look, sir, suppose we close the mouth of the gut with sluice gates. We float the berg in here at high tide, close the gates at low tide, pump out the sea water and leave the berg to melt into the basin pumping out the fresh water as fast as it accumulates.'

'Can you make sluice-gates that size?'

'Yes. It's a shipbuilders' job; some kind of hollow steel caissons. We'd have to sink a concrete sill as mounting for the gates, across the mouth of the gut. It'll be expensive but not ruinous.'

'All this is in your report?'

'It is, sir. I've concluded with a recommendation – that we should start nothing at this end until my colleagues are sure they can deliver icebergs, that is until we've done a dummy run.'

'I shall think about that, Mr Brax. I wish you, in any case, to carry out all the surveys necessary for the drawing of plans, while you're here.'

Jock Drummond arrived to do a quick preliminary survey of the pipeline route. He returned to Farzar after twelve days, to report to Brax that the job would be straightforward; there were no serious problems unless the occasional shepherds and the small bands of horsemen who had watched his progress while remaining aloof and unapproachable raised trouble. By then Simon

Brax had completed that part of his work which could be done for the time being, his underwater and shoreline survey.

They travelled back to London together for a meeting of the Project Icecube team, as Gurling had named it. At home, each found a short letter from Israel Mendes; an invitation to hold their meeting at his house and then to dine with him. The letter concluded 'My wife is abroad so this will be a stag party.' Jock Drummond commented to Emma, 'The poor devil couldn't have the party at all if that bitch were at home.'

Simon found the flat empty. He bathed, changed and walked round to 'The Seven Beeches' – a longish walk but he wanted exercise. As he expected, he found Jocelyn there. He was talking to the big Irish boss known as Leary the Lumper. With them was a slight, pale youth with girlish features and dark, deep-set eyes which he kept modestly lowered. He was drinking Coca-cola and saying nothing. The pair took themselves off to the other bar when Simon appeared.

Simon talked casually for five minutes about what he was doing in Farzar; Jocelyn was not very interested; he had long since lost all inclination to go abroad and no place but that part of London within a mile or two of Marble Arch had any reality for him. He talked about his own business and would have been much offended if Simon had not shown himself keenly interested in it; ten minutes passed before Simon found a chance to say, 'Who's the pretty boy with Leary?'

'Oh, for Christ's sake, Simon . . .'

'I was merely curious.'

'He's a new recruit to Leary's gang. I'm told he's a bricky, I don't know his name, he comes from Cork, and butter wouldn't melt in his mouth. Satisfied?'

'Perfectly.'

Gough, too, found Israel's invitation waiting for him at his Curzon Street flat. He had left Mrs Lulworth in Paris: she had clothes on order and fittings to attend before she could return.

She would telephone him as soon as she arrived in London. She had given the Carlton Towers Hotel as her address, saying that she was living there while hunting for a flat. It had been with difficulty and relief that he had persuaded her to stay for her fittings and not fly back with him.

He was glad to be leaving her and had made up his mind to drop the affair as soon as he decently could: her attitude was becoming tender, she was considering his own comfort before her own, and the gentler she became the less amusing he found her. She was beginning to talk about the state of her feelings and to expect his sympathetic attention; and to ask questions like 'Suppose you were to discover that I'm not at all what I've told you, would you be very angry?' This sort of thing merely irritated him. If there was one thing he did not want it was a woman of her kind – or any woman at all for that matter – in love with him. It had happened before and proved a serious nuisance. One evening she asked him if he had ever been in love and he seized the chance to make his position clear.

'No, never,' he had answered her question, 'it's a state I'm incapable of.'

'You can't possibly know that.'

'I can and do. A lot of nonsense is talked about not being able to know oneself: the truth is that people will not face what they are. One of the wisest things ever said was, *il faut savoir se supporter soi-même.*'

'One must be able to put up with oneself – no comforting illusions, eh? Who said that, David?'

'Toulouse-Lautrec, and God knows it must have been hard to put up with himself.'

'And you . . . you know yourself and put up with what you know?'

'Exactly.'

'And one of the things you put up with is the inability to love?'

'Correct again.'

'I don't believe a word of it,' Gertrud said, 'yours is the pride that comes before a fall.'

He had shrugged: she had been warned.

That warning had been ignored, however, for as he was leaving the house the morning after his return the telephone began to ring. He went back to answer it and was given a telegram from Paris: 'TO HELL WITH FITTINGS PARIS A BORE WITHOUT YOU STOP ARRIVING HEATHROW SIX THIS EVENING PLEASE MEET ME STOP LOVE HILDA.'

He was glad that she had not telephoned: he had no intention of meeting her and a telegram was something one could deny having received. As he walked through the park to his office he considered the question – but why had she wired and not telephoned? Two explanations occurred to him: that she had too little confidence in his attachment to risk giving him the chance to explain that he could not meet her or even see her that night, or to try persuading her to remain in Paris for her fittings; or, she wanted to be free not to face the fact of his indifference by giving him the chance to say that he had not received her telegram. Both explanations implied that she was in love with him. Which meant that he must avoid her or, if she was persistent, tell her to her face that the moment a woman fell in love with him he dropped her, for both their sakes.

The Icecube meeting was held in Israel's workroom at the Regents Park House. Gurling began the proceedings by describing what he had seen and learned and explaining his plan for landing and living on an iceberg while getting it to Farzar. Then Simon Brax dealt with his part of the business by reading aloud his report to Habib Shah. He stressed his concluding recommendation: that there was no point in beginning costly work on the basin until they were sure that they could actually get a berg down to Farzar. There was a discussion about that and Gurling said that it depended on what Israel had to say; and that he had received a directive from the client about it.

'I gather he insisted on you doing all the work required to enable you to draft plans?'

Israel's report was brief: he had an engine which would work under water and would give them a fair measure of controlled movement and of steerage provided they used two of them. The work had been quickly done because it had been a matter of modifying an advanced prototype of his hydroturbine. He said, 'What I don't know is whether we can mount the engines securely. I've worked out a theoretical method but I simply don't know if it'll do. In my view the next step is to try it, I mean make a full-scale experiment.'

He explained how he thought that might be done. It was then resolved that he and Simon should go to Greenland, set up a base, and try to mount one of the modified engines onto a mass of ice. It was important to work fast: September was the last month of the year in which a dummy-run to Farzar could be made. At this point Gurling intervened: he had a letter from the client in which Brax's cautious recommendation was rejected: 'As I told you, a directive from the client.' Habib wrote that he had studied Gurling's latest report and was greatly encouraged by his exposition of the part which would be played by winds and ocean currents; he was confident that a means to drive and steer a big iceberg would be found. He had decided to proceed with the dry-dock scheme at once and he was ready to deposit the sum of two million sterling immediately on receipt of a preliminary and non-binding estimate of the cost.

'He also wants to get on with the pipeline,' Gurling said, 'he points out that the new oil strike near the Curzon Depression has been proved and that if the line doesn't carry water, the greater part of it is on the right line to carry oil.'

'I suppose he can afford this folly?' Brax said.

Gurling smiled; he said, 'His oil revenue in the current year will amount to about fourteen hundred million.'

'Dollars, *rials*?'

'Sterling.'

'In that case,' Gough said, 'ask for a deposit of ten million.'

'I have,' Gurling told him.

'I might have known.'

'Jock?'

'No problems, John. If you want me to get on with it I can start tomorrow.'

'Pipe?'

'The Libyan suspension leaves us with about fifty miles of the stuff in hand. We can simply transfer it. Supplies should be accumulating while we're dealing with what we have.'

Gurling took over again: 'I've been reading everything I can lay hands on about icebergs. There's one possible headache we haven't considered. Icebergs of a certain age tend to roll over, a matter of the centre of gravity shifting as melting proceeds. As far as I can see it shouldn't affect us; we'll be taking a newly-calved berg and moving it much faster than the usual drift.'

There was no more to be said about that for the time being. Jock Drummond said, 'I've got a point, John. Does the ice we're proposing to take *belong* to anyone, legally?'

'Good God,' Gurling said, 'I never thought of that.'

Gough said, thoughtfully, 'I suggest that so long as it's attached to the glacier or is drifting within the three-mile limit or whatever the limit is nowadays, that the bergs belong to Greenland. But once outside that limit, to nobody or anybody.'

'Isn't Greenland politically a part of Denmark?' Jock said.

Gurling replied that it was and said, 'Yes. I'm already in touch with the Danes. They maintain an iceberg patrol and I've arranged with them to keep us informed of the kind of bergs which might interest us. They think it's something to do with meteorology studies – no question of ownership. But now we're thinking about it I'm not happy about David's point that once outside the limit a berg is nobody's property. I'm very much afraid that there's the makings of a lawyers' bonanza here. It's the sort of thing they'd keep going at The Hague for years, with their hands deep in our client's pocket the whole time. Look, as David says, originally a berg is a part of Greenland, that is, it's Danish territory. Suppose for a moment that Land's End broke off from the body of England and floated out into the Atlantic beyond the three-mile limit. You can't tell me that anyone but Britain would have a legal claim to it. The way it looks to me is this: so long as nobody's ever thought of icebergs being anything but a bloody nuisance, the point of ownership simply doesn't arise. But the moment they're seen to be valuable, then the point will be raised. If we sent water in tankers to Farzar as a commodity we should expect to be paid for it. If our client's idea works, then an iceberg becomes a self-contained water-tanker belonging to Denmark. Look at it another way: if it were discovered that one of the Greenland glaciers which calves icebergs were loaded with uranium ore, don't tell me that the International Court wouldn't find that it belongs to Denmark even if a berg carrying the ore were drifting a couple of hundred miles from any coastline – and take a couple of years to hand down the judgement. Jock, that point of yours looks like being a sharp one. Anyone know the market price of water?'

'I pay 20p a thousand gallons for watering the garden here,' Israel said, 'and at that price the whole project becomes impossible.'

'I think,' Gurling said, 'that our client had better get in touch with the Danes.'

'I've another point,' Jock said. 'Is there any question of our operation being regarded as a danger to shipping?'

'I shouldn't think so,' Gurling said, 'a berg under controlled steerage and with men on board and warnings out, is obviously less dangerous than a drifting berg. All right, three resolutions: one, Izzy and Simon to Greenland – I'll clear that with the Danes tomorrow, there won't be any difficulties at this stage. Two, I check with the Admiralty about the shipping question. Three: I advise the client to take the matter up with the

Danish government, I mean the question of title and possible payments.'

They went down to dinner discussing the relative easiness of solving technological problems, by comparison with political and social ones. Gough suggested that this might be because men of the first order of intelligence no longer went into politics: 'Ex-banking men and other kinds of money-lenders, *commerçants*, trade union officials, they do their best but you can't expect much. I gather there are more lawyers in the House than men of any other trade and anyone who's had dealings with lawyers has found them on average depressingly stupid when they aren't merely cunning.'

'If you ask me,' Jock said, 'our job of exploiting natural resources is a bloody sight easier than the politician's job of exploiting greed and fear without letting them get out of hand.'

Israel gave his guests Iranian caviar, a suprême of chicken, a *crême brulée*, a Stilton cheese. The table was decorated with a great silver dish of peaches and grapes which Jock admired extravagantly. When the time came to eat the fruit, Israel explained, 'My father's the last of those Jews *de luxe* of the kind that flourished under Edward VII. These are from his hothouses. I'm afraid he also grows orchids.'

There was an embarrassed silence broken by some kind of bustle in the hall, by Gertrud's voice addressing a servant, then by the door of the dining-room opening; for David Gough there was the confusion of a bad dream as Hilda Lulworth appeared in the doorway and he half rose to his feet. Gertrud started to laugh on a very high pitch; she said, 'Oh no! This looks like the proverbial tangled web. I look for you over half London, give up and come home and find you at my own dining-table.' She ignored everyone but Gough, did not even pretend to listen to Israel, confused but trying, absurdly, to save the situation with,

'Gertrud, what an agreeable surprise. Let me see, I think you all, excepting David, know my wife.' Nor did she notice the other men who were all now standing excepting David who slowly sat down again. Now Israel was saying, 'Have some of the *crême brulée*. Your cook has done us proud.' He sounded like a schoolboy who had invited his friends home to tea without permission. Gertrud simply looked past them all to David, saying,

'I went to your flat. Didn't you get my wire?'

'I did,' Gough said, 'and thought it an impertinent presumption on our acquaintanceship.'

'Did you?' she said, 'I should have thought a couple of weeks in bed together was a fair justification,' and backed out of the room. David began to peel a peach with exquisite care. Israel said, 'Do sit down and have some fruit. I . . . excuse me.' He followed Gertrud out of the room. His guests sat and ate fruit in an awkward silence. They heard the front door slammed violently and then David rose and went out of the room leaving the rest looking hangdog as children who've been smacked.

David found Israel standing in the hall staring at the front door. He said, 'Izzy,' and Israel turned to face him and before he could speak, David said, 'On an aeroplane to Paris I met a woman who made a pass at me. I'd no objection. She told me her name was Hilda Lulworth and that she was divorced. I'd no reason to disbelieve her. I didn't have the faintest idea . . . this sounds very improbable but . . .'

'No it doesn't,' Israel said, 'you did say Hilda Lulworth didn't you?'

'Yes.'

'Her headmistress at school or her tutor at Oxford was called Hilda Lulworth. She's often mentioned her. It was a convenient false name. Did you stay with her or was she just . . .'

'No, we've been together. It was . . . as she said. I'm sorry.'

'For what? David, you're not in love with Gertrud?'

'No. And I told her so.'

'I'm glad. I say it for your sake, not mine. Being in love with

Gertrud's a fate I wouldn't wish on my worst enemy. She seems to be very . . . set on you.'

David shrugged; he said, 'Where's she gone?'

'No idea. Did she give you an address as Hilda Lulworth?'

'Carlton Towers.'

'She may be there.'

She was not: she was waiting for David on the landing outside his flat, the converted second floor of a house; and the moment he appeared she said, with an embarrassing attempt at lightness, 'Don't you know better than to keep a lady waiting?'

'You can't possibly have failed to know that I'm one of your husband's friends,' David said.

'Business accomplices. He has no friends. As a matter of fact I didn't even think of it at the time.'

'Then why give me a false name? You're a mischievous liar and a treacherous bitch. That wouldn't worry me but you're also a bore.'

'Wouldn't it be more comfortable if you were to call me names *inside* the flat?'

'You're not coming inside.'

In the poor light of the landing her face was a pale mask, the features all shadows. He could not see her expression but her voice was shaking as she said, 'You can't mean that, David. Not after . . .'

'None of that. Fucking you, Mrs Lulworth, commits me to nothing.'

He got between her and the door, caught her wrist as she struck at him, held on to it and said, 'If you try that again I shall throw you down those stairs.'

With his free hand he unlocked the door, thrust her away from him, slipped inside and shut the door. Then he stood still, listening. He heard no movement. He went into his living-room, poured himself a large brandy and soda, took it across to his desk, and opened the file containing a draft of his report to the

French flying-boat builders. He noticed that his hands were shaking slightly and frowned at them until they were steady. Only once during the next half hour did he relax his attention, and that was to rise and fetch a dictionary to check the spelling of a French word and to refill his glass on the way. But after half an hour his telephone rang. The call was from the tenant of the third floor, an amiable publisher whose neighbourly advances he had not quite succeeded in discouraging. He said, 'I say, old man, there's a woman, what the police call well-dressed, sitting on your doormat with her back to the door and in tears. I thought she might be drunk or on a trip and spoke to her but she won't answer. Oughtn't one to do something? I mean, is she someone you know?'

'Yes. A Mrs Hilda Lulworth, an acquaintance of mine. She was making a nuisance of herself and I had to ask her to leave.'

'Oh . . . I see . . . well, it's no business of mine, old chap, but she's in a frightful taking.'

'As you say, it's no business of yours. I don't think she'll break in and pinch your first editions, but if you're worried you can call the police.'

David hung up and sat for a moment in thought and then telephoned Izzy.

'Listen, Izzy, your wife's sitting on the floor outside my flat and crying with rage because I told her to go to hell. The neighbours are complaining. I don't mind that, but it's all . . . unsuitable. It's a lot to ask, but could you come round and remove her?'

'No,' Israel said, 'sorry. Look, the fact is I'd help if I could but if I appear she'll simply make a noisy and possibly violent scene.'

David was angry; it seemed to him that Israel was being irresponsible. He said, 'Look, you know very well I shouldn't be asking this if I'd known who she was when I picked her up. I didn't know. The woman I've been sleeping with is a Mrs Lulworth. What you've just said is a pretty shocking confession of failure.'

'It is, isn't it?' Israel said, and hung up.

David went to the front door and opened it a few inches, shoving against Gertrud's weight. She got to her feet with a grace of movement which would have been impossible to most women in such circumstances and said, 'David, please, please let me come in. If you don't I shall kill myself.'

'That would certainly solve your problem, my problem and Israel's problem,' he said and, 'now listen to me. You will leave here at once, go to a hotel . . . as you've no luggage you'd better go to the Ritz or Claridges, the flashy ones don't understand about things like that, get some dinner or supper and a night's sleep, and meet me for lunch tomorrow . . .'

'Here at your flat, David?'

'No. I've told you, you're not coming in here. The Café Royal should be suitable; it's the reverse of intimate. The Café Royal at one.'

'David, if you don't let me in I shall sit here till . . .'

'Till you have to go to the lavatory. Don't be so silly. If you don't do as I say I'll telephone the police and have you removed as a trespasser.'

'Christ, I believe you would, too . . .'

'I'm glad you realize it. You're being tiresome, my dear, and that I will not tolerate.'

'You make yourself very clear, David.'

'I try to.'

Seven

Israel had finished bathing and shaving the following morning when the telephone rang while he was dressing.

'Mr Mendes?'

'Speaking.'

'Mr Israel Mendes?'

'Yes. Who is this?'

'Mr Mendes, this is Dawlish, manager of Burridges Hotel. We have Mrs Mendes staying with us. I understand she arrived very late last night from France and not wishing to disturb the household, took a room with us for the night. I'm sorry to say that she's far from well this morning. Our medical adviser suggested that I should phone you. Mrs Mendes is in no danger, but could you possibly come round and see her?'

'Yes. About half an hour.'

'I'm sorry to disturb you so early but you no doubt understand our position.'

'Very clearly. Thank you.'

This made the third time she had done it; but when it came into his mind to wish that she was not always so successful in calculating the dose which would not kill, he prayed in something like superstitious fear to a God he did not believe existed, *the Lord do so to me and more also if I wish her dead.* The Hebrew he had learned as a child and never used came back to him readily.

The car would be a nuisance; he telephoned for a taxi,

finished dressing, drank a cup of coffee, ran up to the nursery for his morning visit, but had to cut it short when the taxi arrived. He was at Burridges within forty minutes of receiving their call and was shown into Mr Dawlish's office. The manager introduced the other man present, who was young and excessively well-dressed, as 'Dr Daly-Cox, our medical adviser,' and said,

'It seems that Mrs Mendes left strict orders to be called at eight with a pot of black coffee. The chambermaid was unable to wake her and was alarmed by the way she was breathing. This was reported to me and I asked Dr Daly-Cox to see Mrs Mendes.'

The doctor said, 'Does your wife always use sleeping pills, Mr Mendes?'

'Yes. Sombutal.'

'Quite so. I think that she must have taken her usual dose, probably two but possibly three; and later, in a semi-drugged condition, have forgotten that and taken a second dose. Sombutal isn't a drug to treat lightly as I daresay her own physician will have told her. I suggest that you advise your wife to keep the bottle out of reach from the bed. Still, her condition was not serious and in a couple of hours she'll be quite well, but . . .'

He droned on, earning his fee and Israel listened, knowing it had not been like that and that this natty young healer of the rich with the cold eyes and precise diction probably knew it had not been like that. She must have lain awake dwelling on her humiliation, working herself into a state of hysterical despair rendered harmless by an undertow of life-preserving cunning, and so swallowing twice as many Sombutals as were perfectly safe, making once again the gesture of suicide but with just that margin of reserve which, instead of ensuring her death, seemed to leave her life to chance but with the odds well in favour of survival.

'Can I take my wife home?'

'Yes. You have your car here?'

'No, I came by taxi.'

'I shall be glad,' Dawlish said, 'to send you home in my car.'

'That's very kind, Mr Dawlish. Doctor, what do I owe you?'

'The fee is included in your bill, Mr Mendes.'

In the car both of them stared ahead in silence until Israel said,

'Gough told me.'

'Oh, did he?'

'Gertrud, I have to leave for Greenland tomorrow morning. Will you stay at home or go away again?'

She did not answer that; the car was held up by slow-moving traffic and she said fretfully, 'Why did the fool go this way? I need to rest before my luncheon appointment.'

'I thought you expected to be dead,' Israel said.

'Don't you mean hoped rather than thought?'

'Have you never wished me dead?'

'Oh, yes.'

At the office David Gough's secretary said, 'Mr Gurling's been asking for you.'

He went along to Gurling's office. Gurling was studying a map spread on his desk; he said, 'David, ever heard of Ausivit?'

'No, what is it? Sounds like a patent medicine.'

'A place on the east coast of Greenland. I want you to fly there immediately. There's no night life, in fact there's no night, and the food's horrible, but such are the sacrifices we require of you for your fifteen thousand a year. Come round this side and look at this map. Here it is. I've had a telex from the Danish iceberg patrol, there's a newly-calved and very big berg drifting slowly south about . . . here . . . It sounds like the kind we'll be dealing with. Go and take a look at it. It's a question of hull shape, of any points you can observe about shape and behaviour which'll help us solve the problem of steering such a big berg. I've had you booked on the noon S.A.S. flight to Reykjavik and we're arranging for a helicopter from there.

You'll be taken care of at the Ice Patrol station and they'll lay on a launch. Take all the time you need and get all you can.'

'Sending anyone else, John?'

'Not on this job. Izzy and Simon'll be arriving on the following day with a gang of mechanics and fitters and a plane-load of hardware, but they'll be living at the weather station at Kjöge Bay. The Danes are looking after them and their team. I've an appointment with the Danish ambassador at eleven. I was on the blower to Habib at six this morning and I have his agreement to telling the Danes what we're trying to do. Any questions?'

'Photographic gear?'

'Want to take someone from the survey section with you?'

'No. I'll do the work myself. I'll want a Hackenschmidt and the small Mamiya.'

'They'll be here by eleven and there's a car ordered. All clear?'

'Vividly. Who was the imbecile who bore midst snow and ice a banner with a strange device? Jesus, how I hate the cold. I'll go home and pack.'

'At this season,' Gurling said, 'you'll find it quite mild.'

'I'll believe that when I find it so.'

'What are you afraid of – chilblains?'

Back in his office Gough rang for a secretary. He did not know which hotel Gertrud had gone to and was not willing to ring her at Izzy's house, although she might have gone home after all. When the secretary appeared he said, 'Will you do something for me? Telephone the Café Royal, ask for the *maître d'hôtel* of the main restaurant and get him to take down this message to be addressed to Mrs Hilda Lulworth: "I've been sent to the Arctic on an emergency job. Tried and failed to reach you by phone. Apologies about the lunch. David." '

'A table for one, madam?'

'No. I'm lunching with Mr David Gough. Is he here yet?'

'You are perhaps Mrs Lulworth, madam?'

'Yes?'

'I have this message for you.'

Gertrud read it; the *maître d'hôtel* said something; she did not hear but turned her back on him to conceal her face and walked out into Regent Street and turned right and began to walk north, unaware of the people who jostled her or whom she jostled, unaware of the blue sky and strong sunshine hazed by fumes, possessed no longer by the humiliating misery of last night and no longer by the post-Sombutal depression, but an inner, fostered rage which, like sexual pleasure, absorbed all her attention.

She walked the whole way to her house virtually without seeing or hearing anything. Street crossings were made with the precautions which are second nature to the city-bred and did not interfere with the bitter pleasure of nursing her anger.

When Israel reached home that evening he was about to go straight upstairs to do his packing when Ike came unsteadily out of his mother's sitting-room which opened off the hall, followed by his mother herself wearing a floor-length silver-grey chiffon dress and with her long blonde hair tied at the nape of the neck with a piece of black ribbon. Israel picked up his son and talked to him. Ike stared at him and even smiled, but did not try to say anything. Israel said, 'He doesn't seem very talkative.'

'He talks when he has something to say,' Gertrud said; he looked at her and saw that she was smiling timidly. She said, 'Bring him in here,' and turned back into her room. If Israel was surprised at this gentleness he did not show it; he followed her and put the boy down in the middle of the Chinese carpet where he became absorbed in the pattern, following with his fingers the raised elements of the design along their edges. Israel, watching the child, said, 'I used to do that. He's very like your father.'

'I can't see it,' Gertrud said, 'I think he's more like you.' She touched a bell and presently Nanny appeared to take Ike up to the nursery. Gertrud said,

'Would you like a drink?'

'A sherry would be nice.'

'Yes, I'll have the same.'

'You, sherry?'

'It'll make a change.'

She served the drinks and said, 'Please sit down. I want to talk to you.'

'I really ought to be packing.'

'It won't take long.'

'Very well.'

She stood over him and for a brief moment he experienced a faint echo of the powerful drive to possess her, keep her splendour of body to himself, which had moved him when they first met.

She said, 'Izzy, the other day you offered to help me if I'd only let you.' She paused, perhaps waiting for a response; he said nothing and kept his eyes on the golden wine in his glass and she went on,

'Are you still willing to do that? I've behaved . . . badly. I'm asking to be forgiven.'

Although he knew that to trust her would be foolish it was not in his power to say no; still, he did not try to keep the weariness out of his voice when he said,

'What, precisely, are you asking me to forgive?'

'What I did . . . David Gough.'

'Gertrud, one would have to be very old-fashioned or very pompous, nowadays, to feel entitled to the self-indulgence of "forgiving" infidelity.'

He still kept his eyes well away from her and so failed to see the not quite suppressed twitch and flash of contempt. She said, 'But my behaviour in front of your friends . . .'

'Yes. You might have spared me that.'

'It's what I'm asking you to forgive.'

'Very well, I forgive you.' He looked at her now, faintly smiling and adding, 'But on condition that you don't hold that, too, against me.'

'You must take me seriously, Izzy. Or have I done so much damage that you'll never be able to trust me?'

'My dear, forgiveness, trust . . . do you think the words are . . . appropriate to our situation?'

'I'd like to make them so.'

Israel could neither reject nor respond to her advance. He said,

'All right, let's try to be friends. Look, I've a very early start tomorrow, and some papers to go through. I must go and pack. By the way, Harrods should've delivered some special Arctic clothing.'

'They have. I've laid them out in your room. The Arctic . . . I wish I were coming with you.'

'I shall be practically commuting there. Maybe, why not, a later trip . . .' She was refilling their glasses and said, 'May I help you pack?'

'I'd be grateful.'

Her self-blame, her humbleness confused him; he was very suspicious of them but could not face one of those outbursts of rage which would be provoked if he showed it.

Carrying their glasses they went up to his room, inspected the Arctic clothing and went to fetch suitcases. While he found the clothes he must take and she folded them into the cases, he said,

'Packing's one of the many things you do so much better than I do.'

'Thanks. Are you going alone?'

'No. Simon Brax is coming with me. We're sending another man up, but to a different part of the coast. Gough, actually, but I suppose you knew that.'

'Will what happened make it difficult for you to work with him?'

'No.'

'That's because you believe him, I expect he told you it wasn't his fault.'

'Fault. Another of those words. But, well, yes.'

'That he didn't know who I was?'

'He did say that, yes.'

The fact that she remained silent then made him look up from the shirt drawer in which he was rummaging. She was standing over a nearly full case, holding a heavy Irish sweater in her hands, and the tears were running down her cheeks. Israel realized that he did not even know what, exactly, was the cause of her grief or even whether her tears were produced by feeling or by acting. He found that he was taking shirts out and then putting them back again. He said,

'Don't cry, Gertrud.'

'I'm sorry,' she said, 'take no notice. I . . . Christ, it's never any use saying that things aren't fair, is it?'

'None whatever.'

His curiosity was aroused, though; and a measure of compassion despite his underlying distrust. He carried the shirts he had finally chosen over to her, saying, 'It's of merely academic interest to study a detail of God's ways to man.'

'Or woman,' Gertrud said, closing the case and continuing, with her fingers lingering on the catches. 'You know, I don't even know myself whether it's true that he didn't finally, I don't mean at first, know who I was.'

Now Israel understood. He kept his temper – it wasn't difficult, her cunning was so childish – and said,

'We'll forget the whole thing.'

She said, 'I came into our room, David's and mine, and I thought, I'm still not sure, that what he had in his hands before he slipped it back into my case when he heard the door open was my passport.'

He refused her the satisfaction of reacting, of showing even a flicker of interest; he did not believe her, but was far from sure that she was lying.

'I daresay you were mistaken,' he said.

Part Two

Eight

On 1 July it was Israel's turn to accompany the helicopter pilot of the glacier watch on patrol. The Danes of the Iceberg Patrol Service had suggested that the Gurling–Curran team should keep a watch on seven glaciers whose outlets were spaced along one hundred miles of the coast section of Kjöge Bay. Conditions for the calving of big bergs were good: high tides and a steady wind from the south-east were helping to pile the waters of a long, rolling swell whose origin lay in a hurricane off the Bahamas, against the green-edged, white-capped land. The southernmost glacier was the most interesting of the seven for two reasons: it was the nearest to their base; and, as David Gough had been the first to point out, it had a mighty finger which had been growing out from the shoreline for an unknown number of centuries, whose shape, were it to break from the body of the glacier, would make their task easier. It was as they circled above this one, at the start of the 1 July patrol, that the pilot thought that he recognized some new crevasses at the limit of the shoreline. The meteorological signal that morning had forecast an exceptionally high tide and as the hurricane moved north, an increase in the volume of the great swell which was being heaved against the land from the south. Israel decided to remain circling above the glacier for an hour. As a result of that decision he and the pilot became two of the small band of men who have watched the calving of a big iceberg.

After they had been circling for ten minutes he asked the pilot if he could land on and take off from the great finger of ice which pointed out into the sea. There was no particular point in doing so and there was too much wind to make the operation an easy one, but Sigurdson decided that he could do it; and did, with a skill which Israel envied. When the engines were switched off both men were aware of an extraordinary sound, a sustained creaking and groaning of enormous volume which seemed to set the air vibrating and produced yet a third kind of sound, a deep booming note which had no direction. Israel was frightened; the sound was an augury of some colossal impending violence; in the diary he was keeping he wrote later, 'The glacier was in labour and cried out in pain.' That was the sort of thing he kept for his writings and never spoke aloud; even as it was he scratched it out; it had not been like that but rather as if he and the pilot were inside the resonant body of an enormous musical instrument. Israel was relieved when Sigurdson, a young man of very few words, suggested, uneasily, that they would be better airborne. The take-off was awkward; a gust of south-east wind swept them like rubbish under a broom to the cliff edge of the ice, and they dropped fifty feet towards the surface of the sea before their vanes took hold on the thin air and lifted them clear.

They resumed circling; they could no longer hear the extraordinary booming groan of the straining ice, but they could see that the dark fissures running north to south were sometimes a thin line and sometimes much thicker; then they were closing and suddenly the pilot cried out that the whole great cape of ice was heaving to the send of the swell, like a great ship at anchor. As Israel said later, that night in the mess, 'What I saw then I shall never quite believe that I did see,' a remark which provoked a small shrug of impatience from Gough. 'I should,' he went on, 'have been expecting it; the tide had been ebbing for some time and the wind was falling light. But I hadn't been watching the tide or the time.'

The whole gigantic body of the ice-cape, like a crystal of blue glass shot through with yellow light, quite suddenly slid seaward like a launched vessel, and then plunged beneath the water under the impetus of its own colossal weight. This was the calving of Icecube, the breaking away from the body of Greenland and, as the film exposed by their automatic camera showed very clearly when it was projected a couple of days later, it sucked a wide hole in the water, a funnel-shaped whirling hollow as if a plug had been pulled from the sea bottom and the ocean were draining away. For a full minute the new berg seemed to vanish. Then came the surging rise to the surface, the mighty wallowing, the water streaming in cascades and fountains bright with rainbows from the huge body of ice. 'We watched that,' Israel went on, 'watched her steady herself, watched her settle down and cease from rocking and begin to drift.'

There had been, and, curiously, he had forgotten it, one shattering report, very like the sound of a great gun firing; and, what also he did not say, his watching of that imposing spectacle had been fogged by the tears which, he had no idea why, filled his eyes as he witnessed it. Perhaps it was that the titanic movements and sounds, that freeing of an inert mass into motion, implied a kind of life; certainly Israel was never to think of Icecube as 'it'; he had as much respect for the berg as a savage for the lump of stone he worships.

So sure was he that they now had indeed got the berg they wanted, that he signalled to base: 'Relax; we have her; weight at birth about a thousand million tons.' While that signal was being made he was watching the gap widen between Icecube and her glacier dam.

Why was he so sure of her? Well drilled by David, he chose her, as some men choose their women, for her elegant shape; and as some women choose their men, for her size. Four bergs had been calved during their patrol of the coasts; they were rejected because David did not like their shape. But Icecube was triangular, was what David called a 'viable hull'.

As for her size, at first Israel could only estimate it, but during the first days of her drift southward in the East Greenland Current, while the engineers prepared to take her over, she was measured. Icecube's cliff-like faces above the waterline averaged 378 feet; below the waterline she drew about 1,800 feet and was much bulkier than she was above it, spreading to a broad, plinth-like bottom so that although the apex to base measurement of her exposed, plateau-like surface was just under 4,000 feet and she was a little over 2,400 feet across the base, where the breadth was greatest and the depth least, her submerged parallel measurements were very much greater. By Israel's calculations Icecube contained well above twelve hundred million cubic metres of water: thus, frozen into her immense volume was the equivalent of a year's rainfall over an English county; or more than twice Habib's first requirement.

As soon as David Gough had flown the sixty miles from base to inspect the new berg, a signal was made to London and Gurling set out at once to take charge of the operations which had been planned. Israel was glad that he was coming: the atmosphere of the mess while only David and himself were in residence was not easy. It would have been difficult to find two more 'civilized' men than these two, but the business of Gertrud was between them. Israel had decided that Gertrud's hint that David had, after all, known who she was, had been no more than a malignant, that is characteristic, attempt to make mischief and have her revenge on both men. But he found it impossible not to wonder whether, perhaps, it was true. Suppose it were so? It was a long time since any particular stigma had attached to the act of sleeping with a friend's wife and in some regions of subtopia the practice had become a sort of parlour game: it was not wicked; it was unimportant. Yet he could not feel it so; he was a romantic and would never escape the consequences of that misfortune.

There was another source of strain: he had tried playing his guitar in the mess. Very soon he became aware of the deliberate self-control which David was imposing on himself. He had stopped playing and asked, 'Does this get on your nerves?' David had looked up from his book and said, 'It's all right. It's just that I'm completely tone-deaf. I'm told you play very well.'

'Yes, I do,' Israel had said; but he did not play again in David's presence.

Gurling's principal physical contribution to their work was already standing on the naked rock outside the camp of huts which had been erected for the engineers, mechanics and divers. This was the Gurling raft; it looked like a dining-table for Titans, being a hollow rectangle twenty metres square and fifty centimetres thick, of welded light alloy standing on ten legs, steel cylinders which could be telescoped to adjust their length. The raft was to carry all the gear required for the voyage – diesel generators, navigation aids, signalling equipment, radar devices, and fuel-tanks. Beside it were stacked the elements of the huts which were to be erected on it as soon as it was in place on the berg, and in which Icecube's crew were to live and work.

Operation One started shortly after Gurling's arrival at the camp on 3 July, in calm, overcast weather with the thermometer standing at 2°C. Compressors, cement-mixers, pneumatic drills and a gang of fifty men were lifted by helicopter onto Icecube's plateau and the work of letting ten concrete, socketed blocks into the surface of the ice began. For three days the quiet of that coast, normally broken only by the cries of sea-birds, the wash of waves against the beaches and the occasional creak and groan of straining ice, was broken by the throbbing of diesel engines, the ugly clamour of drills and the grind of cement-mixers. One might, as David said, have been in Piccadilly so far as noise was concerned. Each block, as soon as the concrete was set, was wedged into its socket with spring-loaded steel wedges which would expand to take up space left by melting ice. At the end of the third day the Gurling raft was lifted by the helicopter and, with two men standing by each leg, slowly lowered and steered into the sockets. Then came the work of adjustment for level by varying the length of each leg. This went smoothly and took less time than Gurling had estimated, and the rest of the working day was devoted to lifting and installing the big electric generator.

The method of mounting the two hydroturbines which had been worked out in committee, based on a suggestion made by Israel and tested by him and Simon Brax some weeks earlier, was a gigantic version of the familiar Rawlplug method. It entailed drilling holes twenty metres deep into the body of Icecube far below the water level – the actual depth had been worked out by Gough as the most effective at which to apply thrust to the berg; plugging those holes with solid cylinders of a resin which would, when in contact with water, constantly expand to take up any space left by melting or by working wear; and screwing a mounting plate to the ice. It was not a means to inspire confidence in any engineer, but Israel had pointed out that in practice the thrust of the hydroturbines would of itself tend to hold them in place. The mounting plates were hollow, and the edges which pressed against the ice were covered with rubber. Thus, in the unlikely event of the engines having to go into reverse, the entire pressure of the sea at a depth of thirty fathoms would hold the plates in position. For although there should be no question of trying to go astern on both engines, one of them would be going astern every time they had to change course, that is to steer the berg.

Gurling had designed the hollow metal motorized raft from which the engineers, wearing diving suits supplied with air by a compressor aboard the berg, would do their work. Israel had made up his mind to supervise this submarine work himself; it was not necessary and the gang had an able and experienced foreman; but while he had been working out, on paper, the way in which this job could be done, he had realized that the very idea of working deep under the Arctic Sea, or under any water for that matter, terrified him. Because he had discovered, when obliged to play rugger at school, that he was a natural coward, he had never permitted himself to indulge any weakness of that kind; nor was he willing to send men into danger which he was not ready to face himself. He might easily have removed the burden of decision from his own shoulders by reporting his intention to Gurling; he knew that Gurling would forbid him to go down with the raft. Deliberately, he failed to report his intention, he simply embarked, unrecognizable in diving gear, with the rest of the gang and, in the event, was not missed until the raft was submerged.

As the raft, rocking and pitching uncomfortably in the choppy cross-sea raised by the wind, took them round the berg to her stern, trailing their power-supply cable with its cork floats, Israel, isolated inside his diving suit until he chose to switch on the intercom which connected him with the other men and with operational H.Q. aboard Icecube, talked quietly to himself. He was sweating with fear at the prospect of submerging; 'And you think,' he told himself, 'that you are being very brave in facing this terror. But this, also, is a manifestation of self-indulgence.' He remembered that he had learned to ride and jump because he found that he was afraid of horses; and to fly aeroplanes because of that, too, he was afraid. And he reminded himself of the swelling, proud triumph of his first five-bar gate and his first solo spin; and of the pleasure, which he had come to think of as incomparable, of thus ridding himself of fears. 'You're at it again,' he told himself, 'at the game of seeking that joy and pride in doing what any healthy lout unendowed with the imagination which makes a coward afraid of the death he'll never die can do without a qualm: *mazeltov*!' Even so he did not face another explanation of his foolhardy conduct: it is possible that he would have been content to stay on the surface had David Gough not been one of Icecube's company.

When the raft was in position against Icecube's broad stern, Israel himself started the pumps which drove the air out of her hollow body and let water in; as the raft began slowly to sink, she became steadier. He was watching the indicator panel, his eyes on the meter which monitored the balance between air and water; and, at the same time, exerting all the strength of his will to fight off panic which threatened to overwhelm him as, the raft sinking like a lift in its shaft, the water closed over his head. The panic was associated with the idea that something had gone wrong with the air supply and that he couldn't breathe. But, said his intelligence, you can breathe, are breathing and will continue to breathe unless you let yourself be terrified into being unable to breathe. At last he remembered to switch on the intercom and at once heard the foreman, who was watching another meter, say, '. . . another seventy feet, Izzy. How do you like being a fish?'

'I don't,' Izzy said, and slowed the pumps and their rate of fall. The powerful lamp fitted to his diving helmet was on, and he took a quick look around the area of water visible in its beam; he caught a brief glimpse of a small shoal of cod-like fish. Then, for several minutes, he was busy balancing water and air in the body of the raft, hunting slowly up and down past the requisite level until he had the raft stationary in the vertical plane at the chosen point; and suddenly he discovered that he was no longer so desperately afraid.

The ice cliff before them was a confusing glitter in the light from their helmet-lamps. It was difficult to judge their exact distance from what seemed less a surface than a great nebula of diamonds. The foreman took charge of the motor controls and used them very gingerly, inching the raft forward so gently that when its limpets came up against the ice, there was almost no shock; then the motors were driven harder, to keep the limpets as hard as possible against the ice. As the exhaust-pumps sucked the water out from under the limpets, the huge pressure of the sea began to help them, flattening the big rubber discs against the surface until Israel said, 'I only hope the pump's man enough to refill the things, or we'll never get her off again.'

'We can always drill them,' the foreman said.

The men of Israel's team were used to working under water. Israel had never done so before and the silence and deliberation of all their movements, the ponderousness of every action, the ordinary sense of the isolation in which all men live enormously enhanced by their diving suits and the remoteness of voices unassociated with lip movements and facial expression, made it seem to him that he was working in a dream and that nothing they did here would really accomplish any practical result. Yet despite the persistent undertow of fear the dream was not unpleasant; in some way which he did not understand, he was in a world which he could enjoy.

Drilling began and went forward exactly as predicted, the limpets holding the raft firmly to the ice against the counter-thrust of the drill. Having now nothing to do, Israel called Gurling and reported progress. Gurling said, 'What the bloody hell are you doing down there?'

'Learning how the real work's done, John.'

He was conscious, as he spoke, of the strange perverseness of his own satisfaction. Why did the idea of physical prowess still have such dominion? The rigorous discipline of his own work was a thousand times more exacting than the task of drilling holes in a block of ice thirty fathoms under the sea. But it was not work which required him to risk his life. Was the business of the male to risk his life and, perhaps, to lose it while he was still potent? Was a life from which physical risk had been eliminated obscurely unsatisfying? Was every man in an office or workshop like a tiger in a zoo?

He asked Gurling how things were going on the surface. Gurling said, 'The weather's clearing. We might start moving the huts aboard. One thing about these latitudes in summer, we get twenty-four hours of daylight.'

It was fine and still next day with the thermometer at 48°F and with yellow, hazy sunshine penetrating a thin overcast. Israel felt no need to go down with the drilling team again. That underwater work was now being carried on in shifts round the clock, for the mild weather was an enemy, it was costing them water. The southerly drift would soon be creating minor problems, slow though it was; within a week the berg would be south of the base and ferrying supplies would take longer every day. Gurling had to return to London and went reluctantly, for he was enthusiastic about the Icecube project and wanted to stay with it. David Gough took his place as coordinator of works as the elements of the hutments were airlifted onto the iceberg and assembled and welded to the Gurling raft which was now being referred to as the deck. On the forward part of the deck which was being railed with stanchions and nylon rope, was the captain's cabin and the navigation cabin and the signals and radar cabin all together in a single group. On the after part of the deck a second group was erected, which included the mess cabin, galley, sleeping quarters, two bathrooms and two lavatories. And, isolated from the rest but connected by telephone with the captain's cabin, the signals cabin and the navigation cabin, was the cabin from which the engines, and therefore the steering controls, were to be managed. Israel had received permission from the Gurling–Curran board to take control of the engines in person; it was not his job, he was, after all a designer of engines, not a mechanic; but his hydroturbines were so novel and as yet untried that his request was conceded.

These cabins were not the only constructions on the deck: the big electric generator was separately mounted directly into the ice, as already described; but on deck were a second stand-by generator, a big enclosed bank of accumulators for use in emergency, and the fuel tank to supply the turbines. This construction work, and Israel's own immediate task, the sinking of the two engines on the submersible rafts and fixing them to their mounting plates, went forward smoothly, the weather varying from calm and mild to cold and stormy but never so bad that all work had to be stopped.

By 15 July Israel reported that the two miles of steel cable which, as reinforcements to screws and socket plates, had been passed round the berg, through eye-sockets on the engine casings, and winched taut, were in place, and the two huge turbines were ready for use. Gurling flew from London again to be present at the trials; 'trials' is not really the right word, however, for there could now be no question of modifications, they were gambling heavily on Israel's confidence that the engines would do what was required of them. With Gurling came two newcomers to the team: Commander (N) Harland RN; and Commander (S) Hilmar Larsen of the Royal Danish Navy.

The recruitment of these two officers was the outcome of John Gurling's negotiations with the British Admiralty; and of the First Lord's exchanges on the subject of Project Icecube with the appropriate ministries of the Atlantic maritime nations.

Commander Harland was to take charge of Icecube's navigation and act as her captain while at sea; a burly, red-faced, even-tempered man of forty, he had spent the greater part of his time in the Navy on Admiralty surveys, was the author of a textboook on navigation in the Arctic, and of a scholarly illustrated history of navigation charts. A fine linguist, he had represented the British Admiralty on half a dozen international commissions on maritime affairs. In short, as the man in charge of getting a very large iceberg across the Atlantic sea-lanes and shipping routes, he was acceptable to all the interested parties. Both the U.S. and the U.S.S.R. admiralties had raised objections to the whole project; but Gurling had been lucky in the Sea Lord who actually handled the negotiations and who had chosen Harland as his aide. His imagination had, like Gurling's, been fired by Habib's apparently crazy idea; he had contrived, with Harland's help, to play off the objections of the U.S. and the Soviet representatives, and finally reduced both sides to a merely watchful and suspicious rather than actively hostile attitude.

The request to the Danish government for an officer to take charge of Icecube's signals, warning and radar installation had been in the first place a matter of diplomacy, that is to say of courtesy. For it was from their country that the ice was being taken. The whole-hearted help which they had given to the Gurling–Curran teams, and their readiness to lend them Commander Larsen were, however, by-products of the successful negotiations between the Ruler and the Danish ambassador in Farzar. Habib had agreed to pay for the ice to be taken from the Greenland glaciers, at a rate which did not seriously hamper the project and which offered the Danes the prospect of an annual water-royalty revenue, that is revenue from the sale of a commodity which they had not even dreamed of as saleable.

Larsen's responsibility would be a heavy one: the Admiralty-convened international commission on the project had laid it down that throughout the voyage of Icecube and any subsequent iceberg voyages, there must be continuous transmission and emission of effective warning of position and movement. There was also to be an arrangement of lights including floods to outline her entire bulk at night. As David Gough put it, they would make her look like a circus gone to sea. In carefully predefined conditions of poor visibility she was to emit an amplified fog-signal from loud-hailers placed at her extremities at the four cardinal points of the compass. All these arrangements, as also the ordinary work of radio and other signals, radiotelephone communications, and radar watches were in Larsen's charge; he was given a crew of one Petty Officer radio and radar mechanic and three watch-keeping ratings.

From the moment of her calving Icecube's rate of drift had been monitored and charted by David. When Commander Harland assumed command he called Gurling to his quarters to consult over the plan of navigation which he had worked out.

'Well, as you see, your people have made me pretty comfortable. Never expected to sail *de luxe* in an iceberg, I must say. Could you manage a whisky?'

'I could, thank you.'

The two men carried their drinks through into the communicating navigation cabin where Harland had charts spread on the chart table; he said,

'I haven't worked out exact courses. I'll be doin' m' sums later today. I'm assuming, you understand, that your Mr Mendes can give us steering of some kind. What I'm going to give you is a rough general sailing plan. God knows if we'll be able to stick to it, but let's see what you think. At the moment we're here, 61 degrees 2 minutes north, 40 degrees 10 minutes west. As you can see, we're still in the East Greenland Current, cold water; rate of drift with this wind shoving, about one knot. I'm going to try and keep as close inshore as I dare right round Cape Farewell till we're off Cape Desolation – here. Cold water all the way and a five knot current the way we want to go. There's a couple of pilotage problems I won't bother you with. First leg, then, base to Desolation, 450 miles. Any objections so far?'

'I'm not sure,' Gurling said, 'given our final destination we seem to be going a good deal out of our way. Why?'

'Good question and there are three answers. One, current and wind'll be helping us all the way round the south of Greenland and up here into the approaches to Davis Strait. With our weight, we've simply got to be clever with currents. They will be our salvation because unless we're moving however little, I don't fancy Mendes' chance of overcoming our initial inertia; but while we're moving, he can presumably push us along a shade faster. Second answer, we'll be in cold water all the way. Third answer, for the next leg I want to use the Labrador Current . . . here.'

'I've been hoping I was right about that.'

'Ah, you had the same idea?'

'Yes.'

'You should've been a navigator. Right, well, here we are, off Cape Desolation and this is the first real test of Mendes' engines . . . we've to push this little lot across the strait and into the Labrador Cold Current about . . . here.' He indicated a faintly pencilled cross with the bottom of his glass and continued, 'About sixty degrees north fifty degrees west give or take twenty minutes both ways. From Desolation to here is four hundred miles, but we'll be into the southerly drift of the Labrador as soon as we're out of the West Greenland Current – as you can see, they're parallel but opposed.'

'So 850 miles till now.'

'Let's call it a thousand,' Harland said, 'and have another drink on it.'

While Harland refilled their glasses, Gurling studied the chart and as far as he could see from his faint pencillings, his plan was not very different from Gurling's own.

Harland returned from the cupboard saying, 'Here you are, Irish measure, as m' mother used to say and she should've known, being born in Limerick. Now, where were we, yes, from this point six degrees north fifty degrees west we're in the southerly drift of the cold Labrador Current, cold water for a thousand miles and all going our way and we can get our heads down till we're here, due south of Cape Race. Now we face our worst problem.'

'You mean, of course, crossing the Gulf Stream, warm water and with a north component in its drift tending to carry us right out of our way.'

'Yes, well, ignoring drift for a moment and just supposing we're able to steer the shortest course, what I'm aiming at is to get us into the Canaries Current which is cold and going our way. I should try making for this point, south of the Azores, about thirty-eight north forty west. But it's dicey, there are banks here, and we draw a hell of a lot of water, well over the hundred fathoms. But if I can find deep water between the banks we may scrape through and then the Canaries Current will drift us down to Farzar. By the way, have Admiralty passed on to you my opinion that docking this iceberg of yours will probably turn out to be impossible?'

'No. If you think that, why . . .?'

'As the Yanks say, the impossible takes a little longer.

Frankly, I wanted to have a bash, it's not Britain's money and I gather your Arab friend isn't short of cash.'

'Captain, if you meet him, don't call him an Arab. It's the worst insult you can offer a man of Persian blood.'

'I'll remember that, John.'

'Suppose,' Gurling said, 'we reckon on a 2½ knot combined drive and drift all the way, as far as I can see the job will take from forty to fifty days. I'm wondering what our melting losses will be.'

'Not a clue, old boy. There's one thing, it's fairly certain that the bergs which've been sighted as far south as the Bahamas had been drifting about in warm water for months and possibly for years.' Harland looked at his watch and said,

'It's time we found Mr Mendes.'

Jock Drummond had set up three camps and spent a good deal of his time driving from end to end of the pipeline, staying a night or two at each camp. The camps were simply large caravans; one was in the Curzon Depression and for the time being he was sharing it with Dirk Leuwenhoek who was completing drawings for making scale models of the Depression and of the Wilhelm Crater; another, which he shared with Simon Brax, was pitched in the grove of dragon-trees overlooking Abbas Bay; the third was halfway between the two.

Over about a third of the distance there was a tolerable road, which was being improved, roughly parallel with the line surveyed for the pipe and close enough to be useful. The rest of the way was what Jock called jeepable and heavy trucks could use it if they were driven carefully. The country was flat, hard and stony with a meagre vegetation of grey-green grasses, sages, a low, depressed-looking shrub which seemed to be related to the camel-thorn of Asia but had none of its fragrance. In spring, after the few days of meagre rainfall, the floral scene became lively with small, dumpy red tulips, blue and white iris scarcely three inches tall and, among the massifs of eroded tumbled rocks which dotted the plain and where the dew of cold nights condensed to provide moisture, a prostrate, savagely thorned crimson-flowered rose which not even the half-starved goats of the nomads' mixed, lean flocks would touch.

From the Wilhelm Crater to Dragon-tree Bay was 209 kilometres and throughout the whole of that distance Gurling–Curran's work was under continuous observation. Wherever there was activity, there also was a small group of Arabs, men and children, no women. They stood, or sat their camels, very patiently, unsmiling, expressionless, staring. Both Jock and Simon had from time to time made friendly advances, but these people were unresponsive, not even formally polite. 'Lumpen-peasantry,' Jock called them, distressed by the difficulties they put in the way of his impulse to like people. At the inland terminal of the pipe this unnerving audience of the project's progress was more disturbing; there, from time to time, would be a troop of men mounted either on ponies or camels, and once a troop in jeeps; and always armed.

Early in July, when the thermometer rarely fell below forty degrees centigrade and only the extreme dryness of the air rendered the heat tolerable, Jock arrived at the Dragon-tree camp where the temperature was lower but the humidity higher so that staying alive and active was even more difficult. The little tramp-steamer which was being used as a workshop was busy with movement, and there was much coming and going of launches to and from the shore and the underwater work-site where the concrete sill was complete. The huge sluice gates, towed floating round from the Farzar oil terminal where the welding had been completed, were anchored and buoyed in the bay.

The last stretch of track leading to the camp was along the coast of Abbas Bay and Jock saw that the big job of cutting off the projecting granite shelf was in hand, for there were two diving launches and a small floating drilling-rig anchored above the shelf. The work entailed drilling deep into the stone at ten-metre intervals, filling the holes with explosive, and then sealing them with concrete. Specialists were in charge of the work, but as useful auxiliaries, quick and deft at the odd jobs of fetching and carrying to and from the surface, Simon Brax had recruited a family of pearl-divers which he referred to as the 'Ali clan' after the father's name. They got the barest of livelihoods from their diving, for the Japanese cultured pearls nearly killed the trade; most families had drifted back into fishing, and now only the Ali clan remained, their lives made easier by the setting up of a state handicrafts shop for tourists, in Farzar, whose management bought all the pearls the Alis found. Ali and his three sons carried on the business: the youngest son was called Nuri, and was sixteen years old, a youth of touching beauty, an Arabian ephebe. He had attached himself to the European diving team, was paid good wages, combined his work for them with diving for shell and, as he was a cheerful, smiling lad, quick at English, intelligent, a magnificent diver and swimmer, and very warm-hearted, he had become a sort of pet.

When Jock arrived in camp he found Simon resting after a meal, in the big main cabin of the caravan. And seated cross-legged on the floor at his feet, Nuri was laboriously writing the letters of the Latin alphabet in an exercise book, repeating their names as he did so. He jumped to his feet when Jock entered and he and Simon exchanged a quick glance which struck Jock as conspiratorial. He said, 'Starting a school, Sim?' and 'I've had a bloody awful drive and I want a quart of cold beer.' The boy smiled and said, 'I fetch,' and went out to the galley. Jock said, 'What's the idea?'

Simon flushed; he said, 'The kid wants to learn. It seemed to me a good idea to help him.'

'Sodding Arabs,' Jock said, 'after today's little effort, the less I see of the buggers the better.' To which Simon replied, 'Hadn't you better watch that kind of talk?'

'Perhaps. I thought they were going to murder me. I was . . .' Nuri returned and Jock broke off, took the beer, thanked the boy and said, 'Piss off, there's a good lad, I want to talk to Mr Brax.' Nuri looked at Brax uncertainly and Brax said a few words in Arabic and the boy nodded, looking sulky, and left them. Jock saw Simon's eyes following Nuri until he was out of sight; he said nothing, drank a glass of beer, and refilled it. Simon said, 'Well?'

Jock then told Simon that on the last leg of his drive he had suffered a very disagreeable experience: a band of Arabs mounted on camels had emerged suddenly from behind a big massif of rock overgrown with aloes, a mile or so ahead of him along the track, and ridden straight at him; they were armed with what, as they came nearer, he identified as sub-machine guns.

'I didn't want to give these laddies cause for complaint so I pulled up and waited. They surrounded the car and one of them, presumably their leader, bawled a long speech at me. I've never been so frightened in m' life; they were an ugly lot. You know, Sim, it's a bloody stupid thing but although I didn't understand a word I couldn't just sit there saying nothing. I'd run down the window, of course, and I said I was very sorry but I didn't understand what they were talking about. I saw they didn't understand me either and I suddenly got very angry and said listen you big, black, mother-fucking bastard, if you and your mates don't bugger off at once, you'll have Habib's air force to reckon with and I hope they blow your wives and bairns to bits. Why did I say that? I mean, I didna' wish the poor creatures any harm, Christ forbid; maybe it was because I knew they didn't understand. Aye, and they're not black, either; this khaki-faced loon was half off his camel – the brute was farting like a drain – and listens to me and suddenly spits in m' face . . .'

He'd driven on then; there had been some bursts of shots, but either they were not aimed at the car or the Arabs were very poor at shooting.

Simon said, 'I haven't had any trouble of that kind. We're being watched, of course, but that's only natural.'

'Simon, I don't know anything about these people or this country but I've a good notion the shepherds are closing in on the line from both sides. Another thing, there's a muckle of shepherds to a mickle of sheep or goats or whatever the beasties are, they all look alike to me. A kind of drift towards the line. They're beginning to get in my way. It's not two days since one of my own men was badly bitten by two of the bloody great dogs they have with them . . .'

'What did you do?' Simon said, rising, going to the wash-basin and wiping his face with a wet towel.

'Shot the brutes.'

'Jesus, man, you shouldn't've done that.'

'Do you think I don't know it? I lost my temper. I sent the lad into Farzar for anti-rabies injections and it seems he'll have to have three and he's vera sick and vera sorry. Sim, I'm going to see Habib.'

'You're quite sure this movement isn't some kind of seasonal migration?'

'No, I'm not sure of anything. I just don't like their dirty spittle on my face and why should they be converging like this, the green is no greener on our bit of the plain than anywhere else?'

'They may keep on the move to give the grazed areas time to recover.'

'Both ways? Sim, they're stupid, sure, but they're not that stupid.'

'I think you're making mountains out of molehills. The Arabs here are second-class citizens. If Habib and his Persians want to treat them like helots, there's nothing we can do about it. But we don't have to follow their example. I like them, I get on with them and I don't believe it's a good idea to go running to Habib because the *bedu* have funny ways.'

Drummond was astounded at this outburst; he was also tired, hot, dirty and resentful or he would not have said, 'By God, it's that boy Nuri, I knew there was a stink of fish. I . . .'

Simon stood up and said, 'Be careful what you're saying.'

Jock swallowed the rest of his beer and then said, 'Aye, I will. You're right. But I'm going to see Habib, Sim.'

Simon shrugged.

Jock had a meal, a change of clothes; and drove into Farzar. He picked up mail at the Hilton and telephoned the palace secretariat and asked for Caroline.

'Presence, the Khanum is not here. Please to wait.' There was a long wait and then Habib's Farsi secretary, an agreeable young men whom Jock had met and who was called Nadar Azadi, came to the telephone:

'Mr Drummond, how are you? I am sorry you have been kept waiting. Miss Bartrum is not *de service* just now. Mr Drummond . . . how do you say *de service* in English?'

'On duty. Is Miss Bartrum having a holiday?'

'Let us call it that, Mr Drummond.'

'Listen, Azadi, the lass isn't in trouble, is she?'

'Lass . . . that is a nice word. It means maiden?'

'Aye, that's it. She's not in trouble?'

'No, no, no, the opposite of trouble. Can I be of use to you, Mr Drummond?'

'You can. I want an audience, Azadi.'

'His highness is very very busy. It is urgent?'

'I think so.'

'Could I give his highness some idea of the business, Mr Drummond?'

'Yes. One of his subjects spat in my face.'

'But that is terrible, Mr Drummond. We are very very sorry. It was an Arab, of course.'

'It was.'

'They are not couth people, Mr Drummond.'

'Not what?'

'Couth. It is not good English?'

'I expect so. That audience, Azadi . . .'

'Where can I reach you, Mr Drummond?'

'Here, at the Hilton, at three.'

'I will call you back at three.'

'God bless you, Azadi.'

'For your sake, He will, Mr Drummond.'

Jock was in the coffee-room when the call came through.

'I am Azadi, Mr Drummond. Good afternoon, how are you? You have, of course, your car with you?'

'Of course.'

'His Highness will see you at four. The officer of the guard at the Sea Gate will have orders.'

He reached the Sea Gate, so called because it opened into the grounds from the road between the palace and the sea, below Habib's favourite terrace, at ten to four and was allowed to drive the Rangerover into the Court of the Tamarisks. The duty officer, a young man whose wide shorts, neatly rolled shirt sleeves, epaulettes, forage-cap and big moustache all bore witness to a style which had once been east-of-Suez British, led Jock to Azadi's office. On the way, oppressed as he always was by the possibility that silence might imply unfriendliness, Jock said, 'You speak English?'

'A little, sir.'

'Your style . . . Sandhurst?'

'Saint-Cyr, monsieur.'

Thus snubbed, Jock felt that his arrival in Azadi's office was hangdog, but Azadi shook his hand, asked how he was, sent for the inevitable glass of tea, said, 'His highness will receive you in a few minutes.'

Jock said, 'I'm curious about Miss Bartrum, we're old friends.'

'The lass is . . . scheduled for promotion, Mr Drummond.'

A moment later the telephone rang and Azadi answered it, said a word of acknowledgement and hanging up said to Jock, 'His highness will see you now, Mr Drummond.'

Habib was not alone in his office: at a desk under a window

which overlooked the central Court of the Orange-trees, his sister sat talking quietly into a dictaphone. Habib said, 'Mr Drummond, how nice to see you. Azizeh, you know Mr Drummond, I think.' The princess looked up, nodded without smiling, and went on with her dictation. Habib said, 'My sister is my most valuable aide; she is my grand vizier, eh? Please take that chair. I do not have to ask you how the work is going, your weekly reports are a model of clarity and, thank God, of brevity. All is well, I hope?'

'Not altogether, sir, or I shouldn't've had to trouble you.'

'Ah. What seems to be the trouble?'

Jock repeated all he had told Simon. He noticed as he talked that the princess had stopped dictating and was listening to him with her eyes cast down, attentively. When he fell silent it was she who spoke first; not to him but rather as if he were not there.

'Mr Drummond should not have shot those dogs.'

'Perhaps not. But he has his own men to protect. Tell me, Mr Drummond, you have given the matter some thought, what do you suggest?'

'A regular armed patrol, sir. Two tracked armoured cars should be enough. If there are objections to that, what about a helicopter patrol?'

'Neither would be impossible. Either might be unwise. I am not convinced that anything of that kind is necessary.'

'I don't really know your Arabs, sir. It may be that I'm letting my nerves get the better of my judgement.'

'The possibility had crossed my mind, Mr Drummond. Azizeh, you know something of our Arab friends, what is your opinion?'

'That anything of the kind Mr Drummond suggests would be a serious mistake.'

'Why?'

'Because it would be a provocation, a challenge. I think that Mr Drummond will have a certain amount of harassment to put up with. The people are afraid that they are going to lose their grazing. It is surely part of his duty to tolerate it and to exercise great restraint in reacting to it.'

Habib said, 'I wonder if we might not be too respectful of these . . . excessively simple people. They are not above the law, Azizeh.'

'Why provoke them to violence, Habib, if we can avoid it? I have a suggestion.' She broke into Farsi but Habib checked her at once, 'Please speak English, sister. Mr Drummond must understand us.' Azizeh shrugged but said, 'The proper people to have the line policed, if it must be policed, are the seven Cousins. Send for Sheikh Allal and require his help.'

Habib brooded and Jock held his tongue until Habib said,

'Mr Drummoned, leave it to me. I do not know what will be done, but something will.' He rose and Jock rose and Habib said,

'I believe that Mr Azadi has a message for you from a friend. You know where to find him.'

Jock went to Azadi's office, his mind divided between dissatisfaction with the outcome of the audience, resentment at the way the princess had treated him, and curiosity.

Azadi said, 'Mr Drummond, you were asking about Miss Bartrum who would like to see you. I have a servant waiting in the anteroom to conduct you to her.'

'Oh, fine. I'd like to see her.'

'Of course, it will be very nice for her also. You are what they call in English a friend of the family, eh? *Un ami de la maison,*' Azadi laughed and went on, 'and in England at least one can count on the discretion of one's friends.'

The journey through the palace was like walking through a museum of decorative styles. The walls of one corridor and a vast stateroom were a mosaic of looking-glass tiles; from the ceiling hung huge Murano glass chandeliers and on the mirror walls indifferent portraits in the nineteenth century European style of some of Habib's ancestors, shown up for the bad work they were by a great, life-size full-length portrait of 'Omar the Younger by his contemporary Hassan the Shirazi; that painting had cost him his life when it was discovered after the death of 'Omar, for he had been stoned to death by a fanatical Sufi mob for making images.

Another suite of rooms through which the servant led Jock Drummond was all art nouveau, a tribute to Habib's father's taste for whatever happened to be fashionable in Paris or London. Yet another seemed to be a copy of a wing of the palace at Versailles. Then, suddenly, they were in late twentieth-century surroundings: the apartments which were their destination might have been those of a property-developing millionaire in London, with the sense to employ a good interior decorator.

Caroline, wearing a *chador* over her green Irish linen trouser suit, came in from a balcony and slipped off the *chador* worn to keep off the dust stirred and borne by the hot wind from inland. She said, 'Jock, how nice this is,' sounding unnatural. The room was enormous, with a wide view of the sea through arches which had been glazed to form windows. Jock, suddenly lacking anything appropriate to say, admired the huge carpet and she said,

'It was made in Tabriz for Mahomet Shah, the Prince's father. It took eleven years to make.'

She indicated a drinks trolley and said, 'Do help yourself, Jock,' and moved to a big circular divan which occupied the very centre of the room, saying, 'Join me on this very comfortable object; and bring me a tomato juice.'

Jock did so, saying, 'Now what's all this about?'

'All what, Jock?'

'O.K., Caroline, forget it.'

She stared at her drink and said, 'The prince has asked me to marry him.'

'Congratulations . . . and I mean that. I heard rumours . . . will you do it?'

'Yes.'

'I must say you've taken on the devil of a job. I like him. Very much. But . . .'

'Jock dear, would you speak very softly; I have a bad headache.'

'Sorry . . .' He was taken aback and looking at her earnestly saw that she was afraid; or at least unaccountably nervous. Speaking very low and with her head down she said, 'I'm not the only one for whom there may be squalls ahead . . .' Suddenly she smiled and raised her head and said,

'Remember how good I always was at telling fortunes?'

He had never known her do any such thing; he said, 'Wonderful. Go on, do mine now,' and held out his right hand, palm upwards. She raised her own hands to support it and pretended to pore over his palm with conscientious thoroughness, frowning to show how serious she was, and said,

'You're going to receive a large sum of money and be very rich and very happy and cross water. H'm . . . what's this?' She looked up, straight into his eyes and deadly serious for a moment and said,

'I see a beautiful, dark lady and she's very interested in you. Her shadow falls right across your path. Beware of her . . .' and laughed and said, 'There, a gypsy couldn't have done it better. Tell me about the family . . . and you, how's the work going?'

He followed her lead; she either was or thought she was being spied on and she implied that he too was under Azizeh's eye and that she was not his friend; well, he had suspected as much but without any idea why. He talked about his little girls and about the work while she refilled their glasses, saying nothing about the trouble with the Arabs. She showed him a pleasant letter she had received from John Gurling, saying, 'The idea of him living on an iceberg . . . it's fantastic.'

'Not nearly so fantastic as the idea of Izzy Mendes doing likewise.'

'True. I wonder if he plays his guitar among the polar bears.'

'Surely. Soothing the savage breast.'

Jock spent half an hour with her; part of the persistent awkwardness between them was due to the fact that he had never known her except as a brisk and efficient working girl; even when she came to his house to dinner, she played with the children and insisted on doing the washing up. This idle and languid and secretive young woman was a stranger.

When she had summoned a servant to guide him back through the maze of the palace, and he was standing to take leave, he said,

'I wish you all the happiness in the world. By the way, Azadi gave me a hint to keep the news to myself.'

'Would you, Jock, for the time being? The prince must decide when it is to be announced. And Jock . . . take the gypsy's warning seriously.'

'Aye.'

Nine

One of the laws of motion which have been discovered by physicists and which explain the exquisite order and balance of the universe, concerns the conservation of momentum. The simplest way of illustrating it is by the case of gun recoil: the mass of the gun multiplied by the speed of its recoil upon firing is equal to the weight of the shell fired multiplied by its velocity. Or, take the familiar case of the jet aircraft: velocity times mass of the gases jetted out by the engines is equal to velocity times mass of the aircraft in flight. That was only one of the principles involved in Israel's solution to the problem of moving Icecube under control. Another was the principle of inertia, the tendency of a body at rest to remain at rest, of a body in movement to continue in movement along a straight line. Yet another consideration, in which David Gough's collaboration was important, was that of a floating body's resistance to motion due to friction.

Probably man has not yet designed an engine, unless it be the H-bomb, capable of shifting a body weighing a thousand million tons, standing on solid earth. But Icecube was afloat: consider the beautiful universal pattern implicit in the concept of buoyancy. It was Archimedes who, just before some military men treated him in the way the military did treat intellectuals until they discovered that it is better to milk your cow than to slaughter her, discovered that the mass of that part of a body which is immersed in water is equal to the weight of the water displaced; or, in other words that the body immersed in water is lighter than it is in air by an amount equal to the weight of the water displaced. Put it another way: a floating body is one on which an upward vertical force acts to balance the downward vertical force of gravitation. In short, Icecube in sea water was as weightless as a hydrogen balloon in air.

But ice is solidified water: why, then, does not a piece of ice remain motionless in the vertical plane in perfect balance with the water at whatever level it is placed, instead of floating with its surface well above the water surface? Because its density is about one-tenth less than that of water; moreover sea water is denser than fresh water.

All of which does not mean that Israel's engines had nothing to push: inertia and several kinds of friction remain; Icecube's resistance to being pushed was still enormous. Naval architects like David know as one of the basic principles of their trade that the forward thrust applied by engines to a hull – and Icecube had to be considered as a laden hull – is proportional to that mass of water to which sternward acceleration is imparted by the engines, multiplied by the rate of that acceleration. Israel's hydroturbines had been designed, in short, to push as much water as possible as fast as possible away from Icecube's stern.

The most difficult problem on the solution of which he and David Gough had to work together had been that of estimating – accurate calculation was simply impossible because of any iceberg's eccentric shape and manifold anfractuosities – her frictional resistance to motion, a complex factor because there were, so to speak, secondary and tertiary frictions set up by the wave motions which her own movement generated. Israel, David and their Royal Navy collaborators had carried out some singular experiments in Southampton water; one, by way of example, entailed making a number of measured runs in a powerful motor-launch at given throttle settings, and repeating them while towing a triangular block of ice weighing ten tons. By such means they provided themselves with at least some figures to work with, some knowledge of what was entailed in pushing the water out of Icecube's way and of the forces at work in bow-waves, side-waves and wake-waves.

John Gurling and Commander Harland heard Israel's guitar before they opened the door of the engine-control cabin which was his place of work. He stopped playing the moment the door opened and was on his feet, standing rather stiffly as if he had been discovered in some breach of duty. This was not the first meeting between Israel and Harland and they were awkward with each other because Israel had immediately sensed an anti-semite in Harland, while Harland was aware that he had done so. Gurling realized that there was some kind of difficulty between the two men but he had no idea what it was; for him Israel was simply a man, one of the most brilliant he had ever worked with, and not the representative person of a myth.

It need hardly be said that Harland was not the kind of anti-semite who believes in the reality of the Protocols of the Elders of Zion and admires the late Julius Streicher; he would not have countenanced the smallest measure of persecution or even the least shadow of discrimination. Nor would he have allowed his feeling to influence his conduct but he seemed unable to prevent it from stiffening his manner. He had intended to say something about Israel's playing: for he greatly loved classical guitar music. But Israel's manner was correspondingly stiff so that all the Commander said was, 'Are you ready with the engines, Mr Mendes?'

Israel turned to the console of controls and dials, rather like that of a big aeroplane, and said, 'Yes, I am, sir.'

'You know our present rate of drift?'

Mounted on the cabin wall, away from all the other indicators, were three big dials; Israel looked at one of them and said,

'0·97 knots.'

'Are you sure of that? What is that instrument?'

'A gadget of my own, sir.'

'Accurate?'

'At least it's less inaccurate than the standard gear.'

'I see, I have a higher reading in the navigation cabin.'

Harland was aware of a curious conflict within himself; he had an innate respect for good workmanship and skills and it was a part of his antisemitism to believe that Jews were cleverer than other people; on the other hand a distaste for what he took to be Israel's arrogance was impelling him to ignore the fellow's claim. Meanwhile Israel had said nothing to Harland's last remark and Gurling, aware of tension, said, 'What do you say to that, Izzy?'

'John, you know very well that I asked for my own drift-monitor to be installed throughout and was overruled. What can I say, except that in my opinion if we go by the standard gear Commander Harland's going to find some very large navigational errors. It simply isn't suitable for drifting objects of our size. Besides, errors which hardly count when one's speed is twenty or thirty knots, become very important at our speeds.' He turned to Harland and went on, 'Perhaps you'd allow me to explain why I think this monitor here is better than the standard one.'

'Please do, Mr Mendes.'

Israel explained; it took him seven minutes and five diagrams and at the end of the performance Harland said, 'I shall take your readings as correct until I get one of your gadgets in the navigation cabin. Gurling, could you lay that on for me?' He looked at the monitor dial and said, 'So . . . 0·96. Start engines, please.'

Israel sat at the console and began on the starting routine. He said, 'Commander Harland, you understand that there will be no gain for some time?'

'How long?'

'By calculation, two hours . . . we have to set up a very big pressure wave behind us to overcome relative inertia; the power to acceleration ratio will fall exponentially as we get under way.'

'Thanks. Carry on.'

Israel was doing so; he said, 'You won't hear anything in here. Even outside, only a dull rumble.'

Dials all over the console were coming alive, needles rising and quivering. Israel said, 'With your permission, sir, I'll run them dead slow for half an hour before I use full power.'

'What's your total optimum thrust?'

Israel told him, in terms of volume of water pushed aft per second, and the Commander whistled. He said, 'There are two things I want to find out first. How much speed we can add to our drift; and how much steering is possible. Suppose I want to make a turn through ninety degrees, what exactly do you do on receipt of the order?'

'Go full ahead on one, full astern on the other. I believe you'll have to reckon on the change of course being very slow. The factor of momentum inertia is . . . well . . .' he chose a sheet of squared paper covered with calculations and a small graph from the file at his side and concluded, 'See for yourself.'

'Provided I know what to expect, I shall manage, Mr Mendes. Is it essential for you to remain in here while your engines are warming up?'

'No.'

'Then I should like you to come to the navigation cabin and take a look for yourself at what I believe will be our two major problems; crossing the Gulf Stream; and getting through the relatively shallow water south of the Azores.'

The three men went to the navigation cabin and once again Harland explained the problems. Israel listened attentively and said,

'I understand, sir. Just one thing, in this Gulf Stream crossing, shan't we have help from the wind?'

'I'm afraid not. Pressure's likely to be high over Mid-Atlantic and at the critical point the wind's apt to be blowing from the south-west. But it's a thing we'll have to play by ear. Even a hurricane's possible. Or we might be lucky and get the biggest high pressure system south-west of us when we begin the crossing, in which case we'd get a favourable wind for part of the way. Once we're across, then we'll have the north-east trades helping us, quite possibly all the way.'

They returned to the engine-room after Israel had refused a drink which, Gurling saw at once, was a mistake. Israel read his temperature gauges and said, 'I can open throttle now, if you wish.'

'Please do.'

Gurling left the cabin to find the steward – the company included one steward and one cook – to order sandwiches and a a bottle of wine. When he returned Harland was saying,

'. . . in that case, I know your father-in-law. He and I served together some years ago in a Channel Navigation Commission. You know, of course, that he had to live in retirement on the family estate during the war because he wouldn't serve under Raeder?'

'It wasn't Raeder he objected to,' Israel said, 'it was serving under any officer who, as he thought of it, had betrayed Germany to the Nazis. He was no lover of Jews but he was a rigorously just man.'

'I dare say, but I was always sorry for Raeder. Was he to refuse to serve his country because his country was ruled by a scoundrel, a scoundrel who was giving her victories?'

'You don't think, sir, that he'd've done even better to help his country get rid of the scoundrel?'

'You justify political assassination?'

'In such circumstances, yes.'

'Ah, well.'

The next fifteen minutes were occupied in a rapid résumé of Israel's calculation of Icecube's probable very slow rate of response to changes of thrust. As Israel said, it was a question of time taken, given turbines of limited size, to build up enough pressure to deal with such a mass. Harland said, 'I'd very much value a copy of these calculations, Mendes.'

'I have one somewhere. I'll leave it at your room, sir.'

'By the way, to avoid misunderstanding I ought to say that while I'm familiar with your reputation, I haven't read either of your books. To tell you the truth, they're away above my head.'

The moment he had said that Harland regretted the tone which had come into his voice as he was saying it. He had certainly not intended to sneer; yet to him it sounded like a sneer. He went on hastily, 'I regret it; for me mathematics is the supreme discipline. I've sometimes thought it should be the meeting point of art and science, a sort of apex of the triangle . . .'

It was hardly the sort of thing he said naturally; but he had to make some kind of amends. The echo of what he was saying sounded absurd in his own ears and he added, 'Perhaps I mean that it's the basis of science, but like art, depends on insights.'

'I don't know the difference,' Israel said, indifferently. It was an ungracious response, but he could concede nothing. Harland, keeping control of himself, nodded at the guitar propped in one corner of the room and said, 'For you, I see, mathematics and music are one.'

Gurling decided to intervene; he said, 'Izzy's in Bream's class,' and realized he had overdone it when Israel looked shiftily away from him and slightly twitched his shoulders and said, 'Nice of you, John, but you're no judge. I dare say Commander Harland knows that the guitar demands your whole life, not just a little bit of it.'

Harland had his eyes on the three big dials and said, 'I say, we're off . . .' The other two rose to look: the first dial, the drift monitor, now stood at 0·9; the second was at 1·2; the third at 2·1. Israel frowned and said, 'I apologize; it looks as if my calculations were too cautious.'

They sat there, eating their sandwiches and drinking claret. Harland said, 'A very nice wine.'

'From Izzy's cellar,' Gurling said. Very slowly numbers 2 and 3 dials crept slowly up, while number 1 remained steady at 0·9. During the next two hours Israel noted the exact figures at intervals of five minutes and drew a graph. At the end of this time he said,

'Will you look at this curve,sir?' Harland went to stand behind his chair.

'It's not accurate; not enough readings. I'll do it again, over a twenty-hour period. There's a factor I discounted but it looks as if I shouldn't've done. The more we overcome our inertia, the more advantage we're getting from drift. I mean from the current. There can't be any variation in rate of flow of current, can there?'

'No.'

'Then the only answer is, the current's got a better grip on her. I think this may be important, sir. You see what's happening . . . at least I think it is: reduction of the friction which reduces the ratio of drift speed to current speed.'

Gurling said, 'A bonus. We can do with it. Skipper, let's try to steer her now, across the current.'

'Make it so, Mr Mendes,' Harland said, 'I want a ninety-degree turn to port, that is away from the land.'

'Thanks, I know port from starboard,' Israel said. Harland flushed and said,

'Look, Mendes, you're not a sailor and I'm responsible; we've got a lee shore, and I'm certain you know what that is too.'

'Sorry, sir.'

Israel glanced at the compass tell-tale mounted above his head on the ceiling; it was fed from the gyro in the navigation cabin. He said, 'I'm going to go full ahead starboard and full astern port,' and shifted the throttles accordingly. By now David Gough had joined them.

As the four men watched, patient in their intense absorption in the fantastic operation of steering a billion tons of ice, very very slowly the dials began to show changes. In turn, they left the control room and went to dinner in the mess. They spoke less and less. When David went for his meal, Israel picked up his guitar and said, 'Any objections?' Gurling, rolling his tenth cigarette, smiled; Harland, recharging his pipe, said, 'On the contrary.'

Israel had already started the record of five-minute readings to get the materials for a graph; he handed the clip-board to Gurling and said, 'Then would you mind, John?'

Before going to the mess David went to his cubicle in the dormitory and saw that the steward had left a letter from England on his cot; it was addressed to him c/o Gurling–Curran. Arrangements had been made to carry mail with other supplies, to Icecube, by helicopter from one of several centres, during the course of her voyage. The first delivery had just been made, from Reykjavik. David did not recognize the handwriting on the envelope; he slipped the letter into his pocket and did not open it until he was seated, alone as it happened, at the mess table, with a plate of soup before him. In fact he kept the letter to occupy him during the tedious chore of eating.

When he did open it he was startled: it began, 'Dear Izzy' and the first sentence read, 'How I envy you up there in the cool; London has suddenly become intolerably hot . . .' Only then did he look at the printed heading: it was Israel Mendes' address. David put the letter down beside his plate and took three spoonfuls of soup. Then he turned over the single sheet to look at the signature: 'Ike sends his love and so does . . . Gertrud.'

He did not read the body of the letter, not for reasons of honour but because he knew it would not interest him. He put it back into the envelope while the steward removed his soup plate and served him with a helping of chicken, potatoes and peas. Forcing himself to swallow a little of each of these, he set his mind to work. First – deliberate or accidental? Surely no woman would accidentally put a letter to her husband into an envelope addressed to her lover. David called the steward and said, 'Mr Mendes is busy in the control room; asked me to find out if there's any mail for him?'

'I put some letters on his cot, sir. Should I fetch them?'

'No, leave them there. Thanks.'

David had no doubt that there would be a letter from Gertrud among those on Israel's cot; or rather, an envelope addressed to Israel containing a letter to himself. After the damage was done, for she must intend damage of some kind, she would claim that the switch was accidental. But it might be possible to put a spoke in her wheel.

The steward removed his plate and substituted a dish of tinned peaches. David said he did not want them and would not take coffee or tea. He went back to the dormitory and directly to Israel's cubicle which, like the rest, was closed with a heavy nylon curtain. There were five letters on the cot; he sorted them through and found the one he was looking for. He had it in his hand and was turning to leave when the curtain was pushed aside and Israel said, 'Something I can do for you?'

David did not lose his head; he took the other letter from his pocket and handed it to Israel and said, 'I had this letter. As you see, it's addressed to me, but it's for you. It seemed likely there'd be one for me addressed to you. There is . . . here.' Israel took it and looked at it and said, 'It's addressed to me. I shall assume it's for me until I know otherwise. You should've asked me, not just come creeping in here.'

'I didn't creep in, I walked in. I'd better tell you what I think. I don't believe this was a mistake, I think she did it intentionally. If so, the letter you have there'll've been written to make as much mischief as possible.'

Israel was very pale and his hands were shaking. He said,

'You can't possibly know any of that. It's not an uncommon mistake to make. In any case you'd no right to come and take a letter addressed to me.'

'Izzy, you can't really believe this was an accident.'

'I see. You think you know my wife better than I do.'

'No . . . but there's one thing she and I have in common and you're free from.' David smiled to show that he was not more than ninety per cent serious and went on, 'I don't know an English word which describes it so exactly as the French *canaille* – used as an adjective.'

'You mean it takes a shit to judge a shit? I don't know French as well as you do but that seems to be about right.'

'Look, Izzy, I'm not going to give Gertrud the satisfaction of quarrelling with you, however bloody offensive you manage to be.'

'I'm sorry; I shouldn't've said that. Now perhaps you'll clear out and let me read these letters.' As Israel said this he tore open the second envelope and unfolded the letter; it began, 'Darling David.' He said, 'You're right, it's for you.'

'Then please give it to me.'

'I will when I've read it.'

'You . . . look, don't you see she intended . . .'

'Yes, I'm not quite the fool you were about to call me.'

'Well, if you must read it, for God's sake realize what she's trying to do.'

When David had gone to get his meal and Israel had proposed to play his guitar, he had played first a short and brilliant study by Villa-Lobos; then Segovia's arrangement for guitar of Gernsheim's *Elephant March* for piano and drums, which made his audience laugh; finally, a piece of his own composition which made Harland say, 'That's witty stuff. Whose is it?' Israel, stooped over his instrument, touching the strings with love, his eyes wide and empty, had said,

'I've not written it down yet,' and noisily attacked a vivid passage of *flamenco*. John Gurling, still contented-looking, his eyes half closed against the noisome smoke rising, a blue pillar, from his *caporal*, kept his eyes on the three dials and recorded their readings at five-minute intervals. Israel had put away his guitar and said, 'I'm going to eat,' and left them. Some minutes later Gough had returned and immediately looked at the compass tell-tale and the three dials. Harland said, 'Good dinner?'

'All right,' David had said. It was another half an hour before Israel returned; his face was pale and wooden. Gurling said,

'Cold out?'

'Just below freezing,' Israel said.

'Good, colder the better.'

David had relieved Gurling at noting the five-minute interval readings for Israel's graph. Israel went to him and handed over a letter saying, 'This is for you. I'll take over now,' and took the clip-board with its sheet of squared paper and growing columns of figures, saying to Harland, 'The figures'll be distorted, but I can make a separate graph of them and use it to correct the readings for straight cruising.'

Four hours after beginning the manœuvre the compass tell-tale showed them on a course of 119°; the southerly drift was now 0·7 knots and speed was down to 1·9. Harland said, 'Well, she's answering. I'll stay on watch; there's no need for all of us. Why don't you chaps get your heads down?'

'I shan't sleep yet,' Israel said.

They all went out on deck to give the cabin a chance to air. It was 02.30 hours. The orange sun sat on the horizon, a halo of watery haze about it. David said it looked like a poached egg and Harland said, 'Not the poetical type, eh?' The light was primrose yellow, the sea a deep laurel-leaf green with silvery lights on the sun-side slopes of the enormously long smooth, silent waves of the swell. The ice was now white, now golden, now glassy and dazzling, now all the colours of the spectrum. It was exceptionally cold for the season and Harland went to look at the deck thermometer. It was down to −1·3 C. Gurling yawned and shivered and said, 'Better and better, g'night all.'

Only Harland and Israel returned to the engine control room; then Harland went to relieve one of his watch-keepers in the navigation cabin, leaving Israel alone. He was reading Richard Hughes, *In Hazard* but Gertrud's letter to David Gough kept coming between him and that magnificent story. He knew that David was right; that the letter had been written to cause pain and trouble; and that it would be foolish to take a word of it for truth. He knew that what was now at work in him was a venom but he could not utterly reject it; it was as if there was a kind of bitter pleasure in allowing it to poison his mind and spirit.

Two passages in particular hung like confusing clouds upon his mind:

. . . waking to be tormented by wanting you, wanting you inside me, wanting again and again the moments of anticipating with every nerve for you to let the pleasure come by coming. I never knew with him, with anyone till you what it could, should be like.

. . . and even if I really wanted to I couldn't love such a fool. The despicable blind complacency of believing you that you didn't know who I was until I came into the dining-room at Regent's Park. I say blind complacency, or should it be *complaisance*, but is it that, or just dry, dead indifference to personal things, relationships? Your face, that day in Paris when I caught you with my passport. By then it didn't matter, you were as hooked on me as me on you. Suppose you'd known not only then but from the start, suppose I'd never invented Hilda Lulworth, you'd still have wanted to fuck me but would you have done it? No, lover, it's not that I suspect you might be an honest man, what used to be called a man of honour. But you might have jibbed at the prospect of being embarrassed.

At seven Commander Harland, shaved and fresh, returned to the engine control room followed by the steward with a tray of coffee, bacon and eggs and toast. Icecube had been on her new course for half an hour, the ninety degree course Harland had asked for; southerly drift was down to 0·65, and speed on course a small fraction below two knots with both engines full ahead. Harland said,

'Good morning; and congratulations.'

'Thank you.'

'Any reason why we shouldn't get her on course now and really start this voyage?'

'None that I know, sir. We can learn as we go.'

'As soon as I've eaten this lot, I'll go to the navigation room and give you a course.'

Harland telephoned the course to the control room five minutes after finishing his breakfast; 'And, Mendes, will she take about the same time to come about again?'

'I don't think she will, sir. This time the current will be increasingly on our side the more she comes about. Two or three hours, I'd say.'

'Good.'

When Sheikh Allal received Habib's invitation to come again to Farzar to discuss a matter of importance, he sent a message to Azizeh asking for her advice. She sent word that he should come. Once again he was a guest at the palace and once again Habib seemed to treat him with respect, as one equal in authority with himself. At the first session of their talks he said this:

'Presence, I am disturbed. Some of your people are taking a great deal of interest in our Icecube project. It is not a friendly interest. One of our English engineers has been harassed and treated with insufferable rudeness.'

'I know nothing about it, Highness.'

'Could it be that some of your people's acts are withheld from you? Is it possible that the mullah 'Omar is your enemy?'

Refusing to be drawn, Allal said, 'What was the incident you complain of?'

'The leader of an armed band had his men surround Mr Drummond's car and spat in his face.'

'Perhaps the man took him for Simon Brax, highness.'

'Mr Drummond, Mr Brax, what's the difference? Why should Mr Brax be thus insulted?'

'For debauching our children.'

If Habib was surprised he did not show it. He said, 'Please continue. From me, also, it would seem that some things are withheld.'

'The man is a pederast.'

'Are you sure?'

'He has taken a child, a boy of fifteen, as his . . . catamite.'

'Presence, your tone surprises me. Is Mr Brax the only one to do so in our country? Where's the harm? You know as well as I do that particularly among our Arabians, the practice is hallowed by long tolerance. Why should we not extend to our guests the tolerance we yield to each other? Anything less would be hypocritical. It is my earnest wish that we should work together, you and I. If we are to do so you will have to bear with my dislike of hypocrisy.'

Allal said nothing and his face remained closed. Habib said,

'There is another matter. It seems that men of the seven clans have been importing arms illicitly, by way of Senegal. I need not say that I expect this to come as a deeply distressing surprise to you. Dear friend, look to your safety.'

Allal shrugged and said, 'It is a matter of long custom for the desert men to go armed. A few rifles . . .' He shrugged again. Habib said, 'It depends which way the rifles are pointed, wouldn't you say?'

'I will say this much, prince. My people are restive. I can keep my undertaking to hold them in hand. But to do it I shall need help.'

'Money?'

'A subsidy. My friend, what, in the very provocative circumstances, persuasion will not accomplish, money will. I have been and am under strong pressure from a certain faction to destroy the pipeline, and the works of Abbas Bay, and even to raid the oil-field. 'Omar is a man of peace but his words, intended only to instruct, inflame the hotter-tempered men.'

'Send him away.'

'They would rise against me and stone me to death.'

'Then how do you propose to prevent them from waging civil war on me?'

'They do not see it like that. And if they did . . . I know, and most of the Cousins know your strength, but to raise that as an argument with angry bedouin is to be dismissed as a coward. But if certain men found it profitable to talk of peace instead of war . . .'

'How much, Allal?'

'Annually ten million *rials*.'

Habib scribbled the figure idly on his notepad and after it wrote $400,000, its equivalent in international currency. He said neither yes nor no but, 'It has been suggested to me that the works and the pipeline should be policed.'

Allal slowly shook his head; he said, 'I, too, can be candid: the presence of your troops would be dangerously provocative. I do not have to remind you that it is the custom for us to be allowed to police our own territory and ourselves. Last month I hanged a man for murder. At least eleven of the convicts in your prisons were sent there by our courts.'

Habib nodded and said, 'I'm a great respecter of custom, Presence. I invite you and your Cousins to undertake the policing of the line and the works. You would be responsible to me for the safety of the European engineers and their workers and all the works. This irrigation project is for the people, yours and mine. I know that the feeling of your conservatives is against it. But you yourself see all its excellence and all its good sense. Take over the care of what is yours. I'm aware that it cannot be done without money; very well, the state will pay you half a million dollars a year for this special service.'

'I should need the first year's payment in advance.'

'Agreed.'

Excited, Allal remained thoughtful in appearance, and seemed careworn. Habib said, 'Yet another matter. I am about to set up a council of state to which each corporation in the state –

merchants, industrialists, the men of our new scientific institutions, the armed services, will be invited to elect a councillor. I shall myself take the chair, of course; will you accept the place of deputy chairman?'

Allal was disconcerted and did not answer immediately. He muttered something about 'A great honour'. Habib said, 'Think it over,' and when they parted for the day, embraced the Sheikh and kissed him on the mouth.

Then he sent for the Commander-in-Chief of the armed forces, the Emir – the title was a relic of the eighteenth century when Farzar kept a fleet of galleys at sea – of the Navy; and while he waited drafted a cable to John Gurling. When the secretary Azadi showed the Emir into Habib's office, he gave him the cable and said, 'Encode this and send it.'

Two days later the destroyer *Habib*, the frigates *Farzar* and *Ghazvin* and six M.T.B.s began exercises down the coast, using Abbas Bay as their base. And the Gurling–Curran team suddenly acquired a big armed helicopter, with the firm's name in huge letters on her sides, which began regular patrols of the line from Abbas Bay to the Wilhelm Crater. As Habib said to Caroline, 'I am not a bad chap at heart, but to act one hundred per cent in good faith in politics is foolhardy.' To which Caroline replied that she had read somewhere that Oliver Cromwell had told his soldiers to say their prayers by all means but to keep their powder dry.

'Did he now? Sensible fellow.'

Ten

For Harland and the Gurling–Currans life on an iceberg became the commonplace. They even had newspapers at breakfast time on some days of the week, although the first batch did not arrive by the supply helicopter until they were making their ponderous, barely perceptible way round Cape Farewell. The helicopter made her delivery at 03.00 hours, in fine, calm weather. John Gurling, first in the mess, chose *The Times* without glancing at the rest, and so missed being first with the news which was splashed half over the front page of the *Daily Express*; that pleasure fell to Israel, coming unshaven and red-eyed off watch, and carrying the sheets of paper with the readings of his graph of drift-gain. He broke the rule of silence at breakfast to say, 'Seen this, John?'

'Garrulous this morning? Seen what?'

Israel handed him the paper. The headline announced 'OIL PRINCE WEDS LONDON SECRETARY'. Gurling snatched the paper, yielding *The Times* to Izzy. The account began, 'Top London secretary Caroline Bartrum, 24,' followed with her vital statistics (5ft 8ins. 34–24–34) and described the wedding. 'The bride, who wore a flowing white silk jersey dress, designed by Pucci with a veil of priceless Brussels lace last worn in 1898 by the Princess Amelia von Wittelsbach at her wedding to the unfortunate Prince Joachim of Savoy, told me that her ambition was to help her husband in his great task of channelling the country oil wealth, estimated at £1,600,000,000 a year, into agricultural and industrial development for the welfare of their people. Princess Caroline was formerly . . .' Habib, whom Gurling knew as one of the hardest-working and shrewdest business men and politicians he had ever met, was described as 'The billionaire playboy prince with the Omar Sharif profile'. A subhead read 'The man with five million a day'.

Gurling, his mouth full of toast, said, 'Bloody little fool.'

'Oh, come,' Israel said, 'you say he's an agreeable man, he's certainly a beauty, and he's a lot richer than Croesus. What more could a girl want?'

'He's all you say and a European on the outside; but he's an oriental underneath. It's a mistake.'

'If you go on like that I'll inform against you under the Race Relations Act.'

'What the devil am I to send her as a wedding present?'

'I expect Aspreys have something for the girl who has everything.'

'Jewellery won't do; Habib's family collection makes our own crown jewels look like something in a junk shop.'

David Gough had joined them silently but now he said, 'Who's the girl who has everything?'

Israel buried his face in *The Times*. Gurling said, 'Caroline Bartrum's married our client.'

'Has she, though. Good for her. I shall send her my usual wedding present, a copy of Donne, not the *Devotions*, the erotic poetry.'

Gurling, still reading the lively prose of the *Express*, said, 'Nothing here about a honeymoon.'

'People don't have honeymoons now, John. The point has been – er – blunted.'

There was to have been a honeymoon: very careful arrangements had been made for an incognito, secret and very thoroughly guarded three weeks at the walled and rigorously policed villa of a Greek shipowner, on the sea, not far from Delphi.

At the European-style 'breakfast' following the wedding, Habib received a message which, bringing news to compound that of a fatal accident to the boy Nuri at Dragon-tree Bay a week earlier, caused him to excuse himself to his principal guests, go to his private apartments, and send a servant for Caroline.

'Beloved, our Hellenic holiday will have to be postponed.'

'What's happened, Habib?'

'Something bloody unpleasant which I must stay and cope with. Leuwenhoek's been murdered by some of Allal's savages.'

'Oh no. Dirk . . . he was always such a gentle creature. Why?'

'One thing I promise you. They'll pay for this. Not that that'll bring the poor devil back to life.'

'But why Dirk, of all people?'

'He's a European. For Allal and his friends, either a running dog of the imperialists or an unbeliever and a Ferangi.'

'Do you have details?'

'Yes. They'll keep. Listen, go back now to our guests, keep the party going. I think you should be mildly and a little indiscreetly angry . . . your honeymoon's been ruined by a behind-the-scenes oil crisis. You might hint at another dollar devaluation. I've got a little gamble on with German marks and Swiss francs which might be extremely profitable. And send Azizeh to me.'

'Azizeh?'

'Yes, yes. Your beloved sister-in-law. You don't trust her, do you? You think she's too much in my confidence, right? My flower, you shouldn't be jealous of my sister; our dynasty isn't old enough to be incestuous.'

'She dislikes me and I'm afraid of her.'

'She has very tiresome manners. And, of course, delusions of grandeur which, combined with her Leninism, make her a study not to be neglected.'

'You do know that she's . . . against you?'

'You haven't married an idiot, my love. Now go on, get on with it. Efficiency, soul of my heart, and attention to business. What do you think I married you for?'

'To get a perfect secretary for free.'

'Exactly.'

They kissed and she left him, disappointment at the loss of their three weeks of complete mutual absorption lost in the relief of knowing that he was not blind to his sister's treachery. As for Habib, he was at his desk drafting an order to the Emir when Azizeh came in saying, 'You sent for me?'

'Sit down,' he said, still writing. Presently, without looking up, he said.

'Some of your Arabian friends have murdered Dirk Leuwenhoek, and mutilated the body according to their ancient and uncommonly barbarous customs.'

'Habib, Allal and the Cousins can have nothing to do with anything so . . . stupid.'

Habib abandoned his desk and rose and said, 'You think not? A leader, sister, is responsible for what his people do. D'you know what they'll say in Europe and America and the U.S.S.R.? That I have no control over these primitives; that Allal and his tool 'Omar and their friends are getting the upper hand, that an attack on the oil-field is to be expected.'

'First, you're wrong about Allal. He's walking a tightrope. Help him and he'll help you. Second, what are you going to do?'

'I'm going to arrest Allal and shoot him.'

'Are you mad?'

'I'm certainly very angry.'

'Can you never be serious?'

'I was never more serious in my life. However, there's an alternative.'

'Of course.'

'Let me tell you what they did to the Dutchman, who was the most gentle, harmless and useful of men. As archaeologist, anthropologist, sociologist you are, I know, interested in old customs. Tell me, Azizeh, do you remember the place called, I forget why, the gorge of the lion?'

'How could I not? It was called that because . . .'

'Never mind the etymology or whatever it is, you always know these things. What I remember is that we were taken there as children . . .'

'By Aunt Ayami, Habib, to pick tulips and drink the shepherds' *dourch*, the old darling thought it was good for our health and . . .'

'They did not take Leuwenhoek there to pick tulips and drink *dourch*. They took him there to put out his eyes with a bayonet heated in the fire they cooked their kid on. Then they set him free and told him to find his way back to his friends in Farzar and while he, with an attachment to life which, frankly, I find incomprehensible in his circumstances, groped and stumbled among the rocks where we picked tulips, they set their boys to practising their shooting with the blind Dutchman for a target. Shooting him with their new Czech automatic rifles. You're an educated woman, Azizeh; who was the English poet who wrote of the pleasure of teaching the young idea how to shoot? Oh, by the way, the bayonet they used for their ophthalmic operation was also Czech. A prince, being the father of his people, should have no favourites. But, try as I will, sister, I cannot love your playful little friends.'

'Must you always play the buffoon with me? These people have been provoked and feel threatened. You spoke of an alternative . . .'

'To shooting Allal, yes. Mind you, I'd rather shoot him. I dare say it's a failure in my sense of humour, but there are two things which exasperate me, bad faith and incompetence. He's guilty of one and possibly both.'

'The alternative, Habib?'

'You have influence with these people. I want the mullah 'Omar. There is a report he and Allal have quarrelled, that

'Omar has formed a faction of his own. I would like to talk to 'Omar but I'm not ready to arrest him. Go and bring him to me.'

'Supposing I can, what do you want him for?'

'Let's say that I shall talk him into a little common sense; and he will talk me into charity. What a lot of questions you ask, sister.'

What now happened to the mullah did not matter to her nor to Allal; his work was done; if Habib made the blunder of making a martyr of him, so much the better. She said, 'I'll try, Habib.'

'Try hard, sister.'

For the first time in her life she was afraid of him. At the door she turned and said, 'Have you . . . already taken steps?'

'Of course.' He looked at his watch and said, 'The helicopter half-squadron which visited the gorge of the lion should be on the way home by now, with three of the murderers.'

'Brother, they're simple people. They have a long tradition of revenge which to them is honourable. The corruption of the boy Nuri and death in that so-called accident . . .'

'Your advice, sister, is always worth hearing, but nobody has any right to be as simple as that, it's our duty to teach them to be a little more complicated. You know, it's curious, I find in myself less faith in modern penal reform thinking than some of our European friends are good enough to credit me with. Atavism, no doubt; there are precedents in our family for the kind of feelings I have at this moment. I'll confess to you that I have an impulse to take an eye for an eye.'

'But Habib, you have always been so modern, a true man of our age.'

'Precisely, my dear. Think who have been our teachers: Stalin of the purges and labour camps; Hitler of the slaughterhouses; Napalm Nixon, the B52 bombardier. And those ingenious Frenchmen . . . *ah, n'oublions pas la belle France*, who, with Cartesian logic, first applied electrodes to testicles. Besides, I have to deal with people who've committed what in my eyes is the most heinous of crimes.'

'For them, it was not murder, it was . . .'

'Murder? Oh, that . . . no, no . . . these friends of yours, with their mania for post-mortem castration . . . in future I shall hesitate to eat one of their already sufficiently disgusting *ragoûts* . . . have spoilt my honeymoon. *Va, fous-moi le camp.* And bring me your holy man.'

It was two in the morning when the night telephone sounded its low and unalarming buzz beside Habib's bed. He woke at once; Caroline, undisturbed, slept on. He slipped quietly and carefully out of bed to avoid disturbing her. He slept naked and had persuaded her to do likewise; 'It's a matter of natural animal comfort, my flower.'

He went to the telephone in his dressing-room, admiring his own lean nut-brown body in a tall looking-glass as he passed it. He picked up the telephone and said, 'Habib,' and the night secretary said, 'Colonel Said reporting, Highness.'

'I will be with him in five minutes. Put him on the terrace.'

The colonel was twenty-seven and spoke Farsi with an Arabian accent. He jumped to his feet and saluted when the prince, wrapped in a long, black robe, appeared. He wore the falcon insignia of the helicopter branch of the air force sewn to his bush-shirt. Habib embraced him, kissing him on one cheek, and clapped his hands for a servant. He sent for coffee and whisky and then said, 'Well, colonel?'

'Mission accomplished, highness.'

'Admirably terse, colonel, but I did not rise from my bed in the small hours to hear three words. More detail, please.'

'My orders were to shoot their camels, burn their tents but do no harm to women, children and the old; to confiscate all the weapons we could find and explode the ammunition store. And to bring away three prisoners chosen at random among the fighting men, but excluding the sheikh and his family. Those orders were carried out.'

'Excellent. And where are your three prisoners?'

'Here below, Highness, under escort. Those were also the orders.'

'Good again. Help yourself to coffee. Do you drink spirits?'

'No, highness.'

'On religious grounds?'

Said's manner was reserved when he replied, 'I do not like the taste, highness.'

'Pour me a whisky, please.' Habib again clapped hands for a servant and gave the man an order; and presently while the prince was pointing out to the soldier the beauty of the prawn-fishers' big lamps mounted on the boats which fished the bays at night, the night-duty secretary, whose name was Amadi and who was celebrated in the palace secretariat for the beauty of his Italian suits and the silk shirts made for him in Hong Kong, reported. Habib gave him orders which Amadi took down in long-hand. The Prince interrupted himself to ask Colonel Said to supply the names of his prisoners; Amadi wrote them down. He tendered his notebook for Habib's signature.

A part of Habib's orders concerned the official executioner, a functionary whose office had, for some years, been more honoured in neglect than use; common law capital crimes in Farzar are rare and imposition of the death sentence is even rarer. It is a matter of sound economy, the usual sentence for murder being twenty years in the road-making gangs. Where execution of political subversives was required, it was carried out by firing-squads supplied by the army. But the office of public executioner had not been abolished; such abolition would have offended conservative feeling in the country. The conservatives were the men of property whose wealth Habib was coaxing into capitalizing his new industries; property and the hangman are always allies.

Amadi was gone for twenty minutes during which time Habib

questioned Colonel Said in more detail about the punitive raid. Leuwenhoek's body had been disinterred and coffined for forwarding to Holland and Said described the difficulty experienced in persuading the Arabs, cowed though they were, to reveal the grave.

'Persuasion, colonel?'

'The lash, highness.'

When Amadi returned Habib signed the three death warrants and the order to the executioner and said to Said, 'If you will accompany Mr Amadi to his office he will arrange for you to hand over your prisoners to the police,' and to Amadi, 'You'll have to get the fellow out of bed; his work is to be finished before dawn. Their heads are to be taken off and sent to the sheikh, with my compliments. Is that clear?'

'It is, highness.'

Habib yawned and stretched and said, 'Then good night, or rather good morning, gentlemen,' and left them.

Caroline was awake when he returned; she said, 'Where've you been, lover?'

'A little urgent business came up.' As he got back into bed she said, as she began to caress his body, 'I think it's my turn to be on top.'

'Perfect. I have, you know, more than a trace of masochism. How right I was to marry an Englishwoman.'

Simon had been at the wedding reception as a guest of the bride. He was taken in hand, and the long table of Persian dishes explained to him, by the Khanum Firman-Esfandar, wife of the general who was Minister of Posts and Telegraphs, and head of the only publishing house in Farzar, a firm which she had founded when Habib started his policy of encouraging women as well as men of the old landed gentry to put their money and brains into industry or business. Like most of the ladies present she was handsome, brisk and smart in the French style; she had in fact, been educated in Paris. She talked to Simon about the translations from the English, French and Russian classics which she was publishing: 'Sales are small, of course, only half of our people are literate and not one in fifty of them can afford to buy books yet. Fortunately many more will buy than will read. It is chic to have books about, you understand. Our sales of textbooks will pay for our losses.'

It was this lady who was responsible for Simon's receipt of news which made him incapable of continuing to take that pleasure in his work in Farzar, and in Operation Icecube. She had asked him whether he received the English newspapers and when he said no, offered to pass on to him those which she received every day by air. Simon didn't particularly want them but it would have been ungracious to say so and he accepted with a show of gratitude.

The first batch arrived the following morning. Simon opened the package and was confronted with the front page of the *Daily Telegraph*, a good photograph of Jocelyn Quist and the headlines 'TERRORIST MURDER IN LONDON BAR', followed by 'ULSTER KILLERS IN NOTTING HILL'.

> Mr Jocelyn Quist, 38, a building contractor, was shot dead yesterday in a bar of 'The Seven Beeches' public house in Notting Hill, while trying with what a police spokesman describes as 'courage amounting to foolhardiness' to disarm a gunman. The man was an emissary of the Protestant extremist White Boys gang, sent to London to 'execute' Tighe Delaney, 18, for whom the police have been searching. Delaney is wanted to help the police in their enquiries into the murders of the two White Boy leaders, Burke and Whitty, found shot in the back in an empty garage in Londonderry last March . . .

No – this was not the kind of thing, not the order of events, which could possibly ever be true in one's own life. The refusal to believe gave way to shock; he was suddenly shaking, sick; yet still he clung to disbelief – he had written to Jocelyn only ten days ago and that, of course, meant that Jocelyn was still going about his work and pleasures in the usual way; moreover the sky out there, the sea and the land and the dragon-trees were still there, undisturbed. Inconceivable that Jocelyn could be dead and the world unchanged. Nothing had happened.

Simon began to read the story again; and somewhere, in one of the secret places of his mind, fear started to flow, a stream of fear, its source that letter to Jocelyn written just after Nuri had been killed. Simon began to know the two deaths were connected, that the letter about Nuri's death had changed Jocelyn; Jocelyn was not one of those who, with foolhardy courage, try to disarm a gunman. Drunk, he might have done it; but he was never drunk. Desperate? Was there matter in that letter to bring him to the point of desperation? Not for long, he was capable of brief despair in one of his rare moods of self-pity or pique, but not of the long despair which kills. But if he had gone down to the pub just after reading the letter . . .

The most dreadful thing has happened. You'll remember I wrote to you about the diving boy Nuri, the one who was such a beauty and had become so attached to me. He's dead. This morning we fired the charges which had been plugged into that stone ledge I told you about, under the sea. I don't suppose you have the slightest idea what I'm talking about, I know you don't read my letters properly, I only write them for my own satisfaction. Jock was with me. We'd had all the ships and boats withdrawn to a safe distance, and given the siren warning we'd arranged and publicized. Ever since I gave him the skin-diving gear Nuri had been going down under the shelf, from the beach, for shell. It never even crossed my mind that he could be down there at the time. The charges were detonated, it wasn't as spectacular as I'd expected excepting for the wave set up by the fall of thousands of tons of granite which washed out some of the fishermen's hovels along the beach. As soon as the sand had settled and the water had cleared, I went down myself to inspect the result and there he was, or what remained of him, head, one arm and shoulder, the rest of him crushed under the stone. I came up and went to the caravan and I couldn't stop crying. He was not only the most beautiful human being I've ever seen, but the sweetest-natured and most lovable and you'll have to understand this, that I loved him and that I'll never get over this, never. Christ, to remember always that it was I who fired the charges . . .

It was not a letter to have written to a lover as jealous as Jocelyn could be even when he was resenting jealousy of his own skirmishes on the side. Which, of course, was why it was written.

Jock Drummond, arriving that evening at the end of his line patrol, was miserably facing the prospect of breaking the news of Quist's death. He had received mail that morning including a letter from Emma with a full account of what had happened at 'The Seven Beeches'. He climbed up into the big caravan with his heart beating unpleasantly fast. Simon appeared from the galley, his face so white and his eyes so inflamed that Jock, aware of selfish relief, said,

'I see you've had the news. Sim, I can't say how terribly sorry I am. It's an atrocious business.'

'How did you know?' Simon said, without interest.

'A letter from Emma.'

Simon sat at the table and said, 'I hope your little girls are well. Does she give any details? I got it from . . .' he gestured towards the newspapers on the table.

'She does, yes. Are you sure you want to hear them?'

'Why not?'

'This boy, Tighe Delaney . . . it seems he's a killer with a record two years long . . .'

'I believe I saw him once,' Simon interrupted, 'a boy with a soft, girlish face, with the man Jocelyn calls . . . called . . . Leary the Lumper. A picture of innocence, and very shy . . . I thought Jocelyn . . . never mind, go on.'

'The police know he killed those two men in that garage, and then bolted to London, not from the police, from the Protestant gangs. Leary's wife was his first cousin, they gave him a room in their attic and Leary took him on as a bricklayer . . . he was apprenticed as one. Emma says they've arrested Leary.'

'Anything about Jocelyn?'

'According to the locals, Delaney was with three or four of his mates at the bar, Jocelyn was talking business with Leary between them and the door, and this White Boy came through the door with the gun already in his hand and a stocking mask over his face. Jocelyn and Leary were in his way. He said, "Out of the way, you," and they backed towards the wall. Then he turned the gun on Delaney and said something like, "All right, babyface, this is for Burke and Whitty . . ." and at that moment Jocelyn jumped him, there was a struggle, the gun went off and . . .'

'Killed Jocelyn. Go on.'

'They say the gunshot broke the tension, Leary kicked the gunman in the groin and then knocked him down. They sent for the police and it seems that gave Delaney away. They'd lost track of him but when they came in, he tried to make a run for it. They got him of course.'

Simon said, 'What a bloody silly way to die,' and his voice was full of resentment and it crossed Jock's mind, grotesquely, that if a lover's quarrel across the barrier between the quick and the dead were possible, there would have been a flaming row at this moment.

Jock went into the galley to scrape a meal together; he had had three days of diarrhoea and agonizing stomach pains, but he had taken a course of an antibiotic drug and was now, at last, hungry again. While he was cooking rice he heard voices and went out to see who was there. It was a soldier with a dispatch from the palace addressed to him. He sat down to read it and Simon, who was watching his face, said, 'Good God, now what?'

Jock looked up and said, 'Dirk Leuwenhoek. The bloody Arabs have murdered him,' and looked down at the dispatch again and read aloud, 'His Highness Prince Habib bin 'Ali ibn Far has asked me to convey to you his deep sorrow and his condolences for the death of Doctor Dirk Leuwenhoek. I am instructed to inform you that those bedouin responsible for the murder have already been punished with the utmost rigour of the law. I am also instructed to invite you to call on me for an explanation of the circumstances of this most shocking atrocity.' He finished reading; Simon said nothing. Jock said,

'It's signed by Azadi.'

Simon still said nothing. He had no feeling against the Arabs. It seemed to him that they were not 'responsible', that death at the hands of such men, like death at the hands of an Irish terrorist, was a kind of accident. If they had been punished, it must have been for military or political reasons and consequently was of no significance, any more than a hurricane which kills people, or an earthquake, is significant. One does not think of punishing the wind or the waves or the reeling, heaving earth. Babyface Tighe Delaney would be kept in prison for twenty years; the Arabs had been shot or had their necks broken or been choked to death for 'reasons' no more or less weighty than those which had killed Nuri or Dirk. In ancient times, Greek jurists had concluded that if a man were accidentally killed by a ball thrown by an athlete, the only culprit was the ball. Had His Highness Habib bin 'Alī ibn Far taken any steps to have that granite ledge, now at the bottom of Dragon-tree Bay, punished?

The Gurling–Curran men on the berg received the news of Leuwenhoek's murder in a radio-telephone call from their agents in Reykjavik; Gurling was told, at the same time, of the fatal accident at Dragon-tree Bay. The first of these misfortunes was featured largely in their next batch of newspapers, the Icecube operation being news, but the accident which had killed Nuri was not mentioned. As for the murderous affair of 'The Seven Beeches', which was given far more space and prominence than anything else, none of the three men had the least idea that it concerned them otherwise than as citizens. Their attention being much more taken up with the Leuwenhoek murder, the only comment on it was Israel's, 'The man Quist must have had guts.'

The atmosphere in the mess was not comfortable; as Commander Harland might have said, Icecube was not a happy ship. When Israel talked, David became silent, but if David had something to say Israel held his tongue, withdrawing from the circle. On one occasion John Gurling asked Israel to play for them and Harland said, 'Would you, Mendes?' Israel said, 'Sorry, it irritates David,' whereupon David said, 'That's easily disposed of,' and walked out of the room. It was obvious that the two men were on very bad terms; it seemed to Harland that they were behaving like ill-bred schoolboys; of the two he was inclined to blame Israel, but fearing that that might be because the chap was a Jew, he went so far out of his way to be as pleasant as possible to him that his civility was excessive and added to the constraint. Gurling went as far as he could in another direction: when he and David were alone he said, 'If you and Izzy have had a row, it's time you both grew up. Is it that bitch of a wife that's the matter between you?'

'Let's just say my face doesn't seem to fit,' David said; and nothing to the point. Gurling said, 'He's as prickly as a bloody porcupine.'

By this time Icecube was moving at a shade under three knots, with both engines full ahead, in the West Greenland Current, her position being about 320 miles west of Cape Desolation. Harland's navigation had been clever; not that he claimed any merit, it was not in his *moeurs* to say more than that they had been 'Uncommonly lucky, touch wood'. In fact, however, having made a thorough study of everything known about the West Greenland Current, he had manœuvred to take advantage of the fact that its western stream, coming under the influence of friction with the opposed, that is south-flowing, Labrador Current, is drawn first west and then south to make a U-turn and be drawn into it. The steering problem had been difficult, engaging all the knowledge which, by then, both he and Israel and David had gained of Icecube's behaviour. It had entailed giving the starboard engine just that much margin of power over the port one as would hold them in the stream they had chosen, that part of the current which favoured the navigation plan.

It worked: and at 20.00 hours on 21 July Harland came into the mess where the rest of the team were having drinks before dinner, with a slip of paper in his hand, and said, 'Any champers on board, John?'

'Of course. Pol Roger suit you? Is it your birthday or something?'

'I mourn my birthdays, I don't celebrate them.'

'If we're going to celebrate something,' Israel said, 'what about Larsen?'

'He's on watch. We'll send him a glass. Here's what we have to celebrate: our position is 59 degrees 49 minutes north and 57 degrees 40 minutes west; our course is due south; we're well into the Labrador Current and the water temperature's five degrees centigrade down on the last reading. We're making 2·6 knots and we've a prospect – I'm touching wood – of three weeks cruising without foreseeable problems.'

While the steward was fetching the wine they discussed the melting factor, for Gurling was continuously anxious about losses. Whenever the conversation was pure shop, the constraint was less. Moreover it was together that Israel and David had worked out a method of estimating melting losses; though they could not live together they could still work together.

In the nature of the problem it was impossible to get accurate figures but a rough estimate was better than nothing. There was only one place at which they could observe and measure the rate of melting: the sockets drilled in Icecube's plateau to take the cylindrical legs of the Gurling raft, the deck they lived on. At those points melting was enlarging the sockets and, as had been anticipated, it was necessary to pump in liquid concrete under pressure at regular intervals. Since the size of the original sockets was known and that of the enlarged ones measurable, it was easy to work out a rate of melting loss per day for a given surface; and, by extrapolation, get an estimated loss for Icecube's entire surface. A number of corrections had been made, at Israel's suggestion, to allow for the fact that nine-tenths of the iceberg's bulk was under water, and that water temperature had been not only variable, but also different from that other variable, the air temperature which affected only one-tenth of her surface; there was one other important correction to be made: the rate at which ice melts is proportional to the pressure upon it and their criterion for melting rate was taken from a point where the ice was under pressure, to wit the weight of the deck and its load applied at the base of the legs. For the sake of thoroughness similar measurements were made at all the points where machines, like the big generator, and the water and fuel tanks, were mounted directly onto the ice. It was not that these points of pressure added up to a significant figure, but since overall melting loss was being calculated from them, the factor of pressure had to be eliminated from the calculation.

The final result was not alarming: losses were quite tolerable; and in one respect melting was actually helping them, for it was making Icecube's 'prow' progressively smoother, shaping her 'hull' in a way which made her more like a ship and so more manageable.

Although melting loss was not proceeding at a rate to worry them, David's examination of the sockets, to provide Israel with figures, raised in his mind a question touching the security of the engine mountings. Using the formula which Israel had provided, he made some rough calculations based on the colossal pressure which both the weight of the ocean itself, and the titanic thrust of the engines, was exerting on the points of contact of the engine mountings and the big rubber vacuum-limpets. It seemed to him that there was a real danger of the two hydro-turbines literally burying themselves in Icecube's mighty body. He realized that the word of alarm would not be well received if it came from him, and considered speaking first to John Gurling. But there were a number of reasons against that; it smacked – this was absurd and yet could not be ignored – of telling tales out of school; moreover, David had an uneasy feeling that there was something which, in his calculations, he had left out of account; furthermore, he had a great respect for Israel's talents and also for his thoroughness; then there was the professional's decent reluctance to trespass on another professional's field. But over and above all this, he was getting sick and tired of being the one – as it seemed to him he was – to be patient, forbearing and understanding. If he continued in that role he would be admitting that he had been to blame, which obviously he had not. For once Israel would have to put up with being criticized if only by implication.

Israel listened to him with an irritated expression of overtried patience and then said, 'You seem to think I hadn't thought of all this and made the quite elementary discovery that the premises of the argument are wrong. What the hell do you think our trials at Kjöge were for?'

'Izzy, please keep your temper. Nobody's saying you're less than infallible. The trials at Kjöge lasted ten days and, correct me if I'm wrong, were at much lower thrust values.'

'Look, David, this part of the job is my responsibility and I'm not in the habit of taking my responsibilities lightly.'

'For Christ's sake don't be so bloody pompous. All right, you're probably, almost certainly, right. Is there any harm in going down to take a look?'

'Are you volunteering?'

'If you don't like the job, certainly.'

'Since you question my competence you might doubt my report; we'd better put the whole thing to Gurling.'

'We've no idea when he'll be back. It could be weeks.'

Gurling had gone to London by the last helicopter lift. Israel said, 'Then Harland must make the decision.'

'Aren't you making rather much of this, Izzy? I don't think

it would be a good idea to plant doubts about our propulsion in Harland's mind.'

'Very well. If it'll set your mind at rest I'll go down tomorrow and take a look. We'll have to stop engines, which will take some explaining.'

'Tell him it's a routine inspection. I'll come down with you as second hand.'

'If you insist on checking up on me, do so. Otherwise it's not necessary. The submersible rafts are easy enough to manage single-handed.'

'As you wish.'

Harland was in the navigation room; he had watch-keepers on both the lookout and the navigation radars, for there was a cold fog hanging like a silvery curtain between them and the coast of Labrador and far out to sea, so that they seemed imprisoned in a bubble of stillness and silence, reflecting Icecube's brilliant display of lights, which Larsen had switched on, from its watery walls. The commander said, 'Hallo, Mendes, I don't like this weather. Larsen says there are no ships within two hundred miles of us, but there are cod-banks ahead and it's easy for the radar to miss a wooden boat. Something I can do for you?'

'I have to make a routine inspection of the engines as soon as possible. I'd like permission to stop them at, say, eight tomorrow morning.'

'Sorry, out of the question in this weather. Is this inspection necessary?'

'Gough thinks so.'

'Does that mean you don't?'

'I think Gough's making an unnecessary fuss. I could be wrong. They're my engines. I'm prejudiced.'

Harland crossed to the navigation radar and examined the map of the coast to starboard built up of echoes of the pulses the apparatus was transmitting. He muttered a word to the watch-keeper and went to the chart table to mark his chart. He said, 'How do you make this inspection?'

'Put on deep-diving gear and go down on the submersible raft; it's fitted with lights and tools. There won't be anything to do, but it'll take a couple of hours. We've no decompression chamber, so one has to come up to the surface very slowly.'

'Depth?'

'About seventy fathoms.'

'Rather you than me. As soon as I have good visibility you can stop engines.'

'Thanks.'

Israel lingered for a few minutes on the open deck. There was nothing to be seen but silver fog, and grey-green water; its surface scarcely rippled from this height, three hundred feet above it. There was no sense of movement for there were no points of reference; he might have been standing at the cliff-edge of a high and lonely island. Their situation was so extraordinary that there was nothing to do but take it for granted; there is a limit to the endurance of the power to marvel. He looked at the birds which were taking passage with them: there were rarely fewer than a score, of various species, perched somewhere on Icecube's superstructure. Now he counted thirty-four; unafraid of man, they would let themselves be approached quite closely.

Israel stood and looked into the fog and faced the fact that his first dive to the engines had not, though he had been in control of himself while down there, cured him of his terror. This time, moreover, he would be alone. Between now and the moment of the dive, he knew that he would die the thousand deaths of Shakespeare's coward; and there would be the scarcely bearable mental agony of the slow ascent from the depths. Had he not known that he was afraid, he would have resisted David Gough's insistence on an inspection and refused to make the dive. This was so absurd that he smiled.

Later that day Harland took the opportunity of being alone

in the mess with David to say, 'This routine inspection of engines . . . is it necessary?'

'If Mendes said so.'

'I'm asking your opinion.'

'I wonder why? For what it's worth, then – I think it probably is.'

'Very well. Thanks.'

'If you're thinking that Izzy might be making a thing of this being important, forget it. He's not like that.'

On the day following the night of Habib's wedding and of the executions, while he was inspecting the new palace guard, a junior officer, Nadar Gaveti, drew his revolver and tried to kill the prince. He was in a state of near-hysterical excitement – as Habib told his Security Chief, Colonel Mashadi, later, 'Not the type I would choose as an assassin, myself.' As a result his hand was unsteady; moreover, the N.C.O. standing behind him, reacting like lighting, knocked up his arm and so earned immediate promotion and a thousand-*rial* gratuity. Habib's right ear was nicked by the bullet. Gaveti was seized, manacled and handed over to Mashadi's department.

The attempt had been made in the Court of the Orange-trees and the only witnesses were the men of the guard. Habib addressed them: he told them that the attempt to murder him was foolish because, at bottom, he, the prince, and the men of the revolution whether in the army or out of it, had the same goal in mind and sight; and that it was therefore, also, merely criminal inspired by power lust. When what he had said became known in political circles, it inspired admiration. The fact was that Habib knew too well the strength of the revolutionary movement to try blustering. Later that day when Caroline's tears of shock had been dried, he said, 'Who was that English king who dealt with a revolution by becoming its leader?' She couldn't remember, either.

Half an hour later Azizeh, in uniform as Colonel-in-Chief

of the Women's Army Corps, came for orders: Habib gave her a letter for Allal, and she set off in an army Rangerover, with a crew of N.C.O.s. When, nine hours later, she reached Allal's summer camp she went straight to his quarters and delivered the letter. They did not greet each other as lovers; they had had their pleasure of each other and that incident was over. Allal glanced over the letter without comment or expression and said, 'He didn't send you only to deliver this.'

'No. I've orders to take 'Omar bin Mocktar to Farzar. Read the letter aloud – but, first, have you heard about the punitive expedition?'

'Yes. The news reached here this morning,' Allal said, still as if indifferent. Then in a flat voice he read aloud:

We take as read your gratitude for our help in punishing Doctor Leuwenhoek's murderers.

Now we anticipate with the joy which the prospect of your presence always gives us that you will take your seat at our right hand at the first meeting of the Council of State on the tenth day of the new month.

Should you be unable to do so we shall know that only one consideration could prevent your attendance: that the duties of policing the water pipeline which you undertook with such generous enthusiasm have proved so onerous that your personal attention to them cannot be withdrawn.

In that event, anticipating your need as it will always be our endeavour to do, we shall without delay send reinforcements: Saracen armoured cars, light tanks and motorized infantry, all under the command of Colonel Said.

Peace be with you. Habib.

Azizeh said, 'Take the council seat. If he sends this force, we lose control of the territory.'

Then Allal said, 'You don't know my news yet. We may need his help; we may be forced into an alliance.'

Until some days before the princess arrived 'Omar had still sat, during those hours when he was accustomed to make himself accessible, to teach those who came to learn. What they learnt was that he meditated a new lesson; and that very soon he would go to some place apart so that the new message would ripen in his soul. He did not say that the message was from God but at great length he expounded one word: messenger; that is, angel.

'Overnight he disappeared,' Allal told Azizeh.

Nobody knew how: suddenly, he was gone; then news came that he sat beside a well where there were date-palms, and the light shade of tamarisks, known to the shepherds as Safra. Next, two of the Cousins went to Safra to hear what 'Omar now had to say. Lesser men followed, then two more of the Cousins went away in the night, with a large following. All those who went took their arms with them; and the flocks began to move south, grazing their way in the same direction. 'Omar did not preach a *jehad* but soon it was as if an army were encamped about Safra.

Azizeh asked Allal, 'What is the new teaching?'

'That I Allal have betrayed the people; that I am in league with the men of Farzar to take away their grazing land; that whether the land be transformed by Habib and his men of business, or by me saying it is for the people, makes no difference; for they will be enslaved to the plough and the hoe; and there will be no grass for the sheep.'

'What has driven him to do this?'

'Can you ask? Ambition; he wants my place.'

'How bad is it?'

'Two-thirds are left to us; the most of the young men and women – the people who understand us, you and I, when we talk to them.'

Azizeh went back to Farzar; at the palace she was told that the Ruler had gone to Abbas Bay to watch the trials of the great sluice-gates which closed the gut and so formed the iceberg dock. She found him, with Caroline and their guards, three of the Generals, Brax, Drummond and an Englishman she did not know and whom Habib presented to her, John Gurling. Her brother's greetings was ceremonious; he asked after Allal's health and the well-being of the mullah 'Omar.

Gurling was explaining the sluice-gates: at low tide they had been closed and what remained of the sea water pumped out; the fisher children had had the time of their lives catching stranded fish and an over-excited dog joining the game had been stung by a half-dead ray. The bottom of the gut was exposed, a level plain of glittering white sand. Simon Brax's eyes kept going to the huge mass of granite which now lay on the bottom, at the landward end; but the boy's body had been removed for burial, or such part of it as the funeral party could recover.

For two hours they stayed and watched the tide flow and rise beyond the great silver-coloured metal gates and yet not a trickle of water came in. Palace servants had erected a *yort* and there Habib offered his guests champagne or Coca-cola, and canapés, small *mille-feuilles* of spinach and sour cream; yoghourt, cucumber and chopped onion on *croûtons* of bread; Iranian caviar; a pastry made of pounded pistachio nuts, almond and the shells of prawns; tiny, seedless tangerines candied in honey. Azizeh made conversation with Gurling, chiefly for courtesy's sake, asking him how much capital was invested in each gallon of water that was on the way. If she thought the question one he might laugh off, she was mistaken; he said,

'0·009 United States cents. Delivered at the points of irrigation, 0·017 cents. It compares very favourably with desalination. Your brother, highness, has taught us a lesson in economics.'

'What lesson is that, Mr Gurling?'

'Look harder at the world, I suppose.'

Then she asked whether, when the tide was high and the whole weight of the ocean leaned upon the great gates, there would not be seepage.

'Not a significant quantity. You see, princess, we use the weight of the water; the greater the pressure the tighter the seal.' And he explained how the beautiful fin-like steel buttresses on the inner side of the gates conveyed the force of the ocean's weight to the rock bottom of the gut.

Drummond took leave and drove away to the far end of the pipeline where the last mile of pipe was being laid in place and work was beginning on the hydroelectric plant under the lip of the crater. Gurling talked of Icecube's progress; he was returning tomorrow, by way of Grand Canary, to join her for the passage of the Gulf Stream.

Nothing was said about Azizeh's mission until she, with her brother and his wife, were in the motorcar on the way back to the palace, and Habib said, 'I hope our saint likes his quarters.'

'I did not bring him.'

'Explain, please.'

'He is at Safra, surrounded by an army, preaching against you and against Allal. I was to tell you that Allal will come to the council.'

Habib showed no surprise; his security people had followed all 'Omar's moves. He said,

'I will visit you in your rooms, you can give me your report later.'

He gave her time to bath, change and read her letters and she was dictating to her secretary when her brother arrived accompanied by two soldiers escorting a prisoner, a young man who wore officer's uniform from which the badges had been stripped; his face was bruised and both his hands were bandaged. Habib watched his sister's face; she did not know what was expected of her, and looked uncertainly from the prisoner to Habib who said, 'You don't know this man?'

'No.'

Habib told the soldiers to take the man away and his sister said,

'Why do you ask me if I know him?'

'Mashadi tells me you belong to the same club.'

'I? I belong to no clubs.'

'A form of words, sister, the P.D.F.'

She lost colour but could still control her voice when she said,

'Who is that man? What has he done?'

'He is Lieutenant Nadar Gaveti. He tried to assassinate me.' Habib smiled and put a finger on the small piece of plaster which covered the tiny wound on his ear; he said, 'Your friends should choose their assassins with steadier hands.'

Her face expressed no horror; incredulity was followed by a a flush of anger. She said,

'Habib, you cannot, cannot think that I had any part in this . . .'

In a cold voice he said, 'You have killed once. Why not again?'

Deathly pale, she said, 'I killed as a soldier, not as a fratricidal assassin . . .'

Habib said, 'Will you report on your mission?'

'Am I under arrest?'

'No. Perhaps you should be.'

'I knew nothing about . . . could you be mistaken, or Mashadi? It is not our way, in the Front, to assassinate.'

'So Mashadi tells me. But the young man shot at me and cost me a cubic millimetre of ear. Your mission.'

She told him all she knew and after a silence he said, 'Good. You pass the test. Now Allal must work with me; and so must you.'

'I have never . . ..' she began, but he stopped her short, raising his hand and saying,

'Don't say it. Our dossier on you fills a file as thick as my arm. I sent you to Allal to see if you would return.'

'Then you also know how strong the Front is in Farzar.'

'Of course.'

'Yet you have not struck at us.'

'Am I a fool, to start a civil war? What, after all, do you want, you and your friends?'

'A just society.'

'Quite so; but provided that you lead the way to it and that the justice is your own. And answer me this – what, but a just society, do I work for?'

'Provided you remain the fount of its justice.'

'Precisely. Like me, you want power.'

'*L'état, c'est toi,*' she said, bitterly.

'Why not? But you see, Azizeh, where the real, that is the money, power is in the hands of the state, then the only executive power is in the hands of the managers, the bureaucrats.'

'You cannot go that way to justice; justice is the absolute and direct democracy of Lenin's dream.'

'Grow up, little sister. The whole world is abandoning democracy in democracy's name.'

The great bank of silver fog, extending all along the coast of Labrador and down to the Newfoundland Banks and far out to sea, lasted for three days. During the night of the third day it began to thin and break up as the wind rose, blowing very cold from the north-east, fluky and then gusty, but helping them on their way. By nine in the forenoon of the fourth day, the sky being covered by a thin, high sheet of cloud, the sea flat and grey, the air calm and very cold, visibility was unlimited. There was a small iceberg in sight due north of them; and Larsen reported three ships within a radius of forty kilometres, but none nearer than thirty. All had been warned of Icecube's position, course and speed which had fallen to 1·9 knots as Israel reduced thrust in preparation for stopping engines.

He and Gough and one of the navigation hands who was off watch prepared the submersible raft and slung it outboard and lowered it to the water three hundred feet below the deck level. While David and the rating rewound and prepared the hoisting tackle, Israel, with death in his soul, stopped the engines and was then helped into one of the two deep-diving suits carried aboard. David was cheerful; he said, 'Right, over you go. You look like one of those creatures in Doctor Who. I'll be at watch on the pumps and listening out on the blower.' Then he hooked the derrick shackle into the bronze eye between the metal shoulders of the suit, and Israel was lowered to the raft very slowly, like a bale of valuable cargo into the hold of a ship. The last thing Israel saw before the pale grey, glittering ice of Ice-cube's cliff-like side shut off his view, was David's grinning face.

He had thought the grin simply cheerful, but as the raft's pumps which he started as soon as he had freed himself from the tackle, began to submerge her and the water washed about his thighs, it suddenly came to him that the grin had been malicious; and in the dreadful moment when the calm surface of the sea was level with his eyes on the far side of his helmet porthole, it seemed that malicious was not the right word; that grin had been malignant.

Now a nightmare fantasy began to take possession of his mind; that it was a fantasy he knew in that calm centre of the mind round which all his fears raced like the terrible winds of a hurricane about the still and breathless heart of the storm. But that knowledge was powerless against the strength of those fears. What Gertrud had said and written was true; David had known who she was all the time. What of it? There was nothing very wicked nowadays in taking a friend's wife to bed; it was hardly a thing to have feelings about. Ah, but there was worse: David was in love with her, she with him, and they were going to kill him. Sanity asked why should they do anything so extraordinary; was divorce so difficult? But the madness of his transposed terror of the great depths had a cunning answer: what if David had expensive tastes, debts probably, wanted money? With himself, Israel, dead, Gertrud would be a very rich woman; and the man who wanted her and her millions now, at this moment, had his, Israel's life in his hands.

The still centre of this mind-storm was yet intact; from it flowed, as the submerged face of the berg slid up from under the raft whose motors were drawing her progressively away from it so as to follow the outward curve of the berg's mighty snail-like 'foot', the warm stream of reason which said that you did not stop the dive, reverse it, ascend and explain that you did not want to complete the work because you were afraid of being murdered. At the bidding of that reason Israel strove with all the force of his will to thrust back the cloud of darkness spreading across his mind. He read the pressure and depth gauges, the thermometer, the rate of dive gauge; he concentrated on exact regulation of the raft's lateral movement so that its distance from the iceberg's 'foot' was constant; he visually checked the controls, ran over the manœuvring routines in his mind, and adjusted the speed of the pumps to check a slight excess in the rate of fall. But when David's voice inside his helmet said, 'All well down there?' surely there was cruel irony, heartless laughter, behind the words? He sought companionship in his loneliness even from that murderous friend up there, mouthing into the microphone that everything was under control and that there were a lot of fishes about, attracted by the powerful lights of the raft and the diving-helmet.

'Bring some up for dinner,' the voice said, and that was another diabolical joke; for it was not intended that he would ever eat another dinner.

As the raft continued its slow, controlled fall through the waters, Israel began to experience increasingly unpleasant physical sensations. Heartbeat became heavy, breathing difficult. To check his fall into panic he tried to recall whether it had been like this that other time and became sure that it hadn't. From the still centre came the message, 'Ah, but you were not alone.' It did no good, it made him suddenly and utterly aware that that was it, that he was alone, isolated and without a friend; now there were not even any fish, he was too near to the deeps for that, nothing could live here, only he carried the burden of awareness, only he bore on his failing shoulders the huge watery yoke of the task laid on man by God of making Him, in His playful ignorance, conscious of Himself, of what He had made. 'You see?' came the message from the still centre, 'you see? If you can think like Hegel, where's the panic?' But that, too, was no good, knowledge, intelligence was, in the presence of the curse of imagination, an added misery. For would not a creature of instinct turn round, go back, give up, face the cruel aggression of mocking laughter?

He was ultimately lonely; if any man but David Gough had been at the other end of the line which linked him to men, he would have talked, chatted, found something, God knows what, to say; perhaps given away his state of terror and, by so doing, have reduced it and made it manageable. He needed to say that he was afraid: but not to David Gough; and there was Harland. From the still centre in the heart of these dreadful fantasies came a mocking parody: if a Christian face the depths before a Jewish witness, what is his strength? Why, pride. And if a Jew be the one on trial? Why pride; and it shall go hard but be better the example. This was his self-mockery; behind his fears was laughter at his fears and at his striking of attitudes. Oh for the freedom to be abject! He had a vision of David's face, set and cold and merciless; and again it did not help that from the still centre came the word *absurd*. The beast, the hominid in him was stronger than the man at this moment; rightly, perhaps: what he was doing was wantonly dangerous.

His efforts to concentrate, as a way of salvation, on the dials, gauges and controls became useless. Was he not in a lifeless wilderness of waters with not even God knew how many billion tons of the stuff over his head, indifferently crushing the life out of him, only a hemisphere of phosphor-bronze between him and their tale-told-by-an idiot, purposeless, pointless, again indifferent force trying to reduce his dimensions from three to two? He could no longer make sense of what the dials and gauges once used to tell him.

The beating of his heart had become a heavy, laboured pounding in his chest; it was as if he were making a sustained physical effort far beyond his reserve of strength. He became convinced that he could not breathe without a struggle. There was a part of his mind which observed the rest of him and assured him that there was no need for this struggle, that he could breathe normally, that there was nothing to be afraid of. He regained a little of his self-control but breathing still remained a deliberate act, each breath drawn inspired by deep anxiety. The gauges and dials came into focus and made their sense again. The wall of ice glittering and rippling in the lights from raft and helmet crept upwards interminably. Another hundred feet to go.

Precariously, he held onto his self-control, keeping his hands on the raft's switches and levers, his eyes on the gauges, his mind on steady breathing. He was contemptuous of his own condition; this terror must be exorcized. A moment came when, in an attempt to reassert himself, he raised his eyes and made himself watch the slow fall of the raft through the water, by reference to the ice-face; and then to turn about and to look outwards towards the confines of the spherical bubble of light whose bounds were the bounds of his universe. A funnel-shaped motion of bright bubbles led into black darkness; a hideous moment of vertigo and then he was falling, in a slow head-first, quickening dive into the darkness, the eternal watery void. Just before the surge of utter panic which ended in unconsciousness, his hand must have pulled the switch-lever which stopped the motors; he later remembered neither that nor the fact that in the moment of realization of the ultimate misery of loneliness in the dark depths devoid of form and meaning, he had uttered one terrible cry for help.

That faint perhaps saved his life or at least his sanity; freed of mind, the body could carry out the processes of living. The next thing he knew was looking out through the porthole of his helmet at just such another grotesque, ponderous head as his own; for a moment he believed that some trick of water, ice and light was making a mirror in which he now beheld himself. But the voice saying, 'Izzy, Izzy . . .' inside his helmet was not his own. He said, 'Who . . . I'm all right . . .'

It was David, of course; he said, 'I think you passed out. You didn't answer.'

'I couldn't breathe,' Israel said, 'I thought . . .' What he had thought could not be said, no longer mattered, he felt astoundingly happy, this raft was hearth and home and what lay beyond the bubble was just dark water and no longer the ultimate nothingness.

'You stopped the submersion pumps,' David said. He made no answer but restarted the pumps. The ice-wall began again its slow crawl upwards. Joyously, he confessed, 'Christ, I was afraid.'

In the joy of David's company in these depths he did not crow when inspections showed the engines still secure and he took pleasure in conceding, 'You were right in principle, there's some penetration. Not enough to matter . . . yet. It might be tricky before we're home.'

When they began the long, slow ascent he was no longer afraid. Much later in the day, with the engines again at full thrust and while he was alone with David in the mess, he said, 'It's very odd, but down there, God knows why, it came into my mind that you might be in love with Gertrud.'

David looked up from his book and stared at him, unsmiling, and said, 'If I understand the words, I never was, am not and cannot be in love with anyone.'

Unlike Gertrud, Israel did not question that; he was surprised to find in himself pity for his wife and before going to his cot he wrote her a short, friendly letter, saying not much about the dive but a little and adding, 'I can't tell you how terrified I was.'

Eleven

The iceberg drifted by the Labrador Current and driven by her engines to a point on the fifty degrees longitude, due south of the Newfoundland Bank and latitude forty degrees north, began the most difficult part of her voyage: it was at luncheon in the mess that Harland announced that they were now in the Gulf Stream, adding,

'We're thirty hours ahead of schedule but we shall lose all that and more in the next two weeks.'

David asked him to explain the next stage of their navigation: it was very simple. 'Roughly,' Harland said, drawing a triangulation diagram on the tablecloth with one tine of his fork, 'the problem is like this: I want to make a course south-east over fourteen hundred miles. Throughout most of it the Gulf Stream has an easterly component which is worth, to us, about three knots in the right direction: but also a two-knot northerly component. Just drifting we'd probably be carried so far north we'd have to go round the north of Scotland and down through the Channel, which is out of the question and anyway hundreds of miles out of our way. So we use the engines to fight the northerly component . . . right?'

Attentive, the others nodded.

'As far as I can calculate it, that will give us a speed, on course, of 1·5 knots at the best.'

'Forty days before we can change course south into the

Canary Current,' Israel said and, 'it's taking longer than we thought then?'

'I'm afraid it will, yes. On the other hand, once we make that turn we're damn nearly home and dry.'

Four days after that conversation Gurling rejoined their company, by helicopter from St John's, Newfoundland, bringing mail and newspapers. He noticed but did not remark on the improved atmosphere in the mess: Gough and Mendes were no longer at odds.

He brought them news of their increasing fame. Press and broadcasting services had begun by following Icecube's progress closely, and giving a prominent place to news of her. But the painful slowness of her progress made it unsuitable as news and the technical explanations were difficult. It was recognized that the work which the Gurling–Curran team was engaged on was one of great importance to the future of mankind: successful and thereafter followed up, it should add to earth's habitable, food-producing potential, and space and nourishment for several hundred million people. Here was a modern version of the great terracing and irrigation works of the ancients in Peru and Chile, in Baluchistan and in Ceylon. But in the slow drift of Icecube from the Arctic to North Africa there was nothing which could hold the attention: it was not particularly dangerous, nobody was likely to die of it; there was no violence, no sex and the sums of money involved were not even remotely of the order squandered by governments on projects like Concorde. Nor would it affect the price of chocolate, cigarettes, beef, butter or cheese. From time to time the figure of water loss through melting, or an encounter with shipping, provided a small headline and paragraph; Leuwenhoek's murder had given editors a chance to revert to the project; but political killings of insignificant persons had long since been reduced, in the order of news value, to a nine hours' wonder; editors could not go on repeating headlines like 'CUBIC MILE OF ICE TO WATER AFRICAN DESERT'.

Still, Icecube, at day and especially at night, had a visual appeal: now the B.B.C. and C.B.C. were jointly engaged on a ninety-minute feature telling the whole story of Prince Habib's project. Camera crews had already been to Greenland to film the calving of an iceberg, and use was also being made of Gurling's survey films. The work of Jock Drummond in the hinterland had been filmed and he had been interviewed. Leuwenhoek's work and his murder had provided the feature with drama. The works at Abbas Bay had been filmed, with Simon Brax, unsmiling and impatient with the interviewer, to explain them. He had protested against any mention of Nuri's death, had been overruled by Habib, had threatened to resign and abandon the work on the spot, and got his own way. He had told Jock Drummond, 'They wanted to talk of the child *giving his life* for the project . . . Like most of us, he was diving for pearl shell . . . Christ, they make me bloody sick . . .'

Habib had agreed to introduce and then to conclude the programme; he was to be shown floating an icecube in a glass of water.

So now a chartered helicopter was on the way with a camera crew and two journalists, to film Icecube herself and her company, and to talk to Gough, Mendes and Harland. Gurling said, 'But that's not the best or the worst of it. We've got royalty coming for the occasion.'

'Not Princess Anne and her horse?' David said.

'The lady's name is Azizeh. She's our client's sister and she happens to be what my sons call a dish or dolly.'

Before the first meeting of the new Council of State Habib Shah spent an hour with the Emir, his Commander-in-Chief of the armed forces; General Hakim, the ablest of his fighting officers; and Colonel Mashadi, chief of intelligence and security. They studied weapon lists, their own and those of Allal's which Mashadi was able to provide; and the Interior Ministry's estimates of Arab population; then they made marks on the

Emir's big relief map of the hinterland, with special reference to the Curzon Depression.

There was a moment, after the Ruler had drawn a line in red crayon across a part of the map, written a big *aleph* to the south-east of it, and said, '*Aleph* is for Allal,' when the Emir protested. Then Mashadi said, 'Emir, his highness sets a thief to catch a thief.' The Emir, his fingers straying over the panel of medal ribbons on the breast of his light-weight summer tunic, said,

'You, colonel, have no doubt been granted insight into the mind of our Ruler which is denied to me.' It was a joke; there were smiles all round, but only by courtesy; and General Abdul Aziz Hakim, who perhaps had no sense of humour, a rough soldier lacking in refinement, swarthy, black-avised and with a disfiguring facial scar, memorial of a P.D.F. bomb which had only just failed to knock his head off, said, 'Sir, the prince's plan is good. Let the leopard and the untrusted watchdog maul each other; the survivor we face will be weakened.' He turned, then, to Habib and said, 'Unless, highness, it might be safer to deal with 'Omar as one rids one's house of vermin?'

'Napalm, friend, on the encampments and the autumn grass?'

'Why not, sir? It is a question whether we should take the chance that Allal bin Mocktar and his half-brother once again unite against us.'

The Emir was what we call in England a decent man, and had learned his soldiering under the English Field-Marshal Alexander. His fat old face became very red and he said, 'I will not use napalm. When I went as your highness's military observer to Vietnam, I saw what it did to the villagers. I am an old man; if these things must be done, let this cup pass from me. Give my office to one worthier of these times. Besides, it would be bad policy; in the United Nations we should become a byword.'

Hakim, said, 'Vietnam, precisely, Emir. Can the American pot call the Farzar kettle black?'

Habib rose from his place and moved round the table and

embraced the Emir. He said, 'Father in war, we are not barbarians, to burn children alive,' and returned to his place saying, 'My friends, the Americans are a great people, and being so have, like their God, licence to be cruel with impunity. King Solomon wrote – or was it David his successor? – that three things were hidden from him, the way of an eagle in the air, the way of a serpent upon the rock, and the way of a man with a maid. Were he living now, he would doubtless have added a fourth mystery – the way of the Christian with his conscience. We are not, thank God, Christians. But we are little people and our sins will be counted. My mentor in war, our Emir, is wise.'

Hakim said, 'Are not those days passed, highness? They are starving for oil. We have oil. The real strength is ours.'

To which Habib replied, 'General, put that idea from you. Reflect. I will tell you a story: a pious Jew from New York went to visit Israel, as the Zionists call Palestine. He followed the trail of Moses and Jonathan leading their people into the promised land, and expatiated on the beauty and wealth of the orange groves which the Lord God had given to His people. Then the *sabra* who was his guide, a dour man, as these people are, said, "They were fools. If Moses had pointed and Jonathan led to the right instead of to the left, the accursed Arabs would have had the orange groves and we'd have had the oil . . ." '

They laughed, as in duty bound; Habib said, 'Why do you think the strength of the Zionists comes from the Americans? Those great people need a little ruthless people who, if we withhold oil, will take it from us by force. Understand, Hakim my friend, our Emir's meaning: we face very strong men unable to believe that they might be wrong. If they burn children alive, it comes of righteousness. Never forget, friends, that the prophet of the American religion and all but one man of the great Russian religion, were Jews.'

Of course, it was Habib's decision which counted. So that, after this outburst of oratory – that night in bed he said to Caroline that he must be more circumspect for he detected in himself a regrettable tendency to become too fond of the sound of his own voice – and in the Council an hour later, he said to Sheikh Allal, pointing to the map on the table. 'All this territory, Presence, we give into your hands to keep our peace.'

It was not Allal's way to show his feelings but in the sudden relaxation of his body into his chair and into ease, it was manifest that he was surprised and pleased; his enemy had delivered himself into his hands. Azizeh, without his skill in controlling the facial muscles, lost colour and turned angry eyes on her brother. She, in principle, represented the women of her country on the Council. She saw at once the nature of her brother's intentions, and rose to demand the floor. There were some Councillors who scowled; Habib had not been able, or willing, to exclude the conversatives from the Council; for them a woman, albeit a princess and a doctor of philosophy, had no business at such a board as this; or, if in this new age she had, then she should confine her interventions to the things proper to women. But Habib nodded to indicate that she should speak and she said, 'Let the armed forces in both sectors be mixed, half the professional army, half desert men. Surely the agreement between the men of the towns and the Seven, the Shiekhs, the Cousins, should be reflected in the troop dispositions.'

She looked to Allal for immediate support but his face was closed against her and she called him a fool in her heart, raging against the complacent assurance of her brother's control of the game. The Emir caught Habib's eye and said, 'It is certain that her highness's contributions to our deliberations will always be most valuable, but in this matter there are technical considerations of which she is not informed. We cannot mingle regular and irregular forces.'

'There are other reasons, of a political nature, for our dispositions,' Habib said. 'It is my hope that, faced by the example and the arms, of their brethren, those who have been seduced by the dangerous preaching of an ambitious priest will now come to their senses.'

There was no more Azizeh could do. She took no part as they worked through the agenda to the last item: B.B.C. and C.B.C. filming on the iceberg. Habib explained and said, 'You will doubtless agree with me that the government should have a representative of high standing present on the iceberg when the camera crews and journalists visit it. Too much attention is being paid to the firm of Gurling–Curran and too little to ourselves as originators of the project.'

There was a murmur of acquiescence; Habib said, 'I will hear nominations for this mission,' and immediately the *caid* of the merchant's corporation, primed in advance, rose to propose the Princess Azizeh: as a member of the State Council she would represent the whole people; as a woman, the women; and as a member of the royal house, the Ruler. Azizeh half rose to protest but Habib was careful not to see her, attending, instead, to the Councillor, representing the corporations of manual workers, who, also primed, was on his feet seconding the nomination: the princess's learning, her familiarity with European manners and languages, her personal qualities, all fitted her to be seen and heard as her country's spokeswoman by the tens of millions who, no doubt, would see and hear the broadcast. But his own hearty support for the nomination was founded in her highness's well-known and courageous progressiveness and sympathy for the manual workers.

The nomination was carried *nem. con.*; even Allal voted for it. There was nothing Azizeh could do but accept the mission as gracefully as she could force herself to appear. But from the meeting she went to Allal's quarters, allowing him five minutes to get there first. His servants were already preparing his departure, coming and going through the room, furnished only with carpets and cushions, where he received her politely but casually. The servants would understand Farsi, of course, and probably Arabic, possibly some English: she said, in French, 'Are you bent on self-destruction? Allal, you do not see what is in my brother's mind? He sets you and 'Omar to destroy each other.'

'Of course, I'm not blind nor am I a fool. What makes you think that 'Omar's horsemen and camel corps can stand for an hour against the weapons I can use?'

'I tell you,' Azizeh said, angrily, 'that he must know something, have something in mind that you don't know. Suppose he has an understanding with 'Omar?'

'The prince's mind is not so devious. He is crafty but not clever. There can be no composition between him and 'Omar which I should not know about.'

It was his offhand manner as much as what he said that caused Azizeh to lose her temper. She flushed, stamped a foot, but because of the servants controlled her voice when she said,

'Imbécile!'

Allal bowed and smiled and in Arabic said, 'I regret, highness, that you have to leave me so soon. Some other time I hope we may talk together at greater length.'

She turned very pale; Allal, reverting to French, relented enough to say, 'Believe me, I have not forsaken or for one moment forgotten our cause. You must know how strong we are in the army. When 'Omar has been destroyed it will be time to take over Habib. Name your own place on the Council of People's Commissioners.'

Azizeh said, 'Were you behind the attempt to kill him?'

'No. I have a use for him, as I have made clear.'

Larsen got a radar echo off the TV crew's helicopter half an hour before, at 23.00 hours, it came in sight and slowly circled the iceberg. Night, sombre blessing, had been restored to them by their southerly progress; it was remarkable how tempers had improved with the restoration of some hours of darkness out of the twenty-four; the midnight sun had been a strain.

The night approach by the TV team had been chosen deliberately: with all her lights on, Icecube was spectacular. The helicopter circled them a score of times, hovered above them in a dozen different positions, then left them for the land to return the following morning.

Harland, preoccupied, was unable to give much attention to what he called 'these junketings'. For three days there had been a steadily increasing swell, a long, deep, oily and immensely powerful 'send' from the south. It scarcely affected the iceberg – a thousand million tons of ice, albeit floating, has a massive inertia in the vertical plane. But he had to consider what it might mean to his navigation plan. Another preoccupation was the increased melting-rate, entailing a constant watchfulness over all the mountings of the superstructure.

It was while they were standing by to receive the Princess Azizeh that Larsen brought Harland the explanation of that rising swell: Hurricane Dorothy, fourth of the season and now degenerating into a depression a thousand miles south of their present position, had taken a couple of hundred lives in Cuba on her way north-west.

Well, that was that, she could not hurt them; and they weren't to know what her sister Ethel would do for them a couple of weeks later.

Colonel Mashadi brought a tall, dark-skinned Arab, splendid in his white woollen robes, to the prince's private quarters. Caroline received them with coffee and small cakes of pistachio paste and honey. The man spoke Farsi correctly and had very striking blue eyes which betrayed some non-Arab blood: Berber, perhaps. Caroline, not yet showing her pregnancy (but she had written to Maternité in Sloane Street for the clothes she would soon need to conceal her decline from physical grace), talked to him and Mashadi about the week of horse-racing which Farzar was enjoying at the new racecourse, while a servant went to inform the prince that visitors had arrived. When he came both men rose and Mashadi said, "This is the man, highness.'

Habib embraced the Arab. Caroline said, 'I will leave you to your work, gentlemen,' and withdrew. Habib kissed her hands and for a moment sounded absent-minded as he said, 'Captain, you're a very brave man. Not one of our agents has remained in that camp of fanatics as long as you have.'

The captain smiled slowly; he said, 'I am clever with horses, highness. No man of their race suspects a horse leech who loves his charges, of treachery.'

'Very curious,' Habib said. 'Like the English with their dogs. They think, you know, that a dog-lover must be a decent chap.'

All three laughed and then the prince said, 'The colonel tells me you have a plan for our operation?'

'Yes, highness. Colonel Mashadi's people will prepare a letter in which the movement of a convoy of new weapons, giving the date and time, will be referred to. An agent, one of the colonel's men, ostensibly my cousin, will defect to us, I mean to 'Omar, from his office in the Defence Ministry, bringing a letter – the letter – for sale. I shall see that 'Omar receives him and deals with him. And that the letter is acted on. The convoy should be lightly escorted and the officer commanding it must have orders to run away as soon as he plausibly can.'

'There will be casualties,' Mashadi said.

The blue-eyed Arab shrugged: the shrug said that not he but Habib was the power which killed men for the good of man.

'That, highness, cannot be avoided.'

'No. It is not very pretty, this sending our own men to a fraudulent death . . .' The prince sighed; then he said, 'I approve the plan. It is essential that 'Omar be as well armed as Allal.'

Gurling, as Icecube's company stood together to watch the helicopter come in to alight on the iceberg, said,

'Remember – she's "Your Highness".'

And her highness was first out of the machine, wearing a black jersey trouser suit and followed by a young officer in naval uniform, her aide, trying to look as if he were not carrying her sable coat over one arm; Harland stepped forward, saluting to receive the princess; she offered her hand, laughing a little as the wind disordered her hair, looking around, her eyes wide with wonder. She greeted Gurling who made the introductions. Habib would have been amused at his bolshy sister's command of the royal manner: for Harland, 'This must be your strangest but most challenging command, Commander;' for Gurling, 'A long way from Abbas Bay, Mr Gurling; so interesting, our talk there.' David and Israel were presented and Israel, at least, was obviously impressed despite the lady's, 'I had the great pleasure of meeting your colleagues who're waiting for you so eagerly in Farzar.' But the voice was not the well-bred insubstantial one, but had a depth, a bell-like music which seemed to mock the triviality of the words: all this was a charade.

Harland returned to his post and Gurling did the simple honours of their quarters and the iceberg's technicalities . . . and all the time uncouth young men with long hair and wearing jeans, laden with cameras, cables, lights, making absurd demands and talking to each other in a strange jargon, were under everyone's feet; while the two journalists, one English and one American, required first the princess's attention, then Gough's, and then Israel's, to whom they gave more than half their time. Harland, when interviewed on his navigation deck, talked of 'Mendes' outstanding courage in diving to seventy fathoms to inspect engines' and of the 'band of brothers' feeling which had sent Gough down to help him. That brought them back to Israel to ask him what it had been like, what had happened: he said, 'I was terrified and passed out; Mr Gough came down to rescue me.' They left that bit out at the cutting stage; they asked him some questions about his books: he quoted one title and said, 'Not much use to you, is it?' It wasn't, of course, but David, watching and listening, wondered what devil made Izzy take that tone; even the stuff he gave them about the engines was unusably technical. The two patient and experienced journalists gave up and went back to the princess, who had a lively style. David said to Israel, smiling, 'You don't seem to have much sense of public relations.'

'About the democracy I fell like Aristophanes,' Israel said. 'Did you ever read that prophet of our fathers, Aldous Huxley?'

'I know – *Antic Hay*. Believe it or not I had to do it for A-level English and never forgot it. You mean Gumbril's song, "Damn the people, blast the people, rot the lower classes," or some such. Funny to think that their's is the cause Dirk Leuwenhoek died for.'

'And that I nearly died of fright for, come to that.'

'You go on too much about that.'

'I suppose. I've always loathed getting credit where none was due.'

The wind was rising to a measure of force which made Harland and Larsen slightly inattentive to the chatter at the *vin d'honneur*, as David insisted on calling it. When the warning light on the mess-cabin wall flashed three times, he joined Larsen, who had already slipped away, in the navigation cabin, and found the helicopter pilot with him. The pilot said, 'Captain, either I lift this lot off within fifteen minutes, or you've got too many guests for as long as the wind lasts.'

Harland read the wind velocity, glanced over Larsen's latest forecast and went back to the party with his news. Azizeh, sipping champagne, which she detested, was listening, apparently enthralled, to Israel on the subject of Segovia's renderings of Bach. Harland gave her the pilot's ultimatum and she said, 'A gale? Not for me, Captain. It blows one's hair about. Let them go. I shall stay with you.' Harland noticed Israel's face light with pleasure: he saw the point. He went to give the necessary orders.

The big helicopter was only just clear of the superstructure when a gust swept her, looking like a flying crab, south-west. The princess, huddled in her furs which she had reclaimed from her aide before ordering him to leave with the others, almost reducing him to tears, watching the machine's struggle to get back on course, said, 'Now you'll think it was cowardice kept me here. Is this wind helping us or hindering us?'

That 'us' pleased Harland, and he said the wind was helping and, 'You've brought us a fair wind, ma'am.' Israel, standing beside her, the back of his hand caressed by the silky fur of her coat, said that cowardice was the one thing one would never suspect her of.

'The *one* thing, Mr Mendes?'

'I meant . . .'

'Never mind, I forgive you. Can we go inside now, out of this wind?'

By mid-afternoon the wind was at force seven on the Beaufort scale and Larsen reported it likely to increase in violence for some hours. The swell had increased too. Harland's real worry was the pressure of wind under the Gurling raft, that is the deck with all its superstructure; routine injections of fresh concrete and the action of the immensely powerful spring-wedges seemed to be holding the legs steady in their sockets in the ice. But the winds thrown off by the hurricane were warm and the melting-rate would continue to increase, loosening the stanchions in their sockets. The raft, with its load of huts, machines and men was heavy; yet with the wind gusting at force 10 by 20.00 hours, and at force 11 an hour later, and the glass falling, there was real danger. Gurling and Harland decided to increase its weight by pumping its hollow body and stanchions full of water should the wind continue to rise; and to prepare for that contingency at once. All that evening and into the night all hands that could be spared were at work rigging the chain of pumps required to lift water from sea-level. When that was done, hands were set to driving steel stanchions deep into Icecube's body, so that the raft could be anchored by braced steel cables.

It was for this reason that the task of entertaining the

Princess Azizeh fell to Israel: he could not leave his post in the engine control cabin, but there was no reason why she should not sit with him, and the nature of his watch did not prevent him from talking and listening. She had dropped the royal triviality, saying, after they had fought their way, clinging to a safety rope, from the mess to the control cabin, and were seated in shelter,

'If either of us had been asked to forecast our place and occupation at this time and on this day, say a year ago, if there's one guess which we shouldn't have made, it's this. You and I, sitting here on an iceberg in Mid-Atlantic. At least it's not commonplace, Mr Mendes.'

'Certainly not that,' Israel said, and for no particular reason they laughed. She said, 'It makes for a forced intimacy, like people thrown together in an accident or some kind of natural catastrophe.'

What she had said was true: situation and storm created an atmosphere of intimacy which was almost oppressive and the girl was no longer a personage but just a girl; no, not just a girl, her beauty was of the order which confers distinction, an importance greater than her slightly absurd princely standing could ever have done. For a moment he listened to the wind shrieking and battering at their metal walls; it was the sound of primal madness, of the ancient natural disorder.

'Does it frighten you?' Israel said.

'The wind?' She considered that. Israel watching her had increasing difficulty in turning away his eyes to look at the dials and gauges. She said, 'No, not really. Should it?'

'I believe our actual danger is small,' he said, 'but I didn't mean that. There's something else, a horror of the primal idiocy of natural forces.'

'You are too civilized, Mr Mendes.'

'Perhaps . . .' Then, to his own surprise, he told her how his terror of the great deep and the dark waters had driven him to escape into unconsciousness. She listened, never taking her eyes off his face. For a moment the wind's voice had fallen from a shriek to a moan. Azizeh smiled at him and said, 'Poor Israel,' and her use of his first name sounded, in the intimacy of the night-bound, storm-bound cabin, perfectly natural.

He said, 'In other ways, fear has been a spur, but this was something else, panic. There are still men who can pray but I can't, not to mean it. I know I'm alone. What took hold of me was a feeling very old and very humiliating, the feeling that made it necessary to invent God. Have you ever been afraid, princess?'

'My name is Azizeh. Yes, I've been afraid, terrified, but only of men.'

'What men can ever have made you afraid?'

'A foolish question, Israel. I can name one, at least, a certain captain of the Israeli security forces, Yitzak Menassez by name, Have you ever heard of Jasmin?'

She pronounced the name in Arabic – Yasmin. He said, 'Flecker's heroine?'

'I've never heard of Flecker, still less his heroine. It was my *nom de guerre*. For a few days Jasmin had a place on the front pages and TV screens. It was curious: they rave against people who've killed in a cause, but they can't withhold respect. Camus is the only writer of our time who knew that the man or woman who will not kill for the cause, is not . . . *sérieux*.'

He should have been incredulous or amazed; but he was neither; it was impossible not to know, recognize, respect, pay homage to, her integrity. He said, raising his voice against the idiot howl of the wind, 'Tell me about it.'

'No. Time's made it what it makes all heroics, a bore. There's something I want to know, what does this iceberg project mean to you?'

'A technical problem to be solved.'

'Nothing else?'

'I haven't thought about it. I . . . to irrigate arid land must be a good thing to do.'

'Must it? Why?'

'People have to be fed.'

'Are we sure they're not better unborn?'

'What does that mean?'

'A certain number of people have for a thousand years or so lived a certain kind of life adapted to a certain kind of country. Presumably it was more or less satisfactory, for them. Now my brother and of course I, are with your help going to multiply their number by ten, twenty, a hundred and give that multitude . . . what?'

'I suppose, a fuller life.'

'Fuller of what, Mr Mendes . . . Israel?'

'All right, I get it: refrigerators and colour television, given a hundred per cent success. So why are you doing it?'

'What else is there to do?' she said, and, 'Do you know what is meant by the form of words used by Catholic theologians – *invincible ignorance*? As to what we should do we are all invincibly ignorant. I'm a revolutionary because I hate the spectacle of exploitation and I hate the standards of the European and American bourgeoisie. I've been tempted though, to become a Christian. You'll not have suffered that temptation, you're a man of science and your invincible ignorance doesn't trouble you.'

Angry but smiling he said, 'Then instruct me, though that was a judgement made on very short acquaintance.'

'You ask me, who am lame, to lead you, who are blind? No, we face the same . . .' She paused till the maniac wind should be less noisy and then went on, 'We face the same primal idiocy, as you called it, which has penetrated all our societies. We must feed more and more people so that more and more of their children will die of starvation. Might it not be better to refuse to create new wealth than to use people to create wealth which will never be theirs and never enough? Now what's in your mind?'

To protect himself against this kind of talk, against notions which could never become things or actions, he had always had a means; he let himself know that he was bored. He said, 'If I tell you you'll be offended.'

'Don't condescend to me, Israel. It's one of the vices which makes clever Jews unpopular.'

'I apologize. It's in my mind that there's nothing I'd like more, at this moment, Azizeh, than to take you to bed.'

'Better; much better!' She laughed and said, 'What a pity you're on duty. I am glad you've stopped calling me princess. You know, the title doesn't even exist in my language. Do you know what, in my country, the woman you would call a queen is called? *Shahbanu*, king's woman; there's no other word.' She fell silent, listening and went on, 'The wind's quieter. Mr Gurling says you're a musician?'

'You prefer that to scientist?'

'It's not like that; my difficulty's very simply explained. There's no moral difference, only an intellectual one, between inventing a lever and inventing an aeroplane, or inventing a club and inventing an H-bomb, or making a nice noise on a drum and making a nice noise on a symphony orchestra.'

'Perhaps there's all the difference. Hegel thought so. He thought our business was to teach God to know himself.'

'You're a Hegelian?'

'I sometimes think so.'

'I must read him again. Will you play to me?'

Israel rose and crossed the cabin to her and stooped over and kissed her on the mouth, then straightened and went to take his guitar from the fastening he had made to keep it safe, on the bulkhead. Azizeh said, 'That was nice. We must try it again. In Farzar.'

Israel sat at the console, glanced over dials and gauges, listened to the wind whose voice was declining into a whine, then rising again to a shriek. When the wind force declined she could hear a sequence of notes; when it rose, she could hear only a thin ghost of the music. But she seemed content and later

Israel fetched her a sleeping-bag and she got into it, laughing, and slept while he watched and the wind declined and died away to a light breeze.

In the morning the helicopter came again, to take her off the iceberg.

Gurling left too; first for London, then to inspect progress of the work at Abbas Bay and along the pipeline to the Curzon Depression. He had had a long session with Habib and the engineers at which amendments to the contract had been made so that Gurling could give Brax and Drummond reinforcements of skilled men and unlimited local labour. In his most recent letter to the Iceberg's crew he had said nothing of the anxiety in Farzar about the great gathering of Arab fighting men at 'Omar's camp in the south; nor about the rearming and training, by regular army officers, under General Hakim's direction, of the men faithful to Allal and the cause of Islamic Marxism; the young men who followed the P.D.F. line and who understood that Allal was making use of the Ruler to crush 'Omar, before seizing power for the people.

Still, the Icecube crew were not altogether ignorant of hostile Arab activity in the barren steppe south of and inland from Farzar. Broadcast news programmes carried accounts of an attack by a flying-column of camel-men on one corner of the south-eastern oil-field; drilling rigs had been blown up, five Europeans and eleven natives shot dead and several more wounded, and a section of the pipeline to the Farzar sea terminal destroyed. A punitive raid by Habib's air force had killed a number of civilians including women and children and caused an outcry throughout the Arab world. Mashadi was worried by the intensity and persistence of a whispering campaign against Habib in the bazaar and throughout the city. He complained to Habib that mutinous talk of an Islamic Marxist revolutionary coup among junior army officers was being treated too leniently by General Hakim. Habib said,

'Patience. They shall have their revolution – from the top.'

But all this would have seemed very remote to Icecube's crew; they were concerned with a violent event nearer than North-West Africa.

Hurricane Ethel was first spotted by the United States Meterological Radar Watch, on the eighteenth day of Icecube's cruise from the Newfoundland Bank, when the hurricane was near her place of birth somewhere about nine degrees north, fifty-five west. The hurricane's course was a little west of north and her speed well over twenty m.p.h.

Twenty-four hours later Ethel was intercepted and investigated by an aircraft of the hurricane watch, and by then she was 10 degrees further north, still west of the fiftieth parallel of longitude, but on a slightly more easterly course. The aircraft specially built and equipped for the purpose was spewed out of the storm and so badly damaged that it only just made it home to base. The very experienced crew produced readings and reports which showed that Ethel might well turn out to break all records for violence; but she seemed likely to spend her fury over the ocean. Her still centre never came nearer than five hundred miles from Icecube; but her diameter was a little over 520 miles.

Harland, of course, knew that Ethel was on her way. Larsen was following her progress hour by hour and even had he not been doing so, all the classical signs were present – the long, deep, increasing swell while the hurricane was still a thousand miles away; a rising thermometer which was causing all of them, aboard their meltable craft, serious anxiety; a huge and sinister circular halation round the sun, and, at night, round the moon, partially obscured by a sheet of thin strato-cirrus cloud; dead calm and almost unbreathably oppressive air. Shortly before the great wind hit them, they stood and watched the densest blackest bank of cloud which any of them had ever seen, piling up across the south-western horizon. It had all the intimidating power of an aggression, for it seemed informed with malignant intention, as if it hid a being of colossal power and overwhelming evil.

Harland had already taken the precaution, prepared but not used on the occasion of what they called Azizeh's gale, of pumping the Gurling raft full of sea water. As every structure on deck was welded to it, no wind they could survive at all would shift them. The raft now had all its own weight plus four hundred metric tons of water.

Mendes and Gough were with Harland, Larsen and the ratings of the watch, looking out from the navigation cabin at that sinister bank of cloud as it rolled towards them. Larsen's attempt to exorcise the evil in it by giving it its scientific name, failed; they were all painfully uneasy. At last Israel said,

'Frightening, isn't it?'

'Not as frightening as the barometer,' Harland said. 'I've seen barometers do some alarming things, but this is bloody outrageous.'

Larsen's morse buzzer began to chatter like a demented grasshopper and he ran the tape through his fingers. Harland watched him, saying that the barometer had fallen only slowly at first, then faster than he had ever seen it; and crossing to look at it again,

'940 millibars. God damn it, it's not possible.'

Larsen, still running tickertape through his fingers and reading it as he did so, said, 'Oh, yes. It can go lower, captain. In the Pacific it has been as low as 887. But the worst of this is going to miss us, she's moving round us north-north-east. I have her vital statistics – waist, 520 miles; wind speed round the centre, 212 miles an hour . . .'

'Repeat that,' Harland said, looking bleak.

'212.'

Harland ordered all hands into lifejackets. He said, 'If this hits us I'm not too confident that even four hundred tons of water will hold the raft down.'

A number of factors saved them. In the first place they were caught only by the tail of the wind's shirt, as one of the ratings, an Irishman, put it. It is probable that at no time did the speed of the wind which hit them an hour later exceed 150 m.p.h.; by that time Harland's barometers stood at 925 millibars, but he had ceased to be surprised at their behaviour for Larsen had picked up a transmission from Cape Hatteras giving Ethel the impossible barometric gradient of 0·76 per hundred miles.

'Which means?' Israel said.

'For one thing,' David said, 'that the still centre must be damn nearly a vacuum.'

'And that the end of the world must be at hand,' Harland said and, 'd'you play golf, Mendes?'

'I have done.'

'What would you say if I told you Jacklin had gone round in thirty?'

Dusk, with the air hideously darkened by its enormous load of furiously driven water, torrential rain and seaspray mingled, was two hours premature. When the wind did hit them it did so with a sudden, savage blow which bore out that uneasy feeling that this violence was no accident, was purposeful, meant, wicked. All hands were under cover; no man would have survived for two minutes exposed to a wind of that force; it would have burst or collapsed his lungs and tossed his body into the sea which it had flattened. Did God, Israel wondered, hate them for messing about with His distribution of ice and water? Now alone in the engine-control cabin to which he had made his way when the black cloud had shut off half the sky, he knew what chaos and old night meant; in just such violence had earth been born and brought to maturity. The noise was indescribable and almost past belief: all aboard Icecube were more or less deaf for two days after the storm. It was a sustained, relentless, unmodulated roar, of a magnitude beyond experience. There was no light; the atmosphere, turned to a kind of thin mud, was blowing off the earth. Breathing was grinding labour.

Israel thought that only God could know why the whole

Gurling raft with its freight of superstructure and cargo of souls, didn't carry away to be dropped and drowned at the extremity of the wind's throw. What were five or six hundred tons to a force of this order? As it happened he was wrong: David knew the answer; he, standing at a porthole in the mess cabin had seen what few have ever seen, the wind made visible. Because part of the overall illumination rigging had been carried away in the first great blow, Larsen, anxious to do his duty of making the iceberg visible even in the opaque liquid atmosphere, had switched on the great fore and aft searchlights. It was in the after-beam that David had seen the soupy stuff of rain and spray ripped into lines as clear as those an artist might have used, in a futile attempt to draw air in demoniac motion, black in that white brilliance, and precisely defining the way in which the sharp extremity of Icecube, the angular junction of side and plateau, and the slope of ice-face from that point outwards and down to the sea three hundred feet below, had bounced the wind over them. Low of profile, the Gurling raft and all its top structure was in a wind-shadow. Far from building up pressure in the space between the bottom of the raft and the surface of the ice, the wind had exhausted that space, sucked the air out of it, holding the raft down instead of blowing it away. And there was at least a part of the deck where one could have stood in a dead calm; except that one would have been asphyxiated, for the gale was flaying Icecube's deck of its skin of air.

But Israel knew none of this until the following day. Two hours after the first wind had struck, while logging the readings of all his instruments, the drift-plus-drive dial which registered the iceberg's real speed, gave him a shock: it was registering 3·5 knots. He called Harland to check the speed by the reading in the navigation cabin. Then he sat down with paper and pencil and began some calculations.

What made Hurricane Ethel a boon instead of a disaster for Icecube was their relative positions: since the winds of a hurricane go anticlockwise round the centre and since the berg lay on a course almost due south of the storm centre, the wind which roared and battered at her all that night and into the following day was almost due west to east; in short, the berg had what seamen call a following wind; it was blowing at not less than 150 m.p.h. and Icecube presented to its main force a 'stern' of something like seventy thousand square metres.

Israel did not, of course, have all the data he needed; but in his excitement he was prepared to make some reasonable assumptions. In the event, they were not far wrong: oddly enough one of the data he used came from the novel he had been reading, Richard Hughes' *In Hazard* – the pressure exerted per square metre by a wind force twelve. That pressure increases as the square of the wind's velocity. The answer he came up with was startling: the hurricane wind had added a thrust of quarter of a million tons to the thrust of the engines and the eastward component of the current drift.

It was, of course, a wasting asset: by the time, on a day of dead calm, that Icecube was out of the Gulf Stream and into the Canaries Current on a south-easterly course, her speed was down to 2·1 knots, and Israel was trying to calculate how much loss Ethel's feverish high temperature had cost them.

Twelve

Colonel Mashadi, concluding a conference with Habib during which he had been refused permission to use only officers of his own special service, instead of regimental officers on a rota, for guard duty in the royal quarters at night, was disturbed enough to tell the Ruler to his face that he was his own most dangerous enemy.

'Mashadi, I will not live like a frightened old woman. It was General Hakim who was saying recently that nothing so provokes the hostility of the young dissidents among our officers as treating them with suspicion. I agree with him. And I'm determined that they shall see in me a friend. You got your way over that absurd alarm system; we shall leave it at that.'

He was referring to a system whereby either Habib or Caroline could raise the alarm by pressing a button on a small panel at the end of a flex under the pillows of their bed. To Habib's decision Mashadi said only, 'General Hakim's views are always worth attention, highness.'

Mashadi returned to his own quarters in the palace complex: it was after nine in the evening, his clerical staff had long since left the offices, and he was due at ten at a dinner and concert of Persian music by a visiting company from Isphahan, which his wife was giving for the military attachés of the diplomatic missions. Yet he sat down at his desk and rang for the night-duty secretary, a young lieutenant with a hopeless, romantic and as he imagined a secret passion for Prince Habib. Mashadi gave the young man the keys to the strongroom in which were filed the dossiers of all his colleagues in the armed and civil services, and told him to bring the file on General Hakim: these files were supposed to contain only the officers' official records; in fact, they were security police dossiers which Mashadi had compiled as a protection of his own position, and he alone had access to them.

The lieutenant was not a filing clerk and it took him some time to find the file; but Mashadi had great reserves of patience and during the ten minutes he had to wait sat quite still with his hands folded on the desk in front of him and his eyes cast down as if he were praying. He was not praying; there was no being in his universe to pray to. He was critically reviewing his own long distrust of Hakim; critically, because it was not founded on evidence. He did not even consider the possibility that his intuition was at fault; it was simply the case that the general had been very clever in never giving Mashadi's spies the slightest chance to expose his involvement with the Leftists among the officers.

There was not a great deal to help him in the file; he knew it all, of course, but wanted to refresh his memory.

Hakim had been born in 1922 in Izmir, or Smyrna as it was then: his grandfather had been an officer in the service of the Khedive and later military attaché in Vienna; that officer's son, the present Hakim's father, had been on the staff of Enver Bey, and responsible for a particularly frightful massacre of Greek refugees, which it had suited Enver to repudiate. At that time Habib's grandfather, Hassan Reza, had recruiting officers out all over the east Mediterranean region, looking for officers capable of modernizing his army and navy and creating an air force. Enver's arrest of Hakim had been a political expedient; he did not want to execute him; Hassan Reza's agent was given the chance to contrive Hakim's escape and Hakim, with his wife and baby son, fled to Farzar by bribing the captain of a small Danish freighter to carry them as supercargoes. The younger Hakim was sent to the Farzar military academy; he had won all the prizes open to the cadets for riding, shooting and boxing but, the German and English teaching staff being incorruptible, had done very badly in all his examinations; it was only his father's great influence with the prince which gained him a commission in the Ruler's Guards, a crack regiment. As a fighting soldier he had done well enough in action in a number of small frontier wars.

Mashadi reread his own biographical note on Hakim: 'Excels as a military politician. Warm and friendly in manner, articulate, heartless and unscrupulous. Popular with junior officers and other ranks; in his seniors he inspires a kind of carefulness, almost fear, for which there is no specific explanation.'

Mashadi reread that last sentence and sat back, brooding on it: the general was of that small company of men, a high proportion of whom become leaders, who know no law but their own will, who fight their way to the top, though it be the top of a mound of corpses, because, judging all men by reference to themselves, they trust no man in power not to oppress, persecute, perhaps kill them. They are leaders because they are afraid; and Mashadi reflected that General Hakim had anxious eyes.

But there was a more worrying aspect of the case. Hakim's political judgement was excellent; and he was very careful of his own skin. If he were, indeed, committed to or involved with the revolutionary Left it was because he believed it to be serious enough to win; certainly not because he had an ideological conviction. His plotting, if plot he did, was inspired only by personal ambition.

Mashadi sighed, shut the file, sent for the lieutenant to put it away and bring him back the keys. Habib believed that he himself would be able to contain the military revolution when it came, by taking the lead of it; Mashadi did not.

He looked at his watch and rose, wearily, to his feet; he

would be late for his wife's party. He detested music and a poor digestion spoilt his enjoyment of rich food. He sighed again.

Caroline could not sleep that night: a novice and shy mother-to-be, she had a fear which any experienced friend or servant could have told her was absurd, which she perhaps knew to be absurd: should not the child by now be moving in her womb?

Her situation entailed a measure of isolation from the kind of advice she needed. Her physician, Professor Ghadali, treated her with such deference that she felt unable to ask him questions which she feared he might think silly. She had hinted something about her fear to Habib but all he had said was, 'I expect he's bone idle, like his papa.' The fact was, Habib was being rather off-handed lately: that he loved her, and in just the meaning of the word as she understood it, she had no doubt at all; for there was absolutely no other reason why he should have married her: there was certainly no reason to take seriously his own teasing explanation, that he wanted to add a blond son and daughter, preferably twins, to his other beautiful possessions. But her sickness, occasional and not very serious, bored him and he did not conceal this fact; moreover, her timidity in the face of Azizeh's hostility made him impatient. Furthermore he was showing far too much interest in and kindness to a sixteen-year-old boy, one of the Corps of Student Pages which he had revived – it had been one of his great-grandfather's institutions – chiefly in order to have hostages for loyal behaviour from all the richest and most powerful families in the country. She had forced herself to say something, jokingly, about his 'favouritism' and Habib had replied, smiling maliciously, that he 'came from a long line of homosexuals'.

Habib, lying beside her in their enormous bed, was sleeping deeply; he was not exactly snoring, but he was making a faint, intermittent buzzing noise with his nose, and its regularity was irritating. She put out her right hand to touch him gently; without waking he turned onto his right side, so near to the edge of the bed that he was in danger of falling out. Caroline considered waking him; instead she moved towards the middle of the bed to be nearer to him; it was likely that when next he turned in his sleep it would be towards her, into a safer place.

Although there was a nearly full moon that night and the sky was cloudless, the darkness in the bedroom was absolute. The only thing which could keep Habib from sleeping soundly for the six hours he needed was light, however faint; he was particularly susceptible to moonlight – 'You see, my flower, I am a lunatic' – and consequently the windows of their room were very thoroughly curtained with heavy velvet lined with black upholstery satin. So that even when Caroline's eyes were open there was nothing whatever to engage them.

Having given up trying to sleep, she now closed her eyes, to give sleep a chance to take her unawares which it might do if she gave up seeking it. She immediately became aware of a very faint, regular sound which she could not identify. Concentrating her attention, she was unable to distinguish it from Habib's breathing. Perhaps it was her own? She held her breath for half a minute, but she could still hear the sound until the beat of her own heart interfered with her hearing. She became certain that what she could hear was someone breathing.

Caroline was very frightened indeed but she fought down an inclination to scream and she did not lose her head. If there was a man in the room he must be somewhere near the bed; she could not have heard ordinary quiet breathing from across so large a room. An intruder could be only one thing: an assassin. Caroline did not pause to consider what she should do but acted: she reached across the bed under the sheet until she was touching Habib's back with her right hand while she found the alarm button under the pillow with her left. That button would not only sound the alarm it would also switch on all the lights in the room. She pressed it and at the same time shoved Habib outwards with all the frantic strength of her terror.

There was a shattering confusion of simultaneous events: the room was flooded with light, there was a yell of shock from Habib as he hit the floor, the very noisy alarm bell began clanging madly, there was a sharp burning pain in her right arm which doubled when she tried to snatch it back; it was pinned through the skin to the mattress by a long, fine dagger of bright steel. A man was in the act of turning from the bed towards the door as that door was hurled open with a crash; there was a short burst of firing and a scream and the room was full of men in uniform. Habib, stark naked, was drawing the dagger from her arm; and she herself, fantastically, was laughing – in the relief from terror, at the uproar, at Habib's incongruous nakedness, at the indignity of violence, at the man absurdly slumped across the foot of the bed, staining the sheet with his blood.

An hour later Habib, in his black nightrobe, joined Colonel Mashadi in uniform, in the prince's palace offices. Habib had seen a surgeon dress Caroline's wound and give her a sedative. She lay on a clean mattress and under clean sheets, no longer laughing, looking very pale but recovering from her shock. He had said to her, 'I owed you my happiness. Now I owe you my life,' and she had said, 'Our life, Habib, for me we have only one between the two of us.' He had not responded to that but had kissed her and said, 'Try to sleep.' The night-duty maid sat beside her bed; door and windows were guarded by Mashadi's men.

Habib asked Mashadi, 'Is he dead?'

'No, highness. Four wounds but none, as it happens, mortal.'

'Where is he?'

'In the prison block sick-bay.'

'Who is he?'

'Gamal Mamoud Mossadegh; lieutenant, age twenty-two, Hakim's brigade and Hakim's old regiment. Habib Shah Prizeman last year. Excellent record and not on any of our lists.'

'Those lists of yours don't help us much, colonel.'

'Your highness, knowing the difficulties, will permit me not to defend myself.'

'I'm sorry, Mashadi. Have you questioned him yet?'

'Not yet, he's under sedation. When he wakes he'll be told that he's dying of an internal haemorrhage.'

'Why?'

'A dying man has nothing to fear from talking.'

Habib sniffed, and the corner of his mouth twitched.

The telephone from the anteroom buzzed quietly and Habib said, 'Answer it, please.'

'Mashadi.'

The colonel listened for a moment then covered the mouthpiece with his hand and said, 'General Hakim's in the anteroom asking for an immediate audience.'

'We'll see him.'

Mashadi passed the order: Hakim came in, saluted and standing at attention said, 'Highness, I have to report that Lieutenant Mossadegh is dead.'

The colonel had risen; he said, 'Impossible. Who says so?'

'I say so, Mashadi. Highness, my aide called me with this shocking news. The man was my best ensign when I was colonel of his regiment and was the best lieutenant in my brigade. I could not believe what I heard. I went immediately to the prison sick-bay. I found Mossadegh, as I thought, sleeping. Then I saw that he was dead. I called the orderly and sent for Major Gheisari. He confirms that the man is dead.'

'Highness,' Mashadi said, 'Major Gheisari assured me that Mossadegh was in no danger whatever of dying.'

Habib rose; his face was closed; he said, 'Then he seems to have been mistaken. A pity. A dead assassin can't be questioned. Good night, gentlemen,' and left them.

Hakim said, 'Nothing to be done now.'

'Nothing,' Mashadi said and saluted when the general, with a nod, followed the prince out of the room. Mashadi picked up the telephone and dialled the security guardroom.

'Aref? Mashadi. Here are orders for immediate execution. Immediate, is that clear? One: put a strong guard on the prison sick-bay, taking command of it yourself, and remain on duty until I come. Two: nobody, and I mean nobody whatever his rank, is to have access to Mossadegh's body. Repeat your orders.'

The Colonel listened while the orders were repeated.

'Good. Send an orderly to find Major Gheisari; I want to see him here at once.'

The M.O. arrived breathless, pale as a corpse, and stood rigidly to attention like a frightened recruit in front of Mashadi who was lounging behind Habib's desk in the Ruler's chair. For some moments he eyed the other man in silence, his face expressionless. Then he said,

'Your explanation, major.'

'Sir, I have none. None of those wounds could have killed the man.'

'Clearly, you made a mistake; and a serious one, since he's dead.'

'I made no mistake, sir. There was no room for mistakes, all was very simple. I swear it.'

Mashadi continued to stare at Gheisari, but thoughtfully more as if he were thinking aloud he said, 'You could, of course, have killed him yourself.'

The surgeon's pallor became oily with sweat. He said,

'In the name of God, why should I turn murderer?'

The colonel smiled; he said, 'Sit down, man, and stop worrying. We shan't eat you. That's better. Now, describe the wounds, carefully. But no medical jargon, if you please.'

Gheisari sighed deeply, blew out his breath in a comic puff of relief, collected his thoughts and said,

'Four bullets of the burst hit him. The first struck the left hip, badly chipped the bone and emerged in the left buttock. The gun must have been raised slightly in the vertical plane as it was fired, but held steady in the horizontal plane. The second bullet gouged a trench on the left-hand side between the fourth and fifth ribs. It did not enter the body; X-ray shows a hairline crack in the fifth rib. The third bullet went into the left shoulder below the bone and lodged. The fourth chipped the top of the left shoulder.'

'Very clear, admirable,' Mashadi said; he brooded silently for half a minute before saying, 'There's only one possible explanation, of course. Go to your quarters and fetch whatever you need for a thorough examination of the wounds. Meet me in the sick-bay in fifteen minutes. And say nothing about this to anybody. Is that clear?'

Fifteen minutes later the two officers were locked in the sick-bay with Mossadegh's body, stripped and laid out on a plastic sheet on top of the bed. Mashadi said, 'There's only one wound that interests me – this one here, between the ribs.'

Gheisari removed the bandages and dressing, exposing a wound which looked as if a long sharp-edged gouge had been used to scoop skin and flesh from between the two ribs. Mashadi took bandages and dressing and spread them flat on the table and examined them slowly and minutely under the powerful light. Presently he grunted, said, 'As I thought,' and turned his attention to the wound itself, saying that certainly such a wound could not have killed a healthy young man.

'Now take a close look at it, Major.'

'What am I looking for?'

'A small but very deep puncture made into the wound and penetrating the heart.'

Gheisari gave the colonel one startled look and then, taking instruments as he needed them from the bag at his side, began to probe the wound delicately. It did not take him long to find what he was seeking. He stood back, saying, 'How did you know?'

Mashadi shrugged; he said, 'I happen to know that you're very good at your job. If you said the man would not die, then he would not die. Yet he was dead. And at least one man with a possible interest in his death had had access to him. But there was no new wound of any kind. The inference is obvious; one of the old ones had been used to disguise the new one. If you yourself had done it, you'd have used the stiletto before putting on the bandages. But the bandage and dressing are punctured. It was not you.'

'God forbid! But how did the . . . person you have in mind find a suitable weapon in so very short a time?'

'I doubt whether it was like that; I think it probable that possession of the weapon suggested the nature of execution. Now listen to me, Gheisari: I want to warn you as solemnly as I can; if you say one word of this your life will not be worth *that* . . .' He snapped his fingers; watched the surgeon's face turn pale again and added, 'The man you have to reckon with is quick to act and quite merciless. I'm not referring to myself. Do you understand? Yes, I see you do.'

Colonel Mashadi arranged with the Ruler's secretariat to be informed as soon as Habib was accessible on the following morning. The anteroom was crowded but Habib received him at once, out of his turn. Mashadi said, 'I hope that her highness is recovering.'

'A little fever. Nothing serious. What do you want, colonel?'

'A warrant to arrest General Hakim, highness.'

'Do you, though. On what charge?'

'The wilful murder of Gamal Mamoud Mossadegh.'

'Explain.'

Mashadi explained; Habib listened without comment or change of expression; when the colonel had finished, the prince said,

'To silence the young man, of course.'

'Yes.'

'The implication . . .'

'Is self-evident. Highness, we must arrest him. He'll try again. With you out of the way there would be a period of instability – Hakim's opportunity.'

'Or Allal's.'

'No, Sir. Hakim's not for Allal; he's for Hakim.'

'Mashadi, my good friend, we can't arrest him.'

'Why?'

'You know that better than I do. It would be the signal for the very army mutiny and military coup we're trying to avoid.'

Mashadi was silent; the prince, watching his face, said, 'Not that way either, friend.'

'It would be justified, Highness.'

'You cannot suppose that I object on moral grounds? No; it would be inexpedient: with him alive we know whom we're dealing with. And we should be suspected, which would produce an unhealthy state of excitement in the officers' messes and among the students.'

'Sir, with the general free to act I can't guarantee your safety, nor that of the Shahbann Caroline.'

'My dear fellow, of course you can't. I think we must give ourselves a respite, time to think. We shall send the general on a mission.'

Days and nights in the Canaries Current were peaceful but eventful. Three tours operators were running air-and-sea trips to see the iceberg, so strange a sight off that coast, a great, white, glittering mountain-island slowly drifting south, streams of water pouring down its sides. At night, particularly, it was a spectacular sight and sightseeing cruisers and launches became a source of anxiety. Then, too, there were encounters with ordinary shipping; in those relatively crowded waters watch-keeping had to be very vigilant and there were anxious hours for Larsen and his crew. One morning at dawn Icecube received an official salute from the U.S.S. *John Kennedy*, the largest air-craft-carrier afloat. Harland, not at the top of his form, responded to the compliment under British colours and the following day received a sharp rebuke from Farzar and had some careful explaining to do. The Soviet submarine *Kapitza*, which surfaced dangerously close to them the day after that, was saluted under the green and gold colours of Farzar.

Harland, leaving Larsen in command, made a flying visit to Abbas Bay and the Dragon-tree dock to study the pilotage problem on the spot. Petrus Van Kleef was his host, assuring him, with roars of laughter, that it was no more possible to get that great lump of ice into that miserable little dock than for a rich man to enter the kingdom of heaven. The fat Dutchman became more businesslike when he realized that Harland was unresponsive to his rowdiness. The commander returned to the iceberg a little less worried than he had been when he left it. He and Israel and Larsen made a very careful and detailed study of the large-scale chart of Abbas Bay which Harland brought back with him, and especially of the tides and the tidal record which Petrus Van Kleef had compiled for them from his logbooks. Working backwards, from the position they needed to be in by a given time and date, they were able to calculate, with considerable confidence now that they were familiar with the iceberg's behaviour, the exact position from which they must begin to make the long slow turn which would give Icecube the right momentum on the right course to carry her into the Bay and into Simon Brax's new ice-dock in a single, smooth operation.

What worried Harland was that they would have only one chance. If he undershot, the berg would go aground and there be immovable, melting in the subtropical sun to waste her waters in the ocean; if he overshot he might get back into a position from which entry would be possible, by making another of their agonizingly slow turns out of the current and into the open Atlantic, but even supposing they could make a northing at all against the trade wind, the manœuvre would take at least a month and possibly longer, with melting losses now very heavy.

Every variable was studied closely and at length, especially the tides, for the berg would have to be midway in the mouth of Abbas Bay, in the centre of the submerged gorge now known as Brax's Deep, just so many minutes before high tide on a given day as would enable them to be inside the great sluice-gates within fifteen minutes on either side of high water. The conclusion to their repeated calculations and deliberations was that the docking manœuvre would have to begin eleven days, or 554·4 miles, from destination. Harland called the day in question D-day, the hour H-hour.

On D-day minus three Israel Mendes was given three days' leave, was taken off by the supply helicopter, visited Jock Drummond at the Wilhelm Crater reservoir, saw the hydroelectric installations and the Curzon Depression, flew over the region to be irrigated and saw the irrigation grid, followed the pipeline to Abbas Bay in Jock's Rangerover, spent half a day with Simon, still sad and silent, studying the dock installations and their working. Habib received him and spoke warmly and with understanding of his work. Israel and David Gough were together drafting a report on which a simplified and more economical movement of future Icecubes would be based: virtually a handbook of iceberg navigation. Israel went over the plan of the report with the prince and made some minor changes which Habib suggested. He lunched informally with Habib and Caroline who showed no sign of her pregnancy yet, unless in the drawn pallor of her face. Her forearm was bandaged and Israel asked how she had hurt herself.

'A stupid accident,' was all she said.

Israel flew back to the iceberg and a day later Harland began the long and nerve-racking docking manœuvre. A freak tide, a change in wind direction or velocity, an engine failure, any of these could ruin the manœuvre. None was likely but none was impossible or even improbable; only David Gough showed no anxiety, annoying Harland, who was mildly superstitious, by saying that there was a certain point in any big engineering undertaking when success could be counted on.

Five days later, with all going according to plan and the iceberg within less than half a minute of latitude and longitude of her forccast position, the supply helicopter brought Israel a letter from Gertrud, dated from Kempinski's Hotel in Berlin, where she was on her way to her father's estate: the old count had been killed in an extraordinary accident while pigeon-shooting in his own woods. He was standing, at sunset, under an ancient elm, waiting for the birds to come in to roost, the weather being perfectly calm with only the faintest of breezes stirring the great canopy of foliage above, when the tree dropped a huge branch on him, killing him instantly. Gertrud was the heiress and the family lawyers had sent for her. She would write again from the house and was his affectionately. P.S. Ike had German measles but nothing to worry about.

Would this make any change? Would they still continue to live together in mutual hostility exasperated by occasional outbursts of anger and tempered by occasional moments of friendliness? Always until now Israel had found no positive reason to break with Gertrud. As for negative reasons, they were valid only on the assumption that domestic happiness was some kind of right, something everyone should have: that view seemed to Israel to be a vulgarity; a strain of puritanism in his nature was offended by it. But something had wrought a change in him, he no longer felt indifferent to personal happiness; but he did not examine himself to discover the explanation of the welcome his heart was giving to the prospect of change.

Larsen had the means to send a radio-telegram; but Israel had some difficulty in composing it. He had respected the old Graf but had seen him only rarely and there had been no question of any feeling between them beyond courtesy. The old man had once briefly commended Israel for his seat on a horse. On another occasion, a year later, at the end of a very uncomfortable early morning's duck-shooting over the marshes, and as they were about to part, in the hall, to bath and change, Gertrud's father had said, 'Do not think it ill-mannered in me that I have not yet said a word to you about the honour paid to you by scholars for your new book. I have the book in my library and I have tried to read it. It would be impertinent to pretend that I understand it.'

Israel had stood there, mud to the thighs, stroking the beautiful walnut stock of his Purdy twelve-bore and finding nothing to say. A servant appeared with a silver tray carrying a single glass of spirits for each of them; the Graf raised his glass and said stiffly, 'It would give me pleasure if you would autograph a copy of the book.'

'Of course, sir, very willingly.'

That was as near as they had ever come to any expression of feeling; the Graf treated his little grandson with the sort of considerate politeness he used to all, but showed no particular interest in him.

It was remembering these things that Israel composed the telegram: 'Very sorry to hear of your father's death. At least it was of the kind he would have preferred. Write soon.' Then he wrote a note to Nanny, asking for news of his son.

Later, in the night, he thought more about the event and the telegram. Gertrud had disliked her father; and her father had despised her for marrying a rich man instead of a man in their own class; and for her outbursts of hysteria which made him ashamed.

It was from the Emir that General Hakim received his orders.

'They already know, in Prague, that we've more or less made up our minds to buy the Skoda rather than the new Vickers, provided it's as good as they claim. You have yourself to thank for that; I, as you know, favoured the English gun. You'll be given facilities for thorough trials. The Staff Council will require a detailed and careful report from you. You'll stay at our embassy, of course, and our attaché has orders to lay everything on. When can you be ready?'

If Hakim was angry or disturbed he did not show it; he said, 'The day after tomorrow, Emir.'

'Very well. Choose the officers you will need to take with you. And your route.'

The orders received by the attaché in Prague were ambiguous and he had pondered them for a whole day before deciding that he knew what they meant: he was to keep General Hakim in Prague, by whatever means he could contrive, for at least a fortnight.

Thirteen

With the momentum still helping but the current lost and only the last long heave of the tide to replace it, Harland and Israel had allowed for a speed down to one knot from the mouth of Abbas Bay to docking. If they had underestimated it would not matter much; but if they had overestimated they would have to wait for the next high tide and it might be difficult to avoid a drift, with a serious danger of grounding, towards the southern shore of Abbas Bay.

Ten days of the docking approach, the long, steady build-up of a momentum on course which should carry them out of the current and into the still water of the Bay, had gone well. Now only the final forty miles lay before them: had their landfall been high they would, from their considerable elevation, have been able to see it in that clear air; a day or two after entering the Canaries Current they had caught a brief glimpse of Teyde's snowy cone from a distance which Harland calculated as 160 miles. But the coast for a hundred miles north and south of Abbas Bay was low and there were no mountains in the near hinterland.

With the last supply and mail drop came John Gurling wearing what David Gough called a face like a boot. His news was that 'Omar's Arabs had risen in arms, the sophisticated arms captured by a raid on a government arms convoy which turned out to be unaccountably lightly escorted. They had attacked and destroyed two oil-pumping stations, blown up a section of Jock Drummond's new pipeline – Jock was there now, repairing it, or so it was assumed – and attacked the hydroelectric installation between the Wilhelm Crater reservoir and the Curzon Depression basin. The defence of all that territory was in Allal bin Mocktar's hands. Not much damage had been done to the hydroelectric installation: the raiders' German explosives expert, an ex-Nazi wanted by the German and the Israeli police, had been killed early in the raid, with the result that the limpet bombs had been incompetently placed. Casualties had been heavy on both sides but Allal was now said to be in control of the situation, although another and heavier assault was expected.

'Jock Drummond?' Israel said.

'No hard news. He went directly to the damaged section of the line, on the east of the midway camp which, by the way, was destroyed by fire after looting. He has an escort of mixed government troops and Allal's ruffians. I haven't finished yet. There was a smaller but pretty heavy raid on the Abbas Bay end, but there Habib was able to use divebombers which terrify the horses and camels, as well as the men, and I gather the raiders were more or less exterminated.'

'Simon O.K.?' David asked.

'Yes, and looking cheerful for the first time since . . . yes, he's fine.'

'So what do we do now?'

'Carry out our programme, of course.'

'I hope you get paid,' Gough said, 'I hate working for a bankrupt firm.'

'It's none of your business but Habib transferred ten million sterling from his Geneva account to our Zurich subsidiary the moment the trouble started.'

'Probably thought it was safer with us.'

Israel said, 'You're behind the times, David. If my papa were here he'd explain that the international group we have the honour to belong to could absorb an apparent loss of forty or fifty million with much less fuss than the British government. The difference is, they know how to recover it. A sort of conjuring: now you see it, now you don't. What the hell do you think currency crises and inflation are for?'

The expected letter had not come from Gertrud with the mail but there was one from Nanny:

Dear Mr Mendes, Thank you for your letter. When Mrs Mendes had to leave for Germany Ike was rather poorly but quite over it now. It was a mild attack and Doctor Cohen said I could take him out for the first time today so we went to feed the ducks in the park, you know how he enjoys that. You will find him quite changed, very talkative and often asking for his mummy and daddy, and even reading simple words though I am afraid he is inclined to show off by guessing at those he does not know. Elspeth sends her respects. And Ike has drawn you a picture of the kitten – well, I suppose I should say cat now. Yours sincerely.

It was clear from the drawing at the bottom of the sheet that Isaac Mendes would never be an artist; Israel, laughing at it, recalled a line from Thurber: 'I couldn't say what the thing is it's sitting on. It looks broken.'

He was still smiling when David parted his cubicle curtains and said, 'Can you spare a moment? What's the joke?'

Israel showed him the letter and David said, 'The cat sat on the mat.'

'A mat, of course, clever of you.'

'Your son and heir?'

'Yes.'

'Izzy . . . something awkward. Have you – it's a bloody impertinent question – had a letter from your wife?'

'No. But she's in Germany. Why?'

'Yes, well I have and I thought she might have played the same trick again, sort of.'

'You mean . . .'

'Look, please read it,' David said and offered the letter. Israel hesitated, saying, 'I had one by the last mail. Her father's died and she's his heir and she's gone to Germany.'

'Read it.'

'You're sure?'

'Yes.'

It was always difficult not to do what David Gough told you to do; the quality of tense assurance in his light body and neat, fair head, the quality which had seduced Gertrud and a dozen other women, had elements of the certainty, the assurance which unsure men, however 'clever', look for, and look to. It crossed Israel's mind that David would have made a formidable priest, perhaps a fashionable Jesuit wearing purple socks and converting rich Jewesses and even richer Protestants. Shrugging, he took the letter.

It was dated from the *schloss*, was long, carefully written, and began with sham diffidence by supposing that David might think it in poor taste to write him a letter, to an address where Izzy was his daily and hourly companion; 'How I envy him that!'

> As I don't suppose I'm ever mentioned between you and Izzy you won't know that my father having died I've inherited this place. It's an anachronism; not merely a property but a way of life, as they say.

The language was peculiar; English and German alternated. What it said was true, as Israel remembered; the great, sprawling baroque house, the 'French' garden, the stables and smithy and dairy and bakery and carpenters' workshops; the two superficially picturesque, (internally squalid), villages with their thousand acres of well-farmed land and the five or six thousand acres of woodland and marshes rich in game and wildfowl. Goering had once proposed himself for a hunting visit and had been told there were no boar left when the truth was that there were so many that it was dangerous to walk the woods unarmed, and Gertrud's father had sworn that if that vulgar, bloated degenerate forced himself on him, he'd burn the house and the woods. The river, called the Lesser Dahm, was still clean in that country without industry, rich in fat trout and still driving the two sawmills on which the estate's one industry of carpentry and joinery depended; there was even a charcoal-burner left, Gramm by name, who though skilled and shrewd in his trade was mad by the criteria of modern medicine. All these composed a community almost independent of the rest of the world, whose revenues were spent by the count for the use and benefit of all, so that the furniture of the house was old and worn and the carpets threadbare and there was nothing new; the last innovation had been an electric generator also driven by the Lesser Dahm and providing dim light for the house and – but only when the river was in spate during the spring – power for the milking machine. There were other things which Israel remembered observing with a cold eye: the high incidence of such eccentricity as incest between father and daughter, bestiality and wife-beating; and of such diseases as pathological idiocy, goitre and even anthrax. Was Gertrud now proposing to settle into this archaic, narrow, squalid and pretty little world of poverty, religion and ignorance, to become the Gräfin in deed as well as title?

It always seemed to me that I detested all this and as a girl I did all I could to escape, and succeeded. But either I am changed or my father's death has removed the shadow which darkened it for me. Do not think that he was unkind to me as a child. My mother who was Austrian with estates near Trento which now belong to a Milanese Jew property developer, died bearing me; he worshipped her; and I had not even managed to be a boy. Sometimes, without meaning to, he made me feel I didn't even exist and I expect that is why I became a Nazi Mädchen. A maiden, me; you know, they set a high value on chastity and I'd been had, fully cooperating, by our steward's son before I was sixteen. But now the people, the old steward (his son was captured by the Russians when Von Paulus surrendered and is now a Communist bureaucrat across the border), the housekeeper, the tenants, our own farmer come to me for decisions; and it is strange to find in myself the power, and from somewhere the knowledge, to answer them. And to enjoy the responsibility, and find beauty in the land and in the routine of its daily work.

Israel looked up from the letter and said that this was a Gertrud he did not know. 'I didn't even know she existed. Perhaps I should have done?'

As to that David had no opinion; Israel read on to the end and discovered that he could read her conclusion, 'Come if you can: as the shopkeepers say: "No obligation" – I promise!' with no feeling stronger than compassion.

Her 'Come if you can' referred to a paragraph urging David to visit her when the work he was engaged on was done; to allow himself a holiday, stay at the *schloss* for as long as he liked; she could offer him shooting, including wild boar and buck, fishing, riding, if he liked such things – 'I am sad that I really know so little about you' – a good library of books and music if he did not. Israel handed back the letter and said,

'Will you go?'

'Would you, in my shoes?'

'You know . . . I believe I might.'

'Not me, Izzy. I'm afraid of her.'

'She seems – chastened,' and, making an effort to steady his voice, 'You . . . enjoyed each other.'

Gough shrugged and said, 'I've nothing to offer her and she has nothing I want.'

'Then stall for a while. Give her a chance to preserve and strengthen this mood. She seems at last to have something she wants but the mood is fragile; it could easily be destroyed, especially by you. Perhaps if she becomes established as the lady of the manor she'll find strength in that. Be noncommittal for a time.'

'Not very scrupulous, surely?'

'No, but – forgive me – you aren't, are you?'

'Did the old man leave her any money?'

'Not a great deal I imagine. He lived frugally, like a Roman citizen farmer of the Republican era who probably never existed, a Cato, only the old boy shared fair with his people. I'd think that with the E.E.C. farm-support prices at their present level and the annual cull of game and timber, things aren't too bad. Not that it matters now. By arrangement with my father I settled a quarter of a million on Gertrud some years ago. Dodging death duty, really.'

'You're a strange fellow, Izzy.'

'How so?'

'You – it's your turn to forgive me – buy your way out.'

An hour after Caroline's departure – she was in tears and so was Habib – by B.O.A.C. (Habib had steadily refused to squander money on a native airline), General Hakim, whom Mashadi's agents had lost all track of, astounded Mashadi but not Habib by turning up at Habib's G.H.Q. and reporting for duty.

'The moment I received the news, highness, I knew what I had to do. The Chinese Ambassador was on his way to Kinshasa in the embassy aircraft; he was kind enough to give me a lift.'

Hard-faced, Habib said, 'Your orders were to complete your mission, General.'

'Of course, highness. It is finished. Your secretariat already have my report which, I may say, is favourable. As I expected, the gun is exactly what we need.'

'Very well. The report will be discussed by the Staff Council. Be so good as to hold yourself in readiness for orders – in your quarters.'

Hakim saluted and marched out. Habib, whose gamble on the prediction that Allal and 'Omar would so gravely weaken each other that even the victor would be crushed with ease, looked like coming off, sent for Mashadi and said, 'What have you to tell me about General Hakim's return?'

Hakim had been received with enthusiasm by the officers

and men of his brigade. Listening to Mashadi's report, Habib realized that it was now certain that if Mashadi were allowed to arrest him the brigade would mutiny; and that the mutiny might spread to revolutionary sympathizers throughout the services. He was still pondering a decision when the news of a new advance against the Abbas Bay terminal was received: the force was a powerful one, there were motorized columns as well as irregular cavalry and a camel-corps, and some armour. A small flotilla of M.T.B.s was reported working its way up the coast, manned, according to Mashadi's agents, by Egyptian 'volunteers'. The boats were French-built, of a kind which the Israelis had proved effective; their objective was obviously the new sluice-gates and each boat carried one very large and powerful torpedo, as well as other arms.

The Emir still had one destroyer and two frigates at sea off Abbas Bay; but the new M.T.B.s were much faster than these three rather ancient warships. Habib immediately ordered that the air force should send six Phantoms to seek and destroy the boats, and sent for the French ambassador on whom he turned furiously as soon as he appeared and to whom he used language which was far from diplomatic.

'It seems to me that you people, Excellency, would sell bombs to babies if there were a profit in it. I suspect that the industrial bourgeoisie, whom your government is either unable or unwilling to control have been irreversibly corrupted by the *moeurs* of your *boeuf, beurre et fromage* black marketeers of the fifties. Or is it the aim of your government to do all in its power to destroy mine? In that case it might be better that you ask my foreign secretary for your passports. In the present crisis, he who is not with me is against me.'

The ambassador, Monsieur Macon, protested at once: he was astonished and deeply pained that His Highness should permit himself to use such wounding language to a friendly power. He had no knowledge of any sale of M.T.B.s to the Arab rebels and he did not for a moment believe that his government would have permitted such a sale.

'Then where did these people get the boats from?'

'The only sale of such boats in the last two years, highness, has been to the Libyans, on condition of their being used solely for coastal defence against a possible Israeli attack from the sea.'

'The Libyans! Good God, man, you know as well as I do what that means. That any Arab ruffian in the world can have them for the asking provided Qadafi is convinced he means serious mischief. I must request that your Excellency convey to the Quai d'Orsay the strong protest of my government; and request that they seek an explanation from their good friend Colonel Qadafi who has already promised 'Omar the loan of the air force you sold him.'

Habib, while expressing his rage, had seen a possible way to avoid the danger of trouble with the army, at least for the time being. He got rid of the Frenchman, sent for Mashadi and said,

'Have you solved the little problem presented by General Hakim's excessive popularity?'

'There's only one solution, highness – a firing squad.'

'There's an alternative I prefer.'

'And that is?'

'Promotion.'

Habib dismissed the appalled Mashadi, sent for General Hakim and promoted him to divisional command and ordered him to move his division, which included his own brigade and half an armoured division, with air cover, to Abbas Bay, take command of operations there and crush the 'Omari columns.

'And when I say crush them, I mean crush them. Understand, Hakim, I want no prisoners.'

At Hakim's brigade depot a consignment of 'Sleepy Gas' had just arrived in crates labelled 'C.S.'; Hakim alone knew what they were with the result that he had a call from his O.C. stores reporting the delivery of a consignment of riot gas which must be intended for the Security Police department and had been misdirected. Hakim went to inspect the material: the gas was in mortar bombs with the new lightweight polyethylene cases. With the bombs had come a consignment of the special gas masks which his own men would need. Without saying what the stuff was Hakim informed those officers who had to know that it was not what it seemed, had half the consignment put into store, and took the remainder with him on his move south. That move was made swiftly and smoothly. There were no muddles and no delays as the motorized infantry armour, self-propelled artillery, the great convoy covered by an umbrella of Mirages, Phantoms and Harriers took the road. But by the time he had his force deployed and placed to block the Arab advance, that advance was already dangerously close to Abbas Bay – so close that the iceberg crew, from the high platform of the Gurling raft, heard Hakim's opening barrage, could see the flashes of shell and bomb explosions, and occasionally even hear the chatter of machine-guns. Yet at the moment when the battle began they still lay just outside Abbas Bay, moving slowly in on course.

Communication between Icecube and Simon Brax was reassuring, as the berg moved slowly into its destination: there was, he reported, no question of General Hakim not holding the Arab advance although 'Omar's men, under the green flag of the *jehad*, were fighting like demons and casualties on both sides were heavy.

What, of course, Simon could not know was that Hakim was cursing the offshore wind which prevented him from trying his new weapon: the launching mortars were in position and the troops had been given such instruction as was possible under those conditions in the use of the prophylactic masks; but there were not enough masks to go round and it would have been madness to use 'Sleepy G' in that wind.

Then, on the third day of the battle, the wind backed, began to blow briskly but not too briskly off the sea, and was forecast to continue in that quarter for at least a week. It was now blowing straight into the enemy's face and incidentally raising a rough sea and pushing the flow tides higher than normal. That helped Harland but hindered the Emir, at sea with his flotilla and searching for the two remaining M.T.B.s which the air-strike, having destroyed four, had failed to find. There was even some doubt as to whether there ever had been more than four; but Mashadi's agents had persisted in their report of six, and they were reliable men. It became much more difficult to spot the boats, if boats there were, in a grey watery wilderness of spume-topped, ten-foot waves.

Thus Hakim was given his chance to use 'Sleepy G'. The bombardment cost him some casualties. His men found wearing the masks intolerably uncomfortable, and feeling that they were choking, their discipline broke down, some men tore off their masks and, the wind turning fluky although still blowing from the west, some hundreds got a bad dose of the gas. But the effect on the enemy and his animals was astounding; it produced either unconsciousness or a kind of lethargy which so retarded action and reaction that men and beasts became useless as fighters: only about two per cent of those gassed died of the toxin. 'Sleepy G' was, in a sense, a humane weapon; its principal value was that, sparing life, it deprived men of their freedom to resist; and, after all, politicians, worthy men, good husbands and kind fathers, are doing that for the public good every day of the week. Casualties usually recovered completely within four days. But Hakim's orders and natural inclination were to exterminate. He sent in jeeped infantry and light tanks and what followed was systematic butchery of helpless men, a slaughter of which even Hakim's men sickened before it was over, receiving their general's subsequent congratulations in sullen silence.

The only part of Simon's bulletins to the iceberg crew which was not reassuring was the news that two of the M.T.B.s had not yet been caught and were, therefore, if they could continue to evade the air-search and the Emir's lumbering old ships, capable of making an attack on the sluice-gates.

What Simon did not immediately communicate to his friends was a nightmare notion of his own and what nobody else had thought of: might there not be a submarine involved? It was certain that 'Omar had no such vessel; but it was not impossible that some mischief-making government fishing in troubled waters and with the prospect of using 'Omar later, might have lent him one; even the Soviet Union might have done so. For Simon the world's mighty men, the political leaders, were not responsible adults: only the makers, the artists, scientists and engineers qualified for that category. A prejudice, of course, but one in which he took much satisfaction.

He would have taken his fears to the Ruler. But Habib had seized on a report that Allal bin Mocktar had been killed in action as an opportunity to fly east and take personal command of the mixed force there. He decided to ask the advice of Petrus Van Kleef, calling him on the telephone at the Pilot Office.

'Piet, that echo-sounding patrol boat – would it give an echo off a submarine?'

'Perhaps. I don't know. Why? You are afraid of submarines?'

'It's possible they might use one, isn't it?'

'Since I have seen that iceberg it seems to me that everything is possible in this country of nut-cases.'

'Right. Is there some kind of depth-charge which could be manhandled over the side?'

'We have a few old R.N.N. Mark Sevens for breaking up sunken wrecks. The pressure detonators can be preset for depth. Very unreliable.'

'How long would it take you to get round here with the launch and a load of all the charges she can carry?'

'Sim, if you think I'm going to risk even the last hair on my bald head in this potty schemozzle, you think again, friend.'

'I'm not asking you to. I'll use some of my own men as crew. Just get her over here as fast as you can.'

'I am a stupid old fool, but that much I will do for you.'

He arrived before Simon expected him, and so laden with charges that the launch had little freeboard. The charges were like ten-gallon oil-drums and the setting of the detonator mechanism was simple. There was a good deal of corrosion; the things had obviously deteriorated in store. Piet produced a typed paper which he asked Simon to sign: in Gurling–Curran's name it indemnified the Pilot Service for the loss of their survey launch to the extent of £50,000. Reading that figure Simon scowled at Van Kleef and quoted, 'In matters of commerce the fault of the Dutch, is giving too little and asking too much.'

The fat man grinned: 'My friend, my life's work is not finished, I have an ambition to fulfil, I am determined to push the scales past the 140 kilogramme mark before I die. For that I have to keep both my job and my life.'

They unshipped Piet's old Lambretta which he had brought with him in the launch and he chugged off down the dusty road to the city, looking like a barrage balloon on a roller skate, the mere fact that he survived and progressed being a tribute of no mean order to Italian engineering. Smiling, Simon went into the Nissen hut which had been erected beside his caravan to house the European and American overseers who were noisily at their midday meal.

The artillery barrage from the south-east had ceased and relief of tension had released high spirits. Simon yelled for order and got it.

'I want three volunteers for a dangerous job – an antisubmarine patrol off the mouth of the bay. There's the chance of an attempt to torpedo the sluice-gates. I've got an echo-sounder launch and a load of depth charges. God knows if it will work but we'll have to try. Qualifications for volunteers: one, unmarried; two, physical strength; three, good swimmers. There'll be a two thousand dollar bonus for volunteers, payable to dependents in the event of death.'

This was spoken as if he were reading an official but unimportant announcement from head office.

Simon had long maintained in arguments with his colleagues that living safe is a habit; on the whole, a bad one. He had worked at many dangerous jobs in many dangerous places and in all of them he had observed the same phenomenon: the safer, duller and more tedious a man's life, the less was he prepared to risk it. The men in that Nissen hut were of the kind who reckon to earn upwards of 15 to 20 thousand dollars a year for skilled manual work and pay no taxes; they had never known security of employment or limb or life and maybe what you have never known you cannot want.

There were eighteen men in the room and he got eleven volunteers. He was under no illusions about them; they were not heroes but gamblers. He picked three: a powerfully built Polish-American giant named Czolgoz; an Irishman, Griffith by name, who spent his leisure diving with the 'Ali clan for pearl-shell; and a Cornish-born South African named Polderleg who had left Johannesburg in a hurry after killing a Boer policeman who had raped and then beaten up the coloured girl Polderleg was living with.

Less than an hour later Simon and his crew were quartering a mile square rectangle of choppy water off the mouth of Abbas Bay, following a regularly changed series of zigzag courses with Simon at the echo-sounder and Polderleg who had been a seaman as well as a miner, at the wheel.

Icecube, now very close to her destination, her progress almost imperceptibly slow, looked fantastically improbable in those waters, towering like a dazzling cliff of ground glass above the launch. Polderleg held the launch at slow-ahead, stemming the tide, while Simon and Harland talked by loud-hailer: Simon explained what they were up to and Harland told them that they had, in fact, encountered one Soviet submarine further north but there was no reason to suppose it hostile. His voice came booming down from the height of the deck. 'If you get in our way, Brax, remember I can't manœuvre.'

Just at the end of their first hour of patrol Simon got a clear echo from two hundred feet while they were over much deeper water and at a yell from him Czolgoz and Griffith rolled two charges overboard setting the detonators at 200. Polderleg spun the launch on her rudder and opened the throttle wide. The explosions, probably premature, nearly swamped the boat. Some minutes later an eighteen-foot long shark, either stunned or dead, floated to the surface, blood from its mouth staining the sea; with it came hundreds of lesser fish.

'Well, it was good practice,' Simon said. Griffith and Czolgoz began scooping in the fish they could reach.

Halfway through the second hour Larsen made a signal from Icecube: three radar echoes picked up half an hour ago had now been identified, for an M.T.B. followed by two frigates were in sight.

The M.T.B. was gaining on the frigates and there seemed little chance of their getting within range of her, though both were wasting ammunition by firing their forward guns.

Very shortly the M.T.B. was in sight from the launch: she was making a prow-wave of such magnitude that Polderleg estimated her speed at not less than forty knots; he said, 'Now isn't that nice. What now, skipper?'

At the moment the launch was about one mile to seaward of the mouth of the Bay. Simon ordered Polderleg to close to the iceberg, called Harland on the hailer and asked if he knew how many torpedoes the M.T.B. would be carrying. Griffith, who had worked on a naval dockyard project in Israel, said, 'If she's what I think she is, only one but it's as big as the penis of God,' and was echoed immediately by a hail from the berg: 'According to intelligence, one but a big one.'

Brax to Harland: 'Do you know the swimming depth of the torpedoes?'

Harland to Brax: 'Probably on surface if they're intended for the gates. Please tell me your intention.'

Brax to Harland: 'My intention is to stop the bugger. Roger. Out.'

Aboard Icecube, Harland, hard-faced with anxiety, said, 'What's the fool mean by that?' Gurling said, 'Our business is to dock this iceberg. May I use the hailer?' Harland passed him the mike.

Gurling to Brax: 'Are dock and sluice-gates ready and all controls manned?'

Brax to Gurling: 'Ready and manned. Out.'

Simon addressed his crew: his face was flushed, his eyes brilliant with exaltation, his voice clear and sharp and conveying authority as he moved to take the wheel from Polderleg. His order was:

'Overboard the lot of you and prove you can swim. We're about a thousand yards from the nearest land. Watch out for sharks.'

Just as the life these men had lived had prepared them to answer Simon's call for volunteers, so had it prepared them to obey this order. They went without question; if Brax was bent on lonely suicide, that was his business. Alone, Simon put the launch on a zigzag course at half speed, into the bay and towards the sluice-gates. When the M.T.B. came roaring into the mouth of the bay, he was cruising across its course, going about and about to keep between it and the gates. It was long since he had felt so happy and so free and he began to sing. He was so far from being musical that like Squire Weston, but with a different repertoire, he knew two songs: one was the 'Marseillaise' the other was not. It was the Marseillaise he sang now at the top of his unmusical voice, with the throttle wide open and the launch coming about and about again, time after time between the gates and the M.T.B.

The shore batteries, two groups of old but efficient seventy-fives, were firing at the M.T.B. but their shooting was wild.

Simon saw the huge torpedo launched from the M.T.B. which spun on her stern end to change course through ninety degrees and open fire on him with what sounded like an Oerlikon. A shell hulled the launch at the waterline and water began to pour in and strangely enough it was that hit which ensured the success of his plan. Intact, he would have been going too fast to intercept the torpedo which he would have overshot; moreover the torpedo was not on the surface but a little below it, and it is probable that his keel would have just scraped over it. But that torrent of water through the hole in her hull slowed the launch and lowered her in the water.

What the men on the iceberg and the crew of the M.T.B. saw was a colossal, vertical spout of water which actually reached higher than the deck of the berg. The torpedo must have smashed through the hull of the launch and exploded against the cargo of depth-charges, for the explosion blast smashed every window of the shore buildings.

By that moment, so critical for the last minutes of Icecube's journey, the total destruction of the launch and Simon Brax's death had become immediately irrelevant; the point was that, for the time, the gates were safe and the berg at exactly the right point of the tide, and still with the requisite momentum. So that it was with seeming callousness that Larsen, his glasses trained on the shore establishment, said, 'I hope to God Brax's performance hasn't distracted the shore crew.'

Harland picked the mike from its clip beside him and called: 'Icecube to D. Icecube to D. Do you read me?' From the speaker in the bulkhead a voice with a powerful Sydney accent said, 'D to Icecube, we read you loud and clear. Over.'

'Icecube to D. I am coming straight in. Are you fully prepared? Over.'

'D. to Icecube. Come right in and welcome, skipper. Roger and out.'

Very very slowly, in the slack water of the turn of the tide, towering white and majestic above the two low headlands of the gut mouth and the mighty open gates, Prince Habib's cubic mile of ice, diminished of millions of tons but still bearing within her great body the stuff to make a desert green with young wheat and barley and all the fruits of the earth, watched in awed silence by a crowd of the workers who had made this thing possible and a still larger crowd of idlers, made her way into the basin which had been prepared for her. Israel, tense at the console in the engine control cabin, received the order:

'Mendes. For what it's worth, full astern.' He pulled steadily back on the two levers and answered, 'Full astern it is, skipper. It'll probably pull the engines out of her, but I gather we're home.'

Harland's last order, booming over the berg's tannoy system was,

'All hands. Brace yourselves. We shall probably hit the shore pretty hard.'

Six hours later, the tide being at full ebb, the sluice-gates closed and the huge pumps were at work pouring out the small residue of sea water remaining, the great mountain of ice lay still on the sandy bottom, almost filling the dock, melt water pouring down her mighty flanks in rivulets and cascades which glittered in the blazing sunshine. A moment came when David Gough, doing the salinity tests on the mixture of salt and fresh water in the dock, signalled for pumps to be stopped. In three hours' time they would be pumping fresh water into the pipeline. Israel and a shore crew were preparing to go down on derricks and dismount the engines, another shore crew was already at work dismounting the superstructure and the Gurling raft; a big helicopter was standing by to lift the raft ashore; and Harland radioed Habib at his G.H.Q. on the south-eastern front. 'Icecube docked. Shall be ready to start pumping melt water within three hours. Congratulations. Harland.'

At dinner that night in Brax's caravan, Icecube's crew were free at last to dwell on Simon's death. For form's sake they celebrated their success with the last two bottles of their Pol Roger; but it was a joyless celebration. Still later, sleepless, Israel began by flood light and with the help of the night-watch those measurements which would enable him to estimate what their water losses had been during that long voyage from the Arctic.

Fourteen

From the window of the suite of rooms where, the moment Habib was out of the city and on his way to take over Allal bin Mocktar's command, Colonel Mashadi had confined her under guard, Azizeh, using the powerful field-glasses which Habib kept in all the rooms of the palace which commanded a view of the sea, had watched the iceberg's slow drift to land, seen Simon Brax's encounter with the berg's crew, seen the approach of the M.T.B. and the frigates. But the interception of the torpedo, the destruction of the launch, and the sinking of the M.T.B., trapped by the frigates, by a lucky shot from one of the shore-batteries, had all been out of her line of sight. She had heard artillery, and one colossal explosion which had rattled the windows of the palace, but like the spectators and generals in any battle had no idea what was happening.

The soldiers Mashadi had used as escort when he arrested her were blacks from the extreme south-western territory, tall, muscular and stupid, quickly obedient men with nothing in their dark, still eyes which offered hope of sympathetic communication. They were the kind of men of whom European officers in erstwhile colonial services used the adjectives loyal, manly, impassive, dignified; and spoke of them as splendid chaps in a scrap if well led by British (French, Belgian, Dutch) officers; in short, scarcely human. About these of her brother's subjects she knew nothing but that they had sullenly resisted all attempts to persuade them to give up the practice of circumcising their women by excision of the clitoris in the mistaken belief that this would make them faithful; and that they sold prisoners taken on raids into Senegal to those Arab slavers who still found a market for human cattle at prices so hugely inflated by oil revenues as to make the risks of the trade worthwhile.

It had been like being arrested by robots or by trained apes; they had, no doubt, a language of sorts, but she did not know it. Only to Mashadi, their master, could she speak at all and to him she said, 'My brother will break you and perhaps kill you for this.'

'Princess, I know this well.'

'Then why? I am not even the enemy. Hakim . . .'

'Highness, Habib Shah has many enemies. In these confused times I do not think of that but instead I ask myself who are his friends. Well, there's always me.'

She was impressed by his abnegation; for she knew that he understood the strength of Habib's feelings for 'the Family', and that whatever Mashadi could bring against her, it would not be enough; she was, as they used to say in English nurseries, 'only a girl' but a girl of Far blood. Before the colonel left her she said, 'Mashadi, between ourselves and given that we shall both soon be dead, who will win?'

With mock humility he said, 'Am I to answer the Princess Azizeh or Comrade Yasmin?'

'Habib Shah's sister.'

'Then the answer is . . . General Hakim, alas!'

'Ah. And why?'

'If you want to know which of several candidates will get the power all seek, look for the basest, look for the man for whom the whole race of men is the enemy who he believes will cheat him, cuckold him, laugh at him and then club him to death as the venomous little life-hater he, even he, knows himself to be.'

He fell silent, walked to the windows, looked out, on a sea as wine-dark as ever Homer's was. Four fishing boats with curved triangular sails the colour of young poplar leaves were sailing in line ahead for the fishing port. In a low voice the colonel said,

'A very beautiful evening,' and turning to Azizeh again,

'Highness, in the ugly trade I follow for love of your brother, it is very necessary to know how to recognize the leaders; and I tell you Hakim is such a man and Sheikh Allal another. You are Allal's friend, his comrade in revolution, and were once his woman. I have no right, by the only light I have, to trust you. Because you are who you are what I do will cost me my place and perhaps my life. *Inch'allah.* Perhaps I fall short, perhaps I should kill you. That I cannot bring myself to do if only because I love your brother. But I can, in the hope that my own estimate of Habib Shah's chances is wrong, keep you from doing him a mischief at this time of decision. Can I do less?'

Two people received domiciliary visits from Hakim's men that night. Three junior officers presented themselves at the palace guardroom and asked to see Colonel Mashadi; they had, they explained, an urgent and secret dispatch from Habib Shah.

The quarters which had been allotted to Mashadi and his small palace staff were on the sixth floor of that part of the sprawling complex known as the West Tower, a building closely modelled by Habib's grandfather, or rather his Italian–Persian architect, on the Chehel Sutun in Isphahan but later spoilt by the piling of storey upon storey each a smaller version of the last, until it looked like a rectangular wedding cake. The sixth floor was not the trap it seemed, for as well as the principal staircase there was a very narrow spiral cut into the thickness of the rear wall, which emerged into an inner court opening by way of a small arched gateway into the great Court of Orange-trees.

Among the contingencies which Colonel Mashadi had taken into consideration for the immediate future was just such a visit as this midnight call; he was aware that Hakim, having crushed the 'Omaris at the battle of Abbas Bay, was preparing to bring his army to Farzar. To the officer of the guard at the other end of the telephone he said,

'I will come down as soon as I have dressed.'

He picked up the small emergency case which he had ready and went down the spiral staircase to the courtyard, prepared to make his way to the place where he held a Ferret armoured car in readiness to take him south-east out of the city. At the bottom of the staircase he was met by three junior officers. He halted, noted that they did not salute, smiled, shrugged and said,

'Good evening, gentlemen.'

Polite but stern, the three young men led the colonel round through the Court of Orange-trees and back into the guard-room where, joined by the first trio, they escorted him upstairs again to his own quarters. The door into those apartments was guarded by four of the Security Department's black soldiers, men of the tribe he had used to arrest Azizeh. Mashadi could have ordered them to rescue him and it is certain that they would have fought to the death to do so. The same possibility had been open to him in the guardroom. But he reflected that he would be shot dead instantly; that his loyal fellows would lose their lives uselessly; and that so would several of the young officers sent to deal with him. He further reflected that he now had no hope of saving Habib's cause: it was lost because it was not in the fashion of the times: Hakim's was; and that life has to end some time and that whether it be in five minutes or five years hardly matters after a man has passed the age of sixty. He therefore gravely returned the black guard's salute, an example followed by the other officers, and allowed himself to be escorted into his rooms only turning to frown when one of the officers jostled him. The last officer of the escort closed and locked the door behind them.

Mashadi motioned towards the drinks trolley in one corner of the room, indicating that they should help themselves. Their hostile silence implying refusal, he shrugged and said,

'Have any of you gentlemen been students of philosophy? I am wondering if you have read the Austrian Ludwig Josef Wittgenstein: he tells us that death is not a part of life, for it is not lived through. When your time comes, remember that.'

A lieutenant wearing the wings of the glider corps and the ribbon of the Habib crescent for gallantry, said pompously,

'We know nothing of western so-called philosophy; there is but one book.' Perhaps he meant the *Koran*; or perhaps *Das Kapital*. The officer in command of the party, a captain of twenty, a rough fellow from the northern hills who spoke Farsi with a marked accent, said, 'Be silent. Talk is out of place.' Then they laid sudden strong hands on the colonel, picked him up – he made no resistance – and threw him out of the nearest open window. Both the killing and the dying were done silently. Even the sound of Colonel Mashadi's body striking the flagstones seventy feet below was dull.

One officer, a clerkly-looking young man wearing steel-framed glasses, remained behind to go through the colonel's papers; the decorated lieutenant went down the spiral staircase to the court to make certain that the colonel was dead. The captain and the other three lieutenants made their way to the suite where Azizeh was imprisoned.

The first she knew of their visit was a challenge in the corridor, then some kind of altercation; and the sudden crash of two revolver shots. Although it seemed likely that if there was shooting outside her door, it was in her favour, she was immediately terrified; unlike Colonel Mashadi, she was not ready to die. But she was not overwhelmed by her terror; as Comrade Yasmin she had looked frequently into the face of death and she had learnt to control fear as every soldier has to do.

There was a brief silence and then a voice from outside called out to her, respectfully, 'Will your highness unlock the door? We are your friends.' She replied that she was locked in from the outside. They told her to stand well back from the door and shot the lock to pieces with a submachine-gun. When they marched in she stood, deadly pale, facing them, wearing a long blue and gold nightrobe over silk pyjamas. The wall facing the door was starred with bullet holes and the Tabriz carpet with fallen plaster. The captain commanding the intruders said in his uncouth doric,

'We apologize for the violence of our entry, Highness. We bring you this from General Hakim,' and handed her a letter. Leaving the officers standing, she sat down to read it.

From Divisional General and Acting Regent Abdul Aziz Hakim; Highness, you are aware that we have overcome the western army of the 'Omari rebels and that the iceberg has arrived and that even now water for the desert is being pumped inland. This great work for the people and for all humanity will be your brother's monument for all time.

The implication that Habib was dead shook her; she glanced quickly up at the Captain's face but it was impassive. With her heart beating too heavily, she read on,

It is expedient and courtesy requires that the Europeans who have been employed in this work be suitably honoured at a banquet, according to our custom, and that such of our honourable orders as Your Highness considers suitable be conferred on them.

As Regent until such time as the new government be formed to carry on the life of our country until we know whether his late Highness has a male heir and during the minority of that prince, it falls to me to ask Your Highness to overcome the grief which afflicts her and in which I and all our people weep with her, in order to take your brother's place at this reception for the foreigners. Circumstances compel me, alas, to ask that you give me an immediate answer.

I mourn with Your Highness but God's will be done. Now, peace be with you.

Hakim.

Azizeh had no tears; in the brief moment of time in which memory can scan the whole past her mind filled with images of their shared childhood; there was much sweetness and much kindness in it; and she found that it was still hers. The sense of absolute loss was like a hole in the heart, an intense anxiety, a sort of aching hunger. She raised her eyes from the letter and said coldly to the captain,

'I had not been told that Habib Shah was dead.'

'Alas, highness!'

'I do not believe this report. Had it been so Colonel Mashadi would have informed me at once. Send one of your number to bring him to me immediately.'

'Highness, upon learning of the prince's death in battle with the rebels whom God will destroy, in despair he took his own life by casting himself from a high window. We honour his loyalty.'

Azizeh was silent for a full minute; it was clear to her that they had murdered Mashadi; there was a tradition – her grandfather had rid himself of two turbulent ministers by defenestration represented as suicide; she said,

'This is an order. Report to General Hakim that I will take my brother's place at the banquet for the foreign engineers. Present my compliments and ask that he call on me here as soon as his other duties permit to report the details of my brother's death. I take it that the palace will be garrisoned by your general's own men?'

'Your highness's safety requires that.'

'I have been a prisoner here without servants. Be good enough to see that my maids and my secretary are sent to me at once.'

Considering, when the officers had saluted and withdrawn, why she was without tears, she realized that she did not believe that Habib was dead; did not or would not or could not.

For some days in succession, as the enemy weakened and fighting all round the periphery of the territory became sporadic, Habib felt free to have himself driven up to the terminal of the pipeline at the Wilhelm Crater early in the morning and there, in Jock Drummond's company, to watch Icecube's melt water cascading from the two-metre outlet into the growing lake in the ancient crater.

John Gurling flew down to see him; for hours they discussed the Mendes–Gough–Harland report, costs and estimated yields, and having been joined at Habib's H.Q. by the special envoy of the Danish government, they drafted a provisional programme of future iceberg movements based on the rate at which it would be necessary to replenish the reservoir. Gurling and the Dane returned to London and Copenhagen respectively.

On one occasion, standing on the highest part of the old crater's rim which had been given a concrete platform to make a convenient promenade, and looking down past the hydro-electric plant into which and out of which the water cascaded, cool, glittering and beautiful into the lower reservoir of the Curzon Depression whence it would be pumped, by the power it had generated, into the vast irrigation grid, Habib made Jock see, almost as vividly as he himself saw, the splendour of his own vision. He saw the great barley fields and wheat fields and the tasselled maize which followed their harvesting; he saw the stalled cattle and penned sheep and poultry fed from wide fields of alfalfa and grain; he saw the orchards of citrus and almond beautiful and fragrant in flower, and the neat market gardens, the melons ripening on their prostrate vines, the cucumbers and peppers and tomatoes; he saw the clever machines which would teach that half-starved, half-diseased people of shepherds and idlers and raiders to be clever too, and would leave them leisure on a full stomach to break their bondage to meagre grass and a superstition as meagre; he saw the schools and universities and hospitals to be built not out of the squandered capital of oil, but out of the wealth which the land would make for all.

Perhaps the physical beauty, courage and high spirits of his locutor helped Jock Drummond, who had once read economics, to forget the fatal history of such liberalism as this which the prince expounded. Habib said to him,

'Here, Allal was right, my sister is right. You know, Mr Drummond, what I have done to turn our great landlords into modern capitalists. They think it is the final end I have in mind, it is only the first step; I am a better Marxist than they are, I take the way he traced. Capitalism is in its last, greatest and most convulsive crisis. But what we have done here must belong from the beginning to the people and be administered by themselves though in the beginning they will make a mess of it. That and only that will reconcile them to the change; besides it is just.'

And after a silence he said, 'Are you a Christian, Mr Drummond?'

'I suppose, of a kind, sir. I don't go to church; I don't know what I believe; but I suppose I follow the Christian rules; and my two children were baptized – again, I don't know why.'

'Ah. But at least you will understand what I mean when I say that, at the very least, they will say of me that I fed His lambs.'

Telling Emma about that conversation in his next letter Jock wrote that: 'I was moved, my love. He was, or seemed, frivolous and a cynic because of his high spirits; but he was a good man. I said – you will never guess – Sir, you are a good shepherd.'

Then the water at the terminal stopped flowing and almost immediately a dispatch reached him informing him that the last of 'Omar's columns having evaded the patrols, had seized the whole of Section 42 of the pipeline, breached the pipe, and that the water of his iceberg, far from filling the new reservoir, was draining away into the desert sands. He trusted nobody to deal with this but himself.

Against the men – they were Hakim's not 'Omar's but this his intelligence had failed to discover – whom his reconnaissance aircraft found swarming like excited ants all along the southern side of the Section, he sent such aircraft as he could afford loaded not with high-explosive bombs, for he had in mind possible further damage to the pipe, but antipersonnel bombs and, in his passion of vindictive rage against these wanton wreckers, napalm; and half a dozen divebombers. He signalled Gough at Abbas Bay to stop pumping: melting was far from complete, it would take weeks possibly months, completely to fill the water-dock. That stopped the waste of water. Then, under Drummond's directions, he put together a corps of repair teams with all the material they would need and a flying column of armoured cars, light tanks, self-propelled guns and jeeped infantry; and took command of it in person. To Jock, as they set off, he said, laughing, 'Perhaps I shall be the last man of an ancient royal house to lead his troops into battle; and to die.' But he became sober when the news reached him that Hakim was in Farzar with his whole force and that Mashadi had taken his own life.

Habib led the column in a Ferret car and was very soon aware and surprised that the opposition had melted away. He had not expected the air-strike to be so completely effective against men with the 'Omaris' power to, and training in, swift scattering. There were corpses hideously burnt by napalm, but not many and even fewer killed by fragmentation bombs and the dive-bombers' shells. The enemy had not stood to fight; perhaps because the damage he had been sent to do was done, for in Section 42 there were four huge breaches and one whole length of pipe completely destroyed, probably by a limpet bomb or several of them. The Prince noted on his pocket tape-recorder, for later entry in his war diary, that although water had been flowing to waste from the breaches for only forty hours, where it had drenched the arid soil the ground was starred by tiny seedlings.

At each break in the pipe Drummond dropped off a working party and materials and supplies, Habib leaving them a sufficient guard. Habib himself, with the main body of his force, continued west to Section 78, moving at such a speed that the column became shrouded in a cloud of dust turned to translucent gold by the power of the sun. Gough had signalled that he had patrolled the pipe to that section, and that there was no damage. Habib turned his party and set out to return to Section 42. A few minutes later a reconnaissance helicopter of his own air force flew over the length of his column, presumably on the same mission as himself, came low enough for the pilot and observer to salute him as they recognized his head sticking out of the conning tower. He radioed that he had the situation in hand and ordered the machine back to base. The signal was acknowledged and the machine turned and disappeared and it was five minutes later, when the column was at the five-kilometre mark from the last, worst break in the pipe where Drummond himself was in charge of repair work, that a squadron of five big helicopters appeared, one in the lead and four following, the leading machine of a new armed type used for dropping bombs to destroy villages where there was no danger of opposition, the others troopcarriers. It looked to Habib as if the Emir, or perhaps Hakim, unaware of his own swift action though by now they should have received his signals, were intervening to protect the pipeline.

The leading helicopter flew the length of his column, failing to answer his radio call, until it was about half a mile ahead, and up wind. Then, like some huge gravid insect laying its load of eggs, it dropped six canisters like oil-drums in a crescent pattern across the column's course. Habib gave the order to halt. He was puzzled and nervous. His repeated radio calls were still unanswered. The six canisters dropped by the leading helicopter, which after dropping them flew back on a westerly course, did not explode; as far as anyone could see they did nothing, just lay there as if they were indeed some kind of eggs and had yet to hatch; but hatch what?'

When, twenty minutes after the canisters had fallen, the helicopters landed raising small hurricanes of dust and the masked infantry disembarked and advanced slowly in open order towards Habib's stationary column, Habib was unconscious and not a score of his men were in any condition to resist.

First to disembark, a section of men belonging to a far northern regiment of hillmen, people whom Hakim had paid much attention to, made at a steady lope for the leading Ferret car of Habib's column. They were fair-skinned, blue-eyed, bearded, surly fellows who had no particular feelings about the royal house of Far, nor for any other men but those who paid them and kept them supplied with the cannabis which was mother's milk to them. To that section had been given the simple task of shooting the sleeping prince between the eyes. As all six of them were anxious to carry out their orders and so earn the bonus of cannabis, over and above the usual ration allowed to men of their race in the army, it might have been difficult to identify the body of the prince, with most of the head shot away, had it not been for the perfection of the body and the characteristic webbing of the middle toes of both feet. The six were subsequently tried for exceeding their orders to the point of murder, by one of the Regent's courts martial; they were confused by this disaster that had overtaken them and by the enormous amount of hashish they were given in prison; they pleaded their orders, of course, but the court could not understand their jargon and they had nothing in writing – indeed none of them could read. They were convicted and sentenced to be shot; none of them understood what was happening to them until they faced the firing squad and if they understood at that moment that belated breakthrough to intelligence cannot have given them much satisfaction.

Fifteen

The death of Habib Shah was not yet published. There were uneasy rumours in the city but Mashadi's successor Major Mahomet Bagi, a creature of Hakim's, had his police and his spies out on the streets; men who spoke their minds or asked indiscreet questions were apt to disappear suddenly, and there was the beginning of a police terror of a kind new to Farzar: at last the country was really being modernized.

Officially, and in the newspapers, the general's assumption of the title Regent and the fact that the Princess Azizeh was to act as hostess at the banquet in honour of the men of the iceberg enterprise and celebration of the opening of a vast territory of desert to cultivation, were attributed to the Ruler's absence at the head of his army in the south-east. The sudden retirement of the Emir to his estates and the emergence of General Hakim into the place of power were attributed to the Ruler's satisfaction with Hakim's quick and total victory over the rebels on the front which had been assigned to him.

At the banquet Azizeh wore the magnificent cloth-of-gold and night-blue silk dress of the Far princesses of the eighteenth century. Receiving the state's guests she was very pale but in command of her nerves and strikingly beautiful.

It was understood that Caroline Shahbanu was too near her time to come from London. But both Gurling and Curran were there, Gough, Drummond, Mendes, Harland and Larsen. These, and one or two others of the hundred odd guests, had been accommodated with rooms in the palace for one night. And they, the principal guests, had been asked to wear such ceremonial dress as they could manage, which had necessitated flying out a curious collection of garments from London. Curran wore the court dress of a Knight Commander of his Order, John Gurling the academic gown of a Doctor of Science (Oxon.) over evening dress decorated with his D.S.O. and campaign medals. The most David and Jock could manage were their O.B.E.s on evening dress – white tie and tails; they had not thought of their B.Sc. gowns; Harland and Larsen were splendid in full dress uniform. Israel wore evening dress and the one official honour he was proud of, his Order of Merit; and over them the hooded gown of a Doctor of Philosophy (Cantab.).

The room chosen for the reception and the banquet was called the Great Talar; it is an old Persian word meaning a long hall. It was pillared, with arched windows from floor to ceiling. The floor was celebrated, the work of a team of Italian craftsmen who, using coloured marbles from all over the world, had reproduced by inlay the great Tabriz carpet in the throne-room. Walls and pillars were in looking-glass mosaic in the Persian style. There were seven colossal glass chandeliers which had been made in Waterford for Habib's father. The end wall furthest from the great double doors into the Talar was completely covered by an immense tapestry made in Flanders, representing the victory of Habib's ancestor Mamoud Eskandar Shah ibn Far over the Sultan of Morocco at the battle of Tjidjika.

Israel, having made his bow to the princess and exchanged with her a look in which they recalled the strange intimacy of that night of storm aboard Icecube, found himself, having strolled the great length of the room, standing beneath the battle tapestry with a glass of champagne in his hand and, as his self-introduced companion, Professor Darius Tajerbashi, the very urbane old gentleman who held the chair of history at Farzar University.

'It is pleasant,' the professor said, 'to see ladies; and so many ladies! In the time of our prince's grandfather that would not have been possible. No ladies on such occasions. It was our prince's father who made the change. And now we see many changes. We even have a pollution problem.'

'Indeed?' Israel said; he was staring at the tapestry and wondering if he had a special tropism for bores who thought they were wits; and thinking how beautiful she was and that probably she wasn't really.

Tajerbashi said, 'I see you are interested in the battle of Tjidjika. The last battle in history in which war elephants were used.' And, raising his glass gracefully and bowing slightly, 'May I say that it does so young a man as yourself very great credit to be wearing the noblest of all honours which can be won by artistic or scientific genius?'

'You are very kind, Professor. Yes, I was studying the tapestry. Tell me, why are the elephants that curious shade of pale pink?'

She, herself, was a tapestry figure in that gorgeous dress of dark blue and gold. But he had seen her in pants and bra wriggling her way into a sleeping-bag . . .

'I, myself, have often wondered, Doctor Mendes. I have concluded that they must be blushing for shame, for they cost the Sultan, their master, the battle. He had the brutes as a gift from the last of the Moghul emperors. Had I been his historical adviser I should have advised him to cut them up for cat's meat.'

'You have a poor opinion of elephants in warfare?'

What, really, had happened to her brother? There were stories that they had, in their 'teens, been lovers . . .

'No historian, sir, can fail to despise them. They were certainly more trouble than they were worth to Hannibal. And then, consider what Polyaenus has to say of them in the *Stratagemata*.'

'He is not an author I have ever had occasion to look into,' Israel said, falling into the professor's style.

Impossible to think of her, in that dress, as anything but a figuration of the state, a sort of fabulous beast, like Britannia on the old pennies. Try to imagine wooing Britannia . . .

'Why, indeed, should a mathematical philosopher read him? Certainly not for pleasure, he is a dull fellow. But you will perhaps recall the experience of Gaius Metella at Panorma in 215 B.C.; and you will remember that the unfortunate Rajah Porus was not saved from defeat by his elephants at Gaugamela.'

'But there,' Israel said, at last able to recognize a reference, 'his opponent was Alexander in person.'

Princes confronting each other – the lion and the unicorn. Suddenly he remembered, from his fourth or fifth year, coming out of the lavatory and seeing his mother in the corridor and asking, 'Mummy, do God and King George have to go to the lavatory, like us?'

'He was, sir, he was. No, the history of elephants in war is a sorry tale. True, there are the cases of Chandragupta at Ipsus and Pyrrhus' victory at Herakleia twenty years later, yet these are but two exceptions to an otherwise unbroken rule of disaster.'

They admired the pink elephants of the tapestry in silence for a moment. The Talar was filling but it was not noisy for it was the custom for guests to keep their voices low. Israel saw a dozen familiar faces but, as usual with him at parties, was content, once having found a pleasant corner and someone to talk to so that he would be spared hostly attention, to stay where he was. He said,

'There seem to be small bronze cannon mounted on the Sultan's elephants. That, surely, was original?'

They said that Habib, with the modern weapons at his disposal, could not have any serious difficulty with the rebels. But there had been a look of strain in her face, in her eyes. Had she had bad news? Was it true that they had been lovers? Or just the Farzari passion for naughty erotica in gossip.

'As original as it was disastrous, doctor. At the first discharge the creatures wheeled as one and ran for home, scattering the royal cavalry guard and terrifying the horses into bolting. The notion was due to an itinerant Italian engineer known as Il Torinese. He managed to get aboard a ship and out of the country on the night following the battle. I had the curiosity to follow him up and found an account of him as a successful physician in Lisbon. However, his prosperity was short-lived, poor fellow: he was called in to cure the Cardinal Archbishop of syphilis, killed his patient with too much mercury, and was burnt as a heretic. But I see we are going to table.'

The banquet was served in the western fashion, that is the guests sat up to the table. A servant approached Israel, bowed and said something he did not understand. Professor Tajerbashi said, 'Her highness presents her compliments and invites you to sit at her right hand. She honours you by breaking the rule of *taarof*.'

Israel did not have time to ask the professor what *taarof* meant; his heart gave an odd little jolt. Surely Curran, Gurling or Harland should have had the place of honour? Had he known it that was exactly what the professor had meant. Yet it did not occur to Israel that Azizeh was simply indulging a personal preference; or, if it did, he dismissed the thought as fatuous. Nor, after he was seated, was her behaviour such as to make him think so. In fact she seemed absent-minded; at moments almost discourteously inattentive. Twice he caught her staring at his face in a manner which seemed strangely intense. He was soon sure that she was either ill or – the thought occurred to him, afraid.

The ceremony of conferring the Order of Far on the five Englishmen – Curran had refused the honour on the grounds that he had not been personally involved in the enterprise – and Commander Larsen was held in the Little Talar, which adjoined the Great Talar. It had been decorated in the style of the First

Empire during the rule of Habib's ancestor, the prince who had taken Bonaparte's side against the British. At one end of the long, narrow room was a low dais and on it a number of large cushions. On the middle one Azizeh sat cross-legged like a tailor, yet still managing to look dignified; Hakim sat on her right and on her left an aged nonentity, the Minister of Court.

When it was Israel's turn to kneel on the cushion at Azizeh's feet and have the green ribbon with its golden falcon clasp hung over his shoulder, and then to kiss her right hand which she rested in his own, he found a small, very light object lying in his palm. He closed his hand on it, rose, bowed to left and right as he had seen the others do, and returned to his place among the guests who stood, watching the ceremony and talking quietly, in the body of the room. Presently the guests began to drift back into the Great Talar, some to stand talking in groups, to eat sorbets and drink the sweet, heavy wine, very like madeira, which was made in the northern hills, others to take their departure. For five minutes he stood talking with David and Sir Edwin Curran, then found a servant to guide him to his room.

There he was able to look at the object Azizeh had dropped into his hand. It was a small rectangle of the rice-straw paper which the Farzari ladies used to roll their cannabis cigarettes – the habit of smoking them had long been tolerated. It had been rolled into a tiny ball and Israel had to use extreme care in unfolding it. The message it bore was one sentence: 'Be in your room at eleven.' Israel looked at his watch: 9.55.

Curiosity was not the only feeling which tormented him for the next hour and a half. The other was desire; or lust might be the better word. With Gertrud he had had no sexual relations for two years; he had a certain gift for chastity but when the charge of sexuality built up in him to a point at which it became inconvenience so that all women began to seem desirable and the need for sexual relief came between him and his work, he had taken to restoring to a well-run and discreet brothel in Clarges Street. There he had a favourite girl, an Italian called Maria Teresa. The arrangement indulged the least generous trait in his nature – the inclination to avoid emotional obligation; if you paid a woman whose trade it was to sell her body, she had no claim on your feelings.

When, however, there was no question of a commercial transaction but of desire for a woman who was not a whore, he was, in communion with himself, unable to use either of the true words because he had never, in his relations with women, been able to do without the illusion of love. Even his business arrangement with Maria Teresa was sweetened by a mild affection which was no illusion; there was a great deal that he liked and admired in her.

It would be going too far to say that he did literally confuse wanting a particular woman with loving her; yet the moment he discovered that he might have from her what he wanted, he began to use the word love when he thought about her and when he made love to her; it was, perhaps, a kind of cowardice and only his taste for women too independent or too good-natured to exploit the fact that in making love he committed himself, in moments of tenderness, far beyond his true feelings and intention, had kept him out of serious involvement and perhaps even legal difficulties.

It was half past eleven before Azizeh slipped quietly into his room – he had left the door a little ajar. She was dressed in dirty jeans, her hair was tied up in a black silk square, her hands and face filthy, her face flushed, her breathing fast and her eyes brilliant with excitement and rage. She said, 'Lock and bolt the door,' crossed directly to the looking-glass over the dressing-table, said, 'Oh God,' and 'that murdering Turkish *dayus* has my door guarded by two of his niggers.'

'What, in God's name,' Israel began. She said, 'Be quiet and listen,' and sat on the bed and put her feet up and then, eyes cast down as if she were ashamed, 'Habib's dead. Hakim killed him; I know it. He'll have to kill me, now. I'm wondering how.'

Israel sat on the bed beside her but was careful not to touch her. He said,

'How did you get here?'

For the first time she smiled; she said, 'When we were kids my cousin Nadar Khan lived here in these quarters for a year; the rooms were for the pages then. We were in love or thought we were. I used to get out of my window and walk the ledge round the wing and get into one of the corridor windows. He couldn't come to me because my old nurse slept in my anteroom. A little opium in her *dourch* kept her sleeping. I used the old route to-night.'

'Good God.'

His grasp on reality weakened; two hours ago she had been a ceremonial image, gorgeous in night-blue and gold, even her movements hieratic, a living symbol of ancient regality; now . . . watching his face Azizeh laughed, saying,

'Hakim can't have had time to read Mashadi's files yet. Maybe Mashadi destroyed them. Perhaps he doesn't know any more about Comrade Yasmin than you do.'

'What does *dayus* mean?'

'What Hakim is, a bastard, a shit, *le dernier des hommes*, whatever you like that's bad.'

She told him what she knew, supposed, suspected and deduced and when she had done Israel said, 'Yes, you'll have to get out, we'll have to get you out.'

'You want to help me, Izzy?'

'More than anything in the world.'

She sat up, swung off the bed and went into the bathroom, leaving the door open, making a great deal of noise as she washed, and presently emerged with face and hands cleaned of the dirt which Farzar's industries deposited on the stone of all the city's buildings. She said,

'Remember Icecube? We owe each other a kiss.'

He kissed her, but diffidently, and then out of the depth of the self-distrust which drove him meanly to assert that she needn't think she was fooling him, capturing him, said, 'You don't have to bribe me, you know.'

Azizeh stepped away from him, swung back her right arm and smacked his face with such force that he had to take two absurd little dancing steps sideways to keep his balance. She said,

'Never play that Jew part with me.'

He knew precisely what she meant and sat on the bed and waited for her to calm down and until she said, 'Did I hurt you?'

'You bloody nearly broke my jaw.'

'Serves you bloody right,' she said and sat beside him and took his head in her hands and kissed him on the mouth and held his mouth against hers, her tongue playing over his lips. He unfastened her shirt and released his head and began to kiss her breasts. Her breathing quickened and he looked up and said, unsure of his voice, 'Let's go to bed.' She pulled away from him, one hand fastening her shirt, rising, saying, 'Not now, there isn't time,' stroking her hands down her flanks, looking at herself in the mirror.

Israel said, 'By God, you . . .'

'Bitch? I know, I'm sorry, I am truly, I wanted you, I'm not a cock-teaser, you can't think that, but we were foolish, we . . . I've got to climb back into my room. It'll have to wait for London. When you go, I go, but the thing is, the others, your friends must back us up, it's got to be done so that Hakim can't interfere.'

He had recovered his cool. He said, 'Explain what you're talking about.'

'There's an official leave-taking in the Little Talar tomorrow at nine. For that, Hakim has to have me there, I'm his warranty for legitimacy till he can do without me. He won't publish

Habib's death' – the break in her voice was scarcely perceptible – 'until you've all gone. At the ceremony I shall say that I'm going to London and then to Denmark to ratify the contracts for a regular supply of icebergs for our irrigation. You've got to arrange it so that Sir Edwin and Gurling and the others back me up, it's got to be a *fait accompli* and you've got to stay with me so that Hakim can't stop me. Can you do it?'

'Yes. Either that or something else, I could take you now to our embassy and ask for asylum and get you away from there.'

'You're no politician, my friend. Your embassy will know by now who counts here, who will be dishing out the oil and the orders and the industrial contracts, who it pays to love. They'd find a hundred reasons why they couldn't do it. I'm a Far princess or I'm a terrorist with an Interpol record, whichever the aspect General Hakim asks his friends to look at.'

When he had opened the door and seen that there were no guards and nobody else in the corridor, and she was ready to go, Israel, impelled as so often by the fear of being someone's fool said,

'There's a thing, Azizeh . . . did you love your brother?'

She said, 'We shared a happy childhood. It always counts. But it's not the point is it?'

'I don't know.'

'Then take it from me.'

Israel did not say, as they parted, 'Take care,' or 'Be careful' or any of those things. With her it would have been . . . inappropriate. He shut the door after her and stood by it wondering whether to begin with Curran or Gurling. But Curran was only present by way of a commercially motivated courtesy to a very valuable client; and in any case, John Gurling was the man to talk to the old boy.

He stepped into the corridor and locked his door; Azizeh had vanished and there was a cool night air off the Atlantic from an open window. He wondered, as he made for Gurling's room, why he had locked his door and realized that it was just the sense of being watched and threatened which Azizeh carried with her: was she in danger or did she only enjoy believing that she was? Had Hakim 'murdered' Habib, or had Habib died in battle? Was Azizeh a revolutionary or just one of nature's conspirators?

Gurling was not in his room. In David Gough's he found David and Jock Drummond with a bottle of whisky between them. He poured himself a drink and said, 'Where's John?'

'With Hakim,' Jock said and, 'I don't like that man. John was invited to a midnight orgy or something.'

Both men were in pyjamas. Israel said, 'Will he be long? It's serious.'

David, at the table by the window which was open and through which came the quiet wash of the sea on the beach, his small hands very white against the amber of the whisky as he refilled his own glass and Jock's, said, 'There's a rumour Habib's dead.'

Drummond said, 'Last time I saw him he was leading that column west. Once I had got my chaps working on the big break, I went back to see how the other work parties were getting on. Then I went back to the reservoir to check that the water was flowing again; and from there to here.'

Israel, still standing, his whisky undrunk, said, 'It's no rumour. Habib's dead. Hakim had him killed . . .'

Together they said, 'How d'you know?' and he told them about Azizeh's call and what she had told him, realizing as he did so that he had committed himself uncritically to her version of events. Half way through that account he was aware of David's eyes on him; and of the amusement in those eyes. He had been talking very excitedly and with too much feeling. He flushed, hesitated and when he resumed talking did so with deliberate restraint.

Jock said, 'It could be true. John should be told at once.'

'You can't barge into Hakim's private party,' David said.

'You could send a note in,' Jock said; and Israel, 'I'll go and write it now.'

The Regent received John Gurling in the Ruler's private office. Perhaps the associations of the place and the influence of his great office had done something to improve his manners. He said, 'Mr Gurling, I apologize for asking you here to talk business at this late hour.'

'I can work round the clock when I have to, excellency.'

'Of course. You are, in a sense – how do you say? – one of us. You leave tomorrow and I, too, must leave for the south-eastern front to finish the mopping-up which . . . ah, but I forget, you have not heard our most sorrowful news. But please sit down, Mr Gurling. There is whisky there, ice and glasses. You will consent to help yourself. I myself do not drink spirits or wines.'

Gurling did not much want a drink but there was a quality in the general's manner – complacency, insolvence? – which made him drop a single icecube into a tumbler with deliberation and then half-fill the glass with whisky. He said,

'Our doctors are now telling us that after a certain age, whisky expands the arteries. I daresay yours don't need expanding. You said you had sad news?'

Hakim sat himself in the Ruler's chair and said, 'Prince Habib is dead, killed in action.'

'I'm extremely sorry to hear it. There's no doubt about it?'

'None, alas.' The general spread his hands in a gesture of resignation and continued, 'The body has been identified, coffined and is being brought to Farzar for burial in the Far mausoleum. Our loss is a terrible one.'

'Terrible. May I offer my condolences? He will be . . . greatly missed.'

Death, Gurling was thinking, is an anticlimax. Habib had been one of the most vividly alive and one of the most agreeable, as well as one of the ablest, men he had ever met; he was dead and there was no more to say about it than these threadbare banalities.

General Hakim bowed, sighed and said, 'It seemed to me that you should know although the news is not yet public. For the moment it is a burden which I carry with the help of the Council only. You should also know, for it concerns you, that his work will go on.'

'The iceberg enterprise?'

'Precisely – irrigation, land reclamation, transformation of the desert into farmland, all that his highness planned. The next step is already projected and I am expecting – but more of that later. From the point of view of your house, Mr Gurling, there will be only one difference: you will be doing business not with Habib Shah but with me. In the matter of – shall we say amenity? – you will be a loser; but I hope that you will not find me less businesslike.'

'You will forgive me, general, but since we're talking business I must understand the position. As commander-in-chief . . .'

Hakim raised a lean, brown hand; on the middle finger he wore a heavy gold ring set with a single emerald. He said,

'For some time to come the army will be the government. I don't like it but there is no alternative and I must bear that burden, also. My regency was ratified in council one hour before we had the pleasure of entertaining you to dinner.

'Then perhaps I may be the first to congratulate your excellency?'

'Ah, Mr Gurling, but is it, I ask myself, a matter for congratulation? As a simple soldier my responsibilities were heavy but my duty always clear. Will it be so now, I wonder? But when the call comes, we do what we have to do.'

The telephone on his desk buzzed; he listened a moment and said a brief word in Farsi and, covering the mouthpiece with his hand,

'Mr Gurling, I know it is past midnight and you may be tired. But we are, as the French ambassador said to me this evening, *en pleine crise.* There is a gentleman here whom I would like you to meet. It is possible that he will become an important colleague in our great enterprise. Can you bear to prolong our session for half an hour?'

'I am at your service, excellency.'

Hakim spoke into the telephone. Gurling, watching him, was remembering that when Habib Shah had first called on him, had seduced Caroline Bartrum now dowager Shahbanu, and soon to be the mother of Habib's heir; had done that boyish trick with the icecube, had clowned his way into this same 'great enterprise' as if seriousness of purpose was an impertinence only tolerable if covered by frivolousness of manner, it was this crafty and civil ruffian's name he borrowed to cover his incognito. There had been as much augury as irony in that: in the world as it was and would increasingly be, it was General Hakim and not Prince Habib who belonged in that chair across the Ruler's desk.

In the course of his work Gurling had met a fair sample of the world's leading politicians and of all of them respected only the old peasant in Peking. This chap facing him was of the stuff the others, elected or self-imposed, were made of; would know how to do business with his fellow-rogues and scapegoats for the business of their constituents, who now controlled the two great powers; with the lamentable rulers of the Arab states so rich in oil and poor in sense. He would know how to shake his fist at the Jews above the table, and do a deal with them under it; and how to crush the idealism out of the revolution while using its enormous energy. He would know how to fool enough of the people enough of the time to avoid the lynching which, in the long run, his own nature, his own fears, his own ignorance must lead him to deserve.

The new colleague was shown in by one of the general's aides: he was a stocky, forty-year-old Japanese who gave a curious impression of solid mass. His name was Hasegawa. He accepted whisky with a grinning hiss; but did not drink it. Hakim himself poured the drink, marking the visitor's importance by completely filling up the tumbler. He followed up the introduction and civilities by saying,

'Mr Hasegawa's principal interests are in cotton. He is interested in the potentialities of our land, in the fertility which our irrigation enterprise will create. He thinks it possible that we shall be able to grow for him the very large amounts of cotton which he requires for his mills in Japan.'

So much for Habib's dream of a people's cornucopia. Gurling knew nothing about cotton-growing; he had a vision of toiling blacks in Dixieland; he said the first thing that came to mind,

'Won't you have labour problems, Mr Hasegawa?'

Mr Hasegawa smiled; he had strong, square teeth and to Gurling it seemed that they were more numerous than is normal. Speaking good English with an American accent Mr Hasegawa said,

'No, Mr Gurling, no problems: a few of our own skilled men; and a lot of machines.'

With the map of the whole area round the Curzon Depression before them they talked until long after one. The Japanese asked questions; Gurling answered them and in the course of their exchange conceived a great respect for Hasegawa's abilities.

While they talked Hakim's aides came and went with papers, whispered messages; but Gurling was certain that the Regent missed nothing of what was passing between his two visitors. From time to time there was a question which Gurling could not answer; he noted it down. Just before one an aide came in with a sealed letter which he gave to Hakim while keeping his eyes on Gurling. Hakim handed the letter across the desk saying, 'For you, Mr Gurling.' Gurling said, 'Excuse me, gentlemen,' and opened the letter which was in Israel's handwriting. He read it, keeping his face expressionless, refolded it, put it in his pocket and said,

'Sorry for that. It could have been important.'

The inquest continued: by the time Hasegawa announced that he had no more questions Gurling's list of unanswered ones to be investigated back in London was a long one. Gurling, rising, swallowing a yawn and tapping his notebook with a pencil said, 'In addition to all this there'll be some fairly complex and delicate negotiations with the Danes and with the admiralty division of the United Nations.'

'My companies are not concerned in those,' Hasegawa said.

'Agreed, excepting that the terms of any treaty between your group and his excellency's government has a bearing on the terms my company can afford to make with the Danish government. Curran and I have, as it happens, a preliminary meeting with their representatives one hour after we reach London tomorrow. Your excellency, may I suggest that you should have a representative or negotiator to sit in at all our meetings in London for the next few weeks?'

Hakim said, 'A valuable suggestion, Mr Gurling.'

'Then allow me to make another: Her highness princess Azizeh is a trained economist and a woman for whose quickness and ability my colleagues and I have conceived very considerable respect. She has been concerned with the whole enterprise and very much in her brother's confidence from the start. If you ask her to act for you with us in London we shall be delighted; it will be a tribute to . . .'

Mr Hasegawa had risen; he smiled, bowed several times, said,

'Permit me to interrupt you, sir. This business does not concern me. If you will allow me, I shall say goodnight.' He bowed again, once to Gurling, twice to Hakim. As soon as the door closed behind him Hakim said, with a note implying resignation to weariness in his voice, 'Let me see, you were saying, Mr Gurling . . .?'

'That the appointment I suggest would be a tribute to his late highness and . . . here, excellency, I am aware that I may be taking perhaps too much liberty, a public demonstration that Her highness is at one with you in the new government.'

Hakim had taken up a pen and seemed to be only half concealing the fact that he was now reading one of the papers in front of him. He raised his eyes very briefly to say, 'Only a foolish man refuses to listen to well-meant advice from a friend, Mr Gurling, thank you again. You will send the new draft contracts to my secretariat. We shall meet briefly at the formal leave-taking in the morning. Good night to you.'

On his way to his room Gurling looked into Gough's. Jock Drummond had gone to his own room but Israel was again there. Gurling said, 'I've done what I can,' and told them briefly of his suggestion, adding, 'It was probably a mistake. I took your plea, her version of the state of affairs, at their face value. If you've led me into making a bloody fool of myself . . .'

'Will it be all right?' Israel interrupted.

'I don't know. I got snubbed for my interference. I'm going to bed. Just one thing, Izzy, try to remember we're in business and you know what that means. Our client is this country's government. Who and what that government is, is none of our business. Good night.'

David said, 'It's all right. The old man's tired.'

Israel said, 'I'd better let you get some sleep.'

'Just before you go, Izzy – I'm taking three weeks leave. What would you say if I changed my mind and went to see Gertrud playing lady of the manor? I find her letter has made me curious, and it happens I've nothing better to do.'

'Say? I shouldn't say anything. It's no business of mine. Good night, David.'

Back in his room Israel sat on his bed and took his guitar on his knees. Very lightly he touched the strings, made them whisper notes. He could not play, for fear of disturbing his neighbours. He sat there, nursing the guitar, as if waiting for something, until with the pale flush of dawn the tannoy system in the minarets of the Great Mosque carried the muezzin's high-pitched chant all over the city in the call to prayer.

Sixteen

The moment he was back in London Israel's connection with the iceberg enterprise ended. He returned to his own firm within the Group, to the development work on his long-term project, a rotary [i/c] engine fuelled with liquified sewage gases; to the third chapter of his new mathematical treatise, *Purpose and Chance*; to working on a concerto for six guitars.

When, on returning to his house after the day's work, he found Azizeh there or expected, he was happy; his happiness was not serenity, not any kind of calm state, it was a passion, a fever, a drunkenness. With hands and mouth and penis and every square millimetre of his skin he indulged in her body, explored, adored, rejoiced in her body. She took her pleasure in him as he in her and when she said, 'This we share perfectly,' the reservation that was implied did not trouble him until the bad days, the days when she was not there, not expected.

From Gurling he heard that her work on the committees was done well, with conscience as well as skill. Gurling said, 'It's a curious situation. Hakim has every confidence in her work but she's absolutely barred from returning to Farzar.' But the work did not tie her, she would stay one night, three nights, rarely a whole week, but he never knew when he would be alone in their big bed, or when she would be there to share it, their only common domain. Of the future he refused to think: he was afraid of his own addiction to her as well as of his love. When he told her that he loved her she sighed, made some impatient movement; only once did he let himself be driven to ask her if she loved him – she had been absent for ten days. She said, 'I don't know what the word means.' He was sad and hurt but began to consider what it did mean and so said no more.

Ike disliked her, becoming silent in her presence and sulky. About that she said, 'He's very pretty, Izzy. I suppose he takes after your wife.' At that he tried to believe, for an hour or two, that she was jealous of Gertrud, knowing perfectly well that it wasn't so. A day came, after Ike had burst into tears when brought into the room where they were sitting and talking, when she said, 'Izzy, I'm sorry, it's my fault, the fact is I find children a terrible bore and Ike knows it.'

Her absences were wretchedness not merely because he was deprived of her but because of what he knew her to be doing, though only vaguely and in general terms because she did not talk about it enough to enable him to form any clear idea of her activities. As he understood it, and he knew that he might be mistaken, she was off under one of half a dozen different identities – she had once shown him, laughing, insisting that it shocked him, her collection of passports – to Beirut, Tripoli, Cairo, Paris, Damascus, to political or plain conspiratorial meetings of God knew what factions, terrorist groups, splinter parties, militant wings of respectable parties . . . any movement she thought she could use against Hakim. It was not all pride of blood, not all ambition; her revolutionary ardour was as real as her ardour in bed. She hated Hakim for what he was doing to Habib's plans, to the real 'revolution', to 'the people'. But what she did was futile: Israel knew, with a kind of mortal certainty, that the moment she became a danger to Hakim, or even a serious nuisance, one of the Regent's agents would get her, dispose of her. Her revolutionary friends, doubtless fervent in the cause, pure in heart, ardent for justice, were bunglers and amateurs; Hakim's agents, many of them men trained and taught by Mashadi, but who now had a master who was more to their taste, were professionals, needing neither a cause nor hashish, but only law, orders and pay. Not Azizeh but Hakim was the *real*-politician, with his cotton-fields watered by icebergs, his 'pacification' of the Arab shepherds with tanks and divebombers making room for irrigation lines and Mr Hasegawa's tractors; and with his grand projects for motorways, new industrial settlements, steel mills, an airline . . . Israel remembered Professor Tajerbashi's witticism – 'We are so progressive we even have pollution.'

They made only one social call together: no question, when she was with him, of going out or having people in, of allowing any attenuation of their pleasure in each other. But there had to be that one exception: a visit to Caroline would be expected of them; and in any case they were both curious. If there was not much more than that in it, only a modicum of sympathy for her loss, it was because she had cast herself in a grand role; there were enlightening paragraphs in the papers: the Princess Caroline this, the Princess Caroline that – the tragic young royal widow and mother of an heir. *Paris-Match* filled a couple of pages with the royal baby who was also, according to an *Oggi* feature, one of the six richest human beings now living.

What helped to keep Caroline in the news was the ambiguity of the baby's situation: Hakim was still playing the regency game and it was assumed and yet scarcely believed that at any moment now the infant prince would return to his country and people, to learn how, in due course, to rule in the liberal but firm spirit of his father. Following the *Oggi* exposures, one of the English Sunday papers with a research-and-writing team with a good record of discovering the real facts of a case, went into the child's financial position. In London, Paris and Zurich – it seemed that Habib had doubted the stability of the United States – Habib had provided for his wife, independently, a matter of fifteen million dollars; and for his heir, with the mother as trustee, something like sixty million.

As her London house Caroline had bought a 'place' which had once been a royal lodge. It stood in a high-walled garden which had been carved out of Richmond Park. Her servants were all Farzari, the major-domo being a stately old man with white hair and a solemn manner: as Israel said later, 'He isn't real, of course; probably Peter Sellers.' He led them into a great salon decorated and furnished in strictly Persian style – a state apartment rather than a room for living in. Bowing them in, the major-domo said, 'Her Highness the Shahbanu wishes me to say that she will join Your Highness and Mr Mendes in a few minutes.'

They went to the windows and looked out into the garden; it was a small park of lawns, fine trees now passing their prime for Repton had planted them, and a small lake fed by a stream. A number of figures peopled this landscape and at a first, careless glance Azizeh said, 'Gardeners.'

'In uniform, carrying staves, and leading Alsatians? Odd sort of gardeners.'

They saw three of these men, each with his staff and his dog, and since each was obviously patrolling a measured extent of wall, there were probably others out of sight. Israel and Azizeh were so taken up with this strange spectacle that they were startled when Caroline's voice, but curiously measured and controlled, said, 'How kind of you to come and see me.'

She looked very handsome but pale, strained and not friendly, in a long, close-fitting black dress and, by way of jewellery, nothing but a jet seal-ring which had belonged to Habib. She had advanced only one third of the length of the room and halted; it was quite clearly her intention that they should advance to her, not she to them. Israel obligingly complied and her manner was so regal that he only just prevented himself from making a low bow. Caroline did not offer her hand. He asked after her health and that of the boy. She said, 'Thank you, we are well. Azizeh, you would probably like to see your nephew; I have asked Nanny to bring him to us in a few minutes.'

'Good,' Azizeh, her own manner falsified by Caroline's, said, 'I should like to see him. You're not looking well, Caroline. Too pale and thin. You should eat more. We've been watching your guards. What's the idea?'

'The idea? Surely that's obvious. I'm responsible for our country's ruler. He has as many enemies as his father had.' She said this coolly but then suddenly became excited; her face flushed, her eyes glittered and she began to speak much faster and less carefully, saying, 'The disgraceful thing is that I'm not allowed by the English police to arm them properly. I wrote to the Home Secretary about it but his answer was most unsatisfactory. I'd write to Her Majesty but I'm afraid to embarrass her. Now I've asked his excellency to make this house a part of our embassy which will give us extra-territorial rights, of course, and I shall then arm our guards.'

Israel was distressed by her excited manner and her strangely unreal persona. He said, 'But Caroline, who are these men? I mean did you recruit them at a Labour exchange or something?' He spoke gently, with the merest touch of mockery, but she said, 'Why should you treat it as a matter for laughing? It was quite simple, the guards are from a security agency, of course.'

Now he was puzzled by this mixture of near-hysteria and common sense. Azizeh, at last quitting the window and coming towards them, said, 'These enemies you're afraid of . . .'

'You should know, Azizeh.'

'My dear, even my most extremist one-time friends didn't murder babies for no reason.'

'No reason? Why was my husband killed? Do you think I believe the official version? And why has his excellency . . .?'

'*Which* excellency?'

'I'm speaking, of course, of the Regent Abdul Aziz Hakim.'

Azizeh was very pale and her eyes were unnaturally brilliant. She said, 'I see. You were saying?'

'Why has he warned me?'

'Against me?'

'I said no such thing.'

Israel intervened, making his tone as conversational as possible, saying,

'Apropos, what *are* your arrangements with him, with Hakim? What terms are you on with him?'

'I don't understand you. Excellent terms, of course. We're co-trustees for Mahomet Habib's heritage. While I nurse my son's fortune Hakim nurses his kingdom. In a few months I shall be taking him back to our own country, but a regency will be necessary for many years and Hakim is an able and honourable man.'

Azizeh approached very close to her sister-in-law until their noses were only an inch or two apart. Her face was so distorted by the anger she could no longer control that Israel expected Caroline to fall back. But she stood her ground. Azizeh said,

'You fool! The man you keep calling *excellency* in that ridiculous way is Habib's murderer. Do you seriously believe that Turkish swine will ever give up his power for that child or give way to anything but brute force?'

With maddening calm and an expression of distaste, as if Azizeh had bad breath, Caroline stepped back a pace and said,

'That's a monstrous thing to say; but of course you're bound to say it,' and at that moment, as if the whole comedy had been put together by a hack dramatist, the door was opened and the nurse came in carrying Caroline's son. Caroline turned and took the child into her own arms. The nurse said, 'The hand under the head, please, Your Highness,' and Caroline, 'Thank you, Nanny. That will do. Come back in five minutes.'

To Israel even the dialogue seemed curiously thin and unreal. Caroline in her role had imposed the standards of the old musical comedy stage on everyone; how could she not who was living in Ruritania? She ought now to sing a lullaby for the infant prince. But at least the interruption had given them time to get their tempers in hand. Azizeh said, 'He's like his father.' Israel supposed she was relying on the bright blue, quickly moving, apparently curious eyes, and the very dark, almost black hair. Caroline said, 'His father wanted him to be fair. But a blond prince of the house of Far would look rather odd, don't you think?'

Again Israel was disconcerted; for as she spoke tears of which she seemed unconscious were running down her cheeks and ruining her careful makeup. The nurse returned and took the boy from her and left them and then, final surprise, the Caroline Bartrum they had known said, 'Look Azizeh, I was going to offer you tea or drinks, but frankly I don't think it a good idea, do you?'

Azizeh, at her own request, drove the car back to Regent's Park. Neither of them spoke at first. Then, the car stationary at a red light, Azizeh said, 'Stupid bitch. Nothing exasperates me more than wilful blindness . . .'

Israel said, 'If it's a fact that Hakim had your brother killed . . .'

'What d'you mean, *if* . . .?'

'All right, he did. You were bound to tell her.'

'Was I? Now I'm not so sure. I lost my temper. She's probably right. She has to try to do what she has to do, and to do it she has to come to terms, in her own mind at least, with Hakim.'

A couple of days later Israel lunched with Gurling at Gurling's club and told him about that call on Caroline. He said,

'She seems to be in some cloud-cuckoo land, all that common sense she always had . . . gone.'

'Think so?' Gurling said. He bit into a stalk of celery, gave it up, said, 'Why the hell can't one get decent celery nowadays?' and, 'She still consults me about business, you know.'

'Well, that's sensible, anyway.'

'Is it? She's twice as shrewd as I am.'

'Come off it, John.'

Gurling looked at him, but absently. He said, 'You've read,

in the *Times* business pages, the names of the companies Hakim's letting in to get the place really going . . . steel, aluminium, plastics and so forth . . .'

'I saw something of the kind. I didn't pay attention.'

'She's bought the boy into all of them. Sixty or seventy million, his and hers, is still a fairish sum. I think you'll see Prince Mahomet Habib becoming a very big, and in some cases, a majority shareholder in his country's industries. Caroline was remarkably careful, had brokers operating in London, Paris, New York, Tokyo, Berlin and Zurich. Even so, it pushed prices up a bit too much, and for weeks the brokers all over the place were looking at their Dow Jones and wondering where the money was coming from. Habib had been quietly buying gold for years. It seems some metalurgist told him there are only about ten years' supply left in the ground and you know what consumption in the electronics industry is. His average gain was about ninety-eight per cent. The point is there were no sales of stock to account for this big buying. Suppose she keeps ploughing back into the same companies, imagine the size of the boy's holdings in, say, ten, fifteen years.'

'I don't believe I'd've thought of that way,' Israel said.

'Nor did I. Caroline did.'

A silence and then Gurling said, 'Proprietor-prince. Coffee?'

'Please.'

'Downstairs, as usual. Make your way down, you know where it is, while I settle for our lunch.'

On their way through the room to the desk and the door, Gurling said, 'There are some people, women as well as men, who have a tropism for the real centres of power,' and 'By the way, you saw we've docked our second iceberg?'

David Gough telephoned:

'Izzy, I'd like to see you.'

'And I you. How was Gertrud?'

'It's about her I want to have a talk.'

'Can you come to dinner tonight? Just the two of us?'

Had Azizeh been at home Israel would have proposed lunch at a restaurant.

David arrived at half past seven while Israel was up in the nursery being read to by Ike: 'Ant lived with a great friend of his who was a bee. Ant and Bee lived in a Cup. The Cup made a very nice home. Now one day someone Bee and Ant knew asked Ant and Bee to go for a ride on his back. He was a Dog . . .' Ike was passing the stage of reading only the three-letter words in red and being helped out with the rest, but still had to be checked for guessing. Israel interrupted the reading and took Ike down to meet David. Without thinking he slipped the little book into his pocket.

David said, 'He's very like her. I can't see much of you.'

'It's the old Graf, her father, he's really like,' Israel said, 'there's a portrait of him at the age of five by a man called Bruchner in the smoking-room at . . .'

'I've seen it. You're right, the likeness is uncanny. Let's hope he has your brains.'

Ike said, 'Daddy, can I have a drink too, please?'

'Certainly. I'm sorry I forgot.'

Israel gave him a few drops of brown sherry diluted with sodawater, in a liqueur glass. David clinked glasses with him and then with Israel, which made Ike laugh. Nanny arrived to take him upstairs again:

'Say goodnight to Mr Gough.'

'Goodnight Mr Gough.'

'Goodnight Ike.'

Over a second drink David said, 'Azizeh away?'

'How did you know she was living here?'

'Office gossip.'

'Oh God. Yes, she's away.'

They went in to dinner; Israel said, 'I know you don't like eating. I've got an iced soup, asparagus, a mousse of ham and chicken. All cold so we can serve ourselves. All right?'

'My dear chap . . .'

Over the iced soup of yoghourt, cucumber and mint, Israel said,

'Tell me about Gertrud.'

'She's well and . . . different.'

Instead of talking about her David began to talk about her place.

'The woods are magnificent but they're not being properly managed and nor's the game. The forester is eighty and hasn't taken in a new idea for half a century. His younger brother, the head gamekeeper, is seventy-six, and quite as bad. Gertrud could treble her income from those two things and improve them at the same time.'

Israel, removing the soup-plates and serving a big dish of asparagus said, 'I didn't know you knew about such things.'

'Izzy . . . where the hell d'you get asparagus like this? You know as well as I do that a trained technician with an inquiring mind can look at any technical problem with more intelligence and more references than a peasant. And I've been doing some reading. It's the same story all over her property: you know, it's not till you look at farming in the remoter parts of Germany and France that you realize how advanced our own is. If our industrialists were half the men our farmers are, we'd be head of the league.'

The subject led them to a digression. There had been an article in *The Times* business news about the cotton-growing treaty between the government in Farzar and the Hasegawa group of textile companies, and Israel spoke, with an indignation echoing Azizeh's bitterness, of Hakim's betrayal of Habib's dream. David listened, smiling, and then he said,

'Ah, but Hakim's right. He's a brute bastard of a Turk and maybe that's why he's right. The revenue will be bigger, much bigger, than under our friend's régime. You know, that idea of turning shepherds into farmers and letting them manage their own land themselves . . .' He shrugged.

Israel said, 'Hakim's not turning them into farmers but into corpses.'

'The Russian method – Tsarist or Bolshevik it's all the same – when they expanded east and south.'

'Hardly an explanation. Have some more asparagus and go on with what you were telling me.'

'It's the usual thing – combining a lot of small farms into one big one, viable units in modern terms; mechanization, crop modernization to suit the markets, developing industrial farming methods . . . they've still got hens running about the yards picking up a living. Well, simply bringing the farming up to date. Rents ought to be much higher but that depends on getting more out of the place.'

Israel, staring at David, forgetting his mousse, mechanically offering the salad bowl, said, 'You sound like Gertrud's business manager.'

Coolly, helping himself to the salad, David said, 'If I could eat here every day I could get to like eating. It might come to something of that kind, she certainly needs a man who has some business sense. For one thing her capital, the money you settled on her, should be invested in the place. The villages need a rehousing plan, long-term of course; sewers, but their own, so that the sewage can be processed as fertilizer . . . it's obvious enough, to people like us.'

'Like you, perhaps. It wouldn't've occurred to me. David, are you trying to tell me, with proper delicacy, you're going to marry Gertrud?'

David took a long drink from his glass, said, 'How I envy you your cellar, may I help myself?' refilled his glass and went on, 'She did break her promise and ask me to marry her.'

'And you said yes?'

Israel put a hand into a pocket for a handkerchief and found the little *Ant and Bee* book; he pulled it out, frowning, wondering what it was. He put it on the table and idly flicked it open: he read, 'They wanted to go and live with a spider friend who lived in a Web.' He had read somewhere that after copulation the female spider, her end attained, eats the male. Oh, sublime economy and essence of conservation! David was saying,

'Let's say I want to marry the whole place.'

'Of course. Does she know that?'

'I'm always absolutely honest with women, Izzy. With men it would be absurd. But with women it's the only good way.'

'What about your own work?'

'D'you know a man named Von Anklam?'

'The North German shipbuilding consortium?'

'That's the bloke . . . I met him at Gertrud's, a dinner party for the local brass. Had an interesting offer from him. Their yards aren't impossibly far. Would you be inclined to divorce Gertrud if we asked you to?'

'I'd be inclined to divorce Gertrud on almost any terms.'

David laughed. He said, 'Remember you are talking of the woman I love,' and it crossed Israel's mind that it wasn't a question of the male spider but of a hornet in the web. He said, 'There would have to be no question of her having Ike.'

'I'd no idea you were so strongly attached to the boy.'

'That's my business, David. I shouldn't have thought you were in a position to have any ideas of any kind about it. The point is I will not have him brought up by Gertrud.'

'I see that my lover's feelings are not to be spared.'

To hide his disgust Israel went to the sideboard for another bottle of wine. David was saying, 'Mind you, I'm sure you're right and I don't think there'll be any trouble about that if you wouldn't object to us having him for a week or two now and again.'

Remembering that likeness between the child and the portrait Israel said, 'We'll leave that for the future but I must have complete control.'

'I think she'll agree.'

Israel rose and removed the plates, placed clean ones and a

dish of fruit on the table and a bottle of Sauterne in a cooler. He said,

'You've surprised me, David.'

'I've surprised myself. It was odd to discover that I could.'

Azizeh came home the next day: she was in Israel's workroom when he came in that evening, sitting in an armchair with her legs over the arm, smoking a thin cigarette of hemp, and reading the typescript of his book. She put it down when he came in, saying,

'It's mortifying that you can write what I can't make head or tail of.'

'And what d'you make of that mortifying fact?' he asked, trying to match her casualness, his heart beating fast with excitement.

'That what I can't understand can't be important,' she said and jumped up to be taken in his arms and kissed. He held her face between his hands and studied it with intensity, gently pushing the hair off her forehead and temples, running a finger lightly down the side of her nose. He said, 'You look tired.'

'Thank you for nothing. It's only the curse.'

'Oh, hell.'

'Your concupiscence is excessive.'

'My what?'

'Concupiscence, a perfectly good word meaning sexual appetite.'

Neither then, nor at dinner, nor afterwards while watching a television play, a silly piece but their own running critical comment amused them, did he say anything about David's news. They were in bed before he told her about it. She was not very interested; he had not expected that she would be, nothing which did not concern her closely ever held her attention. There was a long silence between them but neither was inclined to sleep. At last Israel said,

'I shall be free, as they say. Would you like to marry me?'

She switched on the light again and pushed herself upright on one elbow so that she could look down into his face and said,

'My dear, have you gone crazy?'

'I don't think so. I have always understood that women are offended if one doesn't offer marriage when one's in a position to do so. It was just an idea.'

'Well, it was a rotten one. Me, marry . . . can you imagine it? It isn't as if you didn't know what I feel about that kind of thing.'

'Forget it. Our silence was becoming oppressive; it was just something to say.'

The nonsense of all this was that although Israel kept his feelings out of his voice he was hurt, as if he and not the institution of marriage had been despised. Azizeh kept the light on and continued to study his face as, earlier that evening, he had studied hers. Still leaving the light on she lay back and said,

'I want you to do something for me.'

'Whatever you like.'

'You aren't going to like it.'

'Don't beat about the bush.'

'All right. I want you to go to Farzar for me. It's not only that I can't go, Hakim would have me shot. By the way, he sent me a cheque which fixes my rating in the Civil Service: grade two. But it's something you can do and I can't.'

'You'd better explain.'

'There's a man called Abdul Saadi, it's not his real name but never mind that. We want him out of the country. It's been very difficult since Hakim took over for any Farzari to get a passport. If Saadi applied for one he'd be very thoroughly gone into and he can't take that risk. There are two reasons for getting him out. He's very badly needed at our headquarters in Paris; and if he stays too long in Farzar events will catch up with him, events he's been organizing there, and he'll be blown, taken, tortured and shot.'

'What has all this to do with me, Azizeh? It was understood that I don't get mixed up in your . . . political business.'

'You won't be. Listen, it's natural that you should want to see how your work for the country is working out, so as you're taking a holiday, you go there. You'll put up at the Hilton and hire a car. Then you'll tell the hall porter that you want a man to act as courier, driver, interpreter, general manservant. That man will be Saadi. You'll find him so satisfactory that you'll want to keep him, bring him to England as a servant. You apply to the Ministry of Police for a permit to take him with you for six months and offer to pay the exit licence, it's fifty pounds which is nothing to you. There'll be no difficulties and, in those conditions, no inquest. You'll get the permit and bring him here and that's all, you'll never even see the man again.'

He knew at once that he ought to refuse; not simply because he could at once see several flaws in the plan but on general principles. Anything which smacked of conspiracy he found distasteful; he also found it futile, he had a very strong feeling inherited from the Jewish past that the strong men in power are in the short run absolutely certain to win. Had he said what he thought, Azizeh would have been reminded of Mashadi. It is probable that if her reaction to his diffident suggestion of marriage had not been what it was, and had it not hurt him though he had known perfectly well what it was bound to be, he would have refused; or at least argued and then insisted on remaking the whole plan himself. As it was he said,

'Very well. When do you want me to go?'

His tone must have offended her because she only replied briskly, as if he were some kind of subordinate, 'As soon as possible.'

'On Wednesday, then.'

His unquestioning compliance forced her to relent and she said,

'You're unbelievably good to me, Izzy.'

Was there a faint note of mockery in her voice? It did not seem to him that she had said it with much conviction; she was preoccupied with thoughts which his own ban prevented her from sharing. Was he doing to her what he had done to Gertrud?

He put up at the Hilton and in a mood of indifference a little enlivened by curiosity as to what would happen, carried out his instructions: he hired a car and asked the head porter to find him a dragoman, offering a high wage. He became less contemptuous of the organization of this nonsense when the porter sent him four candidates for interview and driving test. How the thing was managed he neither knew nor cared. As it happened he would have chosen Saadi had the business been genuine. Saadi was an attractive man of about thirty with a fair skin, a Greek nose and curious red lights in his black hair. His English was good, his driving excellent if a little too dashing, and although his clothes were shabby he was clean and neat in his person. It would be easy enough to spend a couple of weeks in this man's company: he was presumably some kind of political criminal but Israel had never belonged in his heart to any kind of establishment and he did not mind that. The unequal struggle between the hoodlums in power and those seeking to oust them and take their place was not a matter any educated man with serious concern could afford to spend spirit on.

They would now have to go through the comedy of establishing the bona fides of the operation. They drove to Abbas Bay where a new iceberg, number three, had just been docked in the Dragon-tree gut. It was not quite as big as Icecube had been; and its shape must, Israel thought, have made it awkward to handle. He was received by the Farzari engineer in charge with a mixture of deference and enthusiasm, soon discovered that the man was a technician who knew and respected his work, and conceived some respect for General Hakim who, clearly was not making the mistake of putting military-political thugs in charge of big enterprises. He was introduced to the young Danish naval officer who had been appointed for three years to the job which Harland had pioneered, and who talked of a new development which Gurling was investigating – using explosives to break off icebergs of manageable shape. He read the minutes of the desk study preceding the feasibility study; it was labelled 'Caesarean'. He also met the new Welsh engineer officer and talked with him for two hours and promised to examine the practical possibilities of two theoretical improvements to the iceberg engines which the young man had worked out on paper. Israel began to enjoy this holiday.

From Abbas Bay Saadi drove him to the Curzon Depression, keeping as near as possible to the pipeline. Their route swarmed with military and police patrols and was continuously overflown by observation helicopters. Seven times between Abbas Bay and the Depression they were stopped, their papers examined with laborious care, and the car and luggage searched. One patrol officer turned out to be familiar with Israel's name and work and instead of being merely what the French call 'correct' was forthcoming. He apologized for the trouble he was causing and explained that they were not only keeping a general watch against 'Omari sabotage but looking for a Palestinian terrorist known as 'Camal X'. 'Mister, it is looking for a needle in grass. We do not even know his face.'

At the Curzon Depression which was rapidly turning into a great shallow lake from which water was pumped to the irrigation grid, there was no inn or guesthouse. But a small government guest bungalow had been included in the complex of buildings round one segment of the Wilhelm Crater and Israel had been invited by the new Department of the Environment to make use of it.

On the day after his arrival there he walked the complete circuit of the Crater, though in places the going was difficult, leaving Saadi at the guest bungalow; for he did not want company, did not want to talk or be talked to and perhaps to be told things he had no wish to know: he had conceived the suspicion that Saadi was Camal X and the idea had become a nagging worry.

The Crater was now a lake. He had played a major part in bringing the water to this place yet he could not make the connection between that Greenland iceberg and this great body of water, so natural did it look and such a transformation had it wrought. Already a faint fringe of green was appearing round the inner lip of the Crater where wind-borne and bird-borne seeds long dormant were germinating and the young trees planted by the administration showing leaf. Already, as poor Leuwenhoek had foreseen, great numbers of wild fowl were using the water, and it was said that a small flock of flamingoes had been sighted. In his last report before his death Leuwenhoek had suggested stocking the water with certain plants and with some species of fish, notably rainbow trout, and some species of fresh-water shrimps. As for insects, the lake would attract them, so that in time the water would, with help, create its own ecological system. The Dutchman's suggestions had been carried out with expert help from American ecologists and a score of times that day Israel saw fish rising. There were already one or two sailing dinghies on the water, the property of technical and administration staff at the pumping and hydroelectric stations.

On the following day Israel followed, on foot, the channel down which water from the Crater cascaded to the turbines which turned the generators. The music of water, too, he and his friends had added to this barren and silent place, and the rainbows playing in its mist of spray. But for the shadow cast by Saadi, Israel would have been happy that day. The two engineers on duty at the hydroelectric station gave him lunch and then he went on down, noting leaf and flower conjured out of the crumbling rock by the spume of the cascade, to the lower level in the Depression where, again, Arctic water was bringing a lunar landscape alive, touching it with a haze, a faint stubble of green and subtle colours of wildfowl plumage.

During the next several days he and Saadi drove through the western section of the irrigated region, coming and going on a zigzag course. Planting was still in progress here and as they drove the dirt roads the twenty-kilometre avenues of cotton plants seemed to wheel round them like ponderously turning spokes. Planting was being done by big slow-moving machines: each machine had a Japanese driver and a crew of natives, young boys and a few women, who rode the after-platform of the machine, going rhythmically through a series of motions by which the planter was fed.

It was impressive, of course, this great work of agricultural engineering. But where was Habib's version, where the fields of green wheat and barley, lettuces and cucumbers, where the melons and the vines and figs, where the cattle, the poultry, where, above all, the people, the villagers who were to have been working cheerfully in the fields which were to have been their own?

They went back to Farzar; Israel reread his orders. He sent Saadi to bring the forms he needed, completed them, visited the British embassy where a young man called Grandison whom he had met at a palace party endorsed the forms for him and, driven by Saadi, went to the Police Ministry.

Grandison had warned him about what this part of the job would be like. In all its dirty corridors, in all its railed-off open offices with their ranks of desks manned by shabby men working their way indifferently through ever-growing piles of papers, swarmed swirling masses of ill-shaven men in threadbare clothes, women with or without the *chador*, even children, each seeking attention to a personal problem. There were faces bright with laughter at the absurdity of their predicament; faces streaked with tears; but most of the faces were set in concentration on the misery of seeking a solution to a riddle without an answer.

Israel and Saadi queued, pushed, shouted, pleaded. They were, until Israel came to his senses, at a disadvantage, for they expended spirit in this waste of shame whereas the rest of the victims did not. Just as the plant or animal which plays host to a parasite develops a tolerance for that parasite and, albeit debilitated, yet lives, so these hundreds who competed with them for attention had an evolved tolerance of the bureaucratic parasite which lived on them.

But Saadi, after all, was one of them or at least of the same culture, and presently conveyed his understanding of what they had to do by drawing Israel's attention to his right hand and, when he had it, rubbed his thumb and middle finger together.

Israel had never bribed anyone in his life and was terrified of the consequences of trying to do so. But five hours of this inferno and the knowledge that at two in the afternoon business would end until the following morning, had made him desperate. He folded a thousand-*rial* note into the batch of papers, fought his way to the barrier using his superior height and long arms unscrupulously for the first time in his life; and managed to get the papers into the hands of a clerk sharp enough to estimate the value of the clothes Israel was wearing.

Farzar airport: Habib Shah had always refused to spend money on it. The technical equipment was the best to be had but had been paid for by skimping on the amenities.

Things were changing now: Hakim was building an airport which, once its Italian architect, English interior decorator and Mexican muralist had done their exorbitant best, would be the envy of all the world's little Caesars. For the time being, however, international passengers were crammed into a departure lounge in which the sweepers were defeated by the number of feet in the way of their brooms, the Duty Free shop was out of stock of all but a native brandy and two brands of American cigarettes, and the refreshment bar had nothing but tea, coffee and English biscuits.

Israel and Saadi sat side by side on an uncomfortable bench waiting for their flight to be called. There had been no more difficulties over papers than those commonly made by the bureaucrats; no awkward questions; no hint of suspicion, only the routine obstruction by which the parasite manifests the self-hatred provoked by its repressed shame of parasitism. Israel's fears had, it seemed, been vain; now he was no longer afraid and if Saadi was nervous he did not show it.

So that when the arrest came, although it was carried out with a minimum of fuss and quite politely, it came as a fearful shock, a blow totally unexpected and having all the nightmare horrors of a sudden and violent accident.

Four policemen, two in plain clothes and two in uniform, made the arrest. They stood in front of their victims, cutting them off from the rest of the people. Saadi was told to stand and was immediately handcuffed and briskly searched for weapons. He made no resistance and asked no questions, but his face became suddenly stony and very pale. The two uniformed men removed him under the curious and frightened stares of the waiting passengers. The departure lounge had become suddenly quiet, so that the unconnected remarks of people too far away to see what was happening and still unaware of the arrest became suddenly and disconcertingly audible . . . 'I told the guy he was mashuggah' . . . 'Mais non, on a droit à vingt kilos' . . . 'Fourteen per cent for service, I said, what service?' . . .

One of the plainclothes men still stood facing Israel and with his back to the crowd. The other sat down beside him, taking Saadi's place. Israel heard his flight called but made no attempt to move. The seated man said, 'Mr Mendes, we have orders to take you to Major Baji for questioning. We hope that you will please agree to come of your own free will.'

'What is this about? Why should I come with you? My flight has just been called and I wish to board the aircraft.'

'Mr Mendes, that will not be possible, sir.'

'Are you arresting me? Because, if so . . .'

'Why use such a word, sir? We are asking you, Major Baji is asking you, to assist in a matter most serious.'

'I should like to telephone the British embassy.'

It sounded, in his own ear ridiculously like a phrase in a

phrasebook. 'Do you not know your own umbrella? No! I would rather pay a fine.' The policeman said, 'From Major Baji's office that will be possible, I think.'

There was nothing to do but rise and say, 'Very well, let us go.'

The standing man picked up Israel's hand luggage, a dispatch case and a small under-seat bag. They walked one on each side of him out of the lounge and through the controls to the forecourt where a big Mercedes was waiting for them. They were driven, at a hundred kilometres an hour, siren wailing, back into the city and across most of it to the police ministry. Israel's escort took him up in a lift to the tenth floor and through a door which isolated one large suite of offices, forensic laboratories and temporary cells. Israel was now feeling frightened but, knowing himself guilty, could not work up the kind of anger he was going to need. He was taken through a door which had to be unlocked from the inside to let them in, into a large office with dull khaki walls, austerely furnished with metal desks, chairs and filing cabinets.

Behind the largest desk, the only one occupied, sat an officer in uniform, a stout, dark man. His head, completely bald on top, was shaven round the sides; it was pear-shaped and he wore steel-rimmed spectacles. He was writing and did not look up even when one of the escorts reported. He muttered an order in an ill-tempered manner; the escort carrying Israel's bags put them on the nearest desk and then both men withdrew, leaving Israel standing alone. The officer still did not look up and he continued to write but after half a minute said, 'Sit down, Mr Mendes.'

Israel sat in the nearest chair. The officer continued writing. Israel tried to think that this preoccupation was being acted out to frighten and humiliate him with a sense of his own powerlessness; but something told him that it was not like that, that this man had more, and more difficult, work to do than he was sure of being able to accomplish and did not dare begin a new task until he had finished the old one: he seemed to emanate a feeling of chronic anxiety. At last, Israel, clearing his throat, said,

'I should like an explanation of the outrageous way I have been treated, if you please.'

The officer sighed, put down his pen, glanced at his watch, took off his glasses and rubbed his eyes. He said,

'Come nearer, Mr Mendes. I am a little deaf. The result of a bomb one of your friends threw at me.'

Israel rose and moved nearer to the desk and said, 'I do not have bomb-throwing friends, Major Baji, if you are Major Baji.'

'Yes, I am Major Baji. If you do not have such friends what were you doing trying to smuggle a dangerous terrorist known as Camal X out of this country? An abuse of hospitality, don't you think, Mr Mendes?'

'First, I haven't the slightest idea what you're talking about. Second, am I under arrest? Third, I wish to communicate with my embassy immediately and to protest against your intolerably high-handed conduct.'

'I will take your points in that order. First, I think you are lying, Mr Mendes. Second, no, you are not under arrest; you are familiar with your Scotland Yard's formula, helping the police with their inquiries. Third, a representative of your embassy will be here in about half an hour and it is I who will do any protesting that has to be done.'

Israel sat down; for the first time in his life he had a total understanding of the phrase 'at a loss'. He said, 'I have not, I repeat, the slightest idea what all this is about.'

Major Baji looked at him thoughtfully; he rubbed his eyes again. He said, 'I wonder why you are not more indignant. It is well-known that Englishmen are not resigned and calm under an injustice done to themselves however coolly they may accept injustice done to lesser people. It is true that, as a Hebrew, you are of a people who have learnt long patience. But your education, your culture, are English. The man who calls himself Saadi . . .'

'My servant . . .'

'. . . is a terrorist with a police record in three countries. He has killed at least twice with his own hands, a score of times through the hands of others. He is involved in a conspiracy to assassinate His Excellency Abdul Aziz Hakim. Of course, you will say that you knew nothing of all this.'

'I shall indeed. And I shall then want to know why such a man was planted on me.'

Baji looked taken aback. Israel, his spirits rising at once, said, and now he managed to sound angry, 'I asked at the Hilton for a servant, driver and interpreter. Four men were sent to me. I chose the best of the four. During my tour I found Saadi so satisfactory that I offered him a job in England. He accepted. I applied in the correct manner for an exit permit for the man; it was granted. Now, sir, either you knew who Saadi really is, in which case I want to know why I was not immediately informed that I was employing a dangerous criminal; or you did not know, in which case how the hell do you suppose I could?'

'Certain facts, Mr Mendes, have only just been uncovered. The man's identity has only just been established. We believe that you knew those facts and that identity before we did.'

'What possible reason can you have for such an extraordinary belief?'

'You are, I believe, on very friendly terms with the former Princess Azizeh, sister of the late Habib Shah.'

'I know her, yes. I don't see what that has to do with it.'

'Oh come now, Mr Mendes. The woman is living in your house; you certainly know what sort of company she keeps.'

'All I know is that she is your country's representative on certain working committees running the iceberg enterprise.'

'That does not preclude other activities. I suggest that you are familiar with them?' The major was looking at him speculatively as if he were not a very dangerous but possibly vicious animal. He went on, 'Would you demonstrate your good faith, Mr Mendes, by consenting to be searched?'

'Certainly not. The suggestion is outrageous.'

Israel had had to make an enormous effort to avoid showing in his face the shock which this suggestion had given him. He was no conspirator, and was not of the class which takes the possibility of police interference for granted; it had not occurred to him to destroy Azizeh's paper of instructions; it was still in his wallet. Baji was saying,

'Your dispatch case, will you allow me to go through it? I am trying, Mr Mendes, not to use the powers I have, but to enlist your help.'

'My dispatch case contains nothing but the work I am engaged on.'

'Then why do you object?'

'Because your request is an intolerable intrusion into my privacy and implies a suspicion which I resent.'

The telephone on Baji's desk rang. He answered it, listened, gave an order and said, as he replaced the phone,

'Mr Grandison, from your embassy, is on the way up.'

When Grandison came in he nodded to Israel, shook hands with Baji and sank into a chair. He had a languid manner, had adopted a rather old-fashioned style and his real interest in life was bird photography. He said,

'Spot of bother, eh?'

'A very inadequate description of what I . . .'

'I'm, er, seized of the facts, old man. Let's see if we can sort it out, eh?'

Baji said, 'Mr Grandison, Mr Mendes has refused to be searched. If his protestations are genuine, why should he do so?'

'You know, old man, you really shouldn't've suggested such a thing. It was naughty of you. Mendes is a world-famous philosopher and engineer . . . in short what they call a V.I.P., and here you are treating him like a coolie.'

'I am treating him as a suspect because he has behaved suspiciously. Our Islamic justice does not regard rank or riches, it is democratic. Mr Mendes can establish his innocence by letting himself, his papers, be searched, and if he will not do that then I shall be forced to . . .'

'Don't say it, Baji, don't say it. A threat of any kind would put me in a most embarrassing situation.'

'I was about to say that I shall be forced to ask him to remain here until we have the result of Saadi's interrogation.'

Grandison, for all his idle manner, was, as Israel realized, very shrewd: he had not pressed Israel to let himself be searched; and now he immediately rose and said, 'In that case, major, it's above our level. I shall return to the embassy and ask H.E. to have a word with the Regent. I repeat that you don't realize who you're dealing with.'

For some reason which Israel did not know, Baji did not like that. He folded his hands on the desk and sat for some minutes in silence, staring at his hands, brooding. Grandison picked up Israel's two small bags and said, 'These yours Mendes?' Israel took the cue and rose. Baji said, 'One moment, please,' and picked up the telephone and gave an order, put down the phone and said, 'Mr Mendes will be put on the next aeroplane out of Farzar airport wherever it is bound by two of my men. Let me make myself clear. I believe him to be guilty but I know him to be unimportant. He is being deported. Letters will go to your government, and to Mr Mendes' firm, informing them that he is not *persona grata* in this country and will under no circumstances be granted a visa to return.'

Grandison said, 'Well, we shall see. I propose to accompany Mr Mendes to the airport and see him off. Any objections?'

'No.'

'Statesmanlike, Baji. No hard feelings, eh? Don't forget our squash date for Thursday.'

'I am afraid that I shall be un . . .'

'No you won't, old man, you'll keep that date or I'll put it about that you're afraid to lose ten *rials* . . . that was the bet. Besides, you work too hard and need to get your weight down.'

Casablanca: Israel remained on board; Madrid, he spent forty minutes in the transit lounge and drank two manzanillas which exasperated the acid turmoil in his stomach which humilation had provoked. Silently he talked to himself: why have you let this upset you? Who do you think you are? The kids, the counter-culture kids, live like this, with this; and despise it. Have you ever thought of yourself as a pillar of the establishment? It's a joke, no more. The internal disturbance did not abate and his mind despite his will repeated over and over again the things he could and should have said to Baji.

Paris: he had two hours to wait for a connection and to be doing something telephoned his house. Elspeth said that 'Ma'am' – her indicative for Azizeh – had left the house yesterday and Ike had a 'throat' but would be all right in a day or two and the weather in London was lovely. There were still ninety minutes to waste; he spent them drinking brandy. Why brandy, he asked himself; he disliked the taste and it gave him a pain in the stomach. By the time he was aboard the aircraft he felt giddy and lost.

Home was an anticlimax, empty of Azizeh. Ike's 'throat' made him unfriendly and fractious and Israel was not as patient with the boy as he knew he should have been and his own fractiousness made him ashamed.

After three weeks which ever afterwards in his life he tried to forget, when alone in bed he had wept or tried to hold the vision of her in his mind's eye, his skin's memory, while he masturbated, he went to his desk and finished the fourth chapter of *Purpose and Chance*, applied his mind to the next stage of the methane engine, put the concerto for six guitars aside as too ambitious for his measure of talent. Either Hakim had got her and he must grieve for her; or he hadn't, and he must grieve for himself.